About the Authors

ecca Winters lives in Salt Lake City, Utah. With
/ons and high alpine meadows full of wildflowers,
never runs out of places to explore. They, plus her
ourite holiday spots in Europe, often end up as
ckgrounds for her romance novels because writing is
er passion, along with her family and church. Rebecca
oves to hear from readers. If you wish to e-mail her,
lease visit her website at: www.cleanromances.net

Raye Morgan has been a nursery-school teacher, a
travel agent, a clerk and a business editor, but her best
job ever has been writing romances – and fostering
romance in her own family at the same time. Current
score: two boys married, two more to go. Raye has
published more than seventy romances, and claims to
have many more waiting in the wings. She lives on the
Central California Coast with her husband.

The author of over seventy-five titles for Mills & Boon,
Stella Bagwell writes about families, the West, strong,
silent men of honour and the women who love them. She
credits her loyal readers and hopes her stories have
rightened their lives in some small way. A cowgirl
hrough and through, she recently learned how to rope a
eer. Her days begin and end helping her husband on
their south Texas ranch. In between she works on her next
t e of love. Contact her at stellabagwell@gmail.com

Twins

Twins:
Double Trouble

REBECCA WINTERS

RAYE MORGAN

STELLA BAGWELL

MILLS & BOON

First Published in Great Britain 2020
By Mills & Boon, an imprint of HarperCollins*Publishers*
1 London Bridge Street, London, SE1 9GF

TWINS: DOUBLE TROUBLE © 2020 Harlequin Books S.A.

Doorstep Twins © 2010 Rebecca Winters
A Daddy for Her Sons © 2013 Helen Conrad
Daddy's Double Duty © 2011 Stella Bagwell

ISBN: 978-0-263-28216-0

MIX
Paper from
responsible sources
FSC™ C007454

This book is produced from independently certified FSC™ paper
to ensure responsible forest management.

For more information visit: www.harpercollins.co.uk/green

Printed and bound in Spain
by CPI, Barcelona

DOORSTEP TWINS

REBECCA WINTERS

CHAPTER ONE

"I'M SORRY, Ms. Turner, but Kyrie Simonides says he can't fit you in today. If you'll come next Tuesday at three o'clock?"

Gabi's hand tightened around the leather strap of her taupe handbag. "I won't be in Athens then." The outcome of this visit would determine how soon she left Greece…that was if she were allowed to see him now.

She fought not to lose her composure in front of the retirement-age-looking receptionist who was probably paid a lot of money not to lose *hers*. "After waiting over three hours for him, surely he can take another five minutes to talk to me."

The woman with heavy streaks of silver in her hair shook her head. "It's the weekend. He should have left Athens an hour ago."

At twenty after six on a hot Friday evening Gabi could believe it, but she hadn't come this far to be put off. There was too much at stake. Taking a calming breath, she said, "I didn't want to have to say this to you, but he's left me no choice. Please tell him it's a matter of life and death."

Because it was the truth and her eyes didn't blink, the receptionist's expression underwent a subtle change. "If this is some kind of a joke, I'm afraid it will backfire on you."

"This is no joke," Gabi replied, standing her ground at five feet five in her comfortable two-piece cotton suit of pale lemon. She'd already undergone a thorough vetting and security check upon entering the building, so the receptionist knew she didn't pose a threat.

After a slight hesitation the taller woman, clearly in a dilemma, got up from her desk and walked with a decided limp back to her boss's office. That was progress.

While businessmen came and went from his private domain on top of the building complex in downtown Athens, she'd been continually ignored until now. If Gabi had just come out with it in the first place, it might not have taken her most of the day to get results, but she'd wanted to protect him.

Gabi only knew three facts about the thirty-three-year-old Andreas Simonides: First, he was the reputed new force majeure at the internationally renowned Simonides Corporation whose holdings were tied up in all areas of metallurgy, including aluminum, copper and plastics.

Her source confided that their vast fortune, accumulated over many decades, included the ownership of eighty companies. With a population of twelve thousand employees, the Simonides family ruled over a virtual empire extending beyond Greece.

Second, if the picture in the newspaper didn't lie, he was an exceptionally attractive male.

The third fact wasn't public knowledge. In truth no one knew what Gabi knew...not even the man himself. But once they talked, his life would change forever whether he liked it or not.

While she stood there anticipating their first meeting, she heard the woman's footsteps. "Kyrie Simonides will give you two minutes, no more."

"I'll take them!"

"You go down the hall and through the double doors."

"Thank you very much," she said with heartfelt sincerity, then rushed around the reception desk, her golden jaw-length curls bouncing. At first she didn't see anyone as she entered his elegant inner sanctum.

"Life and death you said?" came a voice of male irony from behind her. Though deep, it had an appealing vibrant quality.

She spun around to discover a tall man shrugging into an expensive-looking gray suit jacket he'd just taken from a closet. The play of rip-cord muscle in his arms and shoulders beneath a dazzling white shirt attested to the fact that he didn't spend all his time in the confines of an office. Helpless to do otherwise, her gaze fell lower to the fabric of his trousers molding powerful thighs.

"I'm waiting, Ms. Turner."

Heat stole into her cheeks to be caught staring like that. She lifted her head, but her voice caught as she looked up into eyes of iron gray, half veiled by long black lashes that gave him an aloof quality.

He possessed a healthy head of medium-cropped black hair and an olive complexion. Rugged of feature, his dark Greek looks fascinated her. The picture she'd seen of him hadn't picked up the slight scar partially hidden in his left eyebrow, or the lines of experience she could detect around his eyes and wide male mouth. They revealed a life that had known every emotion.

"You're a difficult man to reach."

After shutting the closet door, he walked across the room to his private elevator. "I'm on my way out. Since you refused to come back next Tuesday, say what you have to say before I leave." He'd already stepped inside the lift, ready to push the button. No doubt he had a helicopter on the roof waiting to fly him to some exotic vacation spot for the weekend.

Standing next to him, she'd never felt more diminutive. Even if she didn't have an appointment, his condescension was too much. But because she might never have another opportunity to get this close to him, she hid her reaction.

Without wasting time she opened her handbag and pulled out a manila envelope. Since he made no move to take it, she undid the flap and removed the contents.

Beneath a set of DNA results lay the front page of a year-old Greek newspaper revealing him aboard the Simonides yacht, surrounded by a crush of people partying the night away. Gabi's elder half sister Thea, whose dark Grecian beauty stood out from the other women on board, was among the crowd captured in the photo. The headline read, "New CEO at Simonides is cause for celebration."

Along with these items was a photograph taken a few days ago of two baby boys wearing diapers and shirts. Gabi had gone to a store to get it enlarged into an eight-by-ten.

She held everything up so he couldn't miss looking at the identical twins who had a crop of curly black hair and gorgeous olive skin like his and Thea's. He'd had his hair cut since the photo.

Up close she picked out many of the other similarities to him, including their widow's peaks and the winged shape of their dark eyebrows. The strong resemblance didn't stop there. She quickly noticed they had his firm chin and wide mouth. Her list went on and on down to their sturdy bodies and same square-cut fingertips.

Yet nothing about the set of his features indicated the picture had made any kind of impression. "I don't see *you* in the photograph, Ms. Turner. I'm sorry if you're in such a desperate situation, but darkening my doorstep wanting a handout isn't the way to get the help you need."

Gabi's jaw hardened. "And you're not the first man to ignore the children he helped bring into the world."

His black eyes narrowed. "What kind of a mother sends someone else on an errand like this?"

Somehow she got around the boulder in her throat. "I wish my sister could have come herself, but she's dead."

The moment the words left her lips, she sensed his body quicken. "That's a tragedy. Now if you'll excuse me."

Andreas Simonides was a cold-blooded man. There was no way to reach him. As his hand moved to the button on the panel, alerting her that this conversation was over, she said, "Are you saying you never saw this woman in your life?"

Gabi pointed to Thea's face in the newspaper picture. "Maybe this will help." She put the items under her arm while she pulled out Thea's Greek passport. "Here."

To her surprise he took it from her and examined the photo. "Thea Paulos, twenty-four, Athens. Issued five years ago." His black brows formed a bar. He shot her a penetrating glance. "Your sister, you say?"

"My half sister," she amended. "Daddy's first wife was Greek. After she died, he married my American mother. After a while I came along. This was the last passport Thea held before her divorce." Gabi bit her lip. "She...celebrated it with friends aboard your yacht."

He handed the passport back to her. "I'm sorry about your loss, but I can't help you."

She felt a stab of pain. "I'm sorry for the twins," she murmured. "To lose their mother is tragic beyond words. However, when they're old enough to ask where their father is and I have to tell them he's alive somewhere— but it doesn't matter because they never mattered to him—*that* will be the ultimate tragedy."

The elevator door closed, putting a definitive end to all communication. Gabi spun around, angry and heartsick. For two cents she'd leave the incriminating evidence with his receptionist and let the other woman draw her own conclusions.

But creating a scandal within the Simonides empire was the last thing Gabi wanted to do, not when it could rebound on her own family, especially on her father whose diplomat position in the consulate on Crete might be compromised. In his work he met with Greek VIPs in business and governmental positions on a regular basis. She couldn't bear it if her presence here brought on unwanted repercussions.

No one had asked her to come. Except for Mr. Simonides himself now, no one knew the nature of this visit, especially not her grieving parents. Since Thea had died in childbirth from a heart condition brought on by the pregnancy, Gabi had taken it upon herself to be the babies' advocate. Every child deserved its own wonderful birth mother and father. Unfortunately not every child was so lucky.

"Mission accomplished," she whispered to the empty room. Her heart felt like an anchor that had come loose and had plunged through fathoms of dark water to the lowest depths of the Mediterranean.

Once she'd put everything back in the envelope and stashed it in her handbag, she left his private office. The venerable receptionist nodded to Gabi before she disappeared into the hall. In a few minutes she arrived at the ground floor of the building and hurried outside to get a taxi back to her hotel.

To her surprise, the chauffeur of a limo parked in front got out and approached her. "Ms. Turner?"

She blinked. "Yes?"

"Kyrie Simonides said you had to wait a long time to get in to see him. I've been asked to drive you wherever it is you wish to go."

Her adrenaline kicked in, causing her pulse to speed up. Did this mean the twins' father wasn't a complete block of ice after all? Who wouldn't melt over seeing a photo of his own flesh and blood? If the boys' picture didn't completely convince him, the printout of their DNA would provide infallible proof of a match.

By sending a limo for Gabi, it could mean he planned for a second meeting with her, but he was forced to be discreet. With his money and power, not to mention his looks, the head man had learned how to keep his former liaisons private.

"Thank you. If you wouldn't mind taking me to the Amazon Hotel?" She'd purposely checked in there because it was near the Simonides building in the heart of the Plaka.

He nodded as he helped her in.

Before carrying out her plan to meet with Mr. Simonides today, Gabi had told her parents that one of her female coworkers from Alexandria, Virginia, was in Athens on a trip. They'd decided to get together and see a little of the sights. Gabi felt awful for outright lying to them, but she didn't dare let them know her true agenda.

Until Thea's fifth month of pregnancy when she'd developed serious heart complications and was hospitalized, Gabi hadn't even known the name of the babies' father. But as the end drew near and it became apparent Thea might not make it, she told Gabi to look in her jewel box at home and bring her the envelope she'd hidden there.

Gabi brought it to the hospital. Thea told her to open it. She took one look and gasped when she realized who the man was. "This is all I have of him. Like everyone else on board, we'd both had way too much to drink," Thea whispered. "We were 'strangers in the night' kind of thing."

Her confession elicited a moan from Gabi.

"It didn't mean anything to him. He didn't even know my name. I'm ashamed it happened and he shouldn't have to pay for a mistake which was as much mine as his. I wanted you to see him so you'll know what kind of genes the children have inherited. Now promise me you'll forget everything."

Gabi understood how Thea felt and planned to honor her wishes. Besides the unsuspecting father, she realized that any news would be exploited if linked to the Simonides family. As they had recently lost the daughter of her father's first marriage, Gabi wanted to save her parents any added grief.

While she sat there deep in thought the rear door opened. Surprised they'd already arrived in front of the hotel, she gave a start before getting out.

"Please thank your employer for me."

"Of course."

Once he'd gone, she hurried inside, anxious to eat something at the snack bar before going up to her room. Whatever Mr. Simonides intended to do, he was in the driver's seat and would be the one to set the timetable for their next conversation. *If there were to be one…*

She could only hope he would make the arrangements before morning. Tomorrow she needed to fly back to Heraklion on Crete and rejoin her family. On top of their sadness, they had their hands full with the twins who'd been born six weeks premature.

When it had looked as if Thea was in trouble, Gabi had taken an undetermined leave of absence from the advertising agency in Virginia to fly to Heraklion. Since then she'd taken over the care of the babies because her busy parents' demanding diplomatic position didn't allow for the constant nurturing of the twins without full-time help.

That was four months ago and Gabi's job as public relations manager had been temporarily filled by someone else at Hewitt and Wilson, so she had a vital decision to make. If Mr. Simonides chose to claim his children, then she needed to get back to her work in Virginia ASAP.

Her immediate boss had been made regional director of the East Coast market and hinted at an important promotion for her. But she needed to get back home if she wanted to expand her career opportunity with him. The only other career more important would be to become the mother to Thea's children. But if she chose to do that, then it meant she would have to give up her advertising career until they were school age.

Having been burned by Texas rancher and oil man Rand McCallister five years ago, Gabi had no intention of ever getting married or having children, but if the twins' birth father didn't want them, then she would take on the responsibility of raising them because they were her family. As such, she needed to go back to Virginia where she could rear them in familiar surroundings.

Her family's home in Alexandria was the perfect residence in a guarded, gated community with other diplomats' families, some of whom had small children. Gabi had always lived in it with her parents when they weren't in Greece on assignment. Since Gabi's father owned the house outright, she wouldn't have to deal with a mortgage payment.

If she combined the savings from her job with her dad's financial help, she could be a stay-at-home mom until they were both school age, then get back to her career. It could all work. Gabi would *make* it work because she'd grown to love the twins as if they were her own babies.

In all likelihood Mr. Simonides wasn't interested in the children and had only made certain she got a ride back to wherever she'd come from. Therefore she would fly the twins to Alexandria with her next week.

After a quick meal, Gabi went up to her room on the fourth floor, reasoning that her mother would go with her to help the three of them settle in before returning to

Crete. The consulate was no place for two new infants. Her parents would never admit it, but the whole situation had grown out of control.

No sooner did she let herself inside with the card key than she saw the red light blinking on the telephone. Her mother could have left a voice message rather than try to get her on her cell phone. Then again…

With an odd combination of curiosity and trepidation, she reached for the receiver to retrieve it.

"Another limo is waiting for you in front of the hotel, Ms. Turner. It will be there until eight-thirty p.m." Her watch said eight-ten. "If you don't appear with your luggage by then, I'll understand this isn't a life and death situation after all. Your hotel-room bill has been taken care of."

Gabi hung up the phone feeling as if she were acting in a police procedural film, not living real life. He'd had her followed and watched. The fabulously wealthy Mr. Simonides inhabited a world made up of secrecy and bodyguards in order to preserve, not only his safety, but the privacy he craved.

She imagined the paparazzi constituted a living nightmare for him, particularly when someone unknown like Gabi materialized. Her intrusion reminded him there were consequences for a night of pleasure he couldn't remember because everyone partying on the yacht had been drinking heavily.

Thea had confided he was a Greek god come to life. Unlike Gabi, who'd inherited her mother's shorter height and curves, Thea had been fashionably tall and thin. Growing up, she could have any boy she wanted.

She'd always had a man in tow, even the bachelor playboy Andreas Simonides touted in the press, now the crowned head of the Simonides empire. When he'd picked Thea out from the other women on board and had started making love to her in one of the cabins, she'd succumbed in a moment of extreme weakness.

How tragic that in celebrating her divorce she'd become pregnant, the consequences of which had brought on her death...

Gabi couldn't imagine Mr. Simonides forgetting her sister no matter what. But if he'd been like Rand, then there'd been many beautiful women in his life. As both sisters had learned, they'd only made up part of the adoring horde. What a huge shock it must have been to discover he'd fathered baby boys whose resemblance to the two of them was nothing short of astounding.

Gabi only had a few minutes to freshen up and pack her overnight bag before she rushed down to the lobby. It was a simple matter since she hadn't planned to be in Athens more than a night and had only brought one other change of outfit with her.

Through the doors she spied a limo with dark glass, but a different driver stood next to it. She assumed she would be driven to an undisclosed location where Mr. Simonides was waiting for her.

"Good evening, Ms. Turner." He opened the rear door to help her in with her case. "I'll be taking you to Kyrie Simonides."

"Thank you."

Before long they were moving into the mainstream of heavy traffic circulating about the old Turkish quarter of Athens. Again she had the feeling she was playing a part in a movie, but this time she experienced a distinct chill because she'd dared to approach a complete stranger who had all the power.

The sky was darkening into night. If she were to disappear, her family wouldn't have a clue what had happened to her. Their pain at such an eventuality didn't bear thinking about. In the desire to unite the babies with their only living parent, she'd been blinded to the risks involved. Now it was too late to pull out of a possibly dangerous situation she'd created.

At this point she wasn't quite sure what she'd hoped to achieve. Unless a bachelor who partied and slept with women without giving it a thought were to give up that lifestyle, he wouldn't make the best father around. But for the sake of the twins who deserved more, she couldn't just take them back to Virginia and raise them without first trying to let their father know he *was* a father. Would he want any part in their lives?

She wanted him to be a real man and claim his children, invite them into his home and his life…be there for them for the whole of their lives. Give them his name and seal their legacy.

But of course that kind of thing just didn't happen. Gabi wasn't under any illusions. No doubt he was convinced she'd approached him to extort money and was ready to pay her off. He would soon find out she wanted nothing monetary from him and would be leaving for the States with her precious cargo.

Before Thea died, she'd asked Gabi to help get the babies placed for adoption with a good Greek couple. She wanted them raised Greek. Both sisters realized the impossible burden it would put on their older parents to shoulder the responsibility of raising the children. For all their sakes Gabi had made Thea that promise.

But after her death, Gabi realized it was a promise she couldn't keep. In the first place, the twins' birth father *was* alive. Legally no one could adopt them without his permission.

And in the second place, over the last three months Gabi had learned to love the boys. She'd bonded with them. Maybe she wasn't Greek, but, having been taught Greek from the cradle, Gabi was bilingual and would use it with them. They would have a good home with her. No one but their own father could ever pry them away from her now.

Suddenly the rear door opened. "Ms. Turner?" the driver called to her. "If you'll follow me."

Startled out of her thoughts, she exited the limo, not having realized they'd arrived at the port of Piraeus. He held her overnight case and walked toward a gleaming white luxury cabin cruiser probably forty to forty-five feet in length moored a few steps away along the pier.

A middle-aged crew member took the bag and helped her aboard. "My name is Stavros. I'll take you to Kyrie Simonides, who's waiting for you to join him in the rear cockpit. This way, Ms. Turner."

Once again she found herself trailing after a stranger to an ultraleather wraparound lounge whose sky roof was open. Her dark-haired host was standing in front of the large windows overlooking the water lit up by the myriad boats and ferries lining the harbor. The dream vessel was state of the art.

Since she'd last seen him in the lift, he'd removed his suit jacket and tie. He'd rolled his shirtsleeves up to the elbow. Thea had been right. He was spectacular-looking.

She understood when the man announced to her host that the American woman had come aboard. He turned in her direction. The lights reflecting off the water cast his hard-boned features into stark relief.

"Come all the way in and sit down, Ms. Turner. Stavros will bring you anything you want to eat or drink."

"Nothing for me, thank you. I just ate."

After his staff member left the room, she pulled the envelope out of her purse and put it on the padded seat next to her, assuming he wanted a better look at everything. He wandered over to her, but made no move to take it. Instead his enigmatic gaze traveled over her upturned features.

She had an oval face, but her mouth was too wide and her hair was too naturally curly for her liking. Instead of olive skin, hers was a nondescript cream color. Her dad once told her she had wood violet eyes. She'd never seen wood violets, but he'd said it with such love, she'd decided that they were her one redeeming feature.

"My name's Andreas," he said, surprising her. "What's yours?"

"Gabi."

"My sources tell me you were christened Gabriella. I like the shortened version." Unexpectedly he reeked of the kind of virile charm to turn any woman's head. Thea hadn't stood a chance.

Gabi understood that kind of potent male power and the money that went with it. Once upon a time she'd loved Rand. Substitute this Greek tycoon's trappings for seven hundred thousand acres of Texas ranch land with cattle and oil wells and voilà—the two men were interchangeable. Fortunately for Gabi, she'd only needed to learn her lesson once. Thea had learned hers, too, but it had come at the cost of her life.

One black brow quirked. "Where are these twins? At your home in Virginia, or are they a little closer at your father's consulate residence in Heraklion?"

With a mere phone call he knew people in the highest places to get that kind of classified information in less than an hour. Naturally he did. She wanted to tell him that, since he possessed all the facts, there was no need to answer his question, but she couldn't do that. Not after she'd been the one to approach him.

"They're on Crete."

"I want to see them," he declared without hesitation, sending Gabi into mild shock that he'd become curious about these children who could be his offspring. She felt a grudging respect that he'd conceded to the possibility that his relationship with Thea, no matter how short-lived, had produced them. "How soon are you due back in Heraklion?"

"When I left this morning, I told my parents I was meeting a former work colleague from the States in Athens and would fly home tomorrow."

"Will they send a car for you?"

"No. I told them I wasn't sure of my arrival time so I'd take a taxi."

He shifted his weight. "Once I've delivered you to Heraklion, there'll be a taxi waiting to take you home. For the time being Stavros has prepared a room for you. Are you susceptible to the *mal de mer*?"

They were going back by sea?

"No."

"Good. I'm assuming your parents are still in the dark about the twins' father, otherwise you wouldn't have needed to lie to them."

"Thea never wanted them to know." She hadn't wanted anyone to know, especially not Thea's ex-husband Dimitri. For the most part their marriage had been wretched and she hadn't wanted him to find out what she'd done on the very day she'd obtained her divorce from him. Dimitri wouldn't hesitate to expose his ex-wife's indiscretion out of simple revenge.

"Yet she trusted *you*."

"Not until she knew she might die." Thea hadn't wanted to burden anyone. "Though she admitted making a mistake she dearly regretted, she wanted her babies to be taken care of without it being Mom and Dad's responsibility. I approached you the way I did in order to spare them and you any notoriety."

"But not my pocketbook," he inserted in a dangerously silken voice.

"You would have every right to think that, Mr. Simonides."

"Andreas," he corrected her.

She took a deep breath. "Money isn't the reason I came. Nor do you have to worry your name is on their birth certificates. Thea refused to name the father. Though I promised to find a good home for the twins with another couple, I couldn't keep it."

"Why not?"

"Because you're alive. I've looked into the law. No one can adopt them unless you give away your parental rights. In truth, Thea never wanted you to know anything."

He shrugged his elegant shoulders. "If not for money, then why didn't you just spirit them away and forget the legalities?"

Gabi stared hard at him. "Because I plan to adopt them and had to be certain you didn't want to claim them before I take them back to Virginia with me. You have that God-given right after all." She took a fortifying breath. "Being their aunt, I don't."

Her lids prickled, but she didn't let tears form. "As for the twins, they have the same God-given right to be with their father if you want *them*. If there was any chance of that happening, I had to take it, thus my presence in your office today. Naturally if you do want them, then I'll tell my parents everything and we'll go from there."

The air seemed to have electrified around them. "If you're telling me the truth, then you're one of a dying species."

His cynical remark revealed a lot. He had no qualms about using women. In that regard he and Rand had a lot in common. But Gabi suspected Mr. Simonides didn't like women very much.

"One day when they're old enough to understand, I wouldn't be able to face them if I couldn't tell them that at the very beginning I did everything in my power to unite them with you first."

His eyes looked almost black as they searched hers for a tension-filled moment. "What's in Virginia when your parents are here in Greece?"

"*My life*, Mr. Simonides. Like you, I have an important career I love. My parents' responsibilities are here on Crete for the time being. Dad has always had connections to the Greek government. Every time they're transferred, I make the occasional visit, but I live at our family home in Virginia."

"How long have you been here?"

"I came a month before the children were born. They're three months old now." *They're so adorable you can't imagine.*

"What's your routine with them?"

Gabi thought she understood what he was asking. "Between naps I usually take them for walks in their stroller."

"Where?"

"Several places close by. There's a small park with a fountain and benches around the corner from the consulate. I sometimes go there with them."

"Let's plan to meet there tomorrow, say three o'clock. If that isn't possible, phone me on my cell and we'll arrange for another time."

"That will be fine," she assured him.

"Good." He wrote a number on a business card and handed it to her. In the next breath he pulled the phone out of his trouser pocket and asked Stavros to report.

Half a minute later the other man appeared. "Come with me, Ms. Turner, and I'll show you to your cabin."

"Thank you." When she got up, she would have taken the envelope with her, but Andreas was too fast for her.

"I'll return this to you later. Let's hope you sleep well. The sea is calm tonight."

She paused at the entrance. Studying him from across the expanse she said, "Thank you for giving me those two minutes. When I prevailed on your receptionist, she said you were already late leaving your office. I'm sorry if I interrupted your plans for the evening."

He cocked his dark head. "A life and death situation waits on no man. Go to bed with a clear conscience. *Kalinihta*, Gabi Turner."

His deep, attractive voice vibrated to her insides. *"Kalinihta."*

* * *

As soon as Stavros saw her to her cabin, Andreas pulled out his cell phone to call Irena for the second time this evening.

"Darling?" she answered on the second ring. "I've been hoping to hear from you."

"I'm sorry about tonight," he began without preamble. "As I told you earlier, an emergency came up that made it impossible for us to join the family party on Milos."

"Well, you're free now. Are you planning to come over?"

He gripped the phone tighter. "I can't."

"That sounded serious. Something really is wrong, isn't it?"

"Yes," his voice grated. In the space of a few hours his shock had worn off enough for agony to take over.

"You don't want to talk to me about it?"

"I will when the time is right." He closed his eyes tightly. *There was no right time. Not for this.*

"Which means you have to discuss it with Leon first."

What did she just say?

"Judging by your silence, I realize that came out wrong. Forgive me. Ever since we started seeing each other, I've learned you always turn to him before anyone else, but I said it as an observation, not a criticism."

She'd only spoken the truth. It brought up a potentially serious issue for the future, but he didn't have the time to analyze the ramifications right now. "There's nothing to forgive, Irena. I'll call you tomorrow."

"Whatever's disturbing you, remember I'm here."

"As if I could forget."

"*S'agapo*, Andreas."

In the six months they'd been together, he'd learned to love her. Before Gabi Turner had come to his office, he'd planned to ask Irena to marry him. It was past time he settled down. His intention had been to announce it at tonight's party.

"S'agapo," he whispered before hanging up.

CHAPTER TWO

THE next afternoon Gabi's mother helped her settle the babies in their double stroller. "It's hot out."

"A typical July day." Gabi had already packed their bottled formula in the space behind the seat. "I've dressed them in their thinnest tops and shorts." One outfit in pale green, the other pastel blue. "At least there's some shade at the park. We'll have a wonderful time, won't we?"

She couldn't resist kissing their cheeks. After being gone overnight, she'd missed them horribly. Now that they were awake, their sturdy little arms and legs were moving like crazy.

"Oh, Gabi...they're so precious and they look so much like Thea."

"I know." But they also looked like someone else. That was the reason they were so gorgeous. She squeezed her mother around the shoulders. "Because of them, Thea will always be with us."

"Your father's so crazy about them, I don't know if he can handle your taking them back home to Alexandria to live. I know I can't. Please promise me you'll reconsider."

"We've been over this too many times, Mom. Dad can't do his work the way he needs to. It's best for both of you with your busy schedules. At home I'll be around my friends and there'll be other moms with their babies to befriend. We'll see each other often. You know that!"

Right now Gabi had too many butterflies in her stomach at the thought of meeting up with Andreas to concentrate on anything else. She slowly let go of her. "See you later."

Making certain the twins were comfy, she started pushing the stroller away from the Venetian-styled building that had become a home to the consulate with its apartments for their family. From her vantage point she could look out over the port of Heraklion on the northern end of Crete, an island steeped in Roman and Ottoman history.

Normally she daydreamed about its past during her walks with the children, but this afternoon her gaze was glued to the harbor. Somewhere down there was the cabin cruiser that had brought her from Piraeus.

The trip had been so smooth, she could believe the sea had been made of glass. She should have fallen into a deep sleep during the all-night crossing, but in truth she'd tossed and turned most of it.

That was because the man she'd labeled bloodless and selfish didn't appear to fit her original assessment. In fact she had trouble putting him in any category, which was yet another reason for her restlessness.

As a result she'd slept late and had to be awakened by Stavros, who'd brought a fabulous breakfast to her elegant cabin with its cherrywood décor. She'd thanked him profusely. Following that she'd showered and given herself a shampoo. After drying her hair, she'd changed into white sailor pants and a sleeveless navy and white print top.

Once her bag was packed, she'd applied lipstick, then walked through to the main salon before ascending the companionway stairs in her sandals. She'd expected to find Andreas so she could thank him for everything, but discovered he was nowhere in sight. Somehow she'd felt disappointed, which made no sense at all.

Since Stavros had let her know her ride was waiting, she'd had no choice but to leave the cruiser from the port side. He'd carried her overnight bag to the taxi and wished her a good day. After thanking him again, she'd been whisked through the bustling city of close to a hundred and forty thousand people. Further up the incline they reached the consulate property and passed through the sentry gate.

After her arrival, she'd made some noncommittal remarks to her parents about having had an okay time in Athens, but she'd missed the children too much and wanted to come straight home. The babies had acted so happy to see her, her heart had melted.

Closer to the park now, she felt her pulse speed up. Though the heat had something to do with it, there was another reason. What if Andreas took one look and decided he *did* want the children? Though that was what she'd been hoping and praying for, she hadn't counted on this pang that ran through her at the thought of having to give them up.

The park held its share of children, some with their mothers. A few older people sat on benches talking. Several tourists on bikes had stopped to catch their breath before moving on. It was a benign scene until she noticed the striking man who sat beneath the fronds of a palm tree reading a newspaper.

There was an aura of sophistication about him. A man in control of his world. One of the most powerful men in Greece actually. Everywhere he went, his body-guards preceded him, but she would never know who they were or where they were hidden.

Today he'd dressed in a silky blue sport shirt and tan trousers, a picture of masculine strength and a kind of rugged male beauty hard to put in words.

She glanced at the twins. They didn't know it, but they were looking at their daddy, a man like no other who wasn't more than ten feet away.

His intelligent eyes fringed with inky black lashes peered over the newspaper at them before he put it aside and stood up.

Gabi moved the stroller closer until they were only a few feet apart. Hardly able to breathe, she touched one dark, curly head. "This is Kris, short for Kristopher. And this…" she tousled the other gleaming cap of black curls "…is Nikos."

Andreas hunkered down in front of them. Like finding a rare treasure, his eyes burned a silvery gray as his gaze inspected every precious centimeter, from their handsome faces to the tips of their bare toes.

He cupped their chins as if he were memorizing their features, then he let them wrap their fingers around his. Before long both his index fingers ended up in their mouths.

Gabi started to laugh. She couldn't help it. "He tastes good, huh. You little guys must be hungry." She undid the strap and handed Nikos to him. "Sit down on the bench and you can feed him." In a flash she supplied him with a cloth against his shoulder and a baby bottle full of formula.

"If you've never done this before, don't worry about it. The boys will do all the work. Let him drink for a minute, then pat his back gently to get rid of the air bubbles. I'll take care of Kris."

For the next little while, she was mostly aware of the twins making noisy sounds as they drank their bottles with the greatest of relish. Afterward they traded babies so he could get to know Kris.

Every so often the sounds were followed by several loud burps that elicited rich laughter from Andreas. When she'd approached him in his office yesterday, she hadn't thought he was capable of it.

Any misgivings she'd had about starting up this process fled at the sight of him getting acquainted with the boys. It was a picture that would be impressed on her heart forever. Wherever Thea was, she had to be happy her sons were no longer strangers to their father, even if he'd never sought her sister out again.

Gabi didn't know the outcome, but this meeting was something to cherish at least.

"We'll have to make this fast because I don't want to keep them out in the sun much longer." She flashed him a quick glance. "Next time—if you want there to be a next time—you can take them for a walk on your own."

He made no response. She didn't know what to think. Another five minutes passed before she said, "There now. They're as sated as two fat cats." Again she heard laughter roll out of him.

Together they lowered them back into the stroller. Her arm brushed his, making her unduly aware of him. She put the empty bottles and cloths away. When she rose up, their glances collided. "I have to go," she said. Maybe she was mistaken, but she thought the light in his eyes faded a trifle. "If you want to see them again, call me on my cell."

Pulling out his phone, he said, "Tell me your number and I'll program it into mine right now."

Maybe that was a good sign. Then again maybe it wasn't. A small shiver ran down her spine in fear that when he contacted her next, he would tell her that, cute as the boys were, he was still signing his rights away and they were all hers with his blessing.

After she'd given him her number, he pushed the stroller toward the path leading out to the street. One of the older women caught sight of the twins and shouted something about them having beautiful children.

"Efharisto," Andreas called back, thanking the woman as if this were an everyday occurrence.

Gabi didn't want to tear herself away, but her mother would worry if she wasn't back soon and would want to know why the delay. "I really have to go."

"I know," he said in a husky tone before giving the boys a kiss on their foreheads. "I'll be in touch."

With those long powerful strides, he left the park going one way while she trundled along with the stroller going the other. The farther apart they got, the more fearful she grew.

He wasn't indifferent to the twins. She knew that. She'd felt it and seen it. But one meeting with his children didn't mean he wanted to take on the lifetime responsibility of parenting them. Between his work and girlfriends he wouldn't have much time to fit in the twins.

She'd told him she'd be leaving for Virginia next week. If he didn't want her to take them away, he needed to make up his mind soon.

Maybe he would compromise. She'd raise them and he'd be one of those drop-in daddies. For the boys' sake Gabi couldn't bear the thought of it, but having a daddy around once in a while, even if he only flew into D.C. from Greece once a year with a present, was better for them than no daddy at all, wasn't it? Gabi loved her own father so much, she couldn't imagine life without him.

The only thing to do now was brace herself for his next phone call.

Accompanied by his bodyguards, Andreas rushed toward the helicopter waiting for him at the Heraklion airport. Once he'd climbed aboard, he directed his pilot to fly him to the Simonides villa on Milos where the whole clan had congregated for the weekend.

Last night there'd been a party to celebrate his sister Melina's thirtieth birthday, but he'd been forced to miss it because of a life and death situation. *Gabi Turner had been right about that.*

Though his married sister had been gracious over the phone, he knew she'd been hurt by his excuse that something unavoidable had come up to detain him in Athens. He'd promised to make it up to her, but that kind of occasion in her honor with extended family in attendance only happened once a year. Now the moment was gone.

Yet, sorry as he was, he had something much more vital on his mind and couldn't think about anything else. Throughout the flight he still felt the strong tug of those little mouths on his fingers. Their touch had sent the most peculiar sensation through Andreas.

Even though he had ten nieces and nephews, he hadn't been involved in their nurturing. The closest he'd come was to hold their weightless bodies as they were being passed around at a family party after coming home from the hospital.

Today had been something totally different. It was as if the blinders had come off, but he hadn't known they existed until contact was made. Kris and Nikos weren't just babies. Those excited bodies with their bright eyes and faces belonged to a pair of little guys who one day would grow up to be big guys. Guys who had the Simonides stamp written all over them.

As soon as he entered the main villa Andreas went in search of his vivacious mother, who was in the kitchen supervising dinner preparations with the cook, Tina.

"There you are, darling," she said the minute she saw him.

He gave her a kiss, already anticipating her next comment. "My absence was unavoidable."

Her expressive dark brows lifted. "A delicate merger?"

"Incredibly delicate," he muttered. The memory of Nikos and Kris so trusting in his arms as they inhaled their formula never left his mind.

"You sound like your father. I have to tell you I'm glad he's finally stepped down and you're in charge. He's a different man these days. Let's just hope that when you're settled down, hopefully soon, your wife will have more influence on you to take time off once in a while. You're already working too hard if you had to miss Melina's birthday party."

His mother could have no idea. He gave her an extra hug. "Where's everyone?" he asked, knowing the answer full well, but he didn't want to sound like anything out of the ordinary was wrong.

"Still waterskiing. Your grandparents are out on the patio watching your father and your uncle Vasio drive the younger children around. We'll eat out by the pool in an hour."

"That gives me enough time to get in a little exercise." After stealing an hors d'oeuvre from the plate

Tina was preparing, he pecked her cheek to atone for his sin before walking through a series of alcoves and walkways to reach his villa with its own amenities farther down their private beach.

The massive family retreat—a cluster of linked white villas in the Cycladic style—had been the Simonides refuge for many generations. Because of business, Andreas didn't escape from his penthouse in the city as often as he wanted and had been looking forward to this time with the family.

Who would have dreamed that, before the lift door closed, an innocent-looking blonde female would sweep into his office like a Cycladic breeze, bringing a fragrance as sweet as the honeysuckle growing wild on the island before she dropped her bomb?

Still charged with adrenaline, he changed into his swim trunks and hurried down to the beach where the family ski boats were in use.

"There's Uncle Andreas!" One of his nieces waiting on the beach for her turn screeched with joy and ran toward him. Her brother followed. "Now that you're here, will you take us? Grandpa hasn't come back for us yet."

His sister Leila's children were the youngest, seven and nine. "What do *you* think?" He grinned. "Climb in my ski boat. We'll show everybody! You spot your sister first, Jason."

"Okay!"

Happy chaos reigned for another half-hour, then everyone left the beach because dinner had been announced. Andreas secured his boat to their private pier. Things couldn't have turned out better than to find his brother Leon the last to tie up his own ski boat. His wife Deline had gone up with the others, leaving them alone for the moment.

"How was the party last night?" Andreas asked as he started tying the other end for him.

Leon shot him a glance. "Fine, but I have to tell you Dad wasn't too thrilled you didn't make a showing. He was hoping to see you there with Irena."

Irena Liapis was a favorite with the family and the daughter of his parents' good friends who owned one of the major newspapers in Greece. It was the same paper that had shown Thea aboard the family yacht.

Everyone was hoping for news that a wedding was in the offing. With his four siblings married, his parents were expecting some kind of announcement from him.

Andreas groaned. No woman had ever been his grand passion. Maybe there wasn't such a thing and he was only deluding himself because he'd been a bachelor for too long. But his feelings for Irena had grown over the months. Besides being beautiful, she was intelligent and kind. He wanted his marriage to work and knew it could if she were his wife.

But last night Gabi Turner's explosion into his life had caused every plan to go up in smoke. Now that a certain situation had developed threatening to set off a conflagration, his whole world had been turned on its side. For the time being he couldn't think about Irena or anything else.

Andreas knew it wasn't fair to keep any secrets from the woman he'd intended to marry, but, as he'd just found out, life wasn't fair...not to the twins who'd lost their mother or to Gabi who'd taken on the awesome responsibility of raising her half sister's children.

By tacit agreement he and his brother started walking up the beach toward the pool area. Using his fingertips, Leon scooped up his sandals lying in the sand. "Your non-appearance was kind of a shocker. Normally Dad gives you a pass."

"It's because he has a soft spot for Melina." She was the baby in the family.

"If you pulled off the Canadian gold-refining merger, I'm sure all will be forgiven."

Andreas frowned. "That might not happen. I'm still debating if it's to our advantage."

"With the kind of revenue it could bring in, you must be joking!"

"Not at all. I think they're in deeper trouble than they've made out to be." He gave his brother a covert glance. "Speaking of trouble, there's something you and I have to talk about in private."

"If you're referring to the acquisition of those mineral rights in—"

"I'm not," he cut him off. "You made a brilliant move on that." Leon was his second in command. "I'm referring to something else that doesn't have anything to do with business. After we eat, come to my villa alone. Make it look casual. You need to see something."

Leon let out a bark of laughter. "You sound cryptic. What's gotten into you?"

"You'll find out soon enough."

For the next hour Andreas joined in with his family and gave Melina the gift he'd found for her on one of his business trips to the Balkans. She collected nesting dolls. The one he gave her proved to be a hit. Once des-

sert was served, he faded from the scene and headed
for his place, nodding to one of the maids on the way.
Not long after, Leon showed up.

"Lock the front door behind you. I don't want us to
be disturbed."

Leon flicked him a puzzled glance as he pushed in
the button. He walked into the living room. "What's
going on? The last time I remember seeing you this
intense was when Father suffered that mild heart attack
last year."

Heart attack was the operative word.

Andreas was still trying to recover from the one Ms.
Turner had given him. Without wasting any more time
he handed the newspaper photo to Leon, who studied
it for a minute before lifting his head. "Why are you
showing me a picture of you? I don't understand." He
handed it back to him.

"If you'll notice the date, this headline is a year old.
When the picture was taken, I happened to be in the
States on business with our big brother. As usual, the
paparazzi got you and me mixed up. That was during
the time you and Deline were separated. This tall, raven-
haired beauty who's looking over at you was the woman,
right?"

Only now did it strike Andreas that Thea bore a
superficial resemblance to both Deline and Irena.
Sometimes it astounded him that he and Leon had similar tastes, not only in certain kinds of foods and sports,
but in women. They were all striking brunettes.

"Yes," he whispered. "And if I hadn't gone to Deline
and told her the truth about that night, it could have
cost me my marriage. I still marvel that she forgave me
enough to give us a second chance."

Leon unexpectedly grabbed the paper out of his hand and balled it up in his fist. "Why are you reminding me of it? Look here, Andreas—" His cheeks had grown ruddy with unaccustomed anger.

"I *have* been looking," he came back in a quiet voice. "Because I love you and Deline, for the last twenty-four hours I've been doing whatever it takes to protect you and keep this news confidential."

"What do you mean?"

"I thought you'd like to know the name of the woman you spent that hour with on the yacht. Her name was Thea Paulos, the divorced daughter of Richard Turner, of the Greek-American Consulate on Crete. Her ex-husband Dimitri Paulos is the son of Ari Paulos who owns Paulos Metal Exports, one of the subsidiary companies we acquired a few years ago."

While his brother stood there swallowing hard, Andreas removed the twins' photo and DNA results from the manila envelope and handed everything to him.

Stunned into silence, Leon sank down on the couch to stare at the children he'd unknowingly produced. Though Andreas had it in his heart to feel sorry for his brother's predicament, a part of him thought Leon the luckiest man on earth to have fathered two such beautiful sons.

"I had our DNA compared to theirs. It's a match."

Leon's face went white.

"I've seen them," Andreas confided. Thanks to Gabi, he'd held and fed both of them, an experience he'd never forget.

His brother's dark head reared back. "You've *seen* them—" He sounded incredulous.

"Yes. They're three months old."

"Three months?" He mouthed the words, obviously in shock. "How did Ms. Paulos contact you?"

"She didn't. Tragically for the children, she died on the operating table giving birth to them."

"She's dead?" He kept repeating everything Andreas said, like a man in a trance.

"It was her half sister, Gabi Turner, who came to my office yesterday. She's the one who arranged for me to see the boys at a park near the consulate today."

His brother jumped up from the couch looking like a caged animal ready to spring.

"Take it easy, Leon. I know what you're thinking, but you'd be dead wrong. In the first place, she believes *I'm* the father."

Leon jerked around. "You didn't tell her *I* was the one in that news photo?"

"No."

His brother averted his eyes. "How much money does she want to keep quiet?" he asked in a subdued voice.

It was a fair question since the same one had dominated Andreas's thoughts when she'd first pulled out the photograph. "Forget about her desire to blackmail me. This has to do with something else entirely."

"And you believed her?" Leon cried, grabbing his shoulders.

Andreas supposed Gabi could have been lying through her teeth. If that were the case… He saw black for a moment before a semblance of reason returned.

"I'd stake my life on the fact that her only agenda for coming to me was to make sure I knew I had two sons before she left Greece."

"Why would she do that?"

He sucked in his breath. "Because she said they deserve to be with their real father if it's at all possible."

Leon's eyes clouded for a moment before he flashed Andreas a jaded look and released him. "It could be a ploy. Where's she supposedly going?"

"Alexandria, Virginia." To her home and her life, as she'd put it. "Her father started his diplomatic career there. I have confirmation of it."

While Leon stood there tongue tied, Andreas's cell phone rang. He checked the caller ID and clicked on. "Mother?"

"Where are you?"

"In my villa." He glanced at his brother. "Leon's with me."

"Can't you two stop talking business for one evening?"

"Yes. We'll be right over."

"Good. Everyone's wondering where you are. Deline's been looking everywhere. We're going to start some family movies."

"Tell her we're coming," Leon called out loud enough for her to hear before Andreas clicked off.

He went into the study and locked the envelope in his desk, then eyed his brother soberly. "Since Gabi thinks I'm the father, we'll leave it that way for now."

As soon as Leon handed the wad to him he set it in an ashtray on the coffee table and put a match to it. When the evidence was gone, he lifted his head. "Before you make a decision about anything, you need to see the twins for yourself."

Another odd sound escaped his brother.

"I'll phone Gabi and see if we can't arrange it for Monday. We'll make up some excuse to the family about a business emergency. We won't have to be gone long."

Leon buried his face in his hands. "How am I going to be able to act like everything's normal until then?"

A shudder passed through Andreas's body. "We're both going to have to find a way."

His dark head reared back. "When Deline finds out about this... I swear I've been doing everything to make our marriage work. It only happened that one time, Andreas. It'll never happen again. I love Deline." The tremor in his voice was real enough.

"I believe you."

"You know the reason why we separated for those two months. We'd been fighting over my working too much. She got on that old rant about my being married to you instead of her. She said she was tired of being neglected and told me I was the reason we hadn't gotten pregnant yet.

"When she told me she wanted a separation because she needed time to think, I was in hell. After weeks of trying to get her to talk to me, she told me she was thinking of making the separation permanent. I was so hurt, I ended up taking the yacht out. Some of my friends came along and brought women. There was too much drinking. I never meant to lose my head."

Andreas had heard it all before. He'd seen his brother was in anguish then, but this news added a terrifying new wrinkle.

After pacing the floor, Leon stopped and faced Andreas. "I know that was no excuse for making the ghastliest mistake of my life." His mouth formed a thin line. "Sorry you got involved in this mess." There was a lengthy pause. "It isn't your problem. It's *mine*, but I don't know what the hell I'm going to do about it yet."

At least Leon had admitted responsibility. "Once you've seen those babies, you'll figure it out." Of course

Andreas could tell himself that now, but there was no sure way to know how his brother would feel after he'd gotten a look at them. "Let's agree that for the moment there's nothing else to be done. You go on back and find Deline. I'll be there in a few minutes."

Though he'd promised his mother he wouldn't be long, he found he didn't want to put off the phone call to Gabi until tomorrow. It surprised him how much he was looking forward to talking to her again.

Gabi had just finished changing the last diaper of the night when she heard her cell phone ring. She'd kept it in her jeans pocket to be certain she'd didn't miss Andreas's call if it came.

A peek at the caller ID and a rush of pleasure filled her body. Since her parents had gone out to dinner with guests, she could talk freely and clicked on.

"Andreas?"

"Good evening," came his deep, compelling voice. She liked the sound of it. Thea had obviously found it attractive, too. The knowledge that she'd had an intimate relationship with him increased Gabi's guilt and anger at herself for having any thoughts or feelings about him.

"Am I calling at the wrong moment?"

"No." She left the bedroom that had been turned into a nursery and closed the door. "It's a perfect time." Gabi was the only person to speak for the children. He sounded eager enough to see them again. "The children are finally down until their three-o'clock bottle, thank heaven."

"Then you're going to need your beauty sleep, so I won't keep you."

She let the remark pass. His only agenda had to do with his children, who appeared to be growing on him. That was the result she'd been hoping for. Leaning against the wall in the hall, she said, "Have you decided you want to see the twins again?"

"Yes. Could we meet at the park on Monday?"

Her pulse sped up. "Of course. When would you like to come? Morning or afternoon is fine with me."

"Morning would be an ideal time for me."

"Then I'll meet you at ten o'clock. After they've been fed and had their baths, I often take them on a walk when it's not so hot."

"I'm anxious to see them again."

That was an excellent sign. "The children love any attention." Especially when it was from their father. "I'll see you then."

"Gabi?" There was a nuance in his voice that caught her off guard.

"Yes?"

She heard him take a deep breath. "Thank you for being there for them."

It was too early for her to get a handle on his vision for their future. After his visit on Monday to see the children, there might not be another one. She had to prepare herself for that possibility. "You don't need to thank me. I wouldn't be anywhere else."

"I've noticed you don't accept compliments graciously, so I'll say it another way. Not everyone would do what you're doing. Not for your sister, not for anyone."

"Before you give me too much credit, don't forget I watched the twins being born. It was a life-changing experience for me."

"I don't doubt it. *Ta Leme.*" She knew that phrase well enough.

Gabi hung up, wishing his visit was as soon as to-morrow instead of Monday. She would like to know his plans because she was leaving with the children next week. It was no good staying in Greece any longer. One way or the other, she needed to get on with her life and her parents needed to get on with theirs.

During Gabi's morning walk with the children, Kris had nodded off. Last night he'd played too hard after she'd gotten up to give him a bottle. Nikos, on the other hand was wide awake and raring to go.

When she reached the park bench beneath the shade, she undid the strap and picked him up. He clung to her as she showed him the fountain. The noise of the babbling water had captured his attention. She looked round to see if Kris was all right. As before, her breath caught to discover Andreas standing over the stroller looking down at him.

Every time she saw the boys' father, she experi-enced a guilty rush of excitement that was impossible to smother. He'd dressed in a light blue business suit with a darker blue shirt and no tie, the personification of male splendor in her eyes. Thea's, too.

There was a time when Gabi hadn't thought there was a man who came close to Rand in his cowboy boots and Stetson. While on her two-week summer vacation with Rachel McCallister, her friend from college, she'd fallen hard for Rachel's cousin and his Texas charm. Two weeks of a whirlwind relationship and she'd thought it would go on forever.

Too late she found out there was nothing deeper to back up his fascinating drawl and the smile in those dancing blue eyes. He'd let her go back to Alexandria without making any kind of plans to see her again. When she learned through Rachel that he was getting married to his old girlfriend, Gabi's heart withered.

Since then she'd met and dated some attractive, successful men at her work and at the consulate, but she took no relationship seriously. Her career had become her top priority, the one thing she could count on.

Thankfully she'd learned her lesson well before meeting the legendary Andreas Simonides. Though there was no male to equal his intelligence or incredible appeal, she wouldn't fall into that trap again. Once had been enough.

She walked toward him carrying Nikos. "Good morning."

"Kalimera." His voice had a lazy, almost seductive quality. She felt his gaze linger on her face before he switched his attention to Nikos. Again his gray eyes lit up. "Do you remember me?" He kissed the baby's cheek.

Nikos's eyelids fluttered in reaction. He was so cute.

"Gabi?" His eyes trapped hers once more. They held a trace of anxiety. "I brought someone with me I'd like you to meet."

Who?

Maybe it was a woman he was thinking of marrying now that he was running the Simonides company. Gabi fought to remain calm. Naturally that woman would be hopelessly in love with him. But when she learned he had two sons, would she be able to accept and eventually love the children he'd fathered with someone else?

Suddenly Gabi was feeling very possessive. No woman could mother them the way she could, but it was none of her business since she had no parental claim to the boys.

He put a hand on her upper arm and squeezed gently. "It's all right," he whispered, noticing how quiet she'd gone. "I trust him with my life."

Him?

While her heart picked up the lost beat, Andreas stepped around the end of the wall. Within two seconds he came back again, but at this point Gabi thought her vision had become blurred because she was looking at two of Andreas.

She blinked in alarm, but nothing seemed to clear her double vision. They came closer, in range now, she realized there was nothing wrong with her eyesight. Moving toward her was Andreas and his mirror image wearing a tan suit and cream shirt, only he didn't have a scar and his hair was the same style and longer length as in the news photo.

Gabi stared at Andreas in surprise. "You're a *twin!*"

"That's right. Gabriella Turner, meet my best friend and older brother by five minutes, Leonides Simonides."

"Hello, Mr. Simonides," she said, shaking his hand.

"Leon? Say hello to your sons."

CHAPTER THREE

Thea had been with Leonides Simonides, not Andreas?

"Ms. Turner? I hardly know what to say." Leon looked as stunned as she felt. In fact he barely got those words out because his gaze had fastened on the boys in visible disbelief.

"Gabi's holding Nikos," Andreas stated, filling in the silence. "Down there is Kris, who looks like he just woke up from his catnap."

Swift as the speed of light Andreas caught Gabi's eye and winked. Warmth flowed through her body as she smiled back, remembering the humorous comment she'd made on Saturday about the children being fat cats.

But she couldn't forget Leon. Though Andreas would have told him about the children ahead of time, this still had to be the most earthshaking moment of his life. She wasn't surprised he sank down on the bench literally stupefied.

"Would you like to hold Nikos?" she asked.

"I won't know what to do if he cries," he murmured, ashen faced.

"He won't." She handed the baby to him. By now Andreas had reached for Kris and was kissing his sweet little neck.

Deciding to give them privacy, she wandered to the other side of the park and sat down to finish reading the biography she'd picked up on the life of the French chef Julia Child.

She hadn't enjoyed a book as good as this in several years. Like Julia, Gabi had experienced an epiphany about food. But it hadn't happened until her father had been transferred to Crete where she'd tasted her first *pastitsio* and developed an instant love of Greek cuisine.

During the last few months she'd been practicing in the kitchen at the consulate, determined she would raise the boys on Greek food in honor of both their parents. By now she could make pretty good *spanakopita*.

When she realized she'd read the next page for the tenth time, she closed the book and looked across the park. The babies had been put back in the stroller. Both men stood next to them. It seemed as if Andreas was doing most of the talking. Gabi wasn't sure what it all meant.

Hesitant to interrupt, she waited until he started wheeling the stroller toward her with a grave countenance marring his handsome features. She put the book back in her purse and stood up, noticing that Leon had walked out to the street.

"Let me apologize for my brother." He spoke without preamble.

"There's no need. It's not every day a man is confronted by instant fatherhood, especially when they're twins." The happiness she'd felt earlier to see the children united with Andreas had dissipated. Not in her wildest dreams would she have thought up a contingency where his twin brother was the father!

Andreas eyed her with a solemn expression. "Especially when he's been married three years."

A small gasp escaped her throat. Had Thea known he was married, or hadn't it mattered to either of them in the heat of the moment?

"Obviously he's going to need some time," she whispered.

"You're a very understanding woman. When he can gather his wits, I'm sure he'll want to talk to you." She was fairly certain Leon wouldn't, particularly when Andreas would have already told him she planned to go home to Virginia and raise the twins. But she didn't say anything.

"Thank you for making this meeting today possible, Gabi."

It sounded like a goodbye speech if she'd ever heard one. Leon had probably told him he couldn't deal with the situation. What man could? One night in a stranger's arms wasn't supposed to end up like this. He wouldn't be the first father to opt out of his responsibilities.

She felt sorry for Andreas, who clearly loved his brother and had done everything he could to support him. "Of course. I approached *you*, remember? Thanks to you I won't ever have to lie to the children."

After clearing her throat, she said, "When I get back to Virginia, I'll be reconnecting the phone and will leave the new phone number on a voice mail for you. That way if your brother ever wants to contact me, you can give him both numbers. One last thing. Please let him know I'll never try to get hold of him for any reason."

His eyes turned as black as his grim expression. "How soon are you leaving?" he asked in a gravelly voice.

"The day after tomorrow." She extended her hand, not wanting to prolong the inevitable. "Goodbye, Mr. Simonides."

Tuesday evening Gabi's phone alerted her to a text message while she was packing the last of the babies' clothes into the big suitcase. Her parents were in the nursery playing with the twins, their last night together for two months or more. Pretty soon it would be bedtime. Her dad wanted to put them down.

Since yesterday when she'd pushed the stroller in the opposite direction from Andreas and his brother, she'd tried hard to put the whole business behind her. She thought she'd been doing a fairly good job of hiding her feelings from her parents. Any pain they'd seen would have been attributed to tomorrow's dreaded departure.

Little did they know she'd met the boys' father. To her dismay he was doing nothing to prevent her from taking his children out of the country, out of his life.

Gabi hurt for his sons.

She hurt so horribly she could scarcely bear it, but she had to handle it because that was her agreement with Andreas. She would honor her commitment even if it was killing her.

With a tortured sigh she reached for the phone on the dresser. Her best friend Jasmin knew she was coming home and probably wanted to find out her flight number and time. But when she saw who'd sent the message, her adrenaline kicked in, causing her heart to thud.

I just arrived in Heraklion. When you've put the twins to bed, meet me at the park. I'll wait till morning if I have to because we need to talk. A.

She had to stifle her cry of joy. This meant Leon had been having second thoughts about letting his children slip away without making some arrangement to see them again. It meant she would have contact with Andreas one more time. Gabi wished her pulse didn't race faster at the thought.

After shutting the suitcase, she hurried to her bedroom to change. She slipped off her T-shirt and jeans, then reached for the tan pleated pants and kelly green cotton top she'd left out to wear on the plane tomorrow.

Once she'd run the brush through her curls and put on lipstick, she poked her head around the door of the nursery. Her parents were absorbed with the children, too busy to be unduly curious about her. "I'm going out for a few minutes to pick up some things at the store."

"Don't be too long," her dad cautioned in between singing to Nikos off-key. The scene melted her heart.

"I won't."

A minute later she waved to the guard at the sentry and headed in the direction of the park. Because of the reflection from the water, twilight brought out the beauty of the Greek islands, but never more so than tonight. It was Andreas's fault. The knowledge he was waiting for her had added that magical quality.

Maybe this was how Thea had felt when she'd met Leon that evening aboard the yacht, as if the heavens were close for a moment and one of the twin gods from Olympus had come near enough for a human to touch.

He'd come close all right, so close he'd touched her with two little mortals, and now his twin, the powerful god Andreas, was here to parlay a deal between the two worlds. When Gabi thought of him in that light, the stars left her eyes and sanity returned.

Tonight he wasn't dressed like a god. She spied him at the fountain wearing a cream sport shirt and khakis. No one else was about. Instead of expensive hand-sewn leather shoes, he'd worn sandals like everyone else walking along the beachfront.

He watched her coming, but didn't make a move toward her. "*Yassou*, Gabi."

"Hi!" *Keep it airy.* "I came the minute I got your message because Mother and I have an early morning flight to Athens."

"I'm aware of that." He stood with his hands on his hips, emanating a stunning male virility. "Before you go anywhere, I have something in mind I'd like to discuss with you."

She blinked. "Why isn't Leon with you?"

Andreas studied her for a long moment. "I think you know the answer to that question."

Gabi was afraid she did, but Andreas's presence confused her. "Then I don't understand why *you're* here."

"Because I don't want you to leave Greece."

She struggled to stifle her moan. Of all the things he might have said, his blunt answer wasn't even on her list. Now if Rand had said, "I don't want you to leave Austin…" But he hadn't said anything. As for Andreas, she knew his agenda had nothing to do with her personally.

"I don't understand."

He took a deep breath. "Leon's in a panic right now, but in another day or two he's going to conquer it. When he does, the children need to be here, not clear across the Atlantic."

Gabi was the one starting to panic and shook her head. "I can't stay on Crete."

His pewter gaze pierced her. "Why not?"

"B-because my parents need to get their life back," she stammered. "The boys and I need our own home."

He took a step closer. "You've had a home here for months. I would imagine your parents will be devastated when the babies are gone. Therefore that couldn't be the real reason you're so anxious to take flight. Do you have a lover in Alexandria waiting for you?"

Taking the out he'd proffered, she said, "As a matter of fact I do. Not that it's anyone's business." While she spoke, she watched a young couple who'd wandered into the park and had started kissing.

"You're lying. Otherwise he'd have flown here to whisk you and the children back to Virginia weeks ago." The comment had come out more like a soft hiss. He would make a terrifying adversary if crossed.

She turned her eyes away from the amorous couple. "If you must know, I want the children to myself."

"So they'll know you're their mother," he deduced. "That makes perfect sense, but you don't have to go to Virginia to do that."

Gabi sucked in her breath. "I don't have the means to earn a living right now and Dad's home in Alexandria is paid for. With my savings and his financial help, it will work until they're in school and I can go to work."

He shook his dark head. "I've learned enough to know your father has the means to help you move into your own place here on Crete where you and the boys can be close by but still independent. Why are you afraid to tell me the truth? What's going on?"

Andreas saw too much. "There are already too many questions being asked about the paternity of the twins. My parents don't know anything. If it got out about your brother and Thea, my family as well as yours would suffer and you know it. That's why I want to take them back with me."

"Out of sight, out of mind, you mean."

"Yes."

He rubbed the back of his neck. "That might work for a while, but it's inevitable the day will arrive when the secret comes out. They always do. By then the damage will be far worse, not only for the families involved but for the twins themselves."

"I realize that, but for the present I don't know what else to do. There's—" She stopped herself in time, but Andreas immediately picked up on it.

"What were you going to say?"

"N-nothing."

"Tell me!" he demanded.

Feeling shaky, she said, "I should never have come to your office."

"That isn't what you were about to blurt."

The man had radar. At this point she had no choice but to tell him. Not everything, but enough to satisfy him.

Taking a few steps, she sank down on the park bench. He followed, but stood near her with his tanned fingers curled around the back railing. "Thea's husband would love to hurt our family for backing her in the divorce. He's capable of making trouble that could make things unpleasant for Leon, too."

"You're talking about Dimitri Paulos."

Gabi got up from the bench. "How did you know?"

His eyes played over her. "I did a background check. Thea's passport alerted me she has an ex. Has he threatened you personally, Gabi?"

She pressed her lips together. "No, but suffice it to say he was furious when Thea divorced him. If not for diplomatic immunity through Dad, I don't even want to think what might have happened to her. Dimitri considered her his possession. Thea was convinced he'd hired a man to follow her everywhere."

One black brow lifted sardonically. "My father and I have had business dealings with Dimitri's father in Athens. I'm familiar with his son's more devious methods."

That shouldn't have surprised Gabi. Andreas knew everything. "The trouble is, before she died she told me he was still out for blood wanting to know who made her pregnant. If he were to learn your brother is the father of her twins, he'd love to feed that kind of gossip to the newspapers just to be ugly."

"He can try," Andreas muttered with unconscious hauteur. After a palpable silence he said, "Since your parents must be waiting for you, I'll walk you back."

Gabi shook her head. "That won't be necessary."

"I insist."

He cupped her elbow and they started walking. Far too aware of his touch, she eased away from him as soon as they reached the street and moved ahead at a more brisk pace, but his long strides kept up with her.

When she nodded to the guard doing sentry duty, she thought of course Andreas would say goodnight. Instead he continued on through the front courtyard with her.

She halted. "You don't need to see me all the way to the front door."

"But I do. I want to speak to your parents."

What? Her body tautened in defense. "No, Andreas! My parents aren't involved in this. That's the way I want it to stay. If Leon decides to claim the children, then I'll tell them everything. If there's any discussion about this, he's the one who needs to do it."

He cocked his head. "In an ideal world, it would work that way, but he's not ready yet."

That was obvious enough.

Reaching out, Andreas grasped her upper arms gently. She wished he wouldn't do that. It sent too many disturbing sensations through her body. Her awareness of him was overpowering.

"I have a plan that will solve our immediate problem, Gabi, but you're going to have to trust me."

Her eyes filled with tears. "Thea trusted me. Now look what's happening because I broke my promise to her. After her wretched divorce and subsequent death, my parents have suffered enough pain." Her voice throbbed. "Please just go." She stepped away from him.

His jaw hardened. "I can't, not when things haven't been resolved yet. You know the saying about being forewarned. If our two families know the truth and unite now, no power later on can shake our worlds. Don't you see?"

Yes. She could see there was no talking Andreas out of this. He wasn't the acting head of the Simonides Corporation for nothing. Gabi had only herself to blame. He'd asked her to trust him. Up until a minute ago she'd thought she could. But to go any further with this was like flying blind.

"I—I don't even know if they're still up." Her voice faltered.

"Then call them on your cell and alert them you've brought someone home with you."

She lowered her head. "I can't do that."

"Then I *will* because they deserve to know exactly what's going on."

A shiver raced through her body. Andreas had just put his finger on the thing tormenting her most. She'd hated doing all this behind her parents' backs. Defeated by his logic and her own guilt, she opened her purse and pulled out her phone. When she pushed the programmed digit, her mother answered on the second ring.

"Hi, darling? Where are you? I thought you'd be home before now."

She turned her back on Andreas. "When I went out, it was to meet a man I arranged to see in Athens the other day. He's with me now and wants to talk to you and Dad. I realize this sounds very cryptic."

The silence on the other end told its own story. "Do we know him?"

Gabi swallowed hard. "No, but you know *of* him by reputation." *You and everyone in Greece.*

"What's his name?"

"Andreas Simonides."

"Good heavens!" When the Simonides yacht was occasionally spotted outside Heraklion harbor, the whole city knew about it.

Gabi closed her eyes tightly for a second. "I realize it's getting late, but this is of vital importance. Prepare Dad, will you?"

"Of course. The babies are asleep. We'll be waiting for you in the salon."

"Thanks, Mom. You're one in a billion."

Andreas eyed her as she put the phone back in her purse. "If you were looking for a job, I'd hire you as my personal assistant on your integrity and discretion alone."

She'd just received the supreme compliment from him, but the last thing she'd ever want to be was his personal secretary or anything else that put her in such close proximity to him for business reasons. No way would she allow herself to be put in emotional jeopardy like that again.

"Shall we go in?" She led the way to the front door and opened it. The salon was to the right of the main foyer where Gabi found her parents. Blonde and fit, she thought they were the most attractive people she knew. Andreas wouldn't be able to help but like their soft-spoken manner.

After she made the introductions, he sat forward in one of the chairs opposite the couch where they were seated. Gabi sat in another matching chair, knowing her parents were dying of curiosity.

"I've noticed you staring at me," Andreas began without preamble. "No doubt you've seen your grandsons' resemblance to me. That's because their father Leonides is my brother. We're identical twins, too. Twins run in the family."

While her parents digested that startling piece of information he said, "Nikos and Kris have an uncle Gus and two aunts, Melina and Leila. Until Gabi came to my office on Friday evening, my parents had ten grandchildren. But after our chat, I realized that number has grown to twelve."

"But this is unbelievable!" Gabi's mother exploded. She actually sounded relieved as she looked at Gabi's father. His burnished face had broken out in a smile, the last reaction Gabi would have imagined from either parent.

Andreas sent Gabi a satisfied glance. "Later, she'll fill you in on all the hows and whys of our first meeting. The important thing to know is that on Saturday, Leon met the children at the park.

"Unfortunately he's not ready to claim them yet. His wife Deline knows about his one-night relationship with your daughter Thea while he and Deline were separated. His pain and guilt over what he'd done drove him to go home the next day and talk everything out with her.

"It took a lot of gut-wrenching sessions and tears, but she eventually forgave him because she wasn't without her faults in the marriage, either. But that was a year ago and she has yet to learn he fathered two children. That's the hurdle facing him as we speak."

Gabi's parents squeezed hands.

"When Leon tells Deline about the twins, it could break up their marriage, possibly for good. The irony here is that they've been trying for a baby since the day they got married. It was one of the reasons they quarreled in the first place. She claimed he worked too hard and wasn't home long enough for them to start a family. So far they haven't been successful."

The added revelation hurt Gabi a little bit more. There'd been too much suffering all the way around.

"They'd been separated a while at the time he met Thea aboard the yacht. She'd come with a big group of friends, but Leon didn't know them. His friends had arranged it in order to party and cheer him up. His wife Deline had just told him she wanted a permanent separation. In his grief, he acted out unwisely. It doesn't excuse him for what he did, but it does explain his actions that night."

Gabi's father sat forward. "I'm afraid my daughter acted just as irresponsibly. Her marriage never took. When she won her divorce after a long battle, she made a wrong choice that night."

Andreas frowned, his brows black above his gray eyes. "Even if he was separated from his wife at the time, my brother's in a bad way because of his shame over making love to a virtual stranger when he was already married. His shame is even worse because he knows your daughter has passed away leaving two beautiful little babies who are his. Believe me, he's in anguish right now."

"He would be," her father murmured.

"Leon's my best friend, Mr. Turner. I know his heart."

Gabi bowed her head. She heard the love and the caring in his tone. He really was a wonderful man.

"In another day or two when he's found the courage to tell his wife, he's going to want to see the children again and meet you. Hopefully at that point he'll be able to make some decisions in their best interest."

"I don't envy him," Gabi's mother murmured.

Neither did Gabi, but her thoughts were also on Andreas. This was no shallow man. The depth to his character kept hitting her harder and faster. Only a few days ago she'd thought he had ice water in his veins.

"I've come here tonight to urge Gabi not to go back to Virginia yet. I believe that if she stays in Greece another week where the children are accessible, something good will come of this.

"But she's told me her fears about Thea's ex-husband, Dimitri Paulos. I know him and his family through business. Apparently he became hostile when your daughter asked for a divorce. That's his way. Gabi's worried he's going to keep nosing around until he finds out who fathered Thea's twins. She's afraid that if he learns it's Leon, he'll expose him to the press."

Her mother nodded. "He'd do it without a qualm."

By now Gabi's father had gotten to his feet. "I'm afraid he turned on me when I helped my daughter obtain her divorce."

"It happens. But by the time my brother comes to grips with this situation one way or the other, it will have lost its sensational value. For now I'd like to suggest Gabi and the children be removed to an undisclosed place that's still close enough for Leon to have immediate access."

Gabi blinked. "Where?"

Andreas shot her a penetrating look. "I know the perfect spot," he said with authority and got to his feet. "It's late. Walk me out and we'll talk about it."

The next few minutes were a blur while her parents thanked him for his frank speaking and dealing with this delicate situation head-on. Before he joined her at the front door, there'd been hugs to welcome the twins' uncle to the family. The man was endowed with charm from the gods.

She went outside with him. The balmy night air seemed to make the moment more intimate somehow. Strange little tingles brought an ache to her hands. When she looked up at him, she felt her body come to life with feelings she'd thought Rand had killed. But it wasn't true.

This couldn't be happening again. It just couldn't!

In the semi-darkness she felt his piercing gaze travel over her features. "Gabi?" he said her name in his deep voice. "Will you continue to trust me for a little while longer?"

It was hard to swallow. "After approaching you first, I'm hardly in a position to refuse now. Do your parents know anything yet?"

"No. Leon wants to tell them when he's ready."

"So you have to continue to be the keeper of all the secrets."

"I don't mind."

No, because she was learning what kind of a man he really was. "You have a lot on your shoulders."

"So do you. In fact you've inherited the bulk by taking care of the twins. I'd like to help you with that. We'll think of it as a vacation time for both of us. After all, they're part my flesh and blood."

"Andreas? Are you married, too?" Before she took another breath she needed the answer to that question. "I haven't seen a wedding ring, but I realize some men don't wear them."

In the silence that followed, she felt his sudden tension. "I'm still single. You don't need to be worried I'm keeping secrets from a wife or neglecting her for Leon's sake."

Single. His answer frightened her because she no longer trusted herself around him. When she'd promised to never let a man get under her skin again, Andreas had already found entrance, slipping past her guard totally undetected.

"W-where is this safe place?" she stammered.

"On Milos, in a little village called Apollonia. I realize you're leaving in the morning, but I hope you'll give my idea serious thought. Either way I'll expect a call from you later tonight. Sleep well, *despinis*."

CHAPTER FOUR

ANDREAS had two phone calls to make. The first was one he'd known was coming ever since Gabi had entered his office, or rather blown in with that head of curly golden hair and eyes like the periwinkle bougainvillea outside his villa door.

Like the Venus de Milo unearthed in the ancient town of Milos where he used to dig around the ruins as a boy, Gabi's feminine shape appealed to his senses. With his six-foot-three height, he'd never been partial to shorter women or blondes until now, a fact that surprised the daylights out of him.

Her guileless honesty combined with her intensity had intrigued him. If he were to admit to all the traits he'd found fascinating and endearing since watching her with the twins, the list would be endless.

Something earthshaking had happened to him. Already he felt a changed man. Right or wrong, his desire to be with Gabi was so profound, he realized he had to break it off with Irena.

To feel this way about another woman wasn't fair to her. He hadn't planned for this to happen. It just did…

Maybe Andreas's feelings for Gabi would die a quick death, but until that eventuality he *had* to explore them because he'd never known this kind of excitement over a woman in his life. Somewhere in his gut he knew these feelings weren't all on his side. Gabi wouldn't have asked him if he was married if her emotions weren't involved, too.

Tonight, when they were outside the consulate, it was all he could do not to pull her in his arms and kiss them both into oblivion.

After his shower he hitched a towel around his hips and reached for his cell. It rang until Irena's voice mail came on. Frustrated because this wasn't something he wanted to do by phone anyway, he started to click off when he heard her speak.

"Andreas—don't hang up. I was in the other room and had almost given up on hearing from you tonight. I've missed you."

Guilt smote him. The last time they'd talked had been Friday. Now it was Tuesday night. In that short amount of time he hadn't missed her at all. Another woman had filled his thoughts to the exclusion of everything else. How could that be?

"Irena? Forgive me."

"You know I do."

Yes, he knew.

"Something's definitely wrong. You sound so different."

Heaven knew his world had changed. "I'm not sure how to say this except to come straight to the point because you deserve my total honesty. Up until last Friday you've been the only woman in my life."

A long pause ensued. "And now you're telling me there's someone else?"

He bowed his head. "Let's just say I met someone." Andreas couldn't believe he'd admitted it to the woman he'd loved and had been planning to ask to marry him.

It meant Gabi had a hold on him more profound than even he had realized. "I swear this was the last thing I ever expected to be saying to you."

More silence. "Does she feel the same way?" Irena finally asked in a subdued voice. There were never any tantrums with her. She wasn't like that. He wished she would rage at him. Instead there was this condemning quiet that underlined her pain.

"I sense she's not indifferent to me, but I haven't acted on my feelings yet."

"But you *want* to?"

He drew in a ragged breath. "I would never hurt you purposely, Irena, but until I explore what's going on inside of me, being with you right now wouldn't be fair to you. That's why I'm calling."

More silence. "Won't you at least come to the house so we can talk about this?"

"I will when I'm back in Athens."

"Where are you?"

His hand tightened on the receiver. "I'm on Crete and can't leave." He was in a hotel, wondering how he would be able to wait until morning when he saw Gabi again.

"Does she know about us?"

There's no us. Not anymore. "No."

"Who is she?"

Irena deserved that much. "An American who came to my office because of a life and death situation. She had business with me no one else could help her with. I'm still helping her solve a very serious problem before she returns to the States."

"I see," she whispered.

Except she didn't see. How could she? Andreas wanted to tell her everything, but he couldn't until he knew what Leon was going to do. Irena was best friends with Deline. The whole situation was more complicated than anyone knew.

He clutched the phone tighter. "I know I've hurt you, Irena, but to be less than honest with you at this point would be unconscionable."

"Your father told me your courage is one of your most remarkable traits. After this conversation I have to say I agree with him. I love you, Andreas. I know you did love me in your own way. But you were never *in* love with me, otherwise—" She broke off talking. He knew what she was going to say, that otherwise they would have married months ago. "I'm going to hang up now." The line went dead.

Horrible as he felt for hurting her, relief swept through him that from here on out he wouldn't be lying to her or Gabi.

Before he let any more time pass, he had a second call to make to Leon, who was vacationing for the next two weeks on Milos with Deline and the rest of the family. With Gabi sequestered in Apollonia on the north end of the island nine kilometers from the Simonides villa, the timing and proximity couldn't be better.

In anticipation of her falling in with his plan, he'd made all the arrangements ahead of time. Now there was nothing left to do but inform his brother, who'd known this call was coming.

As soon as they spoke he'd never heard Leon sound so upset. He hadn't told Deline the truth yet, but knew he had to.

After encouraging him not to wait any longer, Andreas hung up to wait for Gabi's phone call. If she chose to fly back to the States in the morning, then he'd take her and the twins home in the company jet.

* * *

Gabi's father patted the side of the bed and stared at her with solemn eyes. "When did Thea tell you about Leon Simonides?"

With that question she realized it was going to be a long night. She sat down next to him. "Right before she died." After clearing her throat she said, "All along Thea thought the man she'd made love with was Andreas. That's why I went to his office."

Her parents listened intently as she explained what had happened to Thea. "When she swore me to secrecy, I intended to honor my promise to her. But after she died, I kept looking at the babies and thinking how terrible it would be if they never knew their father, either. I realized I couldn't go through life with that kind of a secret."

"Of course you couldn't." Her father pulled her into his arms. "I love you more than ever for what you've done."

"So do I," her mother cried. "It took tremendous courage, darling."

"I'm sorry to have lied about my reason for going to Athens on Friday, but I didn't know if I'd be able to get in to see Andreas."

"Thank heaven you did. Honestly, when he walked in the salon, it was like looking at the children all grown up."

Her dad shook his head. "I'm still amazed by what we've learned. He's a very remarkable man. A good one. No wonder he's at the head of the Simonides empire."

"You should see him with the boys, Dad. The way he responds, you'd think *he* was their father." Her voice shook.

Her mother reached over to press her arm. "What's Leon like?"

"I can't tell yet. He was in shock on Saturday and hardly spoke, but the fact that he came at all speaks of his character." She wiped her eyes.

"Seeing those two brothers together will really be something," her mom said. "That's how it's going to be for Kris and Nikos."

Gabi nodded. "Thea was so beautiful, and they're so handsome already. When they've become men, they'll be as spectacular as Andreas—I mean Leon."

"Does he know Kris will have to undergo a series of surgeries in the future?"

"Not yet, Mom," she mumbled.

"Why didn't you tell him?"

"Because I knew Leon was in shock. When I put myself in his place, I realized how hard it would be for him to tell his wife. I suppose I didn't want to scare him off or have him thinking I was after his money to pay for the medical expenses."

Gabi's father patted her arm. "Tell Andreas. He'll know the best way to broach his brother."

Her dad was right. "I will."

"Do his parents know anything yet?"

"No."

"So where is this safe place he was talking about?"

She slid off the bed, too filled with nervous energy to sit any longer. "On Milos."

"Of course," her father said. "Their family compound is on that island in a private bay that is better guarded than the White House."

"Actually, he mentioned I'd be staying at a nearby village called Apollonia, but I don't know any of the details yet. He said to leave everything to him, but I have to be sure it's the right thing to do. I told him I would have to think about it. He's waiting for a phone call from me tonight."

Her dad cleared his throat. "I guess your mother and I don't have to tell you how wonderful it would be to know you and the children are close by while Leon is deciding what to do. Naturally I'd prefer that you stayed right here and—"

"No, Dad," she interrupted him. "I don't know how you've done your work through all this, but it's time you were able to concentrate on the job you were appointed to. You have too many dignitaries coming and going to put up with so much distraction."

"You and the children are hardly a distraction, Gabi."

"You know what I mean. Your life isn't conventional. You need to get back to it. Andreas told me to think of this as a vacation."

Her mother flicked her a thoughtful glance. "If Leon realizes he wants his children, then you have to admit Andreas has come up with a temporary solution that suits everyone. A week from now and everything could be settled. But it's your decision."

That was what was haunting Gabi. No decision sounded like the right one.

If Leon wanted to claim his children and raise them, then she would be free to get back to her old life in the States. But her world had changed so dramatically since her arrival on Crete four months ago, she didn't know herself anymore.

The twins had come to mean everything to her. As for Andreas... She kneaded her hands. He was waiting for her to get back to him.

She paused in the doorway fighting conflicting emotions. "Andreas is doing everything in his power to unite his brother with his own babies. I started all this and need to finish it, so I'll tell him yes. See you in the morning."

Once out the door she rushed down the hall to her room to make the phone call. He answered on the second ring.

"Gabi?" came the deep voice she could pick out over anyone's. "Did you discuss this with your family?"

"Yes." She struggled to sound calm. "The children need their father. If my coming to Milos will hasten the process, then so be it."

"Good. Now here's what I want you to do. Follow through exactly with the plans you and your parents have for tomorrow morning. But when you arrive at the airport, tell the driver to take you through to the heliport where my helicopter will be waiting. I'll be there to help you and the boys aboard."

"All right." She gripped the phone tighter. "Andreas—there's something else you need to know. I should have told you before now, but I was afraid."

"Of what?"

"That you would believe what you first thought about me—that I was out to get money from you."

"Go on."

"This concerns Kris."

"What about him?" Just now she heard a raw edge to his voice.

"He was born with a defective aortic valve in his heart. No one knows why. He didn't inherit anything genetic from Thea. She didn't develop heart trouble until she became pregnant. His condition is called stenosis."

"I noticed he's a little smaller."

Most people saw no difference in the twins, but nothing got past Andreas. "According to his pediatrician here in Heraklion, he'll have to undergo his first operation next month. I'd planned to have the surgery done in Alexandria with a highly recommended pediatric heart specialist."

"We have one of the best here in Athens," Andreas murmured, sounding far away. "How many procedures will be required?"

"Maybe only one more after that. The doctor said most valves have to be replaced every two to three years, but with non-embryonic stem-cell heart tissue, the replacement valve should grow as Kris grows and no more surgery will be necessary. That's what we're hoping and praying for."

"Amen to that."

She put a hand to her throat. "When do you think you'll tell your brother?"

"Tonight. He needs to be apprised of all the facts before you're settled on Milos. In the next few weeks he and I will start giving blood for Kris's fund."

"Our family plans to give some, too. To look at him you wouldn't know anything's wrong. He's so precious."

"Until now I've never coveted anything of my brother's."

"I know what you mean. If the gods were giving out perfect children, you wouldn't have to look any further than Kris and Nikos."

"No," came the husky rejoinder. "Get a good sleep for what's left of the rest of the night, Gabi. Tomorrow's a new day for all of us."

"Andreas—"

"Yes?"

"I just wanted to say that I think Leon is very lucky to have a brother like you. Would that the twins develop that kind of love for each other. Goodnight."

"We're coming up on the little fishing village of Apollonia, named after the god Apollo." Andreas had been giving Gabi an insider's tour of the Cyclades from his position in the co-pilot's seat.

She'd never been to Milos. As the pilot swung the helicopter toward the beautiful island sparkling like a gem in the blue Aegean Gabi's breath caught. She'd once visited the islands of Mykonos and Kea on the ferry, not by air. To see all the fantastic volcanic formations and colorful beaches from this height robbed her of words.

During the flight from Heraklion, her awestruck gaze had met his many times. Maybe it was a trick of light from being at this altitude in a cloudless sky, but when he looked at her the gray of his irises seemed to turn crystalline, almost like a glowing silver fire.

The twins were strapped down in their carry-cots opposite her so she could watch them. They'd stayed awake during the flight, good as gold.

"Is that Apollonia down there hugging the bay?" she questioned as they drew closer.

Andreas chuckled. "No. That's the home of the Simonides clan. Apollonia is just beyond it."

Gabi was staggered. She stared at the twins. Little did they know the lineage they came from included a kingdom as magical as anything she'd seen in a fairy tale. But instead of towers and turrets and drawbridges, it was a gleaming white cluster of cubical beauty set against an impossibly turquoise-blue sea found only in this part of the world.

Further on lay the picturesque little town where she'd be staying. It was built in the typical royal blue and white motif along a sandy beach, the kind you saw in videos and on postcards advertising the charm of the Greek islands. Before the helicopter landed, she knew she was going to love it here.

She picked out the boats at the village pier. There appeared to be myriad shops and restaurants close by, an idyllic vacation spot if there ever was one. As soon as they landed and the blades stopped rotating, Andreas helped her and the twins into a car waiting by the helipad.

The pilot loaded her luggage and the stroller into the trunk. There was a considerable amount of stuff. She poked her head out the window. "Thank you!" she called to him. "When you travel with babies, there's no such thing as packing light."

Both men flashed each other a grin before Andreas took his place behind the wheel and started the motor. Seated across from his hard-muscled body, Gabi felt an excitement out of all proportion to the reason why she and the twins had been whisked to this heavenly place.

He drove them past tavernas and bars, pointing out a supermarket and a bakery where she could buy anything she needed. In a few minutes they turned onto a private road that wound beneath a cluster of trees and ended at a perfectly charming blue and white house with its own shaded garden and stone walkways.

Gabi let out a sound of pleasure. "This is an adorable place, Andreas."

"I'm glad you like it. From the front door you step right out onto the beach. The house is fully air-conditioned, another reason why I chose it."

"The babies and I will be happy as clams here."

He darted her a curious look. "That's an odd American expression. Do you think clams are happy?"

She burst into laughter. "I have no idea, but I know we will be."

His low chuckle followed her as she got out of the car to open the back door. By now the twins were so awake they were eager to escape their confinement. While she released Kris's carry-cot from the strap, Andreas removed Nikos. Together they walked toward the door where a pretty, dark-haired woman who looked to be in her mid-twenties held it open for them.

"*Kalimera*, Kyrie Simonides."

"*Kalimera*, Lena. This is Gabi Turner." The two women smiled. "Lena and her husband manage this resort. They have a son, Basil, who's five months old."

"Oh—I'd love to see him."

"He's with my husband right now, but I'll bring him out to the garden later in the day. How old are your children?"

"Three months."

"They are very beautiful." Lena's glance slid to Andreas, no doubt trying to figure out their relationship when the wiggling babies looked like *him*, not Gabi. "We have maid service. If you need anything, pick up the phone and the office will answer."

"Thank you. This is delightful."

"I think so, too. Enjoy your stay."

After she walked off, they moved through to the living room whose white interior was accented with dark wood furniture and blue accessories. "What a charming house!" she cried.

"I'm glad you like it." Andreas sounded pleased as she followed him through to one of the bedrooms down the hall where two cribs and a set of dresser drawers had been set up. Everything was impeccably clean.

Andreas helped her lift the boys out of their carry-cots and lay them down in their cribs. "I'll bring in your things."

"That would be wonderful." She kissed Kris. "The babies have been awake for a long time and are getting impatient for their lunch, but first they're going to need a diaper change."

"Afterward I'll help you feed them."

"That won't be necessary."

"What if I want to?"

His playful teasing didn't fool her. "You've done more than enough, Andreas. I can just picture your exceptional receptionist wondering where on earth you've disappeared to."

She watched him kiss Nikos. "Didn't I tell you I'm on vacation? The whole family's here for the next two weeks."

This time her heart really did get a major workout. "As I recall, you were going to give me an appointment at three o'clock yesterday afternoon."

"If *you* recall," he murmured, coming to stand next to her, bringing his warmth and enticing male scent with him, "a life and death situation altered the scheme of our lives."

Gabi gripped the railing of the crib tighter. *Our* lives was right. When she'd gone to his office in Athens on

Friday, the idea that days later she'd be alone with him on Milos would have stretched the limits of her imagination. Yet here she was…

"For the time being, my first priority is to lend Leon moral support." On that succinct note he left the bedroom.

While he was gone she gave herself another lecture about remembering why she'd been temporarily ensconced in this corner of paradise. Leon was blessed to have his brother's backing. As Gabi's father had said, Andreas was a good man. *How* good no one would ever know who hadn't walked in her footsteps since last Friday evening when she'd first confronted him.

In a few minutes he'd returned with the diaper bag and bottles of formula already prepared. They changed the babies before going into the living room to feed them. He was as confident and efficient as any seasoned father. Whether Leon ended up raising them or not, Andreas had claimed his nephews. She had an idea he would be an intrinsic part of their lives from now on.

After they put the twins down for their nap, Andreas announced he was leaving for his villa. "I'll be back with food before they're awake." He flicked her a heavy-lidded glance before disappearing from the house.

While she was taking clothes out of the suitcase to hang up and put in drawers, she heard the car drive off. He'd told her the Simonides compound was only ten minutes away by car, but already she missed him. To keep herself busy she acquainted herself with the rest of the house.

A perfect little kitchen containing snacks and a fridge stocked with drinks connected to the living room. On the other side was a hall with a bathroom separating two bedrooms. Hers had a shady terrace with loungers and a table looking out on the translucent water. The pots of flowers and an overhang of fuchsia-colored bougainvillea on the trellis gave off a subtle perfume.

Gabi hugged her arms to her waist, hardly able to contain the rush of euphoria that swept through her. She was in that dangerous state where the lines were blurred and she was imagining something quite different than the reality of her situation.

The beach was calling to her, so, with Lena's assurance that she would watch over the babies, Gabi changed into her two-piece aqua-colored swimming suit. A month ago she'd wandered into a little shop in Heraklion and had bought the most modestly cut outfit she could find, but it still revealed more than she liked. A tan might have helped, but this hadn't been a summer to relax in the sun.

After smoothing on some sunscreen, she grabbed a large striped towel and left for the beach through the terrace exit. A person could step down to the sand where the sea was only ten yards away, no more. It shimmered like a rare aquamarine. She dropped the towel and ran out, luxuriating in the calm water whose temperature had to be in the seventies.

Gabi swam for a while, then floated around on her back while she watched various sailboats and the occasional ferry in the distance. There were a few other people farther down the beach, but for the most part she had this area to herself. Doing a somersault, she swam underwater to examine the shallow sea floor before surfacing to reach the beach and stretch out on her towel.

While she lay there on her stomach thinking this was pure heaven, she heard a motor that signaled a boat was approaching. When the sound was suddenly cut, she lifted her head from her arms and realized a ski boat had glided right up on the sand.

Her double vision was back as two Greek gods in dark swimming trunks jumped down from the sides with the kind of agility any male would kill for and walked in her direction.

"Andreas—" She sat up with a start, taking the towel with her to give herself a little protection from his all-seeing eyes. Then she remembered her manners, her gaze darting to his brother. "How are you, Leon?"

A faint smile hovered around his lips. "More in control than I was a few nights ago. I apologize for my rude behavior."

She shook her head. "There's no need."

"There's *every* need," he insisted, reminding her of a forceful Andreas. "I should be the one asking you how you are. You've been taking care of my sons all this time and I never knew."

Gabi smiled. "They're my nephews so it's no sacrifice, believe me."

"May I go in and see them?" He was making the effort, she'd give him that.

"Of course. If they start to fuss, there are bottles of formula made up in the fridge. Just warm them up in some hot water. Andreas?" She flicked her gaze back to him. "Why don't you show him their room while I go for another swim? If they wake up, it will be lovely for them to see their daddy."

His white smile had a domino effect that slowly melted every bone in her body. "When you surface again, climb up the back ladder into the boat and I'll take you for a ride. While Leon gets acquainted with them, we'll enjoy a picnic on the water."

"That sounds good. I'm getting hungry." It was already three-thirty. She'd lost track of the time.

"So am I." His husky tone caused a ripple effect through her body.

The second they disappeared through the front door, she hurried into the bedroom via the terrace and grabbed a loose-fitting short sundress with spaghetti straps she often wore over her suit as a cover-up.

Their deep male voices faded as she rushed back to the beach. After shaking out the towel, she walked in the water and chucked her things in the back of the boat before climbing in. By the time Andreas emerged from the house, she was presentable enough to feel comfortable being with him.

He ran toward her, shoving the boat back into the water, then he levered himself effortlessly over the side. His brief glance managed to take in all of her before he started the motor. "We'll head for Kimolos." He nodded toward an island that couldn't be more than a mile away. "The sight of the little village of Psathi is worth the short trip."

Halfway across, he turned off the engine and joined her in the back so they could eat. In the hamper were sodas, fruit and homemade gyros. No food had ever tasted so good. She didn't have to search for a reason why.

"Thank you for a wonderful meal. In fact this whole trip."

Andreas stared at her while he munched on an apple. "Thank *you* for not giving up trying to get in to see me."

Gabi knew what he meant. Her mouth curved in a half-smile. "We need to thank your receptionist. Without her going out on a limb for me, that would have been the end of it." Then a slight frown marred her brow. "But maybe it would have been better if she hadn't had compassion on me."

Lines darkened his striking features. "Don't *ever* say that. I don't even want to think about it."

Neither did she. A world without Andreas was incomprehensible to her. She finished her cola. "What are your brother's feelings by now?"

Letting out a heavy sigh, he closed his eyes and lay back on the padded bench to get the full effect of the sun for a moment. End to end, his toned physique with its smattering of dark hair plus his chiseled profile proved to be too much for her. She turned her head to stare anywhere but at him.

"If the twins hadn't tugged at Leon's heart the first time he saw them, he wouldn't have agreed to my plan for you to bring them here. When I told him Kris has to go in for heart surgery next month, that seemed to jar him to the reality of the situation. But he's terrified because he loves Deline and is afraid he'll lose her when she learns the truth."

"I can't imagine being in his position."

After a silence, "If you were Deline, do you think *you* could handle it?"

His searching question brought her head around. They looked at each other for a long time. "I don't honestly know. She forgave him for what happened a year ago, but now that the other woman's children are involved..."

She bowed her head. "If I loved him desperately, it might be possible. At the time he didn't know he'd gotten my sister pregnant, but I'm not Deline. Do they have the kind of love for each other to deal with it?"

He jackknifed into a sitting position and put his feet on the floor of the boat. His eyes looked haunted. "After he tells her, I guess they're going to find out how solid their marriage really is."

Gabi stirred restlessly. "He needs to do it soon. Every day that passes while he keeps it from her will make it harder for her to trust him."

"I told him that the night he saw the children at the park."

"Andreas—much as I'd love to go sightseeing with you this afternoon to give him more time with the twins, I think we should go back. You need to impress on him that if he waits even another day, it might be too late to convince Deline of anything."

"I agree," his voice rasped.

"Trust is everything. If Leon wants to prove his love, then he needs to approach her *now*."

He nodded. "Not only that, every day he's away from his sons, he's losing that vital bonding time with them." Andreas sprang to his feet. "Let's go."

With the sea so placid, they made it back to the beach in a flash, but Gabi had returned in a completely different frame of mind than when they'd headed for open water. She jumped into the shallows carrying her towel above her head and walked in the front door of the house ahead of Andreas.

To her surprise, Leon had brought the children into the living room. It was a touching scene to see the three of them spread out on the quilt together. Nikos lay next to his daddy, who held Kris in the air, kissing his tummy to produce smiles.

Andreas's eyes looked suspiciously bright as he darted her a glance that spoke volumes. While she held back, not wanting to interrupt, he lifted Nikos from the floor and cuddled him.

Leon stood up with Kris pressed against his shoulder. "I can't believe they're mine." He spoke into the baby's soft black hair. He was totally natural with the children now.

"I dare say you've produced the most beautiful sons in the entire Simonides clan."

He eyed Andreas with a soulful look. "No matter what, I have to tell Deline today. Come with me, bro."

What Gabi had been hoping for had come to pass, yet with those words *no matter what* she felt a door close on her secret dream of adopting the twins herself. It was as if her heart had just been cut out of her body.

CHAPTER FIVE

"GABI?" Leon had turned to her. "I'm not sure when I'll be back. Do you mind being responsible for the twins a while longer? You know what I mean."

Yes. She knew exactly, but by some miracle she didn't give in to the impulse to break into hysterical sobbing. "I've loved taking care of my nephews and want to help you any way I can. Why don't you put the children back in their cribs so I can change them?" she suggested in the brightest voice she could muster.

As they headed for the bedroom she was aware of Andreas's avid gaze leveled on her, but she managed to avoid contact. He could see inside her soul. If she were to make the mistake of looking at him, her composure would dissolve. This was a pivotal moment for Leon. An emotional meltdown on her part now could ruin everything.

Thankful after they'd left the room and she could hear the rev of the boat engine, Gabi put clean diapers on the twins and got them ready for an evening walk around the village in their stroller. Next to the bakery was a deli where she could buy some food ready to go.

Once she'd showered and had dressed in a matching blue skirt and sleeveless top, she wheeled them out of the back door. Lena happened to be pushing her little boy along in his stroller as she did some weeding.

The two of them talked and pretty soon they went into the village together. Gabi enjoyed the other woman's company. It helped not to think about the loss that was coming. If she were honest, it wasn't only the twins she was already missing...

Three hours later she was putting the babies to bed when her cell rang. The sight of Andreas's name on the caller ID caused a fluttery sensation in her chest.

"Hello?" She knew she sounded anxious.

"I called as soon as I could, Gabi."

"You don't owe me anything. H-has Leon told his wife?" Her voice faltered.

"Yes."

His silence made her clutch the phone tighter. "Was it awful?"

"I won't lie to you. It was a great deal worse."

Tears clogged her throat. "I'm so sorry."

"So am I. She's threatened to divorce him and has flown back to Athens in the helicopter. I just drove him to the island's airport so he could take a plane to catch up to her."

A whole new world of pain had opened up for them.

When Thea had divorced Dimitri, Gabi had been overjoyed, but this was an entirely different situation. From all accounts Deline was a lovely woman who didn't deserve to have any of this happen to her. Neither did the babies. But the fact remained Leon and Thea had made a mistake that had caused heartbreak in every direction.

"Does your family know the reason they left Milos?"

"Not yet, but it's only a matter of time," he ground out.

She moistened her lips nervously. "What would your brother like me to do?"

"Stay right where you are. I'll bring the car around at eight-thirty in the morning. We'll drive to the pier where the cabin cruiser will be waiting. I need a solid break and intend to show you the sights of the island. Pack enough formula in case we want to dock somewhere overnight. Stavros will take care of everything else."

Her body trembled.

An invitation to party overnight on the Simonides yacht had proved too much of a temptation for Thea. Gabi wasn't any different. The desire to spend uninterrupted time with the twins' uncle aboard his cabin cruiser filled her with secret longings that had her jumping out of her skin.

When she thought about it, she would never again have the opportunity to be with a man who thrilled her the way Andreas did. In a few days Leon would make definitive plans where the twins were concerned and Gabi would be leaving Greece.

So why not enjoy this time with Andreas? As long as she recognized he was a bachelor who didn't take his relationships with women seriously, then she wouldn't either. She'd learned her lesson with Rand.

In the future she would come to visit her family and the twins from time to time, but she had a career waiting for her back in Virginia. The boys' lives were here with their father. They would need to get used to the nanny Leon would employ to help him.

Gabi couldn't possibly stay around, otherwise none of it would work; therefore this little bit of time on Apollonia was all she was going to get with Andreas. As she'd told his receptionist on Friday, "I'll take it!"

"Eight-thirty's a perfect time. The three of us will be ready. Goodnight, Andreas." She hung up before she betrayed herself and kept him on the phone if only to listen to the sound of his deep, mellifluous voice.

With the babies down until their next feeding, Andreas instructed Stavros to bring the cruiser as close to the cave opening as possible. A side glance revealed that a golden-haired nymph had come to join him on the swim platform and was ready to dive with him.

Her modest two-piece suit only seemed to add to the allure of her beautifully proportioned body. Compared to the bronzed females he'd seen at various beaches throughout the day wearing little or nothing at all, her delicious femininity and creamy skin—unused to so much sun—drew his gaze over and over again.

"Are you sure you want to try this, Gabi? We've done a lot of swimming today. If you're tired, we can explore here in the morning."

She flashed him a mischievous smile that gave his heart a wallop of a kick. "After the big buildup about an evening swim at your favorite beach, you couldn't stop me!"

Without warning she leaped off the side and headed through the cave opening to Papafragas beach at a very credible speed.

Andreas hadn't had this much fun in years and followed her into the cool water. Beyond the opening was a long, natural, fjordlike swimming pool surrounded by walls of white rock. He heard her cry of delight.

"This is fabulous, Andreas!" Her voice created an echo.

He caught up to her and they both treaded water. "You can see the deep caves where pirates used to hide."

Her lips twitched. "Even modern-day pirates like the Simonides twins, I would wager." She kept turning around, looking up at the incredible rock formations. "It's time for the truth, Andreas. Between you and Leon, how many girls did you used to bring here on an evening like this, pretending surprise that you were the only ones about?"

His laughter created another echo. "You've caught me out. We brought our share. It's true that this late in the day most tourists have gone back to wherever they came from." He'd planned it this way because he'd wanted Gabi to himself. "Come on. I'll race you to the beach at the other end."

Another fifty yards lay a strip of sand still warm from the sun, though its rays no longer penetrated here. She reached it first and sank down in it, turning over so she could look up at the sky. "Oh-h-h, this feels so good I'll never want to move again."

"Then we won't." Andreas stretched out on his stomach next to her. He couldn't remember the last time he'd felt this alive.

A come-hither smile broke one corner of her delectable mouth. "We'll have to, if only for the twins' sake."

"They're being watched over. For the moment I'd like to forget everything and everyone and simply concentrate on you." He raised up on one elbow. "You know what I want to do to you."

The little pulse at her throat was throbbing madly. "Yes," she whispered in an aching voice.

A moan sounded deep in his throat. That was all he was waiting to hear before leaning down to lower his mouth to hers. He needed her kiss as much as he needed air to breathe. At the first taste of her, he was shaken by her breathtaking response. After coaxing her lips apart he began drinking deeply. Back and forth they gave each other one hungry kiss after another until it all became a blend of needs they fought to assuage.

Heedless of the fine sand covering their bodies, he rolled her on top of him, craving the perfect fit of her in his arms, the sweet scent of her. "You're so beautiful, Gabi," he murmured against the side of her tender neck. "Do you have any idea how much I want you?"

"Andreas—" The tremor in her voice told him she was equally caught up in the surge of passion sweeping them into a world where nothing existed but their desire for each other.

"What is it?" he whispered after wresting another kiss from her incredible mouth.

"I feel out of control," she admitted against his lips.

He molded her body to his with more urgency. "That's the way you're supposed to feel when it's right. I can't get enough of you." So saying, he kissed her again until they were both devouring each other.

Never having known rapture like this, he wasn't prepared when she suddenly tore her lips away and rolled off him. "Where did you go?" he cried before sitting up. "We're not in any hurry."

"Maybe not, but I'm out of breath and need to slow down before we start back."

He kissed her shoulder. "If you're too tired when we're ready to go, I'll help you."

"You mean you'll get me out of here using the old reliable life-saving technique? Just how far do you think we'd get?" Gabi teased. She'd turned her head, focusing her dark-fringed eyes on him. Their color changed with the surroundings. Right now they'd picked up some of the gray-blue of the water.

"In my condition and the way I'm feeling at the moment, not far, but in time I'd manage it."

"I believe you would," she said with a smile that was too bright after what they'd just shared. His eyes narrowed on the erotic flare of her mouth, an enticement that lured him like Desponia's song. She could pretend all she wanted, but in each other's arms they'd both been shaken by a force that was only going to grow in strength.

"Sometimes I think you're half god the way you make things happen. It's like magic."

"Would that I had the magic to put my brother's world back together."

"I could wish for the same thing."

She got up from the sand and walked into the water to wash off. Bringing her to this spot had been in the back of his mind since last night. He couldn't bear it that they were forced to leave, but they had to get back to the twins.

Although he'd allowed Gabi to believe otherwise, he'd never brought another woman here before, not even Irena. She liked an occasional dip in a swimming pool, but she wasn't adventurous, not like Gabi, who'd sprung onto the canvas of his life with an unexpectedness that had left him reeling.

Until today he could have told Irena that everything he'd done to help his brother through a nightmarish, unprecedented situation had been necessary and it would have been the truth. But being out here with Gabi would have been impossible to explain. More than ever he was thankful he'd broken it off with her.

She would have pointed out that the twins' aunt was already staying in a vacation spot that provided every possible distraction without requiring Andreas's assistance. He would have had no excuse for spending the rest of today and tonight with her on his cabin cruiser. No excuse for coming close to making love to her.

While she treaded water, he threw his head back and looked up at the darkening sky, wishing this night never had to end.

"We'd better go, Gabi." The words came out harsh, even to his own ears. "Do you think you're up to it?"

"I was afraid maybe you weren't and I would have to save *you*," she quipped. So saying, she took off like a golden sea sprite, leaving behind a trail of tinkling laughter he found utterly irresistible.

Gabi gripped the rings that helped her climb the ladder into the boat. After rinsing off in the shower of the swim platform, she wrapped up in a towel and moved toward the rear cockpit where Andreas was talking to Stavros.

She smiled at him. "Did you think we were never coming back and you'd have to deal with two howling babies wanting their feeding in the middle of the night?"

The older man's eyes twinkled. "We would have managed."

"Have they been good?"

"Like little angels."

"I'm glad, then." She raised up on tiptoe to kiss his cheek. "Thank you for being a wonderful babysitter."

Gabi was still trying to catch her breath, as much from the physical exertion of attempting to outdistance Andreas—which was an impossibility—as having been alone with him.

There'd been a moment on the sand when she'd wanted to know his possession so badly, she'd almost expired on the spot. But she knew better than to repeat the mistakes of the past.

She had no doubt Andreas wanted her. He'd been forthcoming about it, and the desire between them had been building until she was ready to burst. Those kisses on the beach were inevitable, but she was wise enough not to read anything more into them. That was why she'd swum for her life back there, so she wouldn't forget the promise she'd made to herself to focus all her energy on her career.

She flicked her host a steady glance. "When I'm back at my job inundated with work, I'll remember this glorious day. Thank you."

"There's more to see tomorrow before we get back to Apollonia," Andreas reminded her.

Gabi knew what that meant. Her pulse throbbed without her permission. "I'm looking forward to it," she said bravely. "Goodnight."

Not daring to meet his eyes this time, she darted down the steps to her cabin off the passageway. Relieved the children lay sound asleep in their carry-cots, she quickly showered again and washed her hair before climbing into bed.

Since spending time on the boat, she'd learned that his stateroom was on the other side of the wall. One more thing she'd picked up from Stavros. This cabin cruiser was Andreas's home when he really wanted to get away on his own.

Gabi realized the older man had let her know she was a privileged person, but she could tell him that without the babies she would never have been given entrée to Andreas's private world.

Almost a week ago today she'd gone to his office. Since then she'd spent some time with him, yet she still didn't know anything about his personal life. He'd only volunteered information on a need-to-know basis. Love for his brother was the sole reason she'd been invited aboard this boat.

With time on his hands, he'd done the natural thing and had kissed her because he knew the attraction was mutual. The same thing had happened with Rand. She'd been a guest on his ranch and he'd enjoyed her to the fullest *as long as she was there.*

Those were the key words to help her keep her head on straight with Andreas until she went back to Alexandria.

Three o'clock was going to be here before she knew it. With the memory of him lying next to her on that sandy beach where she could still feel the taste of his mouth on hers, she closed her eyes, fearing she'd never be able to sleep. But to her shock the twins didn't start crying until seven-thirty the next morning.

Maybe it was the sea air or the gentle sway of the boat. Whatever, they'd actually slept through the night!

After she'd bathed and fed them, she got dressed in shorts and a top before carrying them up on deck one at a time. Already the sun was warm. Stavros had breakfast waiting for her on the up-and-down table, another remarkable invention aboard the cruiser.

"Mmm, that looks delicious. Good morning, Stavros. How are you?"

"Never better."

"I'm glad to hear it. Is Andreas still asleep?"

"No," sounded a familiar voice behind her. She swung around to discover him standing there in a sage-colored polo shirt and white shorts. There couldn't be a more attractive man anywhere in the Cyclades. His slate eyes collided with hers. "I've been waiting for you and the babies to appear. Let's eat. I'm ravenous."

"I'm hungry myself," she admitted. "It must be this gorgeous air." Andreas sat down next to her. Gabi tried to act natural, but after her dreams of him it was close to impossible.

Andreas studied her for a moment. "How did you sleep?"

Was this god from Olympus psychic, too?

"Would you believe these two didn't start crying until seven-thirty? It's the first time I haven't had to get up in the middle of the night. The pediatrician said it would happen when the time was right. Isn't it strange how they both did it at the same time?"

His compelling mouth broke into a lopsided smile. "My mother could tell you endless stories about the mystifying aspect of twins."

"I don't doubt it." She would love to meet the mother of this extraordinary man, but held back from telling him so. Near the end of their meal he chuckled over Nikos, who gave a big yawn. In the next breath he got up and took the twins out of their carry-cots. Propping them in either arm, he moved over to the windows. "What do you think of this sight, guys?"

Gabi had been concentrating so hard on Andreas, she could tell him that the sight of him standing there holding his nephews was the most spectacular one in all

Greece. Terrified to realize how emotionally involved she'd become with him, she found it a struggle not to let him know it.

When she could finally tear her gaze away, she noticed the cruiser was anchored off an unreal white outcropping of elongated rocks set against a brilliant blue sea. She stood up and joined him. "What is this place?"

"Sarakiniko, an Arabic word."

"It looks like a moonscape."

"That's what it's famous for. When we were boys, Leon and I would come here to play space aliens with our friends."

She laughed. "That beats the neighborhood park." Andreas's backyard was unlike any other. "Every time you show me a new place, I think it's the most fabulous spot around. I'll never be able to thank you enough for this tour. I'm very lucky."

He cast her a sideward glance. "Seeing everything through your eyes has taken me back to happier days and times. I'm the one indebted to you, so let's agree we're even."

Once again she sensed he was brooding. If he'd heard from Leon, he would have told her. His change in demeanor had everything to do with his brother.

Gabi knew most men stuck in this unique situation would have left her to her own devices while she waited for word from his brother. Not Andreas. His unselfishness meant he'd put his own needs aside, but it was wearing on him. She wouldn't allow this to happen again.

For the next while they lazed on deck and played with the babies. To convince him he wasn't the sole meaning of her existence she phoned her mother to let her know she and the children were fine. She hoped that if she played it breezy in front of him, he wouldn't suspect how on fire she still was for him.

Her mom was delighted to learn the boys had slept through the night. In front of Andreas she raved about her sightseeing trip and his kindness, then promised to phone again when she knew more about Leon's plans. He could probably see through her attempt to keep everything light and above board, but she had to try.

By the time she hung up, they were coming into port at Apollonia. Since Andreas was still having fun with the babies, she excused herself and went below to pack up the few things in her cabin. She found Stavros and thanked him.

Within a half hour Andreas had driven them back to the house. While he helped her and the twins inside, she sensed he had other matters on his mind. As he was bringing in the last bag, she met him at the door.

"Stop right there. You've done enough." She took the bag from him. "I had the time of my life. Now go. I know you'll get back to me when you have any news."

Gabi felt his gaze travel over her, turning her body feverish. He seemed reluctant to leave. "Promise me you'll phone if you need anything."

His entreaty spoken in that husky tone sent a weakness to her legs. She rubbed her palms against her hips nervously. "You know I will. Now I've got to take care of the babies."

"Before you do that, I need this." In the next breath he pulled her into his arms and started kissing her again. Caught off guard, she was helpless to stop him. Gabi had been dying for his touch since last night. Without conscious thought she slid her hands up his chest and encircled his neck, needing to get closer to him.

He was such a gorgeous man. With every caress her senses spiraled. The heat he created was like a fever in her blood. Another minute and she would beg him to stay. Through sheer strength of will she wrenched her mouth from his and eased away from him, breathing in gulps of air.

"I'll be back. Miss me a little." With another hard kiss to her trembling mouth, he strode off. She shut the door and fell against it while she waited for him to drive away.

As soon as she couldn't hear the car motor any longer, she made fresh bottles of formula, then put the twins in their stroller and headed out the door for a long walk. If her life depended on it, she couldn't have stayed in the house another second, not when she was feeling this kind of pent-up energy. She didn't plan to come back until she'd visited every shop in the village and had worn herself out.

At noon the next day Gabi left the house again, this time taking the twins with her to enjoy lunch in a delightful little restaurant she'd passed last evening. It was a good thing Andreas hadn't come back.

She blushed to realize how wantonly she'd responded to him at the door. Twice now she'd been playing with fire, but only she was going to get burned if she continued to let it happen every time he got near her.

During the delicious meal, the babies created a minor sensation with customers and staff alike. On her way out the door several tourists asked if they could take their picture because they thought the boys were so angelic.

Gabi supposed it didn't matter as long as no one knew they were the sons of Leonides Simonides. In that case their pictures would show up in the newspaper and on television.

Before long she reached the path to the house. As she was about to open the door she heard a female voice call to her. She turned around to see the manager come hurrying up to her. "I'm glad you're back. You have a visitor who's been waiting for a while. She's in the office."

"Who is it?"

"Mrs. Simonides."

Her heart pounded an extra beat. Deline? Was it possible? Where was Leon? Or maybe it was Andreas's mother. Had he dropped her off with the intention of coming by for her later? She could hardly breathe at the thought of seeing him again.

"While I take the children inside, would you please show her over here, Lena?"

"Of course." She rushed off.

Gabi looked down at the children. "Come on, you cute little things. Someone has come to see you. I want you to look your very best."

After wheeling them inside, she brought out the big quilt and put it on the living-room floor where they could stretch out while she changed them. With that accomplished she put them in their white and yellow stretchy suits. The colors brought out the warm tone of their olive complexions. She kissed their necks. "Umm, you smell sweet."

When she heard the knock, she jumped up and darted over to the door to open it. The tall, slender brunette beauty on the other side couldn't be much older than Gabi's twenty-five years. She'd worn makeup but it didn't disguise the telltale signs of pain. Gabi detected a distinct pallor and her eyelids were swollen from too much crying.

"You must be Deline." She spoke first. Her heart ached for the other woman who'd found the courage to come and at least see the children.

"Yes. I understand you're Thea Paulos's half sister Gabriella."

"That's right. Please come in." She had a dozen questions, but didn't ask one. This was too significant a moment to intrude on Deline's personal agony. She followed her into the living room where the twins were lying on their backs making infant sounds. Their compact bodies were in constant motion.

Gabi's lungs constricted while she waited for a reaction from Leon's wife. It wasn't long in coming.

A pained cry escaped her lips and she sank into one end of the sofa as if her legs could no longer support her. Tears gushed down her cheeks. "They look exactly like him, but they should have been *our* children," came her tortured whisper.

By now moisture had bathed Gabi's face. "I'm so sorry, Deline. I wouldn't blame you if you hated me for contacting Andreas. When I went to his office, I thought h-he was their father," she stammered.

"Andreas told me everything." Deline shook her head. "But a situation like this would never have happened to him. Unlike Leon, he doesn't lose his head when he's down or upset. That's why he was made the head of the company over Leon after their father suffered his heart attack."

"I didn't realize." Gabi knew so little really.

"When Andreas is married, his wife will be able to trust him to the death."

The blood pounded in her ears. "Is he getting married soon?"

"Irena's expecting a proposal any day now. She's his girlfriend and my best friend. Her family owns one of the major newspapers here in Greece. She heads the travel section department."

All of a sudden Gabi had to reach for the nearest chair and sit down. Swallowing hard, she said, "Will they be married soon?"

"Irena's hoping so. He's in Athens with her this weekend."

Gabi had to fight not to break down hysterically. It appeared Andreas and Leon had more in common than Deline knew.

Last night Andreas had kissed her senseless. If Gabi hadn't pulled away when she did, she'd have made the same mistake as Thea. When he'd told her he didn't have a wife, she'd taken it to mean he didn't have a romantic interest of any kind at the moment. What a naïve fool she was!

Yet none of it mattered in light of what Deline was going through. Gabi was being incredibly selfish to be thinking about herself at a time like this.

"How can I help you, Deline? I'd like to."

She looked down at the children. "You can't. I've loved Leon forever and always wanted his baby so badly, but it never happened. Now that I'm going to divorce him, there won't ever be that possibility. Life's so unfair." Sobs shook her body.

Gabi's heart sank to her feet. "I agree. My father lost his daughter early, and Thea didn't live long enough to raise her babies. I'm convinced that if she hadn't developed a heart problem, she would never have told me anything and this situation wouldn't have arisen."

"But it did," Deline stated flatly, "and Leon wants his sons, which is only natural. He's told his family, so that's it." She jumped up from the couch. "This morning he came to my parents' home and begged me to fly here and see the children before I did anything else.

"I know what he's hoping for, but he doesn't understand. Even if I wanted to stay with him and was willing to give our marriage one more chance, I don't see *me* in their countenances." Her voice broke. "I'm afraid I'll always see her and resent them even though they're innocent in all this."

Gabi felt such a wrench, she got up and put her arms around Deline. "I admire you for your gut honesty," she cried softly. "I can't tell you how sorry I am."

Deline relaxed enough to hug her back. When they finally let go she asked, "What will you do now?"

"As soon as Leon comes for the children, I'm going back to Crete and then on to the States. My job is waiting for me."

"What do you do?"

"I'm a manager at an advertising agency. It's a fascinating business I like very much." For the twins' sake if nothing else, she had to keep giving herself that pep talk in front of them. If she ever truly broke down, she might not get herself back together again. "Do you work?"

"Not yet, but I have a friend who has offered to let me work in a hotel gift shop. I'm thinking of doing that so I don't fall apart."

Good for her! Gabi could relate. Deline wasn't only wonderful, she had a backbone. "I wish you the very best. I hope you know I mean that."

While they'd been talking, Kris started to whimper. Gabi picked him up to comfort him.

Deline studied her for a moment while dashing the tears off her face. "I was prepared not to like you, but having met you I've discovered that's impossible."

Gabi's eyes filled again. Leon was losing a perfectly fabulous woman. How sad that he and Thea had ever met. Because of that pregnancy, Thea was no longer alive. But following that thought, if they'd never gotten together, there'd be no babies. She would never have met Andreas. No matter how hurt she was, Gabi could never wish the three of them didn't exist.

She walked Deline to the door. "Did you fly here?"

"In the helicopter with Leon. He's gone on to the villa. When he knows I've left the island, he'll be over."

Things were moving fast. "I hope you have a safe flight."

Before she could respond, the baby hiccupped, proving a distraction for Deline, who couldn't help examining his dear little face. "Which one is he?"

"Kris."

"The one who has to have the heart surgery?"

"Yes."

"He looks well."

"I know, but he tires more easily and fusses more than Nikos. He's a little smaller, too. When they're grown, he'll probably be an inch shorter. The doctor said this first operation is going to make a big difference."

Her lower lip quivered. "H-he's so sweet." Her voice caught before she turned away with an abruptness Gabi understood. "I have to go." She hurried off.

"Take care," she called after her.

Oh, Deline…

CHAPTER SIX

WITH a heavy heart Gabi closed the door. After feeding the babies, she put them down for their nap before checking her watch. It was ten after two. She phoned her mother, but all she got was her voice mail. Gabi left a message that she'd be returning to Heraklion without the children.

While she waited for Leon to come for his boys, she checked airline schedules and ferry crossings to Crete. There wouldn't be another flight out of the island airport until tomorrow, but there was a ferry to Kimolos leaving from the pier at five-thirty. From there she would take another ferry to Heraklion.

She needed one more day to be with her parents and get her packing done. Then she'd fly to Athens and make a connecting flight to Washington, D.C. Without the twins to care for, it was imperative she put an ocean between her and Andreas.

A knock on the door broke her concentration. "Gabi? Are you in there?"

It was Leon's voice. She hurried across the room to open it. He looked worse than Deline, as if he hadn't slept in days. "Come in. Your wife said you'd be over."

He followed her into the living room. "I'm not going to have a wife much longer."

There was nothing she could say to comfort him on that score. He knew better than to ask her questions about their conversation since she couldn't answer them out of respect for Deline. "But you do have two little babies who need their daddy. What plans have you made?"

"For the time being I'm going to keep them with me at my villa here. Estelle, the housekeeper, is going to take over as their nanny until I can find a permanent one. Mother will help. The family is around right now, turning one of the bedrooms into a nursery. Everyone's anxious to help me get them settled. Needless to say, my parents are eager to love their newest grandchildren."

"I'm sure they are."

"Gabi?" His bloodshot eyes had gone moist. "I'm aware of how much you and your parents love them. This has to be a very difficult moment for you."

"It is. I won't lie to you about that, but you gave them life. They need you more than my folks and I need them. The sooner you take over, the sooner they're going to become yours, heart and soul."

"You know my home will always be open to you."

"Of course. In two months I plan to fly back to Crete to see my parents for a week. By then Kris will have had his operation and be recovered in time for all of us to have a reunion."

"I'll be looking forward to it. We'll have a family party where everyone can get acquainted."

Gabi wondered how she would live until she saw them or Andreas again. "The next time you're with your brother, please tell him thank you for making the arrangements here. It's been a lovely vacation for me."

"Andreas is the greatest friend a person could have."

I know.

Together they packed up the children's things and put them in his car. Leon had already installed two infant carseats in the back. Then came time to carry the children out of the house and buckle them in.

Throughout the process they stayed asleep, not having any idea that the next time they woke up, they'd be home with their daddy for the rest of their lives. And Andreas would always be their loving uncle...

Such lives they were going to lead being the sons of a Simonides!

She was thrilled for them. For herself, she was dying inside from too many losses in one day. *Don't lose it yet, Gabi. Remember why you sought out Andreas in the first place.*

Leon came around and hugged her hard. "You've been a guardian angel all this time. I'm never going to forget. Before I go, let's program in each other's cellphone numbers. I'm afraid I'll be calling you pretty constantly until I get the hang of being a father. The children will be wanting you all the time."

"For a day or two maybe."

Gabi ran back in the house to get her phone. In a minute they were both set and there was nothing else to detain him. He climbed in behind the steering wheel. She shut the door. Leon pressed her hand one more time before turning on the motor.

Leave now before my little darlings open their eyes.

She waved until everything became a blur.

* * *

The minute the helicopter touched down on the helipad behind the villa on Milos, Andreas climbed out. He'd just come from Irena's, where he'd told her everything. She deserved to know about the twins and the strange circumstances that had brought Gabi into his life.

Even in her pain, Irena demonstrated a rare graciousness before he said goodbye. Now he was anxious to find his brother. He assumed everyone was out at the pool enjoying dinner. After he ate, he'd disappear with his brother.

As he drew closer he could hear his family talking. They sounded more animated than usual. He couldn't help but be curious over the reason why. When he descended the last flight of steps, he saw their large clan congregated around Leon and his parents. To his shock they were holding Kris and Nikos, but the babies weren't happy about it.

Andreas's heart thundered in his chest. He jerked his head to the side looking for Gabi. He felt as if it had been weeks instead of hours since he'd last seen her, but there was no sign of her.

Leon caught his glance and came striding toward him. He pulled Andreas over to the wall where they could talk in private.

"As you can see, the secret is out now. The family knows everything."

Andreas had to admit he was relieved. Now he didn't have to bear the burden of it alone. "Did Deline get a look at the twins?"

"This afternoon. Then she flew back to Athens. I'll be receiving divorce papers shortly."

Unfortunately he'd been afraid of that. "Where's Gabi?"

"On her way home."

It appeared Andreas had just missed her. "You mean the resort."

"No. I mean the States. She said she'd be back in two months for a visit with her folks. That's when I plan to get both our families together."

Two months?

His guts froze. "You mean she's already left Milos?"

Leon stared at him in surprise. "As far as I know."

"And you didn't stop her?"

His brother blinked. "Take it easy, Andreas. Why would I do that?"

"Why *wouldn't* you?" he fired back. "Gabi's been their mother for the last three months. She must be out of her mind with grief right now."

"I'm sure she is, but we both agreed it had to be this way so I could bond with my sons. In this case a complete break was necessary if the babies are going to look to me for their needs now."

Andreas couldn't argue with her logic or Leon's, but after the brief intimacy they'd shared the knowledge that Gabi had left Greece made him feel as if his tether had come loose from the mother ship and he was left to float out into the dark void.

"She asked me to thank you for the vacation arrangements in Apollonia."

He rubbed the back of his neck while he tried to take it all in. When he thought of her response on the beach, and at the door yesterday… Didn't it mean anything to her?

"Bro?" Leon whispered. "Did you hear what I said?"

Yes. Andreas heard him, but he couldn't waste any more time talking. "Leon? Do me a favor and make my excuses to the family while I go inside for a minute. I'll be right back."

While his brother stood there looking visibly perplexed, Andreas raced up the side steps. When he was out of sight of the others he called the resort. "I'd like to speak to Lena. This is Andreas Simonides."

"One moment please." He paced until he heard her voice. "Kyrie Simonides? What can I do for you?"

"I understand Ms. Turner checked out today. Did you order a car for her so she could be driven to the airport?"

"Not to the airport. She went to the pier to get the ferry."

That ferry only went to Kimolos.

His adrenaline surged. "Thank you. That's all I needed to know."

He hung up. Gabi would have to stay there overnight until there was a different ferry to Athens tomorrow. He had time to make plans.

With his pulse racing, he rejoined the family. Two extremely miserable babies were being passed around. They were looking for the one beautiful, familiar golden angel who didn't make up part of the dark-haired Simonides family.

No one—not his sisters, his mother or Estelle could calm them. Leon had to take over, but they still weren't completely comforted. Andreas knew in his gut Gabi wasn't in nearly as good a shape as the twins were.

His mother shot him a curious glance. "Where did you go? Why isn't Irena with you?"

Now was not the time to discuss his breakup or the reason behind it. "She couldn't make it. I had an important phone call to deal with."

"Have you eaten yet?"

"I'm not hungry."

She shook her head. "Your brother told us the saga about the twins and the major role you and Gabriella Turner have played in all of it. You're a remarkable son, Andreas. I love you for your loyalty to him."

"Deline's destroyed all over again."

His mother nodded. "I'm afraid she might not be able to deal with his babies, not when she wants one so badly herself." Her eyes filled with fresh tears. "But the boys are so adorable. It's uncanny how much they resemble you and Leon at that age."

"They have the look of their mother, too. I saw pictures when I was at the consulate."

"The Turner family must be devastated over their loss. Your father and I would like to meet them."

"I'll arrange it." *Just as soon as I catch up to Gabi.*

The splotchy face and swollen eyes that looked back from the hotel-room mirror made Gabi wince. She could only hope that by the time she went aboard the ferry taking her to Heraklion later in the day, all traces of the terrible night she'd just lived through would be gone.

She finished dressing in jeans and a white sleeveless blouse. Her hair, still damp from its shampoo, was already curling. The heat would dry her out in no time. With a coat of coral lipstick, she felt a little more presentable to face the day.

After having given Leon all the babies' things yesterday, she had only her overnight bag to carry down to the pier surrounded with its assembly of fishing boats and other craft. Small groups of tourists were slowly making their way to the same embarkation point where they could see the ferry entering the port.

She hadn't been anywhere without the children for so long, she felt empty. Were they missing her? Her eyelids burned. The only way her parents were handling the loss was because they had each other. They were the great loves in each other's lives.

When she'd thought she'd be raising the twins, she hadn't met Andreas yet and had been glad she was single. Now she had nothing left except her dreams of a god who'd turned out to be too human after all. More than ever she was eager to get back to her career.

"Gabi?"

She thought she was hearing things and kept walking. When her name was called out a second time, she slowed down and turned around. By then it was too late to stifle the cry that sprang from her throat. Her overnight bag dropped to the ground.

Andreas studied her tear-ravaged face. "I thought so," his voice rasped.

Her mouth had gone dry at the sight of him. He looked impossibly handsome wearing white cargo pants and a blue crewneck shirt with the sleeves pushed up to the elbows.

"If something's wrong with the children, why didn't Leon call me? He has my number."

He scrutinized her for a moment. "Whatever happened to hello? How are you? Isn't this a beautiful day!"

Heat spilled into her cheeks, but she didn't look away. "A man with your kind of responsibilities doesn't show up at an obscure port off the beaten track unless there's a dire emergency."

"That's not always true or fair." He stood there with stunning nonchalance. "You're suddenly making judgments about me. What's changed since we last saw each other?"

For him, nothing. Though he had a serious girlfriend right now, he enjoyed being the quintessential playboy up to the very end. Why not? Little did he know the experience with Rand had taught her two could dance to that tune.

"Absolutely nothing. Last week I told you that if Leon decided to claim the children, I had to get back to my job."

He rubbed the side of his hard jaw absently. "I'm the one who brought you to Milos. Why didn't you at least wait until I could make arrangements to get you back to Crete?"

She pasted on a phony smile. "Andreas—I'm a businesswoman, remember? I'm capable of looking out for myself."

His expression tautened even more. "Didn't it occur to you I wanted to do that for you?"

The fact that he'd shown up here proved he was hoping to pick up where they'd left off at the beach. If his girlfriend knew about the other women he played around with, then she had a high tolerance level. Gabi wasn't made the same way.

"It's not a case of occurring to me. You're probably the most generous person I've ever known. But you're also the head of your family's company. Now that Leon's been united with his children, you and I have other fish to fry, as we Americans say. I'm due for a promotion as soon as I return to Alexandria, so it's imperative I leave Greece on the next flight out."

His silvery eyes bored into hers. "Will one more day matter in the scheme of things?"

Yes, considering the convulsion he'd set off by his unexpected presence here. "Since my boss is expecting me, I'm afraid so. Now if you'll excuse me, people are starting to board the ferry."

"Let them," he declared. "My boat will take you wherever you want to go."

She sustained his gaze without flinching. Andreas had an agenda and insisted on taking her to her parents, so there was no point in fighting him. If she kept her wits about her, she ought to be able to handle a few more hours alone with him. Play along for a little while longer. That was the key.

"Okay. I give up. Hello, Andreas. It's lovely to see you again. What brings you to this island on such a beautiful summer morning?"

Laughter rumbled out of him. "That's better."

"I'm glad you think so." The charisma of the man had the power to raise her temperature. "My plan is to go back to Heraklion. I need to pack the rest of my things before I fly home."

He picked up her overnight bag. "Come with me and we'll reach Crete long before the ferry gets there."

Andreas walked her in another direction toward a sleek-looking jet boat tied up in one of the slips. The Simonides family had a different vessel for every occasion. For this trip it was going to be just the two of them. Though she forbade it, she couldn't stop the thrill of excitement that spread through her body to be with him again. She had to be some kind of masochist.

After helping her on board, he handed her a life jacket and told her to put it on. While she buckled up, he undid the ropes and jumped in, taking his place at the wheel. Before he could turn on the engine, she handed him a life jacket. "What's sauce for the goose..." she teased. "Do you know the expression?"

"I know a better one." He smiled back. "Never argue with a woman holding a weapon." He slanted her an amused glance before taking it from her and putting it on his hard-muscled frame. She felt relief knowing that if, heaven help them, something happened on the way to Crete, he was wearing a floating device, too.

The cold, implacable head of the Simonides corporation she'd first confronted at his office was so far removed from the relaxed man driving the boat, she had trouble connecting the two. Before she knew it, they were idling out to sea at a wakeless speed.

"How long are you going to keep me in suspense about what really brought you here this morning?"

Andreas didn't pretend to misunderstand. "Not long." He engaged the gears and the boat burst across the water like a surfaced torpedo.

Gabi had to be happy with that explanation. She *was* happy. Too happy to be with him when he didn't know what it meant to be faithful to one woman. Gabi wished she didn't care and could give in to her desire without counting the cost.

Deline was a much better woman than Gabi. She'd forgiven Leon his one-night stand with Thea. *Until she'd found out about the twins...*

Resigned to her fate—at least until they reached Heraklion—Gabi put her head back to feel the sun on her face. Every so often the boat kicked up spray, dappling her skin with fine droplets of water. She kept her eyes closed in an attempt to rein in her exhilaration.

The problem was, she'd fallen irrevocably in love with Andreas, the deep, painful kind that would never go away. But she'd made up her mind he would never know he was the great love of her life. Nor would she ever dare to say it out loud. An ordinary mortal reaching for the unattainable might bring on the mockery of the gods.

"Tell me something honestly, Gabi. How wedded are you to returning to your old job?"

His question jolted her back to the real world. She sat up, eyeing him through shuttered lids to keep out the blinding sun. "I'm very wedded. Besides being stimulating, it provides me a comfortable living with the promise of great things in the future. Why do you ask?"

He cut the motor, immediately creating silence except for the lapping of water against the hull. In a deft motion he left his seat long enough to produce a couple of sodas from the cooler. After handing her one, he sat down again with his well-honed body turned toward her.

"Thank you. I didn't realize I was thirsty until now."

His eyes, a solid metal-gray at the moment, met hers over the rim of his drink. "I know what you mean." An odd nuance in his low voice caused her to believe he was referring to something else. Memories of the two of them communicating in the most elemental of ways on that beach never left her mind. Trembling, she looked away.

"What do you recall about my receptionist?"

The question was so strange, she thought she hadn't heard him right, but Andreas never said or did anything without a reason. "I suppose I thought she was firm, but fair...even kind in her own way."

"An excellent description," he murmured. "Anna's going to be seventy on her next birthday. She worked for my father forty-five years and never married."

"They must have been a perfect match for her to stay in his employ that long." Gabi imagined the woman had been madly in love with the senior Simonides. If he had a tenth of his son's brilliance and vitality, it all made perfect sense.

"When he stepped down, I kept her on with the intention of asking her to train a new receptionist before I let her go. However, after one day of working with her, I realized what a treasure she was and I refused to consider breaking in anyone else."

Gabi swallowed the rest of her drink. "If it hadn't been for her, the twins would still be without their father. For that alone, I like her without really knowing her."

She heard his sharp intake of breath. "Being a receptionist is only one of Anna's jobs. In a word, she's the keeper of the flame. Do you understand what I mean?"

"I think so," Gabi said with conviction. "She's a paragon of the virtues you admire most."

He nodded gravely. "But she needs to retire and get the knee replacement she's been putting off."

"I noticed her limping."

"It's getting worse every day. The trouble is, I've despaired of finding anyone else like her. Then I met *you*." His piercing glance rested on her, reminding her of something he'd said to her a week ago.

If you were looking for a job, I'd hire you as my personal assistant on your integrity and discretion alone.

The worst nightmare she could conceive of was upon her. She knew exactly where this conversation was going and shook her head.

"Before you refuse me outright," he said, "I'm only suggesting that I could use your help while I look around the company for the right person to replace her. It could take me several months. You'll be given your own furnished apartment on the floor below my office. There's a restaurant on the next floor down for the staff."

"Andreas—" she blurted almost angrily. "What's this really about?"

"I don't want you to leave Greece until we know Kris's heart operation is successful. If there are complications, you'll want to be here."

She didn't want to be reminded of that possibility. "I'm praying everything will go well, but if it doesn't, I'll fly over on the spot."

"That's not good enough."

What was going on inside him? She knew his request couldn't be for personal reasons. Besides his girlfriend, there were legions of women who'd love a fling with him. "Why?"

He seemed fascinated by the pulse throbbing in her throat. "I just came from being with the family. The babies were out of control. We both know they were looking for you." *They were?* "Let's be honest. With the operation coming up, Leon's going to need you. I know it in my gut."

Gabi bowed her head. "They'll get over the separation in a few days and cling to him."

"I don't believe that, and neither do you." Andreas leaned closer to her. "These things take time. I know how much you love the boys. Admit you're dying inside after having to give them up."

"Of course I am." The tears started spurting. Too late she covered her face with her hands.

"Gabi…" Andreas whispered in a compassionate voice.

"When Thea asked me to find a couple who would adopt the boys, it killed me because *I* wanted to be the one to take over. She didn't know that by then I was prepared to give up my career for them. But the law forced me to come to you."

"Thank God it did!" In a sinuous movement Andreas pulled her into his arms. At first she remained stiff, but his gentle rocking broke down every defense and she ended up sobbing against his broad shoulder.

"I know how much you love them," he murmured into her silky curls. "That's why I don't want you to leave. Stay and work for me until Kris has recovered fully from his operation. You and I can visit the twins after work every few days. That way everyone will be happy and it won't interfere with the bonding going on between them and their father."

When she realized she'd be content to stay like this forever, she eased away from him and wiped her eyes with the backs of her hands.

Eventually she glanced at him, never having realized gray eyes could be so warm. His love of the twins produced that translucent glow. "When you put it that way, you manage to exorcize all the demons. Only Andreas Simonides can make everything sound so simple and reasonable, even if it isn't."

"That's all I needed to hear. The matter's settled."

No. It's not. "Nothing's settled. First I have to talk to my boss and determine if that promotion will still be waiting for me if I get back at a later date."

"After knowing you a week, I can guarantee he'll move mountains to accommodate you in order to get you in the end."

Andreas said whatever needed to be said in order to accomplish his objective. That was why he was the head of the family business. There was just one problem. She couldn't figure out his objective. She knew he loved the twins, but he was after something more.

"Tell me the real reason you're asking me to temp for you. By your answer, I'll know if you're telling me the truth or not."

"You're not just anyone. You're the twins' aunt. There's no reason why you shouldn't be able to peek in on them from time to time. That's hard to do from across the ocean." A compelling smile broke out on his striking face. "I want to peek with you."

Andreas…

She averted her eyes. "That's the wrong answer."

"It's the only one I have," he answered with enviable calm.

"You mean the only one you're willing to offer me. Without knowing the truth, I can't stay in Greece even if my boss were willing to give me more time away."

His smile faded. "I didn't know there was more truth to tell unless it's my guilt."

She blinked. "About what?"

He eyed her intently. "About everything. It's my fault my brother's marriage is in trouble again. If I'd left everything alone after you walked out of my office, they wouldn't be headed for divorce and the twins would be in Virginia leading perfectly contented lives with you."

"Except that I couldn't have adopted them."

"They'd have still been yours, Gabi."

"And after they grew up and demanded to know about their father, what then? If I admitted that I'd known his name all along, they might never forgive me."

A strange sound came out of his throat. "You've just put your finger on my greatest nightmare. If I'd kept the secret of the twins over the years *knowing* Leon and his wife could never have children, I wouldn't have been able to forgive myself for playing god with my brother's life."

It was Gabi's turn to moan.

He reached out and grasped her hands. "The truth is, you and I are up to our necks in this mess together. Leon needs our help for a little while longer."

She sucked in her breath. "But you don't really need an assistant."

"Actually I do. Anna's got to get that knee operated on right away."

"You could hire any number of secretaries in your company to replace her."

"I could, but I thought one of the reasons you were leaving Crete was so your parents could get back to the lives they were leading before Thea became ill."

"You're right," she confessed quietly.

"By the time you leave my employ, I'll be hiring a permanent assistant." He kissed the back of her hands before letting them go. A tingling sensation coursed through Gabi's sensitized body and lingered for the rest of the trip to Heraklion.

CHAPTER SEVEN

THE blood donation area of the hospital in Athens had continual traffic. Gabi looked over at Andreas. Both of them were stretched out side by side on cots giving blood. They'd taken the day off from work. It was a good thing since they'd had to wait at least an hour after arriving there before their turn was announced.

In preparation for today she'd eaten a good breakfast and had forced down fluids. Before bringing her to the hospital where Kris would be having his surgery, Andreas had instructed the limo driver to drop them off at a fabulous restaurant in the Plaka for lunch. But instead of ordering the specialty of the house, they'd eaten iron-rich spinach salad followed by sirloin steak.

Andreas was remarkable. In the short time she'd been working for him, she'd learned that when he did something, he always did it right and thoroughly. She loved him with a vengeance. If Kris weren't facing an operation, Andreas wouldn't have asked her to stay on and none of this would be happening.

"This is kind of like lying on the beach at Papafragas."

For him to mention that night—out of the blue—when she'd lost almost every inhibition in his arms came as such a surprise, she almost fell off the cot.

"It's not as warm," she murmured.

"No, and we're not alone. It's a good thing we don't have to swim the length of that fjord later. We're not supposed to do any strenuous activity for the rest of the day. I wouldn't be able to save you."

In spite of that bittersweet memory, she couldn't help but laugh. "Then what are we going to do?"

"I'll tell the chauffeur to drive us back to the office and we'll watch TV in your apartment while we take it easy."

"If you get lightheaded, the long couch is yours," she quipped, but the second the words came out, she regretted saying anything. Since the day he'd shown it to her, he'd never asked to come inside and she'd never invited him. To cover her tracks she asked, "Do you ever watch TV?"

"All the time."

"You're joking—"

He chuckled. "Leon and I are sports nuts."

"I can believe *that*, but when do you find the time?"

"My iPhone. Broadband is everywhere and performs almost every trick known to technological mankind."

"Aha! So in between important phone calls and meetings, you're watching soccer?"

"Or basketball or the NFL."

"How about NASCAR? The Grand Prix?"

"Love it all."

She frowned. "And here I thought you were different."

His smile was too much. "What do *you* watch?"

"When I'm in the States and have time, the History Channel and cooking shows, British comedies and mysteries. I also like bull-riding."

"You're a fan of the rodeo?"

"When I was in college, a friend of mine attending there asked me to go back to Austin with her during our two-week break. We met a couple of cowboys and got talked into going to one. I've been hooked ever since."

He stared at her as if trying to find a way into her soul. "On a certain cowboy?"

"For a time I was," she answered honestly, "but the illness passed."

"Have there been many?"

"Many what?" She knew exactly what he meant.

"Illnesses."

"Probably half a dozen." She didn't want to talk about old boyfriends. The man lying near her made every male she'd ever known fade into insignificance. "Andreas? Speaking of illness, what did Kris's heart surgeon tell Leon when he took him in for his checkup yesterday? You went with him, but you acted differently when you came back to the office."

"Did I?"

"You know you did. If you're trying to spare me, please don't."

Suddenly the curtain was swept aside and two hospital staff came in to finish up and unhook them. "You're all done." They both sat up and put their legs on the floor. "Take your time. There are refreshments outside before you leave the hospital."

When they were alone again, Gabi slid off the cot and turned to him. "I'm still waiting for an answer."

By now Andreas had rolled down his shirtsleeve and was on his feet. "The doctor couldn't promise the operation would be risk free."

"Of course not. No operation is."

"My brother's dealing with too many emotions right now."

They all were. She sensed Andreas was secretly worried, but he hid it well. "On top of Leon's pain, taking care of the twins is physically exhausting work no matter how sweet they are."

His eyes were almost slumberous as they looked at her. "We need time off from our fears, too. Since there's nothing more we can do for the moment, let's go home and relax."

She watched him shrug into his jacket. He sounded as if he meant that they would actually go back to her apartment and spend the rest of the day together, but it was out of the question. Andreas had a playful side that could throw her off guard at unexpected moments, but from the time Deline had told her he had a serious girlfriend, Gabi refused to play.

After they'd been served juice and rolls, the limo took them to the office. They rode his private elevator to her floor. Gabi's heart thudded heavily as they walked across the foyer to her suite.

She opened the door, then turned to him. "Thank you for accompanying me this far in case I fainted, but as you can see I'm fine. If you're feeling dizzy, there's a very comfortable couch to lie down on in the reception room of your office." A smile broke the corner of her mouth. "I know because I spent half a day on it waiting for you to give me an audience."

She heard him inhale quickly, as if he were out of breath and needed more air. "I'm sorry you were forced to wait so long."

"I'm not," she said brightly. "It gave me an opportunity to watch Anna at work. On that day who would have guessed I'd end up filling in temporarily after she left?"

When he still made no move to leave, she said, "Thank you for giving blood with me, Andreas. I'm glad I didn't have to do it alone. See you in the morning and we'll plan that big company party you want to give for Anna after she's recovered from her knee surgery."

Before the weakness invading her body smothered the voice telling her not to let him get near enough to touch her, she stepped inside and started to close the door.

"Not so fast." Andreas had put his foot there, making it impossible to shut it. Quick as lightning he stepped inside and closed it. Her heart thumped so hard, she was afraid he could hear it.

"What is it?"

"What do you think?" he demanded in a silky voice.

Uh-oh. Gabi backed away from him. "I—I'm sure I don't know," she stammered.

He moved toward her. "When I left you at the resort on Apollonia after our night at Papafragas, I held a woman in my arms who was with me all the way. In the blink of an eye I learned she'd left the island. When I went after that woman and found her, she'd changed. Since then I've been waiting for her to re-emerge, but she hasn't. Now I want to know why."

She smoothed her palms against her hips, a gesture his piercing gaze followed while she tried to think up an answer. Unless it was the truth, nothing would satisfy him, but in doing so she would give herself away.

As the silence lengthened a grimace marred his handsome features. "At the hospital you admitted there was no other man in your life, or is that a lie and it's your boss you're in love with?"

Gabi had a hard time believing she'd injured his pride by playing hard to get, because *that* was all this interrogation could possibly be about.

"No," she finally answered with every bit of control she could muster. "Like you, I don't have a significant other I'm keeping secrets from." She'd said it on purpose to watch for the slightest guilty reaction from him. Now was the time for him to admit his involvement with the woman Deline had mentioned, but nothing was forthcoming.

"If that's true, why do you rush away from me the second our business day is over? How come we never share a meal unless it's on Milos while we're checking on the twins?" His eyes narrowed on her mouth. "Have I suddenly become repulsive to you?"

She was aghast. "I'm not going to dignify that absurd question with an answer." If anyone were listening, they'd think he was her husband listing the latest problem in their marriage.

"Then prove it. I told you I'd like to spend the rest of the afternoon with you. We can do it here or at my penthouse."

There was no putting him off. She bit her lip. "Well, as long as you're here, y—"

"My thoughts exactly." He finished her sentence and removed his jacket, tossing it over a side chair. "When we get hungry later, we'll have the restaurant send something up."

She got that excited sensation in her midriff. "Excuse me for a moment."

"Take all the time you need to freshen up. I'm not going anywhere."

That was what she was afraid of as she darted from the living room. The second she saw herself in the bathroom mirror she groaned to see her cheeks were filled with hectic color. After giving blood, she was shocked by her body's betrayal.

When she returned a few minutes later her feet came to a standstill. Andreas had stretched out on her couch with his eyes closed. He'd turned on television to a made-for-TV Greek movie.

He was so gorgeous, she didn't dare move or breathe in case he sensed she was there and caught her feasting her eyes on him. Every part of his male facial structure was perfect. From his wavy black hair to the long, hard-muscled length of his powerful anatomy, he was a superb specimen. But it was the core of the remarkable human beneath that radiated throughout, bringing alive the true essence of what a real man should be.

Maybe it was the combination of giving blood and the many hours of work he'd been packing into each day so they could spend time with the twins. Whatever, it all seemed to have taken its toll. She could tell from the way he was breathing that he'd fallen asleep.

He would never know how much she wanted to lie down and wrap her arms around him, never letting him go, but she couldn't. Feeling tired herself, she lay down on the small couch facing him so she could watch him as he slept.

The movie played on, but she had no idea what it was about. Her lids grew heavy. When next she became cognizant of her surroundings, Andreas had just set a tray of sandwiches and coffee on the table.

Surprised at how deeply she'd slept, she took a minute to clear her head before she sat up. Her watch said five to six! She glanced at Andreas. "How long have you been awake?"

"About twenty minutes. It's apparent we both needed the rest."

"I *never* sleep in the middle of the day!"

She felt his chuckle down to her toes. "You did this time." Did she snore? Help! "I'm going to take it as a compliment you felt comfortable with me."

"In other words it was the proof you needed to realize I don't find you repulsive?"

"Something like that," came the wry comment. "I've already eaten. Have some coffee." He handed her a cup.

"Thank you." She drank half of it before eating a sandwich. In a few minutes she sat back. "That tasted good."

He stood there surfing the channels until he came to another movie. Before she could countenance it, he sat down next to her and pulled her across his lap into his arms.

"This is what I wanted to do earlier."

Andreas moved too fast for her. She could no more resist the hard male mouth clinging to hers than she could stop breathing. Oh—he tasted so good, felt so good. Her body seemed to quicken in acknowledgment that they'd done this before.

Without conscious thought she curled on her side and wrapped her arms around his neck, wanting to get her lips closer to his face. The need to press kisses to each feature took over. She ran a hand into his hair, loving the texture of it.

On a groan he crushed her tighter, then his mouth covered hers again and she thought she'd die of the pleasure he was giving her. "I want you, Gabi. I want to make love to you."

She wanted it, too, more than anything she'd wanted in life, but enjoying a few kisses and sleeping together were two different things. Gabi refused to get in any deeper when she knew she wasn't the only woman in his life. Girlfriend or wife, there *was* someone else. The fact that he still hadn't admitted it revealed the one flaw in him she couldn't overlook.

These last three weeks she'd avoided this situation for the very reason that you couldn't go on kissing each other or it turned into something else. She needed to quit while she could still keep her head. That way she'd have fewer regrets when she got back to the advertising world.

The second he allowed her a breath she eased away from him and stood up. "Much as I'm tempted, I'd rather we didn't cross that line. Remember we're an aunt and uncle to the twins and will be seeing each other on the rare occasion throughout our lives. Many times I've heard you tell potential clients you like keeping things above board and professional. It's my opinion that line of reasoning works well in our particular case."

After his arrival on Milos, Andreas strode through Leon's villa looking for his brother. Estelle told him he was putting the babies down for the night. As he approached the nursery he saw Leon closing the door.

They glanced at each other. "Thanks for coming," he whispered. "Let's go to my room."

"Sorry I couldn't get here any sooner to help with the twins. I had an important meeting." He'd asked Gabi to type up his notes and leave them on his desk before he took off for Milos.

Since the night she'd delivered the coup de grâce, he'd only been functioning on autopilot. Gabi was keeping something from him and he was determined to get it out of her no matter what he had to do.

Leon shut the door behind them. "You're here now. That's all that matters."

Andreas stared at his brother. He'd lost weight and looked tired, but that was to be expected considering he was a new father. The look of anxiety in his eyes was something else again, kindling Andreas's curiosity. "What's this about? I thought you told me Kris was fine after his checkup."

"He is."

"Don't tell me you think they're still missing Gabi?"

"Not as much. After the first few days they both stopped crying for her and accepted me. Now when they see me, they reach for me and don't want anyone else except Gabi when she comes. It's an amazing feeling."

"I can only imagine." Andreas was longing for the same experience himself, but only under the right circumstances. "So what's wrong?"

"Maybe you ought to sit down."

Was it that bad? He remained standing. "Just tell me."

"You won't believe this. Deline called me this afternoon. She's *pregnant*."

The news rocked Andreas back on his heels. In fact it was incredible. He stared at his twin. Leon was now the father of a third child yet to be born.

"The doctor confirmed she's six weeks along. It was the shortest phone call on record. Before she hung up, she said she was still divorcing me, but wanted me to know the baby was due next spring."

"No matter what, congratulations are in order." Andreas gave him a brotherly hug.

Leon looked shell-shocked. "Ironic, isn't it? I've got Thea's children, Deline's carrying mine, yet none of us will be getting together."

He'd left out a heartbroken Gabi who would have had every right to hold on to the twins without telling anyone, but she didn't have a selfish bone in her beautiful body. One thing was evident. Through this experience Leon had learned how much he loved Deline. Andreas could only commiserate with him.

"Don't despair. With time it could all work out the way you want it. As long as I'm here, why don't you fly to Athens and talk to her tonight? I'll do the babysitting duties here until you get back. If you need a couple of days, take it!"

Leon's eyes ignited. "You'd do that?"

His brother was in pain and needed help.

"What do you think?" After today's meeting he didn't have anything of vital importance on for tomorrow. If he went to Gabi's door, she wouldn't let him in. "I'm crazy about my nephews and want to spend some quality time with them."

His brother had difficulty swallowing. "Thanks. It seems like that's all I ever say to you. I haven't been to work in weeks. You've had a double load."

"Don't you remember you've been given maternity leave? As Gabi once said to me, what's sauce for the goose..."

While Leon changed clothes, he shot Andreas a curious glance. "How's she doing as Anna's replacement?"

"Better than even I had imagined."

"Under the circumstances you were wise to break it off with Irena as soon as you did. Everyone in the family knows it now, but I have to tell you it came as a shock to Deline."

Andreas nodded. "Those two managed to grow even closer during the time I was seeing her."

"Deline says Irena is leaving for Italy for a long holiday. Before she does, she wants to take a look at the twins, so don't be surprised if she shows up. Sorry about that if it happens."

"I'm not concerned. If there's any problem with the boys that I don't anticipate, I'll call you."

As soon as Leon left the villa Andreas stretched out on top of his brother's bed and drew the phone from his pocket. He frowned when all he got was Gabi's voice mail. The beep eventually sounded.

"Gabi? Something has come up and Leon needs my help. First thing in the morning I'd like you to reschedule any appointments for the next two days, then I want you to fly to Milos. The helicopter will be standing by. I'll expect you in time to have a late breakfast with the boys."

She would never come for him, but an opportunity to see the twins was something else again.

The apartment in the Simonides office building was more fabulous than any five-star hotel. Every time Gabi stepped out of the shower of the guest suite, she felt as if she were a princess whose days were enchanted because she was allowed to be with Andreas while he worked.

If there was a downside, it came at the end of the day. When Andreas left his office and said he'd see her in the morning, the enchantment left with him. Except for the evening she'd talked to him about not crossing the line, she hadn't been with him in another setting away from the office.

Since she'd come to work for him, the nights had turned out to be the loneliest Gabi had ever known. To stave off the worst of it, she spent time after hours acquainting herself with the files stored on the computer and memorizing the names of his most important clients.

One night last week she'd come across the merger with Paulos Metal Experts. To her astonishment she read that Dimitri had brought several unscrupulous lawsuits against the Simonides Corporation in order to get the judge to intervene.

Andreas had represented his father in court. Every attempt by the opposition was defeated. Photocopies of all the court documents were there. It had been a heated case. She didn't say anything to Andreas, but reading the material gave her a much fuller understanding of the disgusting man Thea had married.

This evening when Andreas had left the office, she could tell he was in a hurry. Naturally she imagined he was planning to spend the night with his girlfriend, a possibility too devastating to contemplate.

With an aching heart she reached for her cell phone to see if there'd been any calls from her parents or Jasmin while she'd been in the shower. To her shock, the only message she'd missed had come from Andreas.

She always loved the opportunity to fly out to Milos so she could hold her precious babies. This time she'd make it a short, drop-in visit and take some pictures of the twins with her cell phone to show her parents. After that she would ask the pilot to fly her to Heraklion for a surprise visit. They'd love to see how much their grandsons had grown.

Since Gabi needed a break to separate herself from Andreas, it was a good plan. In a few more days Kris would be having his surgery. After he'd recovered, she would resign her job with Andreas and go back to Virginia.

That would leave him free to do whatever. Everything would be wrapping up soon and she'd be gone for good.

Twelve hours later Gabi climbed aboard the helicopter atop the office building with her overnight bag. En route to Milos she informed the pilot she would only be there for a brief time. Afterward she wished to be flown to Heraklion.

Armed with her plans, she arrived at the Simonides villa where Andreas stood at the helipad, disturbingly handsome in an unfastened white linen shirt and bathing trunks. She'd been so used to seeing him in a business suit at the office, her heart skipped around, throwing her completely off-kilter.

As he stepped forward to help her out, his penetrating eyes seemed to be all over her, turning her insides to mush. She'd worn a summery print skirt and sleeveless blouse in earth tones on white with white straw sandals. It was an outfit he wouldn't have seen before.

"I'm glad you made it. You smell as delicious as you look this morning."

"Thank you." She hadn't been prepared for a comment like that. Her stomach clenched mercilessly. "It's a new mango shampoo I bought. Your pilot said the same thing. He's going to buy some for his wife."

His white smile was so captivating, her lungs constricted. "I know you can't wait to see the boys. They're in their new swings on the patio. Follow me."

She knew the way as they walked down several flights of steps past flowering gardens to the rectangular swimming pool of iridescent blue.

The Simonides compound was exquisite, surpassing what she'd seen from the air the first time they'd come. Each white villa was terraced with flowers and greenery, one on top of the other all the way down to the sea where the white sand merged with aquamarine waters. She paused on one of the steps to look around.

"Oh, Andreas… I know I say this every time, but this is all so gorgeous, I can't believe it's real." She couldn't believe *he* was real. "With a devoted father like Leon, the children have to be the luckiest little boys on earth."

"The real miracle is that they got their start with you and your family. They're waiting for you."

"I'm dying to see them." She trailed him down one more flight of steps and through an alcove. Out of the corner of her eye she saw the canopied swings propped near each other beneath an overhang of brilliant passion flowers. The seats were moving back and forth to a little nursery-rhyme song.

She ran toward the boys, then slowed down for fear she'd frighten them. They were dressed in identical blue sunsuits. No shoes or socks on because it was too hot.

"They've filled out!"

Andreas chuckled as he undid Kris and handed him to her. "Look who's here."

"Oh, you little sweetheart." She hugged him in her arms, unable to stop kissing his neck and cheeks. While she walked around with him, Andreas extricated Nikos and propped him against his broad shoulder.

"I've missed you," she crooned to him, rocking him gently. Finally she put her head back so she could look at him. "Do you remember me?" He blinked. "I don't think he knows me, Andreas." Her brows furrowed.

"Give him a minute. The sun's so bright. Here. We'll trade." He reached for Kris with one arm and handed Nikos to her with the other.

"How could you possibly be this adorable?" She kissed his tummy. "Do you take cute pills?" She lifted him above her head.

Andreas's happy laughter filled the air. "Kris recognizes your voice. See? He's craning his head to look at you."

"You think?" she cried out joyously. All of a sudden Nikos started getting more excited and made his little baby sounds. "Well, that's more like it." She kissed one cheek, then the other, making him smile each time.

"I'd smile like that if you kissed me that way all the time," Andreas said in a provocative aside. He was back to being playful.

Gabi ignored the comment, but felt the blush that swept into her cheeks. "I'm not sure this was such a good idea. I don't know how I'm going to tear myself away."

"No one's going anywhere quite yet. Estelle will be out in a minute with their bottles. We'll feed them before she puts them down for their naps."

"Maybe the two of you better do it. I don't want my presence to upset them and undo the progress Leon has made."

She lowered Nikos into his swing so she could take pictures. Now that she had an excuse to capture Andreas at the same time, she took a dozen different shots of him and the children in quick succession.

"It's good for them to see you every few days," he murmured, brushing off her worries. "Their psyches have a greater sense of security knowing you haven't disappeared from their lives."

Gabi squinted at him. "Is that based on scientific fact?"

"No." His lips twitched. "I made it up because I know how much you need to hold them."

I love you, Andreas Simonides.

She found a chair beneath the overhang and put Nikos back on her lap so she could examine him. Andreas pulled up another chair next to her and sat down with Kris. Grasping the children's hands, they started to play pat-a-cake with each other. Gabi broke into laughter. Andreas joined her.

"Maybe we shouldn't interrupt them, Estelle. They're having too much fun."

Gabi heard an unfamiliar female voice and looked over her shoulder. She saw two women, each carrying a baby bottle. The older one was dressed for housework. The younger one was the epitome of the fashionably dressed, breathtaking, black-haired Greek woman, making a beeline for Andreas.

"Irena—" Andreas called to her.

Gabi wished she hadn't seen her. Ever since she'd heard about her from Deline, she'd wondered where she'd been hiding. Now that she'd appeared, Gabi found it was much harder than she'd thought to actually meet her. She hugged Nikos to her body.

Deep inside she wished the vision of this incredibly beautiful female weren't permanently etched in her mind. Her brown eyes looked like velvet. Taking the initiative, Gabi said, "You haven't interrupted anything. I'm Gabi Turner, the boys' aunt."

"How do you do?"

"You've come just in time to help Andreas feed the twins. I can't stay any longer. My parents are expecting me on Crete."

She got up and motioned for Irena to sit down before handing Nikos to her. Andreas's veiled eyes followed her movements. By his enigmatic expression, she had no idea what he was thinking. Estelle handed him the other bottle.

Gabi kissed Nikos before turning to Andreas. "When the pilot flew me here this morning, I hope it's all right that I asked him to wait so he could fly me on to Heraklion."

"Of course," came the low aside.

If Gabi had taken license she shouldn't have, she didn't care. This was one time she needed an escape pod. The helicopter would do nicely. She gave Kris another peck on the cheek.

"See you at the hospital, my little darling." Before she lifted her head, the temptation to cover Andreas's sensuous mouth with her own was overpowering, but she resisted the impulse. "I'll let myself out."

As she hurried to retrace her steps back to the helipad she heard Kris start to cry. A few seconds later Nikos joined in. Their cries brought her pleasure as well as pain. In another minute they'd get over it and enjoy the attention of Andreas and his girlfriend.

Gabi, on the other hand, would never get over it. Her cries were loudest of all, but she would manage to stifle them until after she'd reached Heraklion.

By the time Andreas heard the helicopter and felt the paralyzing pang of watching it swing away with Gabi inside, the twins had settled down enough to finish their bottles.

Irena patted Nikos's back to burp him before putting him in his swing. She glanced at Andreas. "Forgive me for intruding on you and Gabi, Andreas. I didn't realize you were here this morning."

"You don't owe me any apology. Leon said you might come by to see the babies."

She nodded. "Deline was right. Leon's children are beautiful. What a tragic situation."

Andreas kissed Kris's head. "It's a painful time for everyone concerned including you, Irena. Heaven knows I never meant to hurt you."

"I'm going to be all right."

He had to believe that. "I understand you're leaving for Italy."

"Yes, but I'm glad I came by here first and happened to see you. The change in you since last month has been so dramatic, I don't know you anymore. When I saw you out here with her just now, I felt an energy radiating. It was like a fire burning inside of you. Seeing you with her explains several things I haven't understood and makes me want that kind of love for myself."

He got to his feet. "There's no finer woman than you. You deserve every happiness. How long will you be in Italy?"

"Why do you ask?"

"Because I'm concerned about you."

"Don't be. Your courage to break it off with me has opened my eyes to certain things about myself I haven't wanted to admit or explore. To answer your question, I'll be in Italy for as long as it takes."

Her cryptic remark surprised him. "Irena?"

"Don't say anything more. We already talked everything out at the house. Please don't walk me to the car. You stay with your nephews. *Adio*, Andreas."

"Adio." In a strange way he couldn't decipher, she'd changed, too. Something was going on… Bemused, he watched her until she disappeared, then he looked down at the twins. The time had come to get them out of this heat. He tucked a baby under each arm and carried them back to Leon's villa. Another diaper change and they'd be ready for their naps.

Once the boys were asleep, he found Estelle and told her he was going to do some laps in the pool. The energy Irena had referred to was pouring out of him. He needed to release it with some physical activity or he'd jump out of his skin.

On his tenth lap he heard the sound of a helicopter approaching. His heart knocked against his ribs to think it might be Gabi returning, but that was only wishful thinking. She'd run for her life earlier, just as she'd run from him at Papafragas beach, and again the evening she'd pushed him away at the apartment. He had yet to understand what was holding her back.

The rotors stopped whipping the air. Any member of his family could be arriving from Athens, a constant occurrence during the summer. It was probably one of his sisters with her children.

To his surprise Leon appeared minutes later and plunged in the pool. He swam like a dolphin to reach Andreas. The second he saw Leon's face, he knew the worst without having to be told anything.

"Thanks for watching the boys for me. It was a wasted effort. Deline couldn't get rid of me fast enough. Even with our baby on the way, the divorce is on."

"That's her pain talking right now."

Leon spread his arms and rested his back against the edge of the pool. "Apparently she and Irena have been discussing you and me. Before I left Athens she said, and I quote, 'It looks like your brother doesn't know how to be faithful, either. It must be another twin thing,' unquote."

Andreas frowned. "I don't understand."

"When Deline visited Gabi and the twins in Apollonia, I guess she didn't know you'd already broken off with Irena."

Air got trapped in Andreas's lungs. "You mean—"

"I mean she told Gabi the family was waiting for the announcement that you and Irena would be getting married."

Andreas swore violently and levered himself out of the pool.

"What's wrong, bro?"

"*That's* the reason Gabi's been fighting me." Now it all made sense.

"Ah." He eyed Andreas mournfully. "I wish my problem could be fixed as easily."

So did Andreas. Being twins, they understood each other too well. "I know how much you're hurting over Deline. Don't give up on her."

Leon gave him a mirthless smile. "I couldn't if I wanted to because she *is* the one woman for me. In the meantime the boys are keeping me sane."

"Gabi was here a little while ago. The children started crying when she left. Fortunately they settled down without too much trouble."

"I'm thinking of stealing her away from you," Leon admitted. "I need her help. The twins love Gabi and that's never going to change because she'll always be their aunt. Let's face it. Estelle's way too old for this sort of thing. She's been run ragged the last three weeks. It's not fair to her."

"I couldn't agree more."

"If nothing changes between Deline and me, I'm going to have to hire a permanent nanny. In the meantime I could use Gabi to bridge the gap, especially with Kris's operation coming up soon."

"Then call her!" Andreas cried excitedly. The very prospect had his adrenaline surging.

Leon lifted hopeful eyes to him. "You mean it?"

"Do it now! She can stay in one of the guest villas. Tell her what you just told me and she'll come in a shot. Let her know you're sending the helicopter for her."

His brother darted him a curious glance. "Who'll help you at the office?"

"Christine."

"Gus's private secretary?"

He nodded. "I like her. She's unflappable like Anna."

"Then she's the perfect choice to fill her shoes."

"I'll talk to our big brother. When he understands everything, he'll arrange for her promotion. As soon as you reach Gabi, tell her it's a fait accompli so she won't have any reason to turn you down."

"Who was that on the phone?"

Shaken by the conversation, Gabi hung up and turned to her mother. They were in the kitchen eating lunch while they looked at the pictures of the babies taken on her cell phone. "It was Leon Simonides. Would you believe his wife is pregnant?"

"You're kidding—"

"No. What's so terribly sad is that she wants the divorce more than ever. He's feeling overwhelmed. His mother has to look after his father, and he's worried because Estelle is too old to keep up the pace. He's asked me to come and help him with the babies until after Kris's operation."

"I don't envy that man the difficult position he's in."

"Neither do I. He's so hurt, Mom." Gabi let out a troubled sigh. "If I'm willing to come, Leon will send a helicopter for me in the morning. All I have to do is say the word and he'll have my personal things moved out of the office apartment to the guest suite on Milos. After the operation he wants me to start helping him interview women for a permanent nanny position."

"That makes sense, but what about your job with Andreas?"

"Leon said not to be concerned. Their other brother's secretary is going to become Andreas's permanent assistant."

He'd already made the arrangements.

Gabi was like a hot potato…so hot Andreas had been willing to let her go without even telling her himself. She couldn't bear it.

Her mother moved around the table and hugged her. "I know you're torn because this means getting closer to the children, but think of it this way. If you decide you want to do this favor for Leon, then staying on Milos will definitely be easier for you."

She looked up at her. "Easier?"

"Oh, darling—I knew you'd fallen in love with Andreas the second he walked in our living room. Knowing he has a girlfriend, this period of time while you've been working for him has to have been very painful."

Gabi buried her face in her hands. "Was I that transparent?"

"Only to your father and me."

After taking a fortifying breath, she lifted her head. "I'll call Leon and tell him yes. With Kris's operation looming, he needs all the support he can get." *And I won't have to face Andreas eight hours out of every day.*

CHAPTER EIGHT

GABI started out her fifth day on Milos with the same routine: baths for the babies followed by a bottle and a morning of playtime out by the pool. As he'd done every morning, Leon had flown to Athens early to put in some work. He always returned by four in the afternoon to take over and give Gabi a break. She'd seen nothing of Andreas, which came as no surprise.

While she was easing Kris into the shallow end of the pool, Estelle appeared. The two of them had developed a friendly rapport. While Gabi did all the carrying and running around, the housekeeper listened for the children when they slept.

"Leonides just phoned. He wants you and the boys to get ready for a boat ride on Andreas's cabin cruiser."

"Did you hear that?" She kissed Kris's cheek. "Your daddy's on his way home!" Kris's surgery was coming up the day after tomorrow. Since she hadn't been able to stop worrying about it, she welcomed the diversion that put a change in their schedule.

"The maids will pack and carry everything down to the pier. While you get ready, I'll stay with the twins. I've already made up their bottles."

Gabi wrapped Kris in a towel and handed him to Estelle. "I'll be right back."

She darted up the steps to the guest villa to throw on her beach cover-up over her swimsuit. In a bag she stashed a change of outfit, plus a towel and other essentials she might need. When she went back to the pool for the babies, Estelle told her they'd already been taken down to the pier. Leon must have arrived in the helicopter while she'd been packing.

"See you later, then."

Gabi hurried down to the beach and walked along the dock past all the different family ski and jet boats to board the cruiser. She frowned when she couldn't see or hear Leon or the twins.

"Hello? Anyone home?" she called out.

"We're all in the main salon."

She jumped at the sound of Andreas's voice and turned in his direction. The sight of his tall, well-defined body squeezed the air out of her lungs. He stood at the entrance to the companionway in a pair of sweats and nothing else. Beneath his hair more black than night, his silvery eyes swept over her. She might as well have been lit on fire.

"What are *you* doing here? I—I mean I thought you were at work," she stammered.

"At the last minute Leon went to see Deline in the hope that they could really talk. Now that he's found out he's going to be a father again, he's anxious to be with her and know how she's doing. I told him not to worry about his children and flew here as fast as I could."

Gabi was at a loss for words, still trying to recover from seeing him when it was so unexpected.

His lips curved upward, drawing her attention to his sensuous mouth. "Shall we start again? How are you, Gabi? It seems like months since we last saw each other.

I've been all right, but, no matter how efficient Christine is, I must admit I've missed my American secretary who charmed all who came in the office or phoned."

Andreas...

He looked around. "I think it's a beautiful day. What do you think?"

It hurt to breathe. "Is Stavros watching the children?"

"No," he said. "Today we're on our own."

Don't tell me that.

Frightened by the primitive feelings he aroused in her, she darted past him and hurried down the stairs to check on the twins. She found them lying on a quilt he'd placed on the floor of the spacious salon. They were sound asleep on their backs, their arms at their sides with their little hands formed into fists. How would it be?

Andreas had followed her down and stood close enough that she could feel his warmth. "What would it be like to sleep like that without cares or worries? Nothing but sweet dreams until their next meal."

He'd read her thoughts.

"Let's get you up to the helm lounge," he whispered. His breath teased the nape of her neck, sending delicious chills to every part of her body. "I've turned on the intercom down here. If they breathe too hard, we'll hear them."

She didn't need an excuse to put distance between her and Andreas, but she felt self-conscious hurrying up the steps ahead of him. Her sundress only fell to mid-thigh, leaving a good expanse of leg showing.

He led her to the cockpit. "Make yourself comfortable while I untie the ropes. Then we'll be off to some other areas around the island you haven't seen yet."

Gabi sat down on the companion seat next to the captain's chair. Being perched this high with the sun roof open was an experience like no other.

"What do you think?" he asked after taking his seat. His arm and thigh brushed hers, increasing her sensitivity to his touch.

"Like I'm master of all I survey."

A chuckle escaped his lips. "It does feel that way." He started the engine and before long they'd idled out from the bay to head for open water. "When Leon and I were boys, he wanted a huge yacht where he could invite all his friends and sail the seven seas like Ulysses, but I dreamed about owning one of these to go exploring for plunder by myself."

"Naturally." She smiled. Andreas had always blazed his own trails, even if he was an identical twin. "A pirate needs to be able to maneuver in and out of coves, yet be able to outrace his enemies in a big hurry. Now that you've achieved all your dreams, it's going to be our little nephews below who will start dreaming their own dreams."

He cast her a shuttered glance. "You think I've achieved all my dreams?"

She averted her eyes. "It was just a figure of speech."

"For your information, I haven't even begun." He had to be talking about his future with Irena. "What about you?"

They were getting into a painful area. The only dream that truly mattered had been shattered when Deline told her Andreas had gone to Athens to spend time with his girlfriend.

"I've achieved a few little ones."

"For instance?" he prodded.

"I made it into the Penguin club when I was in grade school."

"And that was very important?"

"Yes. You had to be a good ice skater."

"Bravo." She laughed. "What else?"

"In high school I tried to make it on the debate team because I thought those kids were really smart. By my senior year I was chosen."

He turned to look at her. "Was it everything you'd hoped it would be?"

"Anything but. I missed too many classes going to meets, and my egghead partner drove me crazy."

"Male or female?"

"Male."

"I take he didn't grow into one of your past illnesses."

"No. Those came later."

"Have you ever been in love, Gabi? I'm talking about the kind you'd sell your soul for and didn't think was possible. The kind that only comes once?"

He'd just described the condition she was in. A band constricted her breathing. "Yes," she said quietly and got out of the chair. "Excuse me for a moment while I check on the twins."

"We haven't heard a sound from them yet."

"Maybe not, but they might be awake wondering where they are and why their daddy isn't with them. I don't want them to feel lonely."

"They have each other." He looked over his broad shoulder at her. The sun shone down, bronzing his skin. "Take it from me, that's the great thing about twins."

Their gazes fused. "Was it hard at first sharing Leon with Deline?"

An odd silence stretched between them. "Do you know you're the first person who ever asked me that question? You have great perception."

He took his sunglasses from a side pocket and put them on. "To answer your question, *yes*, but it helped that Leon and I do business together. Sadly it was Deline who suffered the most for having to share him. They'd been quarreling about it the night he took out the yacht with friends and met Thea."

Gabi moaned low in her throat. "After the twins were born, I bought some books to study up on the subject. One of the things I learned was to dress them differently, put them in different classes. Help them to be individuals. But the books also said that there's a bond connecting them like inner radar and has to be allowed for."

"That's true."

"Do you think it will be as hard on Leon when you get married one day?"

"Yes, because he's not used to coming in second with me."

Gabi didn't like playing second fiddle either. Sucking in her breath, she hurried below deck.

After learning the business alongside his father and grandfather, instinct told Andreas when it was the right or wrong time to make a crucial move. Now was not the moment to tell Gabi he was single. She was too worried about Kris and the upcoming surgery.

When the time came, he wanted her full attention in order to gauge her reaction after she learned he was a free man. Until their nephew had recovered and she couldn't use him for a distraction, Andreas would have to hold back, but the operation couldn't come soon enough to suit him.

"Wouldn't you know Kris was awake just lying there looking around making cooing sounds?" She'd returned to the cockpit holding the wide-eyed baby against her shoulder.

At a glance Andreas took in one head of jet-black hair, the other of spun gold. Gabi and child provided a live painting more riveting than the picturesque town in the distance.

"Look how beautiful, little sweetheart!"

Andreas could only echo the sentiment before he had to tear his eyes away and pay attention to steering the cruiser. He'd brought them into an inlet with a sweeping bay.

"Where are we?"

"Adamantas, the social center of Milos. This part of the island has a natural harbor. Everyone prefers this area because it's sheltered from the north winds."

"I'm sure your uncle knows every square inch of this paradise." She spoke to the baby, kissing his cheeks. For a second Andreas closed his eyes, wishing he could feel those lips against his skin, and jaw and lips and mouth. "Between him and your daddy, the day will come when you and Nikos will explore this place on your own. By then your heart will be as strong as your brother's."

Sunlight caught the well of her unshed tears reflecting the same blue as the deep water. The sight of them tugged at his heart. "He's going to be fine, Gabi." For Leon's sake, he *had* to be.

"I know." But the words came out muffled because she'd buried her face in Kris's neck. "He has no idea he'll be going into the hospital tomorrow to be prepped."

"We'll all be with him. I assume you've informed your parents they'll be staying in the guest suite at the office with you."

She lifted her head. "Yes. They're very grateful for everything."

"I've arranged for the helicopter to fly them from Heraklion."

"I know, but they didn't expect that. It's too much."

"The family insists. Our sisters plan to take turns tending Nikos at our parents' home, so there's no worry there."

"I don't think any babies ever had more love, but this has to be so hard on your brother."

Because Leon was his twin, maybe that was the reason Andreas felt the depth of his brother's anguish. "He needs comfort from the wife he has hurt too deeply. It's a tragedy."

"It *is*," she cried softly. "His pain must be exquisite to know she's carrying their child. I'd give anything to help them."

"Gabi," he said huskily, "don't you know you're saving his life right now?"

Her wet eyes swerved to his. "So are you. But who's helping Deline?"

Andreas loved this woman for her compassion. "She has a big supportive family."

"I'm glad for that." He watched her cuddle Kris closer. The pained expression on her face tore him up. In the midst of feeling helpless over her pain, he heard Nikos start to cry.

"I'll get him." He cut the motor and stood up. "When I come back, I'll bring their bottles and carry-cots. Shall I bring the stroller, too? We could go ashore in Adamantas and have a late lunch."

She stared up at him. "Are you hungry?"

He had to be honest. "No."

"Neither am I. Do you mind if we go back? This is a heavenly spot, but when Leon flies here, he'll expect to find his babies waiting for him."

Chills chased down his spine to realize how often he and Gabi were in sync, speaking each other's thoughts. In some ways it was like his connection with Leon, but much stronger.

Before the surgery, both sets of grandparents lingered in Kris's hospital room, hugging and kissing him. Gabi's father was visibly shaken. She knew he was seeing Thea. With her death so recent, his tears often lurked near the surface.

Leon hadn't let go of his mother. It was very touching. Andreas and their older brother Gus and his wife stood next to their father, who appeared emotional as well. A year ago he'd suffered a heart attack and had to be more aware of his mortality at a vulnerable moment like this.

Gabi found herself studying the impressive, black-haired Simonides family. They were tall people, each one incredibly attractive. Suddenly Andreas looked around and caught her gaze. He gave her a long, un-smiling look that penetrated to her inner core.

She had the feeling he was remembering their first encounter in his office when he was ready to shut the elevator door on her. The newspaper picture and photograph of the twins had changed lives, not only for the families here, but for Deline.

Gabi checked her watch. It was only 6:45 a.m. Kris was the heart surgeon's first patient on the morning docket. She was thankful for that. They'd all been waiting for this day, each of them doing a mental countdown.

The doctor had told Leon that the newest medical technology had made this a quick procedure. In another hour the surgery would be over. Soon life would return to a new normal, but Gabi couldn't go there yet, not when she knew Andreas wouldn't be in it.

You'd better get used to it, her heart nagged. No more thrilling cruises together with the twins like the one they'd gone on the day before yesterday to Adamantas. As long as she'd been helping Leon through this whole process of getting to know his instant family, Andreas had been a part of it. But those days were numbered and she would never experience such joy again.

She finally broke eye contact with him and hugged her mother, who knew her secret. Gabi needed her strength.

When the door opened, she saw the nurse who'd been working with Leon. She said it was time to take the baby and get the anesthetic administered. "There's a waiting room around the corner. If you'll all move there."

A sob rose in Gabi's throat to see tears trickle down Leon's pale cheeks as he kissed his son one last time. He carried such a load of pain, Gabi marveled at his composure. Andreas was right there to steady his brother as the nurse disappeared out of the room with the baby Gabi had seen born. She felt as if a piece of her heart had been taken away.

Her dad reached for her hand and squeezed it. Slowly everyone filed out to the lounge for the long wait. Time was so relative. When Gabi was with Andreas, laughing and sharing while they played with the twins, an hour was but a moment that flew by unmercifully fast. But this hour was going to take a year to pass, she just knew it.

It didn't surprise her that Andreas was the one who brought in drinks and snacks, waiting on everyone. Before long his brothers-in-law arrived and the men congregated while the mothers started talking. Gus's wife Beril sat by Gabi. She couldn't have been nicer. They spoke quietly about Leon.

"Since becoming a father, he's changed for the better, Gabi. But taking responsibility has cost him his marriage. I was just talking to Deline yesterday. It's so sad."

Gabi shuddered. "Even though my sister had been drinking, I can promise you she wouldn't have done what she did if she'd known he was married. She wasn't even aware Andreas had a twin brother, but it's far too late to grieve over that now."

Beril wrapped a commiserating arm around her shoulder. Andreas happened to notice the gesture and left the men to come their way, causing Gabi's pulse rate to pick up.

"You look tired," Beril told him.

"Aren't we all, but Leon's the one on the point of exhaustion."

"I haven't had a chance to talk to him yet. Excuse me, Gabi. I'll be back in a minute."

After Beril walked off, Andreas sat down in her place. He smelled wonderful. The creamy sand-colored suit covered his hard-muscled body like a glove. He took her breath. His leg brushed against hers as he turned to her. "Are you all right?" His velvety voice resonated to her insides.

"I will be when the doctor comes in. It's already been an hour and a half. How are you doing?"

"You heard Beril. What can I do for you?"

She glanced at his striking features. Andreas hid his emotions too well. On impulse she said, "I should be asking *you* that question. You've been the one waiting on everyone else."

"Staying busy helps."

As Gabi nodded one of the doctors who'd assisted with the surgery came into the lounge. Like everyone else, she shot to her feet. He looked at Leon.

"Mr. Simonides? Your son's operation was a success, but he's having a little trouble coming out of the anesthetic." Gabi grabbed hold of Andreas's arm without conscious thought. "If you'll follow me. We've got him in the infant ICU."

Leon's anguish was palpable as he eyed Andreas. "Come with me, bro."

Andreas sent Gabi a silent message that he'd be back and left the room with his twin. Without his support, she hurried over to her parents. Her father hugged her for a long moment.

"I can't believe this is happening, Dad. Leon has already been through so much, and now this… Poor little Kris. He's got to come out of it."

"He will, darling."

When she pulled out of his arms, her mother was there to hug her. "We have to have faith that everything's going to be all right."

While everyone in the room was in agony, Gabi saw something out of the corner of her eye. A dark-haired woman had entered the lounge. It was *Deline*! By then everyone had seen her.

"What's wrong? Where's Leon?" she cried in alarm.

Andreas's mother rushed over to her and explained.

"You mean Kris might not make it?" Deline's voice shook. Her face looked pale.

"None of us is thinking that way."

"But Leon is." Deline's response sounded like a wife who knew her husband better than anyone else. She still loved him, Gabi could feel it. "Where's the infant ICU?"

"Come on, Deline," Gabi answered before anyone else could think. "I'll help you find it."

Together they flew out of the lounge and down the hall to the nurses' station. Gabi spoke up. "This is Mrs. Simonides. She got here late. Her husband is in the infant ICU with Kris who was just operated on. Can she go in?"

"Of course. A baby needs its mother at a time like this." Neither Gabi or Deline bothered to correct the other woman. "Let me get a gown and mask for you."

When Deline was ready the other woman said, "Follow me."

They hurried down another hall and around the corner where they saw Andreas standing outside the door. With the blinds down, you couldn't see inside.

Lines had darkened his arresting face, making him appear older than his thirty-three years. When he saw them coming, his eyes widened in shocked surprise.

The nurse opened the door for Deline who went right in, then she closed it again and walked away.

In the next instant Andreas gripped Gabi's upper arms. He was so caught up in emotions, he had no idea of his strength. "What's going on?"

Gabi shook her head. "I really don't know. Deline came in the lounge looking for Leon. Your mother told her Kris was in trouble. I thought Deline was going to pass out right there, so I told her to come with me and we'd find them."

Andreas couldn't speak. Instead he put his arms all the way around her and crushed her against him. She understood and didn't misinterpret what was going on while he rocked her.

This whole experience, from the first day Andreas had first found out about the twins, had been so fraught with emotion, he didn't know where else to go with all his feelings. Neither did Gabi, who held on to him, for once not worrying about Irena, who hadn't shared in this life and death situation from the beginning.

"Deline wouldn't have come this morning if she didn't still love Leon," he whispered into her silky gold hair. "She's known about this surgery from the start. To show up today has to mean something, doesn't it?"

Gabi had never heard Andreas sound vulnerable before. It was a revelation. "Yes, I believe it does."

"Oh, Gabi, if I thought—"

"That there might not be a divorce?" she finished what he was trying to say.

"Yes," he cried softly, kissing her forehead and cheeks.

"As my mom said a little while ago, we have to have faith." She buried her face in his neck. "Kris has got to make it, Andreas. Nothing will make sense if he doesn't."

She lost track of time while they held on to each other. This amazing man was actually clinging to her as if his life depended on it. His hands roved over her back. One found its way to her nape. His fingers stroked the curls, sending bursts of delight through her body. Gabi nestled closer against him, loving this feeling of safety and comfort. She'd never known anything like it before.

When another nurse came out of the ICU, Gabi had to force herself away from him, but she wasn't ready for the abrupt separation. It was a good thing there'd been an interruption, otherwise she would have stayed right where she was and Andreas would have figured out what was really going on.

"I'd better get back to the lounge and tell everyone there's been no news about Kris yet." Embarrassed to have revealed her terrible weakness for him, she started down the hall. In one long stride he caught up to her.

"We'll both go. There's no telling how long Leon and Deline will be in there. No matter what's going on with Kris, my brother has the person he wants and needs with him right now. As of this moment, we're both de trop."

Everyone's strained faces turned to them the moment they entered the waiting room. Andreas spoke for them. "We still don't know anything about Kris."

"Is Deline with him?" his mother asked anxiously.

"Yes."

Gabi could hear the questions everyone wanted to voice but didn't dare. "The nurse gave her a gown and mask to put on so she could go in with Leon." She saw glances being exchanged.

Andreas didn't miss them, either. "One thing we all know about Deline. She wouldn't be here at a precarious moment like this to cause Leon pain. Quite the opposite, in fact." He'd championed his sister-in-law. Everything Andreas said or did made Gabi love him that much more.

While he talked with his family, Gabi gravitated to hers, still experiencing the sensation of feeling his arms around her. All that strength was encased in one superb male who worried about his family and still had the stamina to carry the bulk of the load for those depending on him professionally.

She checked her watch for the umpteenth time. Another half hour had passed and still no word about Kris. It wasn't looking good. One glance at her parents' expressions and she knew they were thinking the same thing. The room had grown quiet. Like Gabi, who was fighting not to break down, they were all saying their own silent prayers.

While she was deep in thought she heard Leon's voice. "I have good news, everyone." She looked across the room. His gray eyes shone with a new light. "Kris is awake and breathing on his own. He's going to be all right." His voice broke.

Gabi watched Andreas race toward the entrance to give his brother a bear hug.

"Thank heaven!" She broke down and wept for happiness against her father's shoulder. At that point the whole mood of the room changed to one of jubilation.

"They're going to keep him until tomorrow, then I'll take him home. Deline's going to stay with me and help me." Leon's emotions were spilling out. "Thank you all for being here. I couldn't have gotten through this without you."

After hugging everyone, he hurried out of the room taking Andreas with him. No doubt he needed to talk to his twin privately.

Gabi's heart failed as she watched him disappear. Dying inside, she turned to her mother. "Mom?" she whispered. "Do you mind if we go back to the apartment and pack? I'd like to fly to Heraklion today, but let's go by plane. Even though Andreas has put the helicopter at our disposal, I don't want to take advantage now that Leon doesn't need me to help with the babies."

"I think that's a very wise idea." Her mother understood everything. "Let's go."

Once outside the hospital, they took a taxi back to the Simonides office building. Gabi put in the code so they could ride the private elevator to her floor. Relief that Kris was going to be all right took away all their anxiety in that regard, but Gabi was in too much pain over leaving Andreas to talk.

A clean break.

That was what she'd done with the twins a month ago. Now it was time for one more. She turned off her phone.

Her parents traveled a great deal so it didn't take them long to gather up their things and head for the airport in a taxi. While at the Athens airport waiting for their flight, she made the reservation for her trip to Washington, D.C., leaving the next day.

By late afternoon they reached the consulate. After a quick meal, Gabi showered and changed out of her suit into straw-colored linen pants and a mocha blouse in a silky fabric. With too much nervous energy to sit still, she got started on some serious packing. When she'd come here—five months ago now—she'd brought a lot of clothes. Enough to fill two suitcases and an overnight bag.

She'd left home in March and would be arriving in the August heat. An oppressive heat without the relief of a shimmering blue sea wherever you turned—without a pair of black-fringed gray eyes wandering over you like the sun's reflection off the water.

Gabi couldn't breathe for thinking about so many moments with Andreas preserved in her memory. Earlier today her body had memorized the feel of his while they'd held on to each other outside the ICU. She'd known it would be for the last time. That was why she hadn't been able to let go.

"Gabi?" Her father walked in her room. "I guess you didn't hear me. There's a man in the foyer wishing to speak to you. He says his name is Stavros."

She felt a quickening in her body. What kind of errand had Andreas sent him on? Her heart pounded so hard she got light-headed.

"What's wrong, honey? You paled just now. Who is he?"

"He crews for Andreas. I like him very much."

"Then you'd better not keep him waiting."

"You're right."

The urge to fly down the stairs was tempered by her fear that Stavros would know how excited she was. But that was silly because he was observant enough to know she was so hopelessly in love with Andreas, it hurt. He'd watched her in unguarded moments around his boss. She doubted anything got past him, either.

"It's nice to see you again, Stavros."

He smiled. "You, too. I brought the cabin cruiser over from Milos for Kyrie Simonides. A family gathering kept him in Athens longer than expected. His helicopter should be landing any minute now. To save time, he asked me to escort you on board and he'll join you for dinner to say goodbye."

That was the longest speech she'd ever heard him give, but the answer was still "no." No more. She couldn't take seeing him again.

"That sounds lovely. Please tell him thank you, but I'm flying to the States in the morning and have too much to do."

"I'll tell him." He started to leave, then stopped. "I shouldn't say this because it will spoil his surprise, but he's got Nikos with him."

Nikos—

Stunned by what he'd just told her, she was slow on the uptake. "Wait—" she cried because the taxi he'd taken here was about to leave. "I'll come. Give me a minute to grab my purse."

She dashed upstairs for it. When she returned, her parents were talking to Stavros. "We heard," her mom said. "Give Nikos a hug for us."

Five minutes later the taxi dropped them off at the pier where she could see the cabin cruiser moored. As she stepped on deck Andreas came out holding Nikos against his shoulder.

She moaned inwardly because they looked perfect together, but it was all wrong. In an ideal world, Nikos should be Andreas's son...and *hers.*

He flashed her one of his enticing smiles. "We're glad you came, aren't we, little guy?" Andreas turned the baby so he could see her. Nikos's eyes lit up. He acted so happy to see Gabi, she let out a joyous laugh and pulled him into her arms.

"How's my big boy?" After smothering him with kisses, she carried him to the rear cockpit. Over his black curls she studied Andreas, who was standing there with his powerful legs slightly apart, looking impossibly handsome in a black crew neck and jeans. "This was a totally unexpected surprise. Thank you." Her voice caught.

"I knew you had to be missing him." His eyes narrowed on her upturned features. "It appears this was a day of surprises on both our parts, starting with your flight to Heraklion."

All of a sudden Gabi started to feel uncomfortable.

"I won't bother to ask why you didn't use the helicopter or why you didn't stay at the apartment long enough for me to take you and your parents out to dinner."

She hugged Nikos tighter. "We would have enjoyed that, but Leon needed you and you had your whole family to deal with."

"And?" he prodded.

"I didn't say anything else."

"Yes, you did," he came back more aggressively. She moved Nikos to her other shoulder and gave him kisses. "You were going to add Irena's name to the list."

Gathering up her courage, she asked, "What kept her from being at the hospital with you?"

"I didn't invite her."

"Andreas—" She stared at him, baffled. "That doesn't sound like you."

One eyebrow lifted. "An interesting observation. It connotes you're somewhat of an expert on my psyche. I like that," he drawled.

Gabi clung to the baby, growing more nervous by the second. "I shouldn't have said anything."

"You can say anything you like to me."

Exasperated, she cried, "That's what I mean—you're normally so warm and kind about everyone. Did you and Irena quarrel? Otherwise I can't imagine her not being with you this morning w-when—"

"It was a life and death situation?" he finished for her.

"Something like that, yes." Getting agitated, she walked Nikos over to the windows looking out on the harbor. "I'm sure she's been upset since the moment she heard about this whole situation with the twins. But she doesn't have to worry now. The children are settled with their father and I'm leaving tomorrow so—"

"Gabi—" he broke in. "Before you say another word, there's something you need to know."

She struggled for breath. "What?"

"A week ago I learned from Leon that Deline had come to visit you and the twins in Apollonia. I understand she mentioned I'd gone to Athens to see my girlfriend Irena Liapis, the woman who was going to become my wife. Did I repeat that back to you correctly?"

Her body shuddered. "Yes."

He stared her down. "It's too bad Deline wasn't apprised of all the facts at the time."

"What facts?" she whispered.

"That I'd already broken it off with Irena. It's true that she used to be my girlfriend."

Used to be? Gabi's heart jumped. "But Deline said your family was expecting you to marry her."

"Up until you came to my office, that was my intention. Needless to say, my entire world got knocked off its foundation the moment I saw that photo of the twins. In order to deal with the ramifications of your unexpected visit, I was forced to put any plans I had on hold."

"Andreas..."

"As it turned out, it was a good thing. The time away from her made me realize that if I'd loved her the way a man should love a woman, we would have been married months earlier."

"How can you say that?" she cried. "I saw the look on her face when she came to the villa and saw us together with the children."

"What you saw was surprise that we were both there instead of Leon. She's very close to Deline and came by to see the famous Simonides twins before leaving for Italy on vacation."

By now Andreas had made himself comfortable on the leather bench with his arms outstretched and his hard-muscled legs extended in front of him. "Now that Kris is out of the woods, I thought we could relax over dinner and talk."

"There's nothing to discuss." She sank down opposite him, still holding Nikos, who seemed to be content for the moment.

"You've made up your mind to leave, then?"

Her brows met in a frown. "You *know* I have."

"Would you mind putting it off one more day?"

Yes, she'd mind. It would kill her to be around him any longer. "I can't. After I got back with my parents, I phoned my boss at the advertising agency. He's meeting me for lunch the day after tomorrow to discuss my new promotion."

"I'm sorry to hear you're flying out that soon," he murmured. "Nikos and I will be disappointed. We were hoping to enjoy your company for another day."

Another day is all he wants, Gabi. Not a lifetime.

She kissed the top of the baby's head. "Why isn't he with your sisters?"

"They've already taken turns watching him. Now it's my turn to be responsible. If all goes well, Leon's bringing Kris home from the hospital tomorrow. He and Deline will need time alone with him, so I won't return Nikos until the day after tomorrow and could use your help. Our little nephew loves the sea. What better way to tend him than to cruise around parts of the island tomorrow you haven't seen?"

He sat forward with his hands clasped between his strong legs, staring at her in that disturbing way that made her palms ache. "If you hadn't turned off your phone, I wouldn't have had to come all this distance to ask for your cooperation."

Her cheeks went hot.

"I'd like to think we can return him to Leon in good shape. Of course if another day away from Virginia jeopardizes your chances of being promoted, then I'll call for a taxi to drive you to the consulate. The decision is up to you."

Another twenty-four hours with Andreas... Unlike Leon with Thea, Andreas hadn't proposed they spend a night of passion together and then go their separate ways. Otherwise he wouldn't have brought the baby with him.

To Gabi's shame, *she* was the only person who couldn't be trusted in this situation. Andreas had asked her to help him take care of Nikos as a favor to his brother, nothing more. Tears stung her eyelids. Gabi loved Andreas desperately, but he didn't love her.

She nestled Nikos closer. What this all added up to was that Andreas had a kind streak, stronger than most people's. He'd known she would have adopted the children if things hadn't worked out. This last twenty-four hours had been offered as a gift before he let her go back to where she came from.

Clearing her throat, she said, "I didn't bring anything with me except my purse."

"That's not a problem," came his deep voice. "Your cabin has cosmetics. There's a robe and extra swimsuits for guests. You really won't need anything else."

She was dressed in her linen pants and blouse. Since they weren't going to do anything but be on the cruiser, she supposed he was right and could feel herself weakening. She hated her weakness.

"I'll have to phone my parents and my old boss." She also needed to change her plane reservation.

Andreas reached for the baby. "While you do that, I'll feed this little guy. It's after seven. He's starting to look around for his bottle."

She waited until he'd gone below deck before phoning her family. After three rings her mother answered. Gabi explained she was still with Andreas, but her mom sounded upset when she told her about his plans.

"Darling? You're a grown woman capable of making your own decisions, but for what it's worth, I don't think this is a good idea. You have to look after yourself now. You're going back home with a broken heart. Do you really think it's wise to prolong the inevitable?"

"No."

"Of course you want extra time with Nikos, but Andreas doesn't need you to help him tend the baby."

"I know."

"I can tell I've said too much. Forgive me. All I want is your happiness, and there hasn't been a lot of that since you flew to Greece after Thea became so ill."

She gripped the phone tighter. "You haven't said anything I haven't been telling myself since I first met him. Thanks for being my mom." Her voice caught. "When I hang up, I'll give Nikos a kiss and come home. See you in a little while."

CHAPTER NINE

A BRUSH through her curls and a fresh coat of lipstick helped Gabi pretend she was in control before she went down the companionway to say a final goodbye. Midway to her destination she could hear the sounds of bossa nova music playing quietly in the background.

Before she stepped onto the floor of the main salon, a slight gasp escaped her throat to see an elegantly decorated table with candles and fresh pink roses. Their sweet scent filled the room.

As she looked around her gaze caught sight of Andreas coming out of the galley with two plates of food. Her heart thumped loud enough for him to hear. "Where's Nikos?"

Andreas put the plates on the table. "Good evening, Gabriella Turner. I'm glad you could make it. Nikos fell asleep after his bottle waiting for you. I put him in my stateroom, but left the door open in case he wakes up for some reason."

The next thing she knew he held out a chair for her. "Please sit down and we'll take advantage of this wonderful Brazilian meal Stavros has prepared for us. It's a specialty of his due to his part-Brazilian nationality." She didn't know that. "He's really outdone himself tonight."

No one in the world had charm like Andreas. Now more than ever she needed to keep her wits about her. The romantic ambience was too much. "I agree everything's lovely, but—"

"No buts or you'll hurt his feelings. He's grown very fond of you and the twins. So have I. Since you first came to my office, all you've done is sacrifice for me and Leon, not to mention our entire family. It's time you were waited on for a change. With this meal, please accept the gratitude of the Simonides clan."

Gratitude?

Suffering another heartsick pang, she sat down across from him. When the meal was over she would thank him and Stavros. Following that, she would leave the cruiser without tiptoeing in the other room to give Nikos one last kiss.

The fabulous *churrasco*, a beef barbecue served on skewers, made a wonderful change from the Greek food she'd enjoyed for the last four months, yet she had to force herself to eat. To her chagrin she'd lost her appetite knowing she wouldn't be seeing Andreas again. His keen eyes couldn't help but notice.

He lifted his wineglass and took a sip, eyeing her over the rim. The candlelight flickered in his eyes, bringing out the flecks of silver that made them so beautiful. "Who would have dreamed when you swept into my office, things would turn out the way they have?"

She wiped the corner of her mouth with a napkin. "We can only hope Deline's decision to go back to Leon is permanent."

Andreas breathed in sharply. "He's a changed man. By the time baby three comes along, he ought to be an expert in fatherhood. That ought to be good for something."

Gabi heard the concern in his voice and wanted to comfort him. "Since Thea isn't alive, I'd like to think it will be easier for Deline to love the babies for themselves, especially after she's had their baby."

"Let's hold that thought," he said in a purring voice. "More wine?"

She shook her head. "I haven't even finished what I have." Her gaze happened to flick to the half-full glass. She noticed the liquid moving. It suddenly dawned on her she could hear the motor of the cruiser. They were skimming the placid water at full speed!

Only now and then did she feel the vibration from another boat's wake. Gabi had been so deep in thought about Deline and Leon, she hadn't noticed.

"We've left the port—" she cried in panic.

He nodded, not acting in the least perturbed. "Why are you so surprised?"

Her hand went to her throat in a nervous gesture. "Because I'd decided to go home after dinner. You don't need me to help take care of Nikos. I realize you only did this to let me have a little more time with our nephew, but the gesture wasn't necessary."

Though he didn't move, if she weren't mistaken his eyes darkened with some unnamed emotion. "We're at least a third of the way to Milos, but if you want Stavros to turn back, I'll tell him."

"No—" She rubbed her temples where she could feel the beginnings of a tension headache coming on. "Since we're that far out to sea, I'm not going to ask you to change your plans now." She was such a little fool.

"You look pale. What's wrong?"

"Probably nothing a walk up on deck in the night air won't cure. Please excuse me. The dinner was outstanding. I'll be sure to let Stavros know."

She pushed herself away from the table and rushed up the stairs. When she reached the rear cockpit, she could still hear the Latin music. Her blood throbbed with the beat. The urge to dance right into Andreas's arms was becoming a violent need.

Out here on the water there was a stark beauty to the seascape. It provided another haunting memory to take home with her.

"Feeling better?"

She hadn't realized he'd come up on deck. Andreas moved with the quiet stealth of a gorgeous black leopard. Swallowing hard, she said, "Much, thank you."

"I checked on Nikos. He's in a deep sleep."

"That's good." He stood too close to her. She moved to the leather bench and sat down to look out of the windows.

"Aside from missing your parents and the twins, are you looking forward to going home to the States?"

"Yes," she lied. "I love the work I do."

"They'll be lucky to get you back. If you ever need a reference, I'll vouch for you in the most glowing terms."

"Thank you." Unable to sit still, she stood up again. "If you'll excuse me, I'm going to go to bed."

"It's not that late. There's going to be a moon like the kind you don't see very often."

"I'm sure that's true." She clasped her hands together. "But I'm afraid I won't be able to stay awake. It's been a long day, and the wine has made me sleepy."

He rubbed the pad of his thumb along his lower lip. "You only drank half a glass."

Nothing escaped him. "It doesn't take much for me. Goodnight." She made it as far as the entry when he called her name. She swung around and looked back at him. His hooded gaze disguised any emotions he was feeling. "Yes?"

"I'm curious about something. How did working for me compare to the work you do for your boss?"

Gabi couldn't understand why he'd asked her that. "They're both very challenging in their own ways." If she stayed on deck any longer, he'd break her down and get the truth out of her. Then she'd really want to sink in a hole and hide from him. "Where will we be docking in the morning?"

"Why?" he demanded with an edge to his tone. "Are you hoping it will be at the villa so you can fly back to Heraklion in my helicopter?"

"Only if it won't put you out."

"How could it do that?"

His mood had changed. She'd angered him when it was the last thing she'd wanted to do. "I think you're tired, too. The strain of Kris's surgery has caught up with both of us. Get a good sleep, Andreas. I'll see you in the morning."

Without waiting for a response, she went down to her cabin. Once she'd checked on the baby to make sure he was still sleeping comfortably, she showered and went to bed using the guest robe hanging on the bathroom door. Surprisingly, she slept until Nikos woke her up at six wanting to be fed.

After dressing in the same outfit she'd worn last evening, she took off his diaper and bathed him. He loved the water and wanted to play. Finally she dressed him and put him in his carry-cot. On the way to the cockpit, she got his bottle out of the fridge in the galley and carried him up on deck to feed him.

To her surprise the cruiser was moored at a pier along a stretch of beach she'd never seen before. Because it was dawn, the layers of hills in the light above the sand took on lavender to purple hues with each receding line.

At the top of the first hill a small, white cycladic church was silhouetted against the sky. The sheer beauty of it stood out and drew her gaze. She realized she was looking at a sight quite out of this world. A glimpse of Olympus?

"This is my favorite spot on Milos in the early morning," came the familiar male voice she loved. "Before you went home I wanted you to see it at first light."

She cast him a sideward glance. "I can see why. It would be impossible to describe this to anyone and do it justice. This is something you have to experience for yourself."

Andreas lounged against the entry, focusing his gaze on the church. "I was a boy when my parents first brought me here. I thought it had to be the home of the gods."

"Would you believe I thought the same thing when I came up here just now?"

His eyes found hers. They seemed to be asking something of her. "How would you like to go up there? It's a bit of a climb, but not difficult and won't take long. Stavros will watch Nikos for us."

All the warning bells were going off telling Gabi not to go, but she sensed this was too important to Andreas to turn him down. He wanted her to see a place that had deep meaning for him. She knew he didn't show this private side of him to very many people.

She felt honored. Even if she could never have this man's love, she had garnered his respect and that was something to treasure. "I'd like that."

Andreas pulled out his cell phone and told Stavros they were going ashore for a little while. Within seconds the older man arrived at the cockpit with a smile.

"I'll take good care of the little one."

Gabi thanked him for the lovely dinner and his willingness to tend Nikos. "We won't be long," she assured him.

"Shall we go?" Andreas led the way off the boat and along the pier. This morning he was wearing white pants and a sport shirt in a dusky blue silk. She couldn't take her eyes off him.

As he ambled up the path she could imagine him as a boy. She ached to think she'd only known him a short time. All those years when she'd missed the in-between part were gone. She would never know the rest of the years yet to come...

A debilitating stab of pain took the wind out of her. She had to stop halfway up the path in order to gather her strength so she could keep moving. Finally they reached the top. From this vantage point she had an incredible view of the Aegean a thousand feet below.

Andreas turned to her with those penetrating eyes. "What do you think?"

"You didn't really need to ask me that."

A smile broke out on his face so beautiful, she had trouble breathing. "Years ago couples wound their way up from the village on the other side to be married here, but the tradition dwindled out because the guests weren't up to it."

She laughed, still out of breath herself. "Nowadays it would have to be the rare couple who..." The rest of the sentence didn't come out. Why did he mention that subject? Bringing Gabi here was too cruel. She knew he hadn't meant to be, but she couldn't take anymore.

"I—I think we'd better get back to Nikos."

"We just got here." His unflappable manner was starting to unnerve her. He moved closer. "I want to take you inside. The priest came early and opened it especially for us. He's anxious to meet you."

Gabi blinked. "I don't understand."

"Maybe this will help." In the next breath he pulled her into his arms and lowered his compelling mouth to hers in a kiss of such intense desire, he set off a conflagration inside her. It went on and on, deeper and longer and so thrilling, her legs shook.

"With every breath in my body, I love you, Gabi Turner. I want you for my wife and have asked the priest to marry us. Everything's been arranged."

"But I thought—"

"You think too much. I've wanted this since the moment you came into my life."

His electrifying tone and the fire in his eyes caused her to tremble. She could hear him talking, but she couldn't believe any of this was really happening.

"Little did I know that the minute Kris survived his operation, you would try to get away from me. You do love me, don't you? Say it—I've been dying for you to admit it."

"I would have said it weeks ago," she cried, throwing her arms around his neck so she could cover his face with kisses. "I'm in love with you, darling. I don't know if you're in my dream, or I'm in yours, but it doesn't matter because I've needed this forever."

His mouth sought hers again and they clung in a rapture that swept her away. He cupped her face in his hands. "Tell me I'm the man you were talking about," he demanded almost savagely. "Admit it," he cried.

"You *know* you are," she said with her heart in her eyes reflecting the lavender light. "I love you so desperately you can't imagine, Andreas." Now that he'd kissed her again, she was addicted to his mouth, seeking it over and over in an explosion of need, yet the terrible hunger they had for each other kept on growing.

At last he drew in a harsh breath. "There's no way I would ever let you go. I'm in love with you, Gabi. The kind I didn't think would ever happen to me. The way I feel about you, we have to get married *now*."

Gabi needed no urging. He grasped her hand and led her inside the small, seventeenth-century church where he'd come as a boy. The robed priest was waiting for them. She felt as if she were floating in a dream, but it seemed real enough by the time he'd pronounced them husband and wife.

Andreas turned to her with a look of eager, tremulous joy. "Let's go, Mrs. Simonides."

Like happy children let out of school, they ran down the path to the waiting cruiser far below. When they reached the bottom, Andreas swept her in his arms. "I've been wanting to do this for weeks."

"Congratulations on your marriage," Stavros called out while her husband was kissing her senseless. "Don't worry about Nikos. He's up in the cockpit with me learning the ropes."

* * *

"Have I worn you out yet?" Andreas whispered against her throat. It was already early evening. Only temporarily sated, they were wrapped together on their sides, still unwilling to let each other go, even to sit up.

She stared into his adoring eyes. "I'm ashamed to admit that will never happen. I can't remember when I wasn't in love with you."

"The evening you stood at the elevator in my office fighting for our nephews' lives, I found out what the meaning of real love was all about. It hit me so hard and fast, I'll never be the same."

Her eyes misted over. "I knew how deeply I loved you when I saw you interact with the twins. The kind of caring you showed them and your brother told me this was a man above the rest and the woman lucky enough to win his love would be the happiest woman alive."

She caressed the side of his firm jaw. "I'm that woman, Andreas. You make me so happy, I'm frightened."

His expression sobered. "So am I. Joy really does exist for some. We have to guard it with our lives, *agape mou*."

She nodded, pressing her mouth to his, loving the taste and feel of him. "It's so sad that Thea never found it."

He pulled her on top of him. "My poor brother came too close to losing it. I swear I'll love you till the day I die."

The second his hungry mouth closed over hers, Gabi let out an ecstatic sigh, needing her husband's possession. How had she lived this many years without him? Time didn't exist as they gave each other pleasure almost beyond bearing.

"Uh-oh," she whispered into his hair some time later. "I think I heard a little cherub who's been ignored too long."

Andreas bit her earlobe playfully. "I'll get him."

In half a minute he'd brought the baby to bed with them. He lay him on top of his chest, a position Nikos didn't like as well as on his back.

"Oh, Andreas…isn't he the most adorable child you ever saw?"

"Thea and Leon did good work, didn't they?"

"Yes," she admitted with a gentle laugh.

His smoldering gaze found hers. "I can do good work, too."

Emotion made her voice husky. "I already know that."

"Will you be disappointed if our first baby isn't a twin? I'm not unaware you'd planned to adopt these two."

"That was the original plan." She kissed Andreas's shoulder. "But when I saw Leon with them in Apollonia, the ache for them passed because another ache had taken over. I discovered I wanted my own babies with you."

"Gabi…"

Somehow they got lost in another kiss, but Nikos didn't like being caught between them and made his discomfort known.

"It's okay, little guy." Andreas lifted him in the air and got to his feet. "Estelle's waiting to take care of you tonight." He put him in his carry-cot and got dressed.

Gabi sat up in the bed, taking the sheet with her. "She is?"

"Since we're on our honeymoon, she insists. When we get back in the morning, we'll fly to Athens with

Nikos and tell everyone our news, then we'll head straight to Crete. In the meantime, I want you to stay in that bed and wait for me. I won't be long."

"You'd better not be. I already miss you."

He shot her a sizzling glance. "You don't know the half of it, but you're going to find out."

A thrill ran through her body. She ached with love for him. The moment he disappeared with her precious Nikos, she got out of bed and threw on her robe. Her purse was in her cabin. She padded out of the stateroom to get her phone and call her parents, who were delighted with the happy news.

"Well, we'll see you tomorrow, then, darling," her dad said, clearing his throat. "Tell Andreas welcome to the family."

She already had...in ways that would make her blush over the years.

"I will. See you tomorrow. Love you."

No sooner had she hung up than she could hear Andreas calling to her. "I'm in my cabin!"

He came to the door out of breath, his eyes alive. "What are you doing in here?"

"I was just letting Mom and Dad know our news. They're thrilled out of their minds."

"So am I," he murmured, taking her down on the bed with him. "I told Stavros to head for Papafragas beach. If no one's around, I want to make love to you there. It's one of my many fantasies since you blew into my life."

She kissed his eyes and nose. "That's twice you've used that expression."

"Because you're like a fragrant breeze that blows across the island, filling me with wants and needs beyond my ability to express."

"I love you so much I'm in pain, Andreas."

"So am I, and plan to do something about it right now. We can either swim in like we did before, or we can take the shortcut down the steps to the sand from the other side."

She let out a squeal. "There's a shortcut?"

He burst into deep laughter, the kind that rumbled out of him. "So I *have* worn you out."

"Never. But right now I'd rather reserve all my energy for loving you. How long before we get there?"

Andreas undid the sash on her robe. "Long enough, my love."

CHAPTER TEN

AFTER making love over and over again, they lay entwined on the sand until it gave up all its heat. By the middle of the night, Andreas had to throw a light blanket over them.

"Look at those stars, darling. With the walls on either side of us, it's like viewing the heavens through a telescope."

"I *am* looking," he answered her. "They're in your eyes." He couldn't believe he was actually holding his wife, his lover, his best friend. His *life*.

She gave him that special smile he felt wrap right around his heart. He needed to love her all over again. "When we bring our children here one day, we can never tell them...well, you know."

Gabi could be bold one minute, shy the next. Always the giver. There was so much to learn about her. Thank heaven this was only the beginning.

"You mean how we consecrated this spot for our own?" he whispered against her throat.

"Yes."

"I came close to ravishing you on this sand before."

"I came even closer to letting you," she confessed. "You'll never know how much I wanted you that night."

He expelled a sigh. "I wasn't sure of you then. Irena told me that when she saw us together, she felt this energy radiating from us like a fire had been lit."

"Andreas—" She clasped him tighter. "Here I am with you—all of you—I have you totally to myself— and I still want more. Maybe there's something wrong with me to love you this much."

He kissed her trembling lower lip. "If there is, I don't ever want you to get well."

"This night is enchanted. I wish we could hold back the morning. It's going to be here before we know it."

"The morning will always have its enchantment, Gabi. That's because, no matter where we are, we'll always wake up to each other."

"Promise me," she cried urgently.

His adorable wife loved him as much as he loved her. Before the joy of it gave him a heart attack, he proceeded to convince her that this was only the beginning.

A DADDY FOR
HER SONS

RAYE MORGAN

This is dedicated to Lauri, for everything
wonderful that comes out of her oven!

CHAPTER ONE

A NIGHTMARE. That was what this had to be. She must be
dreaming. But what had she expected from a blind date?

Jill Darling was no shy innocent, but her face was
blazing. She could feel it. The man was trying to…
Ugh, it was just too creepy to even try to name what he
was doing. She couldn't really be sure unless she took
a look under the table. And that would cause a scene.
She couldn't do that. She knew people in this restaurant.

But…was that really his foot sliding up and down
her leg?

He was leaning close, talking on and on, his breath
hot on her neck. Okay, maybe that was all in the game.
But what the heck was that foot doing?

She tried to move away, but she was trapped, hud-
dled right up against the edge of the planter that sat
right beside their table, tickling her nose with its palm
fronds. They were eating in the restaurant of the nicest
hotel in this part of town. It had Irish linen tablecloths,
real sterling silverware and a small combo playing for
dancers on a tiny dance floor to the side.

She took a long drink from her water glass, then

looked over at him. She tried to smile, but she knew it was wobbly and pretty darn unconvincing if he should happen to actually notice it.

Karl Attkins was his name. Her friend's brother. He was good looking enough, but somehow cold, as though she could have been anyone with an "available female" label stamped on her forehead. Should she ask him about the foot? And maybe warn him not to lose sight of his shoe. It wouldn't be easy to replace that here in this crowded restaurant.

Oh, Lord, he was using his toes now. She was going to have to say something. If she didn't, her nice steak dinner just might come back up. And all that wine she drank, trying to keep busy. This just wasn't cool. She took a deep breath and tried to think of a way to say it without being insulting.

But then he gave her the out she needed.

"Would you like to dance?" he asked, cocking an eyebrow as though he knew she must consider him quite debonair.

Dance. No, not at all. But she steeled herself to the effort. Dancing ought to give him a reason to put his shoe back on, and if so, it would all be worth it.

"Sure," she said breathlessly. "Why not?"

Well, the fact that they were playing a tango at that very moment might have been a reason to sit this one out. But it hardly mattered. At least the man was shod once more. She tried to keep the electric smile painted on her face as he led her to the proper position. And then she glanced at her watch and wondered how much longer she was going to have to endure this torture. She had to put in a good chunk of time or the friends who'd got her into this wouldn't believe she'd really tried.

Oh, Mary Ellen, she groaned silently as Karl pushed her to and fro dramatically across the dancing floor, leaving her to lunge about like a puppet with its strings cut. *I love you dearly, but this is just too high a price to pay for your friendship.*

"But, Jill," all her friends had counseled solemnly, "you've got to do it. You've got to get back into the swim of things. It's been over a year since Brad...well, since you've been alone." The timing had helped make her receptive. Changes were making her feel vulnerable. Her sister was probably moving away, and her younger half-sister had recently died. Loneliness was looming large in her life. "Time is streaking by," another friend lectured. "Don't let it leave you behind. Don't be a coward. Get out there and fight!"

Fight? For what?

"A man, of course," said Mary Ellen. "Once you hit your age, they don't come a dime a dozen any more. You've got competition."

"But, what if I...?"

"No! You can't give up!" her friend Crystal had chimed in. "Your kids need a father figure in the home."

Mary Ellen had fixed her with a steely stare. "And you want to show old Brad, don't you?"

Show old Brad. The need to do just that surged in her. Of course she wanted to show old Brad. Sure. She would date. If he could do it, so could she. Stand back. She was ready for the challenge.

But where would she find someone to date? Mary Ellen knew just the man for her.

"My brother Karl is a real player," she said airily. "He'll get you back into the swing of things in no time. He has so many friends. You'll be dating like crazy before you know it."

Dating. She remembered dating. The way your heart raced as you waited for him to come to the door, the shy pauses, the way your eyes met his and then looked quickly away. Would he kiss you on the doorstep? Were you really going to let him?

Fun!

But that was then. This was a completely different thing, seemingly from a galaxy far, far away. She was older now. She'd been married and she had two kids. She knew how things worked. She could handle it. Or so she thought.

No. This was a nightmare.

At least her dress was pretty, and she didn't get many chances to wear something like this anymore. A sleek shift dress in teal-blue, it was covered with sequins and glistened as she walked, making her feel sexy and pretty and nice. Too bad she was wasting that on a man who spent more time looking at himself in the mirror than she did.

The tango was over. She turned back toward the table in relief, but Karl grabbed her free hand and twirled her around to face him. The band was playing a cha cha. He grinned. "Hey mambo!" he cried out and began to sway. He seemed to consider himself quite the ballroom dancer, even if he couldn't tell one Latin dance from another.

Jill had a decision to make. Would she rather dance, or go back to playing footsie? She wasn't sure she knew how to cha cha. But she knew she didn't want to feel that foot on her leg again.

What the hell.

"Everybody loves to cha-cha-cha," she murmured as she let him twirl her again.

And then she looked up and saw Connor McNair staring at her in horror.

Her blood ran cold. She was still moving, but no one could accuse her of dancing at this point. The music didn't mean a thing.

Connor. Oh, no.

First, it appalled her to think that anyone she knew might see her here like this. But close on that thought came the shock question—was Brad with him?

No. She glanced around quickly and didn't see any sign of her ex-husband at all. Thank heaven for small blessings. Connor must have come to town and was staying here at the hotel—alone. But still, it was Connor, Brad's best friend, the one person most likely to report to him. She could hardly stand it.

He was mouthing something to her. She squinted, trying to make it out. What was he trying to say?

She couldn't tell, but he was coming out onto the dance floor. Why? She looked around, feeling wild, wanting to run. What was he going to do?

"May I cut in?" he asked Karl.

He was polite, but unsmiling, and Karl didn't seem to be in a friendly mood.

"What? No. Go get your own girl," Karl told him, frowning fiercely. And just to prove his point, he grabbed Jill and pulled her close.

She looked over his shoulder at Connor. He offered a safe harbor of sorts, but there was danger there, too. She didn't want to talk to Connor. She didn't want to have anyone close to Brad anywhere near. The pain of Brad's desertion still ached inside her like an open wound and she didn't want anyone from his side of the rift to see her like this—much less talk to her.

So she glared at Connor. Let him know she didn't need him or his rescue. She was doing fine. She was here enjoying herself. Sort of.

She got back to dancing, swaying her hips, making her sequins sparkle, and trying hard to smile at Karl. Let Connor see that she was having the time of her life. Let him take that bit of news back to Brad, if that was what he was after.

"Mambo!" she cried out, echoing Karl. Why the heck not?

Connor gave her a look of disbelief as he stepped back to the sidelines, but he didn't leave. The next dance was a simple two-step, but that meant Karl's arms around her again, and she couldn't disguise the shudder that gave her.

And there was Connor, taking in every nuance. She glowered at him. He was very handsome in his crisp white shirt with the dark slacks that looked tailor-made. But that was beside the point. Didn't he have a table to go to? What gave him the right to stand there and watch her? Biting her lip, she tried to keep him out of her line of vision and blot him out of her head.

But then he was back, right at Karl's elbow again, stopping them in their tracks.

"Excuse me," he said, looking very serious. "Listen, do you have a silver BMW in the parking lot?"

Karl blinked. His eyes narrowed suspiciously, but he couldn't resist the question. "Why, yes I do. What about it?"

Connor's brows came together in a look of sorrow. "I'm afraid your car's on fire."

Karl dropped Jill like a hot potato and whirled to face Connor. "What?" he cried, anguish contorting his face.

Connor was all sympathy. "I think they've called the fire department, but you might want to get out there and…"

No more words were necessary. He was already gone.

Connor took Jill by the arm, looking annoyed when she balked and tried to pull away.

"Come on," he said impatiently. "I know a back way out."

Jill shook her head, not sure what he thought he was doing here. "But…I can't just leave."

Connor looked down at her and suddenly grinned, startling her. She'd forgotten how endearing he could be and she stared up at him. It was like finding a beloved forgotten toy in the attic. Affection for him trembled on the edge of her mood, but she batted it back.

"Why not?" he said. "Do you want to spend the next two hours with the guy?"

She tried to appear stern. She wanted to deny what he was implying. How could she go? What would she say to her friends? What would she tell Mary Ellen?

But in the end, his familiar grin did her in. "I'd rather eat dirt," she admitted, crumbling before him.

"There you go." He led her gently across the dance floor, only hesitating while she scooped up her sparkly little purse. They headed for the exit and he winked at a waiter who was holding the door for them, obviously primed to help with the escape. He paused only long enough to hand the man some folded money and then they were out the door.

"But what about his car?" Jill asked, worrying a bit. She knew the sense of guilt would linger long after the evening was gone. "He loves that car."

"Don't give it a second thought," he advised, steering her toward his own souped-up, twenty-year-old Camaro, a car she remembered from the past, and pulling open the passenger door.

"His car isn't really on fire, is it?" she asked as she plunked down into the leather seat.

"No." He sank into the driver's seat and grinned at her again. "Look, I'll do a lot for an old friend, but setting a guy's car on fire...no, that's a step too far."

She watched him start the engine and turn toward the back exit.

"But you will lie to him about it," she noted.

"Oh, yeah."

She sighed and settled back into the seat. All in all,

at least she didn't have a naked foot exploring her leg at the moment. That alone was worth its weight in gold.

"Rickey's on the Bay?" he asked in the shorthand they both remembered from earlier years.

"Of course," she responded without thinking. That was where everyone always went when the night was still young enough to make the last ferry to the island. She turned and looked at the lights of Seattle in the distance. If only you could go back in time as easily as you could go back to the places where you hung out in your youth.

"I can't believe I'm letting you do this," she said with a sigh.

"I can't believe you needed me to do it."

She laughed. "Touché," she muttered. So much for the great date that was supposed to bring her out of her shell and into the social whirl.

She pulled her cell phone out of her purse and checked it.

"What are you doing?" Connor asked with just a hint of suspicion in his tone.

She glanced up at him and smiled impishly. "Waiting for Karl to call. I've got to explain this to him somehow."

He shuddered. "Is Karl the mambo king?" he asked.

She gave him a baleful look.

"Don't worry. I gave the waiter a little money to tell old Karl what the score was."

She raised an eyebrow. "And just what is the score, pray tell?"

He hesitated, then shrugged. "I told him to tell Karl I

was a made guy from the mob and we didn't take kindly
to outsiders poaching on our women."

"What?"

He looked a little embarrassed. "Yeah, I know. Definitely corny. But it was the best I could think of on the
spur of the moment."

She had to hold back her laughter. He didn't deserve
it.

"I didn't even know you were Italian."

"There are a lot of things you don't know about me."
He gave her a mocking wink. "A lot of things you don't
want to know."

"Obviously."

She frowned, thinking the situation over. "So now
you've single-handedly destroyed my chances of dating
anyone ever again in this town. Thanks a lot."

"I'm just looking out for you, sweetheart."

She rolled her eyes, but she was biting back a grin.

Rickey's was as flamboyant as a fifties retro diner
should be, with bright turquoise upholstery and juke-
boxes at every table. They walked in as though they
ought to see a lot of old friends there, but no one looked
the least bit familiar.

"We're old," he whispered in her ear as he led her
to a booth along the side with windows on the marina.
"Everyone we used to hang out with is gone."

"So why are we still here?" she asked, a bit grumpy
about it. This was where so much of her life had played
out in the old days. And now, the waitresses didn't know
her and the faces all looked unfamiliar.

"Lost souls, searching for the meaning of life," he said, smiling at her across the linoleum-covered table. His smile looked wistful this time, unlike the cheerful grin from before.

"The meaning of life is clear enough," she protested. After all, hadn't everyone been lecturing her on it for months? "Get on with things. Make the world a better place. Face reality and deal with it. Or something along those lines."

He shrugged. "Sounds nice, until you start analyzing definitions. What exactly does 'better' mean? Better for whom? How do you get the whole world involved, anyway?"

She made a face at him. "You always were the great contrarian," she said accusingly. "And now I've let you kidnap me. Someone should call the police."

The waitress, a pretty young girl in a poodle skirt who'd just arrived at their table blanched and took a step backward.

"No, no," Jill told her quickly. "I'm only joking. Please don't take me seriously. Ever."

The waitress blinked rapidly, but risked a step closer in to take their order. She didn't hang around to chat, however.

"You scared her," Connor suggested as she hurried away.

"I scare everyone lately," Jill admitted. "What do you think? Am I too intense? Are my eyes a little wild?"

He looked at her uncertainly, not sure if the truth would be accepted in the spirit he would mean it. His gaze skimmed over her pretty face. She had new lines between the brows, a new hint of worry in her eyes. Her hands were clenched around her water glass, as though she were holding on to a life preserver. Tense was hardly a strong enough word. His heart broke just a little bit. What had happened to his carefree girl?

But that was just it. She wasn't "his," never had been.

He knew she'd been through a lot since Brad had left her. She had a right to a few ragged edges. But when you came right down to it, she was as beautiful as she'd ever been. Her golden hair sprang into curls in an untamed mass all around her head. Her dark eyes were still warm, her lips were still full and sexy. Still gorgeous after all these years.

And looking at her still sent him over the moon. It happened every time. She was like a substance he had to be careful he didn't mess with, knowing it would be too dangerous to overdose.

But he could see a difference in her and silently he swore at himself. Why had he stayed away so long? She probably could have used a friend. She'd lost her young girl sparkle and he regretted it. He loved that sparkle.

But now he frowned, studying her face as though he was worried about what he found there. "How are you doing, Jill?" he asked her quietly. "I mean really. How've you been?"

She sat back and really looked at him for the first time, a quiver of fear in her heart. This was what she really wanted to avoid. Silly banter was so much safer than going for truth.

She studied his handsome face, his crystal-blue eyes sparking diamond-like radiant light from between those inky black eyelashes that seemed too impossibly long. It had been over a year since she'd seen him last and he didn't seem quite so much like a kid living in a frat house anymore.

He'd always been such a contrast to Brad, like a younger brother who didn't want to grow up. Brad was the serious one, the ambitious one, the idea man who had the drive to follow through. Connor was more likely to be trying to make a flight to catch a party in Malibu or volunteering to crew on a sailing trip to Tahiti. Brad was a man you could count on. Connor—not so much.

Only that had turned out to be a lie, hadn't it? It was hard to trust anything much anymore once the man you'd considered your rock had melted away and wasn't there for you anymore.

She closed her eyes for a moment, then gave him a dazzling smile. "I've been great," she said breezily. "Life is good. The twins are healthy and my business is actually starting to make a profit, so we're good."

He didn't believe her. He'd known her too long to accept the changed woman she'd become. She'd always been careful—the responsible sort—but she'd also had a sense of fun, of carefree abandon. Instead, her eyes, her tone, her nervous movements, all displayed a wary tension, as though she was always looking over her shoulder to see what disaster might be gaining on her now.

"So good that you felt it was time to venture out into the dating world again, huh?" he noted, being careful to smile as he said it.

"Why not? I need to move on. I need to...to..." She couldn't remember exactly what the argument was, though she'd heard it enough from her friends lately. Something about broadening her horizons. Something about reigniting her womanly instincts. She looked at Connor as though she might read the words in his eyes, but they just weren't there.

"So who talked you into that fiasco tonight?" he asked her.

She frowned at him. "It was a blind date."

"No kidding. Even *you* wouldn't be nutty enough to go out with that guy voluntarily."

"Even me?" His words stung. What did he think of her, anyway? Her eyes flashed. "Just how nutty am I, Connor?"

He reached out and grabbed her hand, gazing at her earnestly. "Will you stop? Please?"

She glanced back, her bottom lip trembling. Deep breaths. That was what she needed. And no matter what, she wasn't going to cry.

"So where have you been all this time?" she asked, wishing it didn't sound quite so petulant.

"All what time?" he said evasively.

"The year and a half since I last saw you."

Her gaze met his and skittered away again. She knew he was thinking about exactly what she was thinking about—that last time had been the day Brad left her. Neither one of them wanted to remember that day, much less talk about it. She grimaced and played with her spoon. The waitress brought their order so it was a moment or two before they spoke again.

"So you said your business is doing okay?" he noted as he spread his napkin on his lap.

"Yes." She stared down at the small dish of ice cream she'd ordered and realized she wasn't going to be able to eat any of it. Her throat felt raw and tight. Too bad. It looked creamy and delicious.

He nodded, reaching for a fork. It was pretty clear he wasn't going to have any problem at all. "What business?"

She blinked at him. "Didn't you know? Didn't Brad tell you?"

He shook his head and avoided saying anything about Brad.

She waited a moment, then sighed. "Okay. When Brad left, he took the electronics business we had developed together. And told me I might as well go out and get a job once the babies were born."

He cringed. That was enough to set your teeth on edge, no matter who you were.

She met his gaze with a touch of defiance in her own. "But I gave birth to two little boys and looked at them and knew there was no way I was handing them over to someone else to raise for me. So I racked my brain, trying to find something I could do at home and still take care of them."

He nodded. That seemed the resourceful thing to do. Good for her. "So what did you decide on?"

She shrugged. "The only thing I was ever really good at. I started a Bundt Cake Bakery."

He nodded, waiting. There had to be more. Who could make a living baking Bundt cakes? "And?"

"And that's what I'm doing."

"Oh." He frowned, puzzled. "Great."

"It *is* great," she said defensively. She could hear the skepticism in his voice. "It was touch and go for a long time, but now I think I'm finally hitting my stride."

He nodded again, wishing he could rustle up some enthusiasm, but failing on all fronts. "Okay."

The product Jill and Brad had developed together had been a bit different from baked goods and he was having a hard time understanding the connection. Jill had done the bookkeeping and the marketing for the business. Brad had been the electronic genius. And Connor had done some work with them, too. They'd been successful from the first.

With that kind of background, he couldn't imagine how the profits from cakes could compare to what they'd made on the GPS device for hikers to be used as a map App. It had been new and fresh and sold very well. He wasn't sure what he could say.

He looked up across the restaurant, caught sight of someone coming in the door and he sighed. "You know how legend has it that everyone stops in at Rickey's on a Saturday night?"

Her eyes widened warily. "Sure."

"I guess it's true." He made a gesture with his head. "Look who just walked in. Mr. Mambo himself."

She gasped and whirled in her seat. Sure enough, there was Karl starting in their direction. He was coming through the restaurant as though he thought he owned the place, giving all the girls the eye. He caught sight of her and his eyes lit up.

Her heart fell. "Oh, no!"

CHAPTER TWO

AND THEN, KARL'S jaunty gaze fell on Connor and he stopped dead, visibly paling. Shaking his head, he raised his hands and he seemed to be muttering, "no, no," over and over again, as though to tell Connor he really didn't mean it. Turning on his heel, he left so quickly, Jill could almost believe she'd been imagining things.

"Wow." She turned back slowly and looked at Connor accusingly. "I guess he believed your cockeyed story." She put a hand to her forehead as though tragedy had struck. "Once he spreads the word, my dating days are done."

"Good," Connor said, beginning to attack his huge piece of cherry pie à la mode. "No point wasting your time on losers like that."

She made a face and leaned toward him sadly. "Are they all like that? Is it really hopeless?"

"Yes." He smiled at her. "Erase all thoughts of other men. I'm here. You don't need anybody else."

"Right." She rolled her eyes, knowing he was teas-

ing. "You'd think I would have learned my lesson with
Brad, wouldn't you?"

There was a catch in her voice as she said it. He
looked up quickly and she knew he was afraid she might
cry. But she didn't cry about that anymore. She was all
cried out long ago on that subject.

Did he remember what a fool she'd been? How even
with all the evidence piling up in her daily life, she'd
never seen it coming. At the time she was almost eight
months pregnant with the twins and having a hard time
even walking, much less with thinking straight. And
Connor had come to tell her that Brad was leaving her.

Brad had sent him, of course. The jerk couldn't even
manage to face her and tell her himself.

That made her think twice. Here was Connor, back
again. What was Brad afraid to tell her now?

She watched him, frowning, studying his blue eyes.
Did she really want to know? All those months, all the
heartbreak. Still, if it was something she needed to deal
with, better get it over with. She took a deep breath and
tried to sound strong and cool.

"So what does he want this time?"

Connor's head jerked back as though what she was
asking was out of line. He waved his fork at her. "Do
you think we could first go through some of the nice-
ties our society has set up for situations like this?" he
asked her.

She searched his face to see if he was mocking her,
but he really wasn't. He was just uncomfortable.

"How about, 'How have you been?' or 'What have
you been up to lately?' Why not give me some of the

details of your life these days. Do we have to jump right into contentious things so quickly?"

So it wasn't good. She should have known. "You're the messenger, not me."

His handsome face winced. It almost seemed as though this pained him more than it was going to pain her. Fat chance.

"We're friends, aren't we?" he asked her.

Were they? She used to think so. "Sure. We always have been."

"So…"

He looked relieved, as though that made it all okay. But it wasn't okay. Whatever it was, it was going to hurt. She knew that instinctively. She leaned forward and glared at him.

"But you're on his side. Don't deny it."

He shook his head, denying it anyway. "What makes you say that?"

She shrugged. "That day, the one that ended life as I knew it, you came over to deliver the fatal blow. You set me straight as to how things really were." Her voice hardened. "You were the one who explained Brad to me at the time. You broke my heart and then you left me lying there in the dirt and you never came back."

"You were not lying in the dirt." He seemed outraged at the concept.

She closed her eyes and then opened them again. "It's a metaphor, silly."

"I don't care what it is. I did not leave you lying in the dirt or even in the sand, or on the couch, or anything. You were standing straight and tall and making jokes, just like always."

Taking a deep breath, he forced himself to relax a bit. "You seemed calm and collected and fine with it. Like you'd known it was coming. Like you were prepared. Sad, but okay." He shook his head, willing her to believe what he was saying. "Or else I never would have left you alone."

She shrugged carelessly. How could he have gotten it all so wrong? "And you think you know me."

He pushed away the pie, searching her eyes, looking truly distressed. "Sara was with you. Your sister. I thought…"

He looked away, frowning fiercely. He remembered what he'd thought. He'd seen the pain in her face and it had taken everything in him not to reach out and gather her in his arms and kiss her until she realized…until she knew… No, he'd had to get out of there before he did something stupid. And that was why he left her. He had his own private hell to tend to.

"You thought I was okay? Wow." She struck a pose and put on an accent. "The corpse was bleeding profusely, but I assumed it would stop on its own. She seemed to be coping quite well with her murder."

He grimaced, shaking his head.

"I hated you for a while," she admitted. "It was easier than hating Brad. What Brad had done to me was just too confusing. What you did was common, everyday cowardice."

He stared at her, aghast. "Oh, thanks."

"And to make it worse, you never did come back. Did you?"

He shook his head as though he really couldn't understand why she was angry. He hadn't done anything to make her that way. He'd just lived his life like he always did, following the latest impulse that moved him. Didn't she know that?

"I was gone. I left the country. I…I had a friend starting up a business in Singapore, so I went to help him out."

She looked skeptical and deep, deep down, she looked hurt. "All this time?"

"Yeah." He nodded, feeling a bit defensive. "I've been out of the country all this time."

Funny, but that made her feel a lot better. At least he hadn't been coming up here to Seattle and never contacting her.

"So you haven't been to see Brad?"

He hesitated. He couldn't lie to her. "I stopped in to see Brad in Portland last week," he admitted.

She threw up her hands. "See? You're on his side."

He wanted to growl at her. "I'm not on anybody's side. I've been friends with both of you since that first week of college, when we all three camped out in Brad's car together."

The corners of Jill's mouth quirked into a reluctant smile as she remembered. "What a night that was," she said lightly. "They'd lost my housing forms and you hadn't been admitted yet. We had no place to sleep."

"So Brad offered his car."

"And stayed out with us."

"We talked and laughed the whole night."

She nodded, remembering. "And that cemented it. We were best buds from that night on."

Connor smiled, but looked away. He remembered meeting Jill in the administration office while they both tried to fight the bureaucracy. He'd thought she was the cutest coed on campus, right from the start. And then Brad showed up and swept her off her feet.

"We fought the law and the law won," he noted cynically.

"Right." She laughed softly, still remembering. "You with that crazy book of rules you were always studying on how to make professors fall in love with you so they'd give you good grades."

He sighed. "That never worked. And it should have, darn it all."

Her eyes narrowed as she looked back into the past a little deeper. "And all those insane jobs you took, trying to pay off your fees. I never understood when you had time to study."

"I slept with a tape recorder going," he said with a casual shrug. "Subliminal learning. Without it, I would have flunked out early on."

She stared at him, willing him to smile and admit he'd made that up, but he stuck to his guns.

"No, really. I learned French that way."

She gave him an incredulous look. *"Parlez-vous francais?"*

"Uh...whatever." He looked uncomfortable. "I didn't say I retained any of it beyond test day."

"Right." She laughed at him and he grinned back.

But she knew they were ignoring the elephant in the room. Brad. Brad who had been with them both all through college. Brad who had decided she was his from the start. And what Brad wanted, Brad usually got. She'd been flattered by his attention, then thrilled with it. And soon, she'd fallen hard. She was so in love with him, she knew he was her destiny. She let him take over her life. She didn't realize he would toss it aside when he got tired of it.

"So what are you doing here?" she asked again. "Surely you didn't come to see me."

"Jill, I always want to see you."

"No kidding. That's why you've been gone for a year and a half. You've never even met the twins."

He looked at her with a half smile. Funny. She'd been pregnant the last time he'd seen her, but that wasn't the way he'd thought of her all these months. And to tell the truth, Brad had never mentioned those babies. "That's right. I forgot. You've got a couple of cookie crunchers now, don't you?"

"I do. The little lights of my life, so to speak."

"Boys."

"Boys." She nodded.

He wanted to ask how they got along with Brad, but he wasn't brave enough to do it. Besides, it was getting late. She had a pair of baby boys at home. She looked at her watch, then looked at him.

"I've got to get home. If you can just drop me at the dock, the last ferry goes at midnight and…"

He waved away her suggestion. "You will not walk home from the ferry landing. It's too late and too far."

She made a face. "I'll be fine. I've done it a thousand times."

"I'll drive you."

She gave him a mock glare. "Well, then we'd better get going or you won't make the last ferry back."

"You let me worry about that."

Let him worry—let him manage—leave it to him. Something inside her yearned to be able to do that. It had been so long since she'd had anyone else to rely on. But life had taught her a hard lesson. If you relied on others, they could really hurt you. Best to rely on nobody but yourself.

The ferry ride across the bay to the island was always fun. He pulled the car into the proper space on the ferry and they both got out to enjoy the trip. Standing side by side as the ferry started off, they watched the inky-black water part to let them through.

Jill pulled her arms in close, fending off the ocean coolness, and he reached out and put an arm around her, keeping her warm. She rested her head on his shoulder. He had to resist the urge to draw her closer.

"Hey, I'm looking forward to meeting those two little boys of yours," he said.

"Hopefully you won't meet them tonight," she said, laughing. "I've got a nice older lady looking after them. They should be sound asleep right now."

"It's amazing to think of you with children," he said.

She nodded. "I know. You're not the only one stunned by the transformation." She smiled, thinking of how they really had changed her life. If only Brad...

No, she wasn't going to start going back over those old saws again. That way lay madness.

"It's also amazing to think of how long we've known each other," she added brightly instead.

"We all three got close in our freshman year," he agreed, "and that lasted all through college."

She nodded. "It seemed, those first couple of years, we did everything together."

"I remember it well." He sighed and glanced down at her. All he could see was that mop of crazy, curly blond hair. It always made him smile. "You were sighing over Brad," he added to the memory trail. "And I was wishing you would look my way instead."

She looked up and made a face at him. "Be serious. You had no time for stodgy, conventional girls like I was. You were always after the high flyers."

He stared at her, offended despite the fact that there was some truth in what she said. "I was not," he protested anyway.

"Sure you were." She was teasing him now. "You liked bad girls. Edgy girls. The ones who ran off with the band."

His faint smile admitted the truth. "Only when I was in the band."

"And that was most of the time." She pulled back and looked at him. "Did you ever actually get a degree?"

"Of course I got a degree."

She giggled. "In what? Multicultural dating?"

He bit back the sharp retort that surfaced in his throat. She really didn't know. But why should she?

He had to admit he'd spent years working hard at seeming to be a slacker.

"Something like that," he muttered, thinking with a touch of annoyance about his engineering degree with a magna cum laude attached. No one had been closer friends to him than Brad and Jill. And they didn't even realize he was smarter than he seemed.

It was his own fault of course. He'd worked on that easygoing image. Still, it stung a bit.

And it made him do a bit of "what if?" thinking. What if he'd been more aggressive making his own case? What if he'd challenged Brad's place in Jill's heart at the time? What if he'd competed instead of accepting their romance as an established fact? Would things have been different?

The spray from the water splashed across his face, jerking him awake from his dream. Turning toward the island, he could see her house up the drive a block from the landing. He'd been there a hundred times before, but not for quite a while. Not since the twins were born and Brad decided he wasn't fatherhood material. Connor had listened to what Brad had to say and it had caused a major conflict for him. He thought Brad's reasons were hateful and he deplored them, but at the same time, he'd seen them together for too long to have any illusions. They didn't belong together. Getting a divorce was probably the best thing Brad could do for Jill. So he'd gone with his message, he'd done his part and hated it and then he'd headed for Singapore.

He turned to look at her, to watch the way the wind blew her hair over her eyes, and that old familiar pull began somewhere in the middle of his chest. It started slow and then began to build, as though it was slowly finding its way through his bloodstream. He wanted her, wanted to hold her and kiss her and tell her.... He gritted his teeth and turned away. He had to fight that feeling. Funny. He never got it with any other girl. It only happened with her. Damn.

A flash of panic shivered through him. What the hell was he doing here, anyway? He'd thought he was prepared for this. Hardened. Toughened and ready to avoid the tender trap that was always Jill. But his defenses were fading fast. He had to get out of here.

He needed a plan. Obviously playing this by ear wasn't going to work. The first thing he had to do was to get her home, safe and sound. That should be easy. Then he had to avoid getting out of the car. Under no circumstances should he go into the house, especially not to take a peek at the babies. That would tie him up in a web of sentiment and leave him raw and vulnerable to his feelings. He couldn't afford to do that. At all costs, he had to stay strong and leave right away.

He could come back and talk to her in the morning. If he hung around, disaster was inevitable. He couldn't let that happen.

"You know what?" he said, trying to sound light and casual. "I think you really had the right idea about this. I need to get back to the hotel. I think I'll take the ferry right on back and let you walk up the hill on your own. It's super safe here, isn't it? I mean..."

He felt bad about it, but it had to be done. He couldn't

go home with her. Wouldn't be prudent, as someone once had famously said.

But he realized she wasn't listening to him. She was staring, mouth open, over his shoulder at the island they were fast approaching.

"What in the world is going on? My house is lit up like a Christmas tree."

He turned. She was right. Every window was ablaze with light. It was almost midnight. Somehow, this didn't seem right.

And then a strange thing happened. As they watched, something came flying out of the upstairs window, sailed through the air and landed on the roof next door.

Jill gasped, rigid with shock. "Was that the cat?" she cried. "Oh, my God!"

She tried to pull away from him as though she was about to jump into the water and swim for shore, but he yanked her back. "Come on," he said urgently, pulling her toward the Camaro. "We'll get there faster in the car."

CHAPTER THREE

JILL'S HEART WAS racing. She couldn't think. She could hardly breathe. Adrenaline surged and she almost blacked out with it.

"Oh, please," she muttered over and over as they raced toward the house. "Oh, please, oh, please!"

He swung the car into the driveway and she jumped out before he even came to a stop, running for the door.

"Timmy?" she called out. "Tanner?"

Connor was right behind her as she threw open the front door and raced inside.

"Mrs. Mulberry?" she called out as she ran. "Mrs. Mulberry!"

A slight, gray-haired woman appeared on the stairway from the second floor with a look close to terror on her face. "Oh, thank God you're finally here! I tried to call you but my hands were shaking so hard, I couldn't use the cell phone."

"What is it?" Jill grabbed her by the shoulders, staring down into her face. "What's happened? Where are the boys?"

"I tried, I really tried, but...but..."

"Mrs. Mulberry! What?"

Her face crumpled and she wailed, "They locked me out. I couldn't get to them. I didn't know what to do...."

"What do you mean they've locked you out? Where? When?"

"They got out of their cribs and locked the door. I couldn't..."

Jill started up the stairs, but Connor took them two at a time and beat her to the landing and then the door. He yanked at the handle but it didn't budge.

"Timmy? Tanner? Are you okay?" Jill's voice quavered as she pressed her ear to the door. There was no response.

"There's a key," she said, turning wildly, trying to remember where she'd put it. "I know there's a key."

Connor pushed her aside. "No time," he said, giving the door a wicked kick right next to where the lever sat. There was a crunch of wood breaking and the door flew open.

A scene of chaos and destruction was revealed. A lamp was upside down on the floor, along with pillows and books and a tumbled table and chair set. Toys were everywhere, most of them covered with baby powder that someone had been squirting out of the container. And on the other side of the room were two little blond boys, crowding into a window they could barely reach. They saw the adults coming for them, looked at each other and shrieked—and then they very quickly shoved one fat fluffy pillow and then one large plastic game of Hungry Hungry Hippos over the sill. The hippos could be heard hitting the bricks of the patio below.

"What are you doing?" Jill cried, dashing in as one child reached for a small music toy. She grabbed him, swung him up in her arms and held him close.

"You are such a bad boy!" she said, but she was laughing with relief at the same time. They seemed to be okay. No broken bones. No blood. No dead cat.

Connor pulled up the other boy with one arm while he slammed the window shut with the other. He looked at Jill and shook his head. "Wow," was all he could say. Then he thought of something else. "Oh. Sorry about the door. I thought…"

"You thought right," she said, flashing him a look of pure relief and happiness. Her babies were safe and right now that was all that mattered to her. "I would have had a heart attack if I'd had to wait any longer."

Mrs. Mulberry was blubbering behind them and they both turned, each carrying a child, to stare at her.

"I'm so sorry," she was saying tearfully. "But when they locked me out…"

"Okay, start at the beginning," Jill told her, trying to keep her temper in check and hush her baby, who was saying, "Mamamama" over and over in her ear. "What exactly happened?"

The older woman sniffled and put a handkerchief to her nose. "I…I don't really know. It all began so well. They were perfect angels."

She smiled at them tearfully and they grinned back at her. Jill shook her head. It was as though they knew exactly what they'd done and were ready to do it again if they got the chance.

"They were so good," Mrs. Mulberry was saying,

"I'm afraid I let them stay up longer than I should have. Finally I put them to bed and went downstairs." She shook her head as though she still couldn't believe what happened next. "I was reading a magazine on the couch when something just went plummeting by the bay window. I thought it was my imagination at first. Then something else went shooting past and I got up and went outside to look at what was going on. And there were toys and bits of bedding just lying there in the grass. I looked up but I couldn't see anything. It was very eerie. Almost scary. I couldn't figure out what on earth was happening."

"Oh, sweetie boys," Jill muttered, holding one closely to her. "You must be good for the babysitter. Remember?"

"When I started to go back in the house," the older lady went on, "one of these very same adorable children was at the front door. As I started to come closer, he grinned at me and he…" She had to stop to take a shaky breath. "He just smiled. I realized what might happen and I called out. I said, 'No! Wait!' But just as I reached the door, he slammed it shut. It was locked. He locked me out of the house!"

Jill was frowning. "What are you talking about? Who locked you out of the house?"

She pointed at Timmy who was cuddled close in Jill's arms. "He did."

Jill shook her head as though to clear it. He's only eighteen months old. "That's impossible. He doesn't know how to lock doors."

Mrs. Mulberry drew herself up. "Oh, yes he does," she insisted.

Jill looked into Timmy's innocent face. Could her baby have done that? He smiled and said, "Mama-mama." No way.

"I couldn't get in," Mrs Mulberry went on. "I was panicking. I didn't know what I was going to do." Tears filled her eyes again.

Jill stared at her in disbelief and Connor stepped forward, putting a comforting hand on her shoulder. "We believe you, Mrs. Mulberry," he said calmly. "Just finish your story. We want to know it all."

She tried to give him a grateful smile and went on. "I was racing around, trying all the doors, getting more and more insane with fear. Finally I got the idea to look for a key. I must have turned over twenty flower pots before I found it. Once I got back into the house, I realized they were up here in the bedroom, but when I called to them, they locked the bedroom door."

She sighed heavily, her head falling forward on her chest. "I thought I would go out of my mind. I tried to call you but I couldn't do it. I thought I ought to call the police, but I was shaking so badly…" She shuddered, remembering. "And then you finally came home."

Jill met Connor's gaze and bit her lip, turning to lay Timmy down in his crib. He was giving her a warning glance, as if to say, "No major damage here. Give her a break."

For some reason, instead of letting it annoy her, she felt a surge of relief. Yes, give her a break. Dear soul, she didn't mean any harm, and since nothing had really happened, there was no reason to make things worse. In fact, both boys were already drifting off to sleep. And why not? They'd had a busy night so far.

Turning, she smiled at the older woman. "Thank goodness I got back when I did," she said as lightly as she could manage. "Well, everything's alright now. If you'll wait downstairs, I'll just put these two down and…"

Connor gave her a grin and a wink and put down the already sleeping Tanner into his crib as though he knew what he was doing, which surprised her. But her mind was on her babies, and she looked down lovingly at them as they slept. For just a moment, she'd been so scared….

What would she do if anything happened to either one of them? She couldn't let herself think about that. That was a place she didn't want to go.

Connor watched her. He was pretty sure he knew what she was thinking about. Anything happening to her kids would just about destroy her. He'd seen her face when she first realized she was losing Brad. He remembered that pain almost as if it had been his own. And losing these little ones would be ten times worse.

He drove Mrs. Mulberry home and when he got back, all was quiet. The lights that had blazed out across the landscape were doused and a more muted atmosphere prevailed. The house seemed to be at peace.

Except for one thing—the sound of sniffles coming from the kitchen where Jill was sitting at the table with her hands wrapped around a cup of coffee.

"Hey," he said, sliding in beside her on the bench seat. "You okay?"

She turned her huge, dark, tragic eyes toward him.

"I leave the house for just a few hours—leave the boys for more than ten minutes—the first time in a year. And chaos takes over." She searched his gaze for answers. "Is that really not allowed? Am I chained to this place, this life, forever? Do I not dare leave…ever?"

He stared down at her. He wanted to make a joke, make her smile, get her out of this mood, but he saw real desperation in her eyes and he couldn't make light of that.

"Hey." He brushed her cheek with the backs of his fingers. "It's not forever. Things change quickly for kids. Don't let it get you down. In a month, it will be different."

She stared up at him. How could he possibly know that? And yet, somehow, she saw the wisdom in what he'd said. She shook her head and smiled. "Connor, why didn't you come back sooner? I love your smile."

He gave her another one, but deep down, he groaned. This was exactly why he had to get out of here as soon as he could. He slumped down lower in the seat and tried to think of something else reassuring to say, but his mind wouldn't let go of what she'd just said to him.

I love your smile.

Pretty pathetic to grasp at such a slender reed, but that was just about all he had, wasn't it?

Jill was back on the subject at hand, thinking about the babysitter. "Here I hired her because I thought an older woman would be calmer with a steadier hand."

She rolled her eyes. "A teenage girl would have been better."

"Come on, that's not really fair. She got a lot thrown at her at once and she wasn't prepared for it. It could have happened to anyone."

She shook her head as though she just couldn't accept that. "I'm lucky I've got my sister close by for emergencies. But she's getting more and more caught up in her career, and it's a pretty demanding one. I really can't count on her for too much longer." She sighed. "She had to be at a business dinner in Seattle tonight, or she would have been here to take care of the boys."

"Family can be convenient." He frowned. "Don't you have a younger sister? I thought I met her once."

Instead of answering, she moaned softly and closed her eyes. "Kelly. Yes. She was our half sister." She looked at him, new tragedy clouding her gaze. "Funny you should remember her tonight. She was killed in a car crash last week."

"Oh, my God. Oh, Jill, I'm so sorry."

She nodded. "It's sad and tragic and brings on a lot of guilty feelings for Sara and me."

He shook his head, not understanding. "What did you have to do with it?"

"The accident? Oh, nothing. It happened in Virginia where I guess she was living lately. The guilt comes from not even knowing exactly where she was and frankly, not thinking about her much. We should have paid more attention and worked a little harder on being real sisters to her."

There was more. He could tell. But he waited, letting her take her time to unravel the story.

"She was a lot younger, of course. Our mother died when we were pretty young, and our father remarried soon after. Too soon for us, of course. After losing our mother, we couldn't bear to share our beloved father with anyone. We resented the new woman, and when she had a baby, we pretty much resented her, too." She shook her head. "It was so unfair. Poor little girl."

"Didn't you get closer as she got older?"

"Not really. You see, the marriage was a disaster from the start and it ended by the time Kelly was about five years old. We only saw her occasionally after that, for a few hours at a time. And then our father died by the time she was fifteen and we didn't see either one of them much at all after that."

"That's too bad."

She nodded. "Yes. I'm really sorry about it now." She sighed. "She was something of a wild child, at least according to my father's tales of woe. Getting into trouble even in high school. The sort of girl who wants to test the boundaries and explore the edge."

"I know your father died a few years ago. What about your stepmother?"

"She died when I was about twenty-three. She had cancer."

"Poor lady."

"Yes. Just tragic, isn't it? Lives snuffed out so casually." She shook her head. "I just feel so bad about Kelly. It's so sad that we never got to know her better."

"Just goes to show. Carpe diem. Seize the day. Don't let your opportunities slip by."

"Yes." She gave him a look. "When did you become such a philosopher?"

"I've always been considered wise among my peers," he told her in a snooty voice that made her laugh.

A foghorn sounded its mournful call and she looked up at a clock. "And now here you are, stuck. The last ferry's gone. You're going to have to stay here."

He smiled at her. "Unless I hijack a boat."

"You can sleep on the couch." She shrugged. "Or sleep in the master bedroom if you want. Nobody else does."

The bitter tone was loud and clear, and it surprised him.

"Where do you sleep?" he asked her.

"In the guest room." Her smile was bittersweet. "That's why you can't use it."

He remembered glancing in at the master bedroom when he was upstairs. It looked like it had always looked. She and Brad had shared that bed. He looked back at her and didn't say a word.

She didn't offer an explanation, but he knew what it was. She couldn't sleep in that bed now that Brad had abandoned it.

He nodded. "I'll take the couch."

She hesitated. "The only problem with that is, I'll be getting up about four in the morning. I'll probably wake you."

"Four in the morning? Planning a rendezvous with the milkman?"

"No, silly. I've got to start warming the ovens and mixing my batter." She yawned, reminding him of a sleepy kitten. "I've got a day full of large orders to fill tomorrow. One of my busiest days ever." She smiled again. "And hopefully, a sign of success. I sure need it."

"Great."

"Wait here a second. I think I've got something you can use."

She left the room and was back in moments, carrying a set of dark blue men's pajamas.

He recoiled at the sight. "Brad's?" he said.

"Not really." She threw them down in his lap. "I bought them for Brad but he never even saw them. That was just days before he sent you to tell me we were through."

"Oh." That was okay, then. He looked at them, setting aside the top and reserving the pants for when he was ready for bed. Meanwhile, she was rummaging through a linen closet and bringing out a sheet and a light blanket. That made her look domestic in ways he hadn't remembered. He thought about how she'd looked with Timmy in her arms.

"Hey," he said gently. "That's a pair of great little boys you've got there."

She melted immediately. "Aren't they adorable? But so bad!"

"I'll bet they keep you busy every hour of the day."

She nodded. "It's not easy running a business from home when I've got those two getting more and more mischievous." She sighed and sat back down. "Can you believe they were locking doors? I had no idea they knew what a lock was."

"Time to dismantle some and add extra keys for others," he suggested.

"Yes. And keep my eyes on them every minute."

"Can't you hire a daytime babysitter?"

"Yeah, hiring a babysitter really works out well, doesn't it?" She shook her head. "Actually Trini, my bakery assistant, helps a lot. She doubles as a babysitter when I need her to, and does everything else the rest of the time. And then, Sara comes by and helps when she has a free moment or two." She gave him a tremulous smile. "We manage."

He resisted the impulse to reach out and brush back the lock of hair that was bouncing over her eyebrow. The gesture seemed a little too intimate as they sat here, alone in the dim light so late at night.

But Jill didn't seem to have the same reservations he harbored. She reached out and took his hand in hers, startling him. Then she gazed deep into his eyes for a moment before she spoke. His pulse began to quicken. He wasn't sure what she wanted from him, but he knew he couldn't deny her much.

"Well?" she said softly.

He could barely breathe. His fingers curled around hers and he looked at her full, soft lips, her warm mouth, and he wanted to kiss her so badly his whole body ached with it. The longing for her seared his soul. What would she do if he just…?

"Well?" she said again. "Out with it."

"What?" His brain was fuzzy. He couldn't connect what she was saying to what he was feeling.

"Come on. Say it."

He shook his head. What was she talking about? Her brows drew together and her gaze was more penetrating.

"My dear Connor," she said, pulling at his hand as though to make him say what she wanted to hear. "It is time for you to come clean."

"Come clean?"

He swallowed hard. Did she know? Could she read the desire in his eyes? Did she see how he felt about her in his face? Hear it in his voice? Had he really let his guard down too far?

"On what?" he added, his voice gruff with suppressed emotion.

"On why you're here." She was looking so intense. "On why Brad sent you." She searched his eyes again. "Come on, Connor. What exactly does he want this time?"

Brad. His heart sank, and then he had to laugh at himself. Of course that was what she was thinking about. And why not? What right did he have to want anything different? What he wanted didn't mean a thing. This was all about Jill—and Brad. As usual. He took a deep breath and shook his head.

"What makes you think Brad sent me?" he said, his voice coming out a bit harsher than he'd meant it to.

"You're his best friend." She frowned and looked pensive. "You were my best friend once, too."

There you go. Too many best friends. He was always the odd man out. That was exactly why he'd opted for

Singapore when he had the chance. And maybe why he would go back again.

He raised her hand and brought it to his lips, touching her gently with a kiss, then setting her aside and drawing away.

"Jill, you've had enough excitement for tonight. Let's talk in the morning."

"No, tell me. What does Brad want me to do?"

It was the question in her eyes that scared him— the hint of hope. She didn't really think that there was a chance that Brad might want her back....did she? It wasn't going to happen. He'd seen it with his own eyes.

Brad was a selfish bastard. It had taken him years to accept that. Maybe Jill didn't realize it yet. Brad was a great guy to hang out with. Playing poker with him was fun. Going waterskiing. Box seats at a Mariners game. But as far as planning your life with him, he wouldn't recommend it.

"Jill, I didn't come for Brad. I came to see you because I wanted to come."

Okay, so that was partly a lie. But he had to say it. He couldn't stand to see the glimmer of hope in her eyes, knowing it would only bring her more heartbreak. He had a message from Brad all right. But right now, he wasn't sure if he would ever tell her what it was. She thought he was on Brad's side, but she was wrong. If it came to a showdown, he was here for her—all the way.

He just wasn't sure how much she cared, one way or the other. She still wanted Brad. He could see it in her face, hear it in her voice. He shouldn't even be here.

No worries. He would leave first thing in the morning. He couldn't leave before six when the ferry started to run, but he would slip out while she was busy. No goodbyes. Just leave. Get it over with and out of the way and move on. That was the plan. He only had to follow it.

The couch was comfortable enough but he could only sleep in short snatches. When he did doze off, he had dreams that left him wandering through crowds of Latin American dancers in huge headdresses, all swaying wildly to exotic music and shouting "Mambo!" in his face.

He was looking for something he couldn't find. People kept getting in his way, trying to get him to dance with them. And then one headdress changed into a huge white parrot before his eyes, the most elegant bird he'd ever seen. He had to catch that parrot. Suddenly it was an obvious case of life or death and his heart was beating hard with the effort as he chased it through the crowd. He had to catch it!

He reached out, leaped high and touched the tips of the white feathers of its wings. His heart soared. He had it! But then the feathers slipped through his fingers and the bird was swooping away from him. He was left with nothing. A feeling of cold, dark devastation filled his heart. He began to walk away.

But the parrot was back, trailing those long white fathers across his face—only it wasn't white feathers. It was the sleeve of a lacy white nightgown and it was Jill leaning over him, trying to reach something from the bookcase behind the couch.

"Oh, sorry. I didn't want to wake you up," she whispered as though he might go back to sleep if she was quiet about it. "It's not time to get up. I just needed this manual. I'm starting to heat the ovens up."

He nodded and pretended to close his eyes, but he left slits so he could watch her make her way across the room, her lacy white gown cascading around her gorgeous ankles. The glow from the kitchen provided a backlight that showed off her curves to perfection, making his body tighten in a massive way he didn't expect.

And then he fell into the first real deep and dreamless sleep of the night. It must have lasted at least two hours. When he opened his eyes, he found himself staring into the bright blue gaze of one of the twins. He didn't know which one. He couldn't tell them apart yet.

He closed his eyes again, hoping the little visitor would be gone when he opened them. No such luck. Now there were two of them, both dressed in pajamas, both cute as could be.

"Hi," he said. "How are you doing?"

They didn't say a word. They just stared harder. But maybe they didn't do much talking at this age. They were fairly young.

Still, this soundless staring was beginning to get on his nerves.

"Boo," he said.

They both blinked but held their ground.

"So it's going to take more than a simple 'boo,' is it?" he asked.

They stared.

"Okay." He gathered his forces and sprang up, waving the covers like a huge cloak around him. "BOO!" he yelled, eyes wide.

They reacted nicely. They both ran screaming from the room, tumbling over each other in their hurry, and Connor smiled with satisfaction.

It only took seconds for Jill to arrive around the corner.

"What are you doing to my babies?" she cried.

"Nothing," he said, trying to look innocent. He wrapped the covers around himself and smiled. "Just getting to know them. Establishing pecking order. Stuff like that."

She frowned at him suspiciously. To his disappointment, she didn't have the lacy white thing on anymore. She'd changed into a crisp uniform with a large apron and wore a net over her mass of curly hair.

He gestured in her direction. "Regulation uniform, huh?"

She nodded. "I'm a Bundt cake professional, you know," she reminded him, doing a pose.

Then she smiled, looking him over. "You look cute when you're sleepy," she told him, reaching out to ruffle his badly mussed hair. "Why don't you go take a shower? I put fresh towels in the downstairs bathroom. I'll give you some breakfast before you leave."

Leave? Leave? Oh, yeah. He was going to leave as fast as he could. That was the plan.

He let the sheet drop, forgetting that his torso was completely naked, but the look on her face reminded him quickly. "Oh, sorry," he said, pulling the sheet back. And then he felt like a fool.

He glanced at her. A beautiful shade of crimson was flooding her face. That told him something he hadn't figured out before. But knowing she responded to him like that didn't help matters. In fact, it only made things worse. He swore softly to himself.

"You want me gone as soon as possible, don't you?" He shouldn't have said it that way, but the words were already out of his mouth.

She looked a little startled, but she nodded. "Actually you are sort of in the way," she noted a bit breathlessly. "I…I've got a ton of work to do today and I don't really have time to be much of a hostess."

He nodded. "Don't worry. I'm on my way."

He thought about getting into his car and driving off and he wondered why he wasn't really looking forward to it. He had to go. He knew it. She knew it. It had to be done. They needed to stay away from each other if they didn't want to start something they might not be able to stop. Just the thought made his pulse beat a ragged rhythm.

She met his gaze and looked almost sorry for a moment, then took a deep breath, shook her head and glanced at her watch.

"So far, so good. I'm pretty much on schedule," she said. "It can get wild around here. My assistant, Trini, should show up about seven. Then things will slowly get under control."

Despite her involuntary reaction to seeing him without a shirt—a reaction that sent a surge through his bloodstream every time he thought of it—there was still plenty of tension in her voice. Best to be gone before he really felt like a burden. He shook his head as he went off to take a shower.

It can get wild around here, she'd said. So it seemed. It couldn't get much wilder than it had the night before.

That reminded him of what those boys were capable of, and once he'd finished his shower, he took a large plastic bag and went outside to collect all the items the boys had thrown down from the bedroom. Then he brought the plastic bag into the house and set it down in the entryway.

"Oh, good," Jill said when she saw what he'd done. She looked relieved that he'd changed back into the shirt and slacks he'd been wearing the night before. "I forgot. I really did want all the stuff brought in before the neighbors saw it."

"This is quite a haul," he told her with a crooked smile. "Are you sure your guys aren't in training to be second-story men?"

"Very funny," she said, shaking her head at him, then smiling back. "There are actually times when I wonder how I'm going to do it on my own. Raise them right, I mean." She turned large, sad eyes his way. "It's not getting any easier."

It broke his heart to see her like this. If only there was something he could do to help her. But that was impossible, considering the situation. If it weren't for Brad... But that was just wishful thinking.

"You're going to manage it," he reassured her. "You've got what it takes. You'll do it just like your parents managed to raise you. It comes with the territory."

She was frowning at him. "But it doesn't always

work out. Your parents, for instance. Didn't you used to say…?"

He tried to remember what he'd ever told her about his childhood. He couldn't have said much. He never did. Unless he'd had too much to drink one night and opened up to her. But he didn't remember anything like that. Where had she come up with the fact that his parents had been worthless? It was the truth, but he usually didn't advertise it.

"Yeah, you're right," he said slowly. "My parents were pretty much AWOL. But you know what? Kids usually grow up okay anyway." He spread his arms out and smiled at her. "Look at me."

"Just about perfect," she teased. "Who could ask for anything more?"

"My point exactly," he said.

She turned away. She knew he was trying to give her encouragement, but what he was saying was just so much empty talk. It wouldn't get her far.

"Come on," she said. "I've got coffee, and as long as you want cake for breakfast, you can eat."

The cake was slices from rejects—Dutch Apple Crust, Lemon Delight and Double Devil's Food—but they were great and she knew it. She watched with satisfaction as he ate four slices in a row, making happy noises all the while.

The boys were playing in the next room. They were making plenty of noise but none of it sounded dangerous so far. Her batters were mixed. Her first cakes were baking. She still had to prepare some glazes. But all in all, things were moving along briskly and she was feeling more confident.

A moment of peace. She slipped into a chair and smiled across the table at him.

"You look like a woman expecting a busy day," he noted, smiling back at her and noticing how the morning light set off the faint sprinkling of freckles that still decorated her pretty face.

She nodded. "It's my biggest day ever. I've got to get cakes to the charity auction at the Lodge, I've got cakes due for six parties, I've got a huge order, an engagement party at the country club today at three. They want 125 mini Bundt cakes. I was planning to get started on them last night, but after the baby riot, I just didn't have the energy." She shook her head. "As soon as Trini gets here, we'll push the 'on' switch and we won't turn it off until we're done."

He grinned at her. "You look like you relish the whole thing. Or am I reading you wrong?"

"You've got it right." She gave him a warm look. "I really appreciate you being here to help me last night," she said, shaking her head as she remembered the madness. "That was so crazy."

"Yeah," he agreed, polishing off the last piece of Lemon Delight. "But nobody got hurt. It all turned out all right."

She nodded, looking at him, at his dark, curly hair, at his calm, honest face. She felt a surge of affection for him, and that made her frown. They'd been such good friends at one point, but she hardly knew anything about what he'd been doing lately. He'd walked out of her life at the same time Brad had. Both her best friends had deserted her in one way or another.

What doesn't kill you makes you stronger. Yeah, right.

"So the way I understand it," she said, leaning forward, "you've been in Singapore for the last year or so."

"That's right."

"Are you back for good?"

"Uh…" He grimaced. "Hard to say. I've got some options. Haven't decided what I want to do."

She thought about that for a moment. Did Connor ever have a solid plan? Or was it just that he kept his feelings close to the vest? She couldn't tell at this point. She resented the way he'd walked off over a year ago, but that didn't mean she didn't still love him to death.

Best friends. Right?

She narrowed her eyes, then asked brightly, "How about getting married?"

He looked at her as though she'd suddenly gone insane. "What? Married? Who to?"

She laughed. She could read his mind. He thought she was trying out a brand-new idea and he was ready to panic. "Not to me, silly. To someone you love. Someone who will enhance your life."

"Oh." He still looked uncomfortable.

"I'm serious. You should get married. You could use some stability in your life. A sense of purpose." She shrugged, feeling silly.

Who was she to give this sort of advice? Not only was she a failure at marriage, but she'd turned out to be a pretty lousy judge of character, too. "Someone to love," she added lamely.

His blue eyes were hooded as he gazed at her. "How do you know I don't have all those things right now?"

She studied his handsome face and shook her head. "I don't see it. To me, you look like the same old Connor, always chasing the next good time. Show me how I'm wrong."

She knew she was getting a little personal, but she was feeling a little confused about him right now. What was he doing here? Why was he sticking around?

In the bright light of day she thought she could see things more clearly, and that fresh sight told her he'd come with a goal in mind. If he'd just wanted to see her, make a visit, he'd have called ahead. No, Brad had sent him. Coming face-to-face in the hotel dining room had been a fluke. But what did Brad have in mind? Why didn't Connor just deliver the message and go?

She was beginning to feel annoyed with him. Actually she was becoming annoyed with everything. Something was off-kilter and her day was beginning to stretch out ominously before her.

"Okay, let's stop avoiding the real issue here." She stared at him coolly. "No more denials. What does Brad really want?"

CHAPTER FOUR

"BRAD?"

Jill saw the shift in Connor's eyes. He didn't want to talk about this right now. He was perfectly ready to avoid the issue again. Well, too bad. She didn't have all the time in the world. It was now or never.

"Yes, Brad. You remember him. My ex-husband. The father of my children. The man who was once my entire life."

"Oh, yeah. That guy."

She frowned. He was still being evasive. She locked her fingers together and pulled.

"So, what does he want?" she insisted.

Connor looked at her and began to smile. "What do you think Brad wants? He always wants more than his share. And he usually gets it."

She shook her head, surprised, then laughed softly. "You do know him well, don't you?"

Connor's smile faded. He glanced around the kitchen, looking uncomfortable. "Does he have visitation rights to the boys? Does he come up here to see them or does he…?"

"No," she said quickly. "He's never seen them."

For once, she'd shocked him. His face showed it clearly. "Never seen his own kids? Why? Do you have a court injunction or...?"

The pain of it all would bring her down if she let it. She couldn't do that. She held her head high and met his gaze directly.

"He doesn't want to see them. Don't you know that? Didn't he ever tell you why he wanted the divorce?"

Connor shook his head slowly. "Tell me," he said softly.

She took a deep breath. "When Brad asked me to marry him, he told me he wanted a partner. He was going to start his own business and he wanted someone as committed to it as he was, someone who would stand by him and help him succeed. I entered into that project joyfully."

Connor nodded. He remembered that as well. He'd been there. He'd worked right along with them. They'd spent hours together brainstorming ideas, trying out options, failing and trying again. They'd camped out in sleeping bags when they first opened their office. They'd been so young and so naive. They thought they could change the world—or at least their little corner of it. They'd invented new ways of doing things and found a way to make it pay. It had been a lot of hard work, but they'd had a lot of fun along the way. That time seemed a million miles away now.

"I knew Brad didn't want children, but I brushed that aside. I was so sure he would change his mind as time went by. We worked very, very hard and we did really well together. The business was a huge success. Then I got pregnant."

She saw the question in his eyes and she shook her head. "No, it was purely and simply an accident."

She bit her lip and looked toward the window for a moment, steadying her voice.

"But I never dreamed Brad would reject it so totally. He just wouldn't accept it." She looked back into his eyes, searching for understanding. "I thought we could work things out. After all, we loved each other. These things happen in life. You deal with them. You make adjustments. You move on."

"Not Brad," he guessed.

"No. Not Brad." She shrugged. "He said, get rid of them."

He drew in a sharp breath. It was almost a gasp. She could hear it in the silence of the kitchen, and she winced.

"And you said?"

She shrugged again. "I'd rather die."

Connor nodded. He knew her well enough to know that was the truth. What the hell was Brad thinking?

"Suddenly he was like a stranger to me. He just shut the door. He went down to Portland to open up a branch office for our business. I thought he would think it over and come back and…" She gave him a significant look. "But he never came back. He began to make the branch office his headquarters. Then you showed up and told me he wanted a divorce."

Connor nodded. His voice was low and gruff as he asked her, "Do you want him back?"

She had to think about that one. If she was honest, she would have to admit there was a part of her—a part she wasn't very proud of—that would do almost anything to get him back. Anything but the one thing he asked for.

She stared at him and wondered how much she should tell him. He was obviously surprised to know about how little Brad cared about his sons. A normal man would care. So Brad had turned out to be not very normal. That was her mistake. She should have realized that and never married him in the first place.

She also had to live with the fact that he was getting worse and worse about paying child support. There were so many promises—and then so many excuses. What there wasn't a lot of was money.

The business was floundering, he said. He was trying as hard as he could, but the profits weren't rolling in like they used to in the old days—when she was doing half the work. Of course, he didn't mention that. He didn't want her anywhere near the business anymore.

She knew he resented having to give her anything. After all, he'd given her the house—not that it was paid off. Still, it had been what she wanted, what she felt she had to have to keep a stable environment for the boys.

But now she was having a hard time making the mortgage payments. She had to make a go of her cake business, or else she would have to go back to work and leave the boys with a babysitter. She was running out of time.

Time to build her business up to where it could pay for itself. Time to stabilize the mortgage situation before the bank came down on her. Time to get the boys old enough so that when she did have to go for a real, paying job, it wouldn't break her heart to leave them with strangers.

So, yes. What Brad wanted now mattered. Had he gone through a transformation? Had he come up with second thoughts and decided to become a friend to the family? Or was it all more excuses about what he couldn't do instead of what he could? Women with husbands in a stable situation didn't realize how lucky they were.

Funny. Sometimes it almost seemed as though Brad had screwed up her marriage and now he wanted to screw up her single life as well.

She shook her head slowly. "I want my life back," she admitted. "I want the life I had when I had a loving husband. I want my babies to have their father. But I don't see how that can ever happen."

Her eyes stung and she blinked quickly to make sure no tears dared show up.

"Unless…" She looked up into Connor's eyes. "Unless you have a message from Brad that he wants it to happen, too."

Whistling in the wind. She knew how useless that was. She gave Connor a shaky smile, basically absolving him of all guilt in the matter. She saw the look in his eyes. He felt sorry for her. She cringed inside. She didn't want pity.

"Don't worry. I don't expect that. But I do want to know what he sent you for."

Connor shook his head. Obviously he had nothing

to give her. So Brad must have sent him on a scouting expedition, right? To see if she was surviving. To see if she was ready to hoist the white flag and admit he was right and she was wrong. She couldn't make it on her own after all. She should have listened to him. And now, she should knuckle under and take his advice and give it all up.

She bit her lip. She wasn't disappointed, exactly. She knew the score. But she was bummed out and it didn't help her outlook on the day.

A timer went off and she hopped up to check on her cakes. This was where she belonged, this was where she knew what she was doing. The realm of human emotions was too treacherous. She would take her chances with the baked goods.

Connor watched her getting busy again and he wished he could find some way to help her deal with the truth—that Brad didn't want her. He couldn't say it might never happen. Brad could change his mind. But right now, he didn't want Jill at all. What he wanted was to be totally free of her. At least, that was how he'd presented things a few days ago when they'd talked.

Brad wanted that, and he wanted her to give up her remaining interest in the company. That was the message he was supposed to make her listen to. That was the message he just couldn't bring himself to tell her. Maybe later.

He took his cup to the sink, rinsed it out and headed back into the living room. He was folding up the covers he'd used when the front door opened and a young woman hurried in.

Connor looked up and started to smile. It was Sara Darling, Jill's sister, and she stopped dead when she saw who had been sleeping on her sister's couch.

"You!" she said accusingly, and he found himself backing up, just from the fire in her eyes.

He knew that Sara and Jill were very close, but he also knew they tended to see things very differently. Both were beautiful. Where Jill had a head full of crazy curls that made you want to kiss her a lot, Sara wore her blond hair slicked back and sleek, making her look efficient and professional. Today she wore a slim tan linen suit with a pale peach blouse and nude heels and she looked as though she was about to gavel an important business meeting to order.

"What are you doing here?" she demanded of him. "Oh, brother. I should have known you'd show up. Let a woman be vulnerable and alone and it's like sharks smelling blood in the water."

"Hey," he protested, surprised. He'd always been friendly with this woman in the past. "That's a bit harsh."

"Harsh? You want to see harsh?"

He blanched. "Not really."

Okay, so Sara was being extra protective of her sister. He got it. But she'd never looked on him as a bad guy before. Why now? He tried a tentative smile.

"Hey, Sara. Nice to see you."

She was still frowning fiercely. "You have no right to complicate Jill's life."

He frowned, too, but in a more puzzled way. That was actually not what he wanted to do, either. But it seemed he was right. Sara was circling the wagons around her sister. How to convince her she didn't need to do that with him?

"Listen, staying for the night wasn't how I planned this."

"I'll bet." She had her arms crossed and looked very intimidating. "Just what *did* you have in mind, Casanova?"

What? Did she really think he was hovering around in order to catch Jill in an emotional state? If only! He wanted to laugh at her but he knew that would only infuriate her further.

"Listen, I saved your sister from a blind date gone horribly wrong. Seriously. Do you know the guy she went out with?"

Sara shook her head, looking doubtful.

"I think his name was Karl."

She shook her head again.

"Well, if you knew him, you'd see why Jill needed rescuing. He was flamboyantly wrong for her."

"Okay." Sara looked a little less intimidating. "Good. I'm glad you were there to help her out."

He breathed a sigh of relief. She was approachable after all.

"So I brought her back here, planning to drop her off and come back to see her in the morning, but there was a riot going on in the house. The twins had taken the babysitter hostage. I had to stay and help Jill regain the high ground. There was no choice."

It was as though she hadn't heard a word he'd said.
She paced slowly back and forth in front of him, glar-
ing like a tiger. It was evident she thought he was ex-
aggerating and she'd already gone back to the root of
the problem.

"So…what's the deal?" she said, challenging him
with her look. "Brad sent you, didn't he?"

Uh-oh. He didn't want to go there if he could help
it. He gave her a fed-up look. "Why does everyone assume I can't make a move on my own?"

She glared all the harder. "If he's trying to get her to
come back to him, you can tell him…"

He held up a hand to stop her. It was time to nip this
supposition in the bud. "Sara, no. Brad is not trying to
get her back."

"Oh." Her look was pure sarcasm. "So the new honey
is still hanging around?"

He ran his fingers through his thick, curly hair and
grimaced. "Actually I think that was two or three hon-
eys ago," he muttered, mostly to himself. "But take
my word for it, Brad isn't looking for forgiveness. Not
yet, anyway."

Her dark eyes flared with outrage, but she kept her
anger at a slow simmer. "That's our Brad. Trust him
to make life and everything in it all about him and no
one else."

He nodded. That was one point they could agree on.
"Brad does like to have things go his way."

Sara's gaze had fallen on the plastic bag of items
picked up in the yard. She scowled, touching it with
the toe of her shoe.

"What's all this?"

"Oh. Uh. I left it there. I'll get it...."

She looked up in horror. "What are you doing, moving in?"

Now he couldn't help it. He had to laugh. "Sara, you don't need to hate me. I'm not the enemy."

"Really? What are you, then?"

"A friend." He tried to look earnest. He'd always thought Sara liked him well enough. He certainly hadn't expected to be attacked with guns blazing this way. "I'm Jill's friend. And I really want what's best for her."

"Sorry, Connor. You can't be a true friend to Jill while you're still any sort of friend to Brad. It won't work."

His head went back and he winced. "That's a little rigid, don't you think?"

She moved closer, glancing toward the kitchen to make sure they weren't being overheard. "If you'd seen what she's gone through over this last year or so, you might change your tune."

"What?" He caught her by the upper arm. "What happened?"

She shook her head, looking away.

"Has Brad been here to see her?"

She looked up at him. "Not that I know of. But he manages to make life miserable for her by long distance."

He frowned, wishing she would be more specific.

She looked at him, shook her head and her shoulders drooped. All her animosity had drained away and tears rimmed her eyes. "Oh, Connor, she deserves so

much better. If you could see how hard she works…
And every time she turns around, there's some new
obstacle thrown in her path. I just can't stand it anymore. It's not fair."

She pulled away and he let her go. And now he was
the one whose emotions were roiling. Damn Brad, anyway. Why couldn't he just leave her alone?

He ran his hand through his hair again, tempted to
rip chunks of it out in frustration. He had to get out of
here. If he wasn't careful, he would get caught up in the
need to protect Jill. From what? He wasn't even sure.
Life, probably. Just life. As Sara had said, it wasn't fair.
But it also wasn't his fight. No, he had to go.

He would drive back to his hotel, check out and head
for Portland. He would tell Brad he couldn't help him
and advise him to leave Jill alone. Maybe he would even
tell his old friend what he really thought of him. It was
way past time to do that.

Jill was in a hurry and things weren't working out.
She had Tanner dressed in his little play suit, but she
couldn't catch Timmy, and now he was streaking around
the room, just out of her reach, laughing uproariously.

"Timmy!" she ordered. "You stop right there."

Fat chance of that. He rolled under the bed and giggled as she reached under, trying to grab him.

"You come out of there, you rascal."

She made a lucky grab and caught his foot and
pulled him out, disarming grin and all. "Oh, you little munchkin," she cried, but she pulled him into her
arms and held him tightly. Her boys were so precious

to her. She'd given up a lot to make sure she would have them. Tears stung her eyelids and she fought them back. She couldn't let herself cry. Not now. She had a day to get through.

She had a huge, wonderful day full of work ahead. A day like this could turn things around, if it started a trend. She heard Sara's voice downstairs and she smiled. What a relief. Good. Sara was here. She would be able to help with the children.

She so appreciated Sara giving her some time like this. She knew she was applying for a promotion. She'd been a contributing editor to the design section of *Winter Bay Magazine* for almost two years and she'd done some fabulous work. If she got the new job, she would be working more hours during the week and wouldn't be able to help out as much. Still, she hoped she got it. She certainly deserved the recognition.

She was thankful for small blessings. Right now, if she had Sara here to help with the twins, and then Trini coming in a half hour to help with the baking and delivery, she would be okay. She would just barely be able to fulfill all the commitments she'd made for the day.

It was a challenge, but she could do it. In fact, she had to do it.

Sara appeared at the doorway just as she finished dressing her boys and sent them into the playroom.

"Hey there," she said, ready to greet her sister with a smile until she saw the look on her face. "What's the matter? What's wrong?"

Sara sighed and shook her head.

"Did you see Connor?" Jill asked brightly. "He looks

so much the same, you'd never know he'd been gone for a year and a half, would you?"

Sara gave her a look. "Jill, we've got to talk."

Jill groaned and grabbed her sister's hand. "Not now, sweetie. Not today. I've got so much I've got to get to and…"

Sara was shaking her head. "You've got to get rid of him, Jill."

She frowned. "Who?"

Sara pointed back down the stairs as though he were following her. "Connor. You've got to make him go right away."

Dropping her hand, Jill turned away, feeling rebellious. She'd been thinking the same thing but she didn't want to hear it from anyone else. Connor was hers. She resented anyone else—even her beloved sister—critiquing their relationship. She would make him go when she was good and ready to make him go.

Sara grabbed her by the shoulders. "You know he's just here spying for Brad," she said in a low, urgent voice. "You don't want that, do you?"

Sara had never warmed to Jill's ex-husband, even during the good times. And once he'd gone off and left her high and dry, she'd developed what could only be described as a dogged contempt for the man.

Jill took a deep breath and decided to ignore everything she'd said. Life would be simpler that way.

"What are you doing here so early?" she asked instead, trying to sound bright and cheery. "I appreciate it, but…"

"Oh." Sara's demeanor changed in an instant and she

dropped her hold on her sister's shoulders. "Oh, Jill, I came early to tell you...I'm so sorry, but I won't be able to help you today. They want me to fly down to L.A. There's just no way I can get out of it. I'll be meeting with the editorial staff from Chicago and..."

"Today?" Jill couldn't stop the anguish from bursting out as she realized what this meant.

Sara looked stricken. "It's a really bad day, right?"

"Well, I told you I've got a huge stack of orders and..." Jill stopped herself, set her shoulders and got hold of her fears. "No, no." She shook her head. "No, Sara. It's much more important for you to go do this, I'm sure."

Sara grabbed her hand again. "Oh, honey, I'm so sorry, but I really can't turn them down. They want to see how I handle myself with the visiting members." She bit her lip and looked as though she was about to cry. A range of conflicting emotions flashed through her wide dark eyes and then she shook her head decisively. "Oh, forget it. I'll tell them something has come up and I just can't do it. Don't worry. They'll understand. I think."

Jill dismissed all that out of hand. "Don't be ridiculous. Of course you have to go. This is your career. This is something you've worked so hard for."

"But I can't leave you if you really need me."

"But I don't." Jill dug deep and managed a bright smile. "Not really. Trini will be here soon and we'll be able to handle it."

Sara looked worried. "Are you sure?"

"Positive." She smiled again.

"Because I can stay if you really need me. I can tell them…"

"No." She hugged her sister. "You go. You have to go. I will lose all respect for you if you let silly sentiment keep you from achieving your highest goals. Say no more about it. You're gone. It's decided."

"But…"

"Come on. Do it for me. Do it for all of us. Make us proud."

Her smile was almost painful by now, but doggone it—she wasn't going to stop. Sara had to go. No two ways about it. And she would just have to cope on her own. Thank God for Trini.

"So she's really going?" Connor had watched Sara rushing off and then turned to see Jill come down from upstairs with a tense look on her face.

"Yes. Yes, she is."

He noted that her hands were gripped together as though she could hardly stand it. He frowned.

"Do you think you can do it without her?"

She took a deep breath. "It won't be easy. But once Trini gets here, we'll put our noses to the grindstone and work our little tushes off for the next twelve hours. Then you'll see."

He was bemused by her intensity. "What will I see?"

She looked up at him wide-eyed. "That this is serious. Not just a hobby job. It's real."

He frowned. He wanted to tell her that he respected her immensely and that he was impressed with what she was attempting to do here, but before he could get a word out, she went on, pacing tensely as she talked.

"You know, I thought I had everything pretty much under control. My life was running on an even keel. I was beginning to feel as though I might make it after all." She stopped and looked at him with a sense of foreboding wonder. "And then you hit town. And everything went to hell."

She was trying to make it sound like a joke, but there was too much stress in her voice to carry it off. He winced.

"So you blame me now?"

"Why not? There's nobody else within shouting distance. You're going to have to take the fall." She tried to smile but her mouth was wobbly.

He looked at her, saw the anxious look in her eyes and he melted beyond control. "Jill…" He took her hands in his and drew her closer. "Listen, why don't I stay? I could help you with the boys. I could run errands, answer phones."

She was shaking her head but he didn't wait to hear her thoughts.

He pulled her hands up against his chest. "I want to help you. Really. I know you've had a lot of setbacks lately and I want to help smooth over some rough spots if I can. Come on, Jill. Let me stay."

Her lower lip was trembling as she looked into his eyes. He groaned and pulled her into his arms, holding her tightly against his body. She felt like heaven and he wanted the moment to go on forever, but she didn't let it happen. She was already pulling out of his embrace, and he could have kicked himself for doing it.

Too blatant, Connor old chap, he told himself ruefully. *You really tipped your hand there, didn't you?*

"No, Connor," she said as she pushed him away.

She looked at him, shaken. She'd wanted to melt into his arms. She still felt the temptation so strongly, she had to steel herself against it. She knew it had to be mostly because she was so afraid, so nervous about her ability to meet her challenges. If she let him hold her, she could pretend to forget all that.

And then there was the fact that it had been so long since a man—a real man, a man that she liked—had held her. Karl didn't count. And she hungered for that sort of connection.

But not with Connor. Not with Brad's best friend.

"No. It's sweet of you to offer, but I really can't let you stay. We are going to need to focus like laser beams on this task and having you here won't help." She smiled at him with affection to take the bite out of her words.

He stepped farther from her and avoided her eyes. The sting of her rejection was like a knife to his heart. "Okay then. I guess I'd better get going."

"Yes. I'm sorry."

He started to turn away, then remembered. "Hey, I didn't fix the door I kicked in last night."

She shook her head. "Don't worry. I've already called a handy man I use."

"Oh." He hesitated, but there didn't seem to be much to say. He was superfluous, obviously. Just in the way. Might as well get the hell out.

"Okay. It was good to see you again, Jill."

She smiled at him. "Yes. Come back soon. But next time, don't stop off to see Brad first."

He nodded. "You've got my word on that one," he said. He shoved his hands down into the back pockets of his jeans and looked at her, hard.

"What?" she asked, half laughing.

"I just want to get a good picture of you to hold me over," he told her. "Until next time."

The look in her eyes softened and she stepped forward and kissed his cheek. "Goodbye," she whispered.

He wanted to kiss her mouth so badly, he had to clench his teeth together to stop himself from doing it.

"Goodbye," he said softly, then he turned and left the house.

Outside, he felt like hell. He'd had hangovers that hadn't felt this bad. Everything in him wanted to stay and he couldn't do it. He looked down at the ferry dock. There was a ferry there now, loading up. He'd catch it and then it would be all over. How long before he saw her again? Who knew. He would probably go back to Singapore. At least he knew where he stood there.

Swearing softly with a string of obscenities that he rarely used, he slid into the driver's seat and felt for the keys.

"Goodbye to all that," he muttered, then turned on the engine. About to back out, he turned to glance over his shoulder—just in time to see a small economy car come sailing in behind him, jerk to a stop, and block him in.

"Hey," he said.

But the young woman who'd driven up didn't hear him and didn't notice that his engine was running. She flew out of the car and went racing up the walk, flinging herself through the doorway.

Okay. This had to be the famous Trini he'd heard so much about. She'd trapped him in his parking space and he wasn't going to make the ferry. Now what?

CHAPTER FIVE

JILL HADN'T RECOVERED from Connor leaving when Trini came bursting in. The boys ran to her joyfully and she knelt down and collected them into her arms, then looked up. Jill knew immediately that something was wrong.

"Trini, what is it?" she cried.

Trini was young and pretty with a long, swinging ponytail and a wide-eyed expression of constant amazement, as though life had just really surprised her once again. And in this case, it seemed to be true.

"You'll never guess!" she cried, and then she burst into tears. "Oh, Jill," she wailed, "this is so good and so bad at the same time."

"What is it, sweetheart?" Jill asked, pulling her up and searching her face. But she thought she knew. And she dreaded what she was about to hear.

"Oh, Jill, I just got the call and…" She sobbed for a moment, then tried again. "I got in. I was on the wait list and they just called. I got accepted into the program at Chanoise Culinary Institute in New York."

"But…hasn't the quarter already started?"

"Yes, but they had two people drop out already. So they called and said if I could get there by tomorrow, I'm in."

"Trini! That's wonderful! You deserve a space in the class. I always knew that."

But did it have to be today? She couldn't help but wish the timing had been different. Still, this was wonderful for Trini.

"What can I do to help you?"

Trini shook her head. "You've already done enough. You wrote the recommendation that got me in." She sighed happily, and then she frowned with worry. "The only bad part is I have to leave right away. My flight leaves at noon. The Jamison engagement party…"

"Don't you think twice, Trini. You just get out of here and go pack and prepare for the best experience of your life. Okay?"

Trini threw her arms around Jill's neck and Jill hugged her tightly. "I'm so excited," Trini cried. "Oh, Jill, I'll keep you posted on everything we do. And when I come back…"

"You'll teach me a thing or two, I'm sure." She smiled at her assistant, forcing back any hint of the panic she was feeling. "Now off with you. You need to get ready for the rest of your life."

"I will. Wish me luck!"

"I'll definitely wish you luck. You just supply the hard work!"

Trini laughed and dashed out the door. Jill reached out to put her hand on the back of a chair to keep herself from collapsing. She could hardly breathe. She saw

Connor standing in the entryway. She didn't know why he'd come back and right now, she couldn't really think about it or talk to him. She was in full-scale devastation meltdown mode.

What was she going to do? What on earth was she going to do? She couldn't think a coherent thought. Her mind was a jumble. She knew she was standing on the edge of the cliff and if she lost her balance, she was going over. She couldn't let that happen. She had to get herself together.

But what was the use? She'd fought back so often. So much kept going wrong and she kept trying to fix things. They just wouldn't stay fixed. She was so tired. Today, right now, she wanted to quit. There had to be a way to give up, to surrender to reality. She just couldn't do this anymore.

Looking at her reflection in the hall mirror, she muttered sadly, "Okay. I get it. I'm not meant to do this. I should quit banging my head against the wall. I should quit, period. Isn't that what a sane, rational person would do?"

She stared at herself, feeling cold and hollow. She knew Connor was still watching her, that he'd heard what she said, but she hardly cared. She was in such deep trouble, what did it matter if he saw her anguish? But a part of her was grateful for his presence—and that he was keeping back, not trying to comfort her right now. She didn't need that since there was no comfort, was no real hope.

She stared at herself for a long moment, teetering between the devil and the deep blue sea. That was how it felt. No matter what she did, disaster seemed inevitable.

Then, gradually, from somewhere deep inside, she began to put her strength back together and pull her nerve back into place. She took a giant breath and slowly let it out. She wouldn't surrender. She would go down fighting, no matter what it cost her. Let them try to stop her! She had glaze to prepare. She had cakes to bake. She would try her best to get this done and on time. She could only do what she could do—but she would do the best she could.

She looked at herself in the mirror again and gave herself a small, encouraging smile. She needed a joke right now, something to help her put things into perspective. She was a baking woman—hear her roar! They would have to pry her baking mitts off her cold, dead hands.

Revived and reinvigorated, she turned to face Connor. "There," she said. "I'm better now."

He still appeared a bit worried, but he'd watched her mini-breakdown and the instant rebuild in awe.

"Wow," he said. "Jill, you are something else."

She sighed. "You weren't supposed to see that."

"I'm glad I did. I've got more faith in you than ever."

She laughed. "I've got to get back to work." She frowned. "Why are you still here?"

"Because I'm not going to go while you still need me."

"What makes you think I need you?" Turning, she headed into the kitchen.

"So," he said tentatively, following her. "Now your

number one assistant has bailed on you. And your sister has bailed on you." He shrugged. "Who you gonna call? You need someone else. Who can come to your rescue?"

She met his gaze. "There's nobody. Really. I've tried to find backup before. There's really nobody. This island is too small. There aren't enough people to draw on."

He nodded. "That's what I thought." He picked up an apron someone had thrown on the chair and began to tie it on himself. "Okay. Tell me what to do."

Her eyes widened. "What are you talking about?"

His face was so earnest, she felt her breath catch in her throat. He really meant it.

"How can I help you, Jill? What can I do?"

This was so sweet of him, but it couldn't work. He didn't have the skills, the background. And anyway, he wasn't here for her. He was here for Brad. There was no denying it.

"Just stay out of the way." She shrugged helplessly. He shouldn't be here at all. Why was he? "Go back to your hotel. You don't belong here."

He shook his head. "No."

"Connor!"

He shook his head again. "You're like a fish flopping around on the pier, gasping for breath. You need help, lady. And I'm going to give it to you."

She shook her own head in disbelief. "You can't cook."

"The hell I can't."

Her gaze narrowed. "I don't believe it."

He stepped closer, towering over her and staring down with cool deliberation. "There are a whole lot of things about me you just don't have a clue about, Miss Know-it-all."

She shook her head, still wary. "Look, just because you can fry up a mean omelet after midnight for your Saturday night date doesn't mean you can cook. And it certainly doesn't mean you can bake."

"I'm not proposing to be your baker. You've got that slot nailed. I'm signing on as an assistant. I'm ready to assist you in any way I can."

He meant it. She could see the resolve in his eyes. But how could he possibly be a help rather than a hindrance? There was no way he could get up to speed in time. Still, she was in an awful bind here.

"So you can cook?" she asked him skeptically.

"Yes."

"There's a difference between cooking and baking."

"I know that." He shook his head impatiently. "Jill, you're the baker. But you need a support staff and I'm going to be it."

"But...what are you planning to do?"

"Prep pans, wash pans, drizzle on glaze, pack product for delivery, deliver product, go for supplies, answer the phones..."

She was beginning to smile. Maybe she was being foolish, but she didn't have much choice, did she? "And the most important thing?" she coached.

He thought for a moment, then realized what she was talking about.

"Keep an eye on the boys," he said and was rewarded with a quick smile. "You got it. In fact, I'll do anything and everything in order to leave you room to practice your creative artistry."

"My what?" She laughed and gave him a push. "Oh, Connor, you smooth talker you."

"That's what it is." He took her by the shoulders and held her as though she was very, very special. "I've eaten some of your cake wizardry, lady. *Magnifique!*"

The word hung in the air. She gazed up at him, suddenly filled with a wave of affection. Had she ever noticed before how his eyes crinkled in the corners? And how long his beautiful dark lashes were? Reaching out, she pressed her palm to his cheek for just a moment, then drew it back and turned away so that he wouldn't see the tears beginning to well in her eyes.

"Okay," she said a little gruffly. "We'll give it a try. As long as you turn out to be worth more than the trouble you cause." But she glanced back with a smile, showing him that she was only teasing.

"I won't get in your way, I swear. You just wait and see. We'll work together like a well-oiled machine."

She blinked back the tears and smiled at him. "You promise?"

"Cross my heart and hope to die."

"Ooh, don't say that. Bad vibes." She shook her head. "Okay then. Here's the game plan. I'm going to go back over all my recipes and check to make sure I've got the right supplies before I start mixing new batters. You go and see what the boys are up to. Then you come back and help me."

He saluted her like a soldier. *"Mais oui, mon chef."*

"Wow. Those sleepy-time French lessons really did do some good. And here I was a non-believer."

He looked a bit nonplussed himself. "Every now and then a few French words just seem to burst out of me, so yeah, I guess so."

He turned his attention to the twins not a moment too soon. There was a ruckus going on in the next room. The boys were crying. Someone had pushed someone down and grabbed away his toy. The other one was fighting to get it back. Happened all the time. They needed supervision.

But there was really no time today to deal with it properly. He went back to discuss the situation with Jill.

"If you can think of any strenuous activities, something that might make them take their naps a bit earlier..." she mused, checking the supply of flavorings and crossing them off a list, then handing the list to him to start working on an inventory of the flour she had in storage.

"Say no more," He gave her a wise look. "I've got a trick or two up my sleeve. As soon as I finish counting up the canisters, I'll deal with those little rascals."

Time was racing by. Her convection oven could accommodate four cakes at a time, but they had to be carefully watched.

"We've got to get these done by noon," she told him. "I can't start the mini Bundts any later than that. We've got to get the minis done by three, glazed and packed by four-thirty, and off for delivery by five."

He nodded. He knew she wasn't completely resigned

to him being there with her. This was her biggest day
and her eyes betrayed how worried she was. Her shoulders looked tight. She wasn't confident that they could
do it, even working hard together.

He only hoped he could—what? Help her? That went
without saying. Protect her? Sure. That was his main
goal. Always had been. If only he'd realized earlier that
his vague distrust of Brad was based on more than jealousy. It seemed to be real in ways that were only now
becoming more and more clear to him. It was a good
thing she'd reconciled herself to accepting his help, because he knew he couldn't go. He couldn't leave her on
her own. He had to be here for her.

Meanwhile, he had to find a way to wear out the
boys. He tried to recall his own childhood, but eighteen months old was a little too far back to remember
much. Still, he had a few ideas.

He took the boys out into the backyard. There was a
big sloping hill covered with grass. Improvising, he set
up a racetrack with different stations where the boys
had to perform simple modified gymnastic elements in
order to move on to the next station.

They loved it. They each had a natural competitive
spirit that came out in spades as they began to understand the goals involved. Each wanted to win with a
naive gusto that made him laugh out loud. They were
a great pair of twins.

They were so into it. Running up the hill took a lot of
their time. Shrieking with excitement was a factor. And
Connor found he was having as much fun as they were.

At one point, he had them racing uphill, each pulling a red wagon filled with rocks to see who could get to the top first. He'd brought along lots of prizes, including pieces of hard candy that they loved. He knew they were sure to rot teeth, but he would only use them today and never again. Or not often, anyway. He also made sure to keep the winnings pretty equal between the two of them, so that each could shine in turn.

But, as he told Jill a bit later, the one drawback was— no matter how tired he made them, he was even more so. He was pitifully out of shape.

But it was fun. That was the surprising part. The boys were a couple of great kids, both so eager, so smart. He wondered what Brad would think if he could see them. How could he possibly resist these two?

He brought them back in and settled them down to watch an educational DVD while he went down to the kitchen to see what he could do to help Jill. She had recently pulled four cakes out of the oven and she was ready to put on a glaze.

"Show me how," he told her. "You're going to need help when you glaze all those small cakes for the engagement party, aren't you?"

She looked at him with some hesitation, and he saw it right away. Reaching out, he took her hands in his.

"Jill, I'm not here to take over," he said. "I don't expect to start making decisions or judging you. I'm here to do anything you tell me to do. You talk. I'll listen."

She nodded, feeling a little chagrined. She knew he meant well. He was just here to help her. Why couldn't she calm her fears and let him do just that?

As she glanced up, her gaze met his and she had an

impulse that horrified her. She wanted to throw herself into his arms, close her eyes and hold on tightly.

The same thing she'd felt before when he'd held her came back in a wave and she felt dizzy with it. She wanted his warmth and his comfort, wanted it with a fierce craving that ached inside her. She couldn't give in to that feeling. Turning away quickly, she hoped he couldn't see it in her eyes.

She was just feeling weak and scared. That was what it had to be. She couldn't let herself fall into that trap.

"Okay. I'm going to teach you everything I know about putting on a glaze," she said resolutely. "And believe me, it's simple. We'll start with a basic sugar glaze. You'll pick it up in no time at all."

He learned fast and she went ahead and taught him how to make a caramel glaze as well, including tricks on how not to let the sugar burn and how to roast the chopped pecans before you added them to make them crisper and more flavorful. She then showed him how to center the cakes on the lacy doilies she used in the fancy boxes she packed the cakes in before transporting them.

"Each cake should look like it's a work of art on its own," she told him. "Never ever let a cake look like you just shoved it into a box to get it where it needs to go. They should look like they're being carried in a golden coach, on their way to the ball."

He grinned. "Cinderella cakes?"

"Exactly. They have to look special. Otherwise, why not pick up a cake at the grocery store?"

That was when his phone rang. It made him jerk. He

knew before he even looked at the screen who it was. Brad. Brad wondering how things were going. Brad, wondering if he'd talked her into committing to his plan. Brad, trying to control everything, just like always.

He put the phone on vibrate and shoved it into his pocket.

Once they'd finished the glazing, he went back to babysitting, making peanut butter and jelly sandwiches for the boys. They looked so good, he made one for himself. Then he raided the refrigerator and made a cool, crisp salad for Jill.

"Lunchtime," he told her, once he'd set the boys down to eat at their little table in their playroom.

She gave one last look at her boxed creations, snuck a peek at the new cakes in the oven and turned to him with a smile.

"So far, so good," she said as she sat down across from him at the kitchen table. "Though one disaster can throw the whole schedule off."

"Relax," he said. "No disaster would dare ruin this day for you."

"Knock on wood," she said, doing just that. She took a bite of salad and made a noise of pleasure. "Ah! This is so refreshing." She cocked her head to the side. "The boys are being awfully good."

He nodded. "So it seems. I gave them their sandwiches."

She frowned. "You left them alone with food?"

"They seemed to be doing great when I looked in on them." He glanced toward the doorway. "Though they sure seem quiet."

Jill's eyes widened. "Too quiet," she cried, vaulting out of her chair and racing for the playroom. Visions of peanut butter masterpieces smeared on walls and teddy bears covered in sticky jam shot through her head.

Connor came right behind her. He didn't have as much experience with what might go wrong, but he could imagine a few things himself.

They skidded around the corner and into the room, only to find a scene of idyllic contentment. The peanut butter sandwiches were half eaten and lay on the table. The boys were completely out, both lying in haphazard fashion wherever they were when sleep snuck up on them. Jill turned and grinned at him.

"You did wear them out. Wow."

They lifted them carefully and put them down in the travel cribs that sat waiting against the far wall. Jill pulled light covers over each of them and they tiptoed out of the room and back to the kitchen.

"They look like they'll sleep for hours," she said hopefully.

"Maybe days," he added to the optimism, but she laughed.

"Doubtful. Besides, we'll miss them if they stay away that long."

"Will we?" he questioned, but he was smiling. He believed her.

She glanced at her watch. "We've got time for a nice long lunch," she said. "Maybe fifteen whole minutes. Those cakes have to be delivered by noon, but the church hall where they're going is only two blocks away. So let's sit down and enjoy a break."

She watched as he settled in across from her and began to eat his sandwich. She was so glad he'd talked her into letting him stay to help. Without him, she would surely be chasing her children up and down the stairs by now, with cakes burning in the background. She raised her glass of iced tea at him.

"To Connor McNair, life saver," she said. "Hip, hip, hooray."

He laughed. "Your Bundt cakes aren't all out of the fire yet," he told her with a crooked grin. "Don't count your chickens too soon."

"Of course not. I just wanted to acknowledge true friendship when it raises its furry head."

He shook his head and had to admit it was almost as covered with curls as hers. "Anytime," he told her, then tried to warble it as a tune. "Anytime you need me, I'll be there."

Her gaze caught his and she smiled and whispered, "Don't get cocky, kid."

His gaze deepened. "Why not?" he whispered back. "What's the fun of life if you don't take chances?"

She held her breath. For just a few seconds, something electric seemed to spark between them. And then it was gone, but she was breathing quickly.

"Chances. Is that what you call it?" she said, blinking a bit.

He nodded. "Chances between friends. That's all."

She frowned at him. "Some friend. Where were you to stop me from marrying Brad?"

The look in his face almost scared her. She'd meant it in a lighthearted way, but being casual about a subject that cut so deep into her soul didn't really work. Emotions were triggered. Her joke had fallen flat.

"I tried," he said gruffly, a storm brewing in his blue eyes.

He was kidding—wasn't he?

"What do you mean?" she asked, trying to ignore the trembling she heard in her own voice.

He leaned back in his chair but his gaze never left hers. "Remember? The night before your wedding."

She thought back. "Yes. Wait. You didn't even go to the bachelor party."

He snorted. "I went. Hell, I was hosting it." He seemed uncomfortable. "But I couldn't stay. I couldn't take all the celebration."

"Oh."

"So I went off and left all those happy guys to their revelry. I got a bottle of Scotch and took it to a sandy beach I knew of."

She nodded slowly, thinking back. "As I remember it, you were pretty tanked when you showed up at my apartment."

He took a deep breath and let it out. "Yes. Yes, I was. I was a tortured soul."

"Really? What were you so upset about that night?"

He stared at her. Couldn't she guess? Was she really so blind? He'd been out of his head with agony that night. He knew what a wonderful girl Jill was, knew it and loved her for it. And he knew Brad wasn't going to make her happy. But how could he tell her that? How could he betray a friend?

The problem was, he had to betray one of them. They

were both his best friends and he couldn't stand to see them getting married. And at the same time, he didn't think he should interfere. It was their decision. Their misfortune. Their crazy insane absolutely senseless leap into the brave unknown.

But he knew a thing or two, didn't he? He knew some things he was pretty sure she didn't know. But how could he hurt her with them? How could he explain to her about all the times Brad had cheated on her in the years they'd all been friends?

She would chalk it up to pure jealousy, and in a way, she would have been right. He was jealous. He wanted her. He knew Brad didn't value her enough. He knew Brad didn't deserve her. But how could he tell her that? How could he tell her the truth without ending up with her despising him more than she now did Brad? If she really did.

Besides, what could he offer her in place of her romance with Brad? He wasn't even sure he would ever be ready for any sort of full-time, long-term relationship. Every now and then he thought he'd conquered his background and the wariness he felt. But then he would see examples among his friends that just brought it back again. Could you trust another human in the long run? Was it worth the effort, just to be betrayed in the end?

And so—the Scotch. The alcohol was supposed to give him the courage to do what had to be done. But it didn't work that way. It made him sick instead, and he babbled incoherently once he had Jill's attention. She never understood what he was trying to say.

He couldn't even tell her now. She'd asked him a direct question. What was he so upset about that night? And still, he couldn't tell her the truth.

Because I knew you were marrying the wrong man. You should have been marrying me.

Reaching out, he caught her hand and looked deep into her eyes.

"Jill, tell me what you want. What you need in your life to be happy."

She stared back at him, and he waited, heart beating a fast tattoo on his soul.

"Connor," she began, "I… I don't know how to explain it exactly, but I…"

But then she shook her head and the timer went off and they both rose to check the cakes. Whatever she'd been about to say was lost in a cloud of the aroma of delicious confections.

The last full-size cakes came out and were set to cool and they began to fill the large mini Bundt cake pans. Twelve little cakes per pan. And each had to be filled to exactly the same level.

"They'll take about fifteen to twenty minutes," she told him nervously. "Then the ovens have to be back up to temperature before we put the next batch in. If we time it right, we might just make it. But it's going to be close."

One hundred and ten little cakes, she thought with a tiny surge of hysteria. Oh, my!

Connor left to deliver some of the full-size cakes. Jill checked on the babies. They were still sleeping in their travel cribs. She was thankful for that. Back to the kitchen, she began to prepare the rectangular boxes with the small dividers she was going to put the mini cakes in once they were ready to go. Then Connor was back and they pulled a batch out.

"These are perfect," she said with a sigh of relief. "You get the next batch ready. I'll make the Limoncello glaze."

They both had their eyes on the clock. Time seemed to go so quickly. Minutes seemed to evaporate into thin air. Jill was moving as fast as she could.

And then the phone started ringing. People who hadn't had their deliveries yet were wondering why.

"We're working as fast as we can," she told them. "Please, every minute I spend on the phone means your cake will get there that much later."

It was starting to feel hopeless. A batch overflowed its pan and they had to pull it out, clean up the mess and start again. She mixed up three batches of glaze and accidentally knocked them over onto the floor. That had to be done again.

And the clock was ticking.

She felt as though the beating of her heart was a clock, racing her, mocking her, letting her know she wasn't going to make it. Biting her lip, she forced back that feeling and dug in even harder.

"Last batch going in," Connor called.

She hurried over to see if it was okay. It was fine. Connor was turning out to be a godsend.

It was almost time. The phone rang. It was the Garden Club wondering where their cake was.

"Their party isn't until seven tonight," she said in full annoyance mode. "Can't they wait?"

"I'll run it over," Connor offered.

"You will not," she told him. "The engagement party is next. We have to deliver to them by five or we will have failed."

The twins woke up and were cranky. Connor tried to entertain them but there was very little hope. They wanted their mother.

Jill had to leave Connor alone with the cakes while she cuddled her boys and coaxed them into a better mood. She knew they needed her and she loved them to pieces, but all the while she felt time passing, ticking, making her crazy. She had to get back to the cakes.

Connor had his own problems. His phone was vibrating every fifteen minutes. Every call was from Brad. He knew that without even checking. He had no intention of answering the phone, but every time it began to move, he had that sinking feeling again.

Brad. Why couldn't he just disappear?

Instead he was texting. Connor didn't read the texts. There was no point to it. He knew what they said.

Brad wanted answers. He wanted to know what was going on. He wanted to get the latest scoop on Jill. All things Connor had no intention of giving him. But knowing Brad, that wasn't going to satisfy him. He was going to intrude, one way or another. And he wouldn't wait long to make his influence felt. Connor looked at his phone. If only there was some way to cut the link to Brad and his expectations.

CHAPTER SIX

IT WAS TIME. They had to move. But the twins wouldn't stop clinging to Jill.

Connor had an idea. He brought in a huge plastic tub he found in the garage, placing it in an empty corner of the kitchen, far from the oven and the electric appliances. Using a large pitcher, he put a few inches of barely warm water in the bottom.

"Hey kids," he called to them. "Want to go swimming?"

He didn't have to offer twice. They were excited, getting into their swimsuits and finding swim toys. Jill could get back to packing up her cakes and Connor could supervise the play area while he worked on glazing at the same time.

The long, rectangular boxes were filled with cakes for the Jamison engagement party. It was time to go. Connor packed them into Jill's van and took off. Jill sat down beside the tub of water to watch her boys pretend to swim and she felt tears well up in her eyes. They had made it. Now—as long as they didn't poison everyone at the engagement party, things would calm down. There were still a few cakes to deliver, but nothing was the hectic job the engagement party had been. She'd come through. And she couldn't have done it without Connor.

She wrapped her arms around her knees and hugged tightly. "Thank you, Connor," she whispered to the kitchen air. "You saved my life. I think I love you."

And she did. Didn't she? She always had. Not the way she loved Brad. But Brad was always such a problem and Connor never was.

She remembered when Brad had been the coolest guy around. The guy everyone looked up to, the hunk every girl wanted to be with. He drove the coolest convertible, had the best parties, knew all the right people. At least, that was the way it seemed back then. And he had chosen her. It was amazing how much you could grow up in just a few years and learn to see beyond the facade.

"Cool" didn't mean much when you had babies to feed in the middle of the night. And it only got in the way when it was time to separate your real friends from the posers. Back then, she'd been a pretty rotten judge of character. She'd improved. She had a better idea of what real worth was.

A half hour later, Connor was back. She rose to meet him, ready to ask him how it went, but he didn't give her time to do that. Instead he came right for her, picked her up and swung her around in a small celebratory dance.

"You did it," he said, smiling down into her face. "The cakes are delivered and the customer is in awe. You met the challenge. Congrats."

"We did it, you mean," she said, laughing as he

swung her around again. "Without you, all would be lost right now."

He put her down and shrugged. "What do we still have to get delivered?" he asked. "I want to get this job over with so we can relax." He looked down at the boys, still splashing about in the water. "Hey, guys. How are you doing?"

Timmy laughed and yelled something incomprehensible, and Tanner blew bubbles his way.

"Great," Connor said back, then looked at Jill. "Your orders, *mon chef?*" he asked.

"We do have two deliveries left," she said. "The last cakes are baking right now. We should be ready to call it a day in about an hour. Can you make it until then?"

"Only if I get a fair reward," he said, raising an eyebrow. "What are you offering?"

"I've got nothing," she said, making a face. "Unless you'll take kisses."

She was teasing, just having fun, but it hit him like a blow to the heart. "Kisses are my favorite," he told her gruffly, his eyes darkening.

She saw that, but it didn't stop her. Reaching up, she planted a kiss on his mouth, then drew back and laughed at him.

He laughed back, but his pulse was racing. "Hey, I'll work for those wages any day," he told her, and then he had to turn away. There was a longing welling up in him. He'd felt it before and he knew what it was.

He'd been yearning for Jill since the day he met her. His own background and emotional hiccups had worked against him letting her know over that first year, and by the time he actually knew what he wanted, Brad had taken over, and it was too late.

"What kind of glaze are we putting on these last cakes?" he asked her.

Jill didn't answer right away. She'd seen the look that had come over his face, noticed his reaction to her friendly kiss. For some reason, her heart was beating in a crazy way she wasn't used to.

"Those get a rum caramel with roasted chopped pecans sprinkled on top," she said at last.

They worked on it together, but there was a new feeling between them, a sort of sense of connection, that hadn't been there before. And she had to admit, she rather liked it.

He took out the last deliveries and stopped to pick up a pizza on his way home. She had the boys dried and put into their pajamas by then. They got their own special meals and then were put into the playroom to play quietly and get ready for bed. Jill set out the pizza on the kitchen table and she and Connor ate ravenously.

"Wow," he said with a groan. "What a day. I've worked in a lot of places, but I've never been put through the wringer like I was today."

"You did great," she responded. "I couldn't have met the deadlines without you."

He sighed. "What's the outlook for tomorrow?"

Tomorrow? She hadn't allowed herself to think that far ahead. Was he going to leave tonight? She didn't think so. He didn't seem to be making any of the pertinent preparations. And if he stayed tonight, what about tomorrow? Would he stay then, too? Should she let him?

"Just a couple of orders," she said. "And then, for the rest of the week, not a thing."

"Oh." He looked at her with a guilty grimace. "Uh, maybe you'd better take a look at some of the orders I took over the phone today. I wrote them down somewhere."

That started a mad scramble to locate the paper he'd written them down on.

"I have to set up a system," she muttered once they'd found it. "What if you'd gone and never told me about these?"

Gone? Where was he going?

Their gazes met and the question was there and neither of them wanted to answer it.

She looked at him, at his handsome face, his strong shoulders, and she felt a wave of affection. There was no one else she would have rather spent this day with. It had to be him.

She stopped in front of him and smiled, putting a hand flat on his chest. "Thank you," she said solemnly. "I can never stop thanking you enough. You really did make the difference today."

He didn't smile, but there was a dark, cloudy look in his eyes and he put his own hand over hers. "I wish I could do more," he said, and she could have sworn his voice cracked a little.

She shook her head, wishing she had the right to kiss him the way you would a lover. "You saved me from the nightmares," she murmured.

He frowned. "What nightmares."

She shrugged, wishing she hadn't brought it up.

"Sometimes I have this dream where I'm all alone on an island that's being attacked by huge black birds. They look sort of like vultures. They peck away at me. I run and run and they swoop down. Every time I turn to fight one off, others attack from behind me." She shuddered.

His hand tightened over hers. "Bummer."

She tried to smile but her lips were trembling. "No kidding."

"Hey." He leaned forward and dropped a soft kiss on her mouth. "I had a dream about birds last night, too. Only my dream was about a beautiful huge white bird with lacy wings. I was desperately trying to catch her. And you know what? That bird was you."

She smiled, enchanted, and he kissed her again. "Connor," she whispered warningly, trying to draw back, and a shout from one of the boys gave her statement emphasis. He straightened and watched as she left him.

They both went up to put the boys to bed.

"They're just going to climb out of these cribs again," Connor whispered to her.

"Shh. Don't remind them of the possibilities."

They covered the boys and turned out the lights and left, hoping for the best.

"How about a glass of wine?" he asked her.

She hesitated, knowing it would put her right to sleep. "I'd better not," she said. "But you go ahead."

The phone rang. She sighed. She was completely exhausted and ready to go to bed early and try to recoup. Hopefully this wasn't one of her friends asking about the date last night. She'd already ignored a couple of those calls on her cell. And if it was an order for a cake, she only hoped she would be able to get the facts straight.

"Hello?" she said, stifling a yawn. "Jill's Cakes."

"Oh, thank goodness," said the lady on the other end of the line. "You're there. Now please, please don't tell me you're closed for the night."

Jill frowned. What the heck did that mean? Was it someone at the engagement party who thought some of their order was missing? Or something different? "Well, uh, we're here and cleaning up but our workday is pretty much over. Was there something you needed?"

"Oh, Jill, this is Madeline Green," she responded in a voice that could summon cows. "You know me from the church choir."

"Of course." She pulled the phone a bit away from her ear and glanced up at Connor who had come close and was listening. She gave him a shrug. "Nice to hear from you, Madeline."

"Honey, listen. I'm here at the Elks lodge. We've had a disaster. Our caterer has failed us. We have one hundred and two people here for dinner and we have no dessert."

"Oh." No. Her brain was saying, *"No!"* Her body was saying, *"No!"* "I see. Uh....maybe you should go out and buy some ice cream."

"Impossible. We have to have a special dessert. It's traditional. People expect it. This is Old Timers' Night. Some only come to this annual award dinner because of the fancy desserts we usually serve. It's everyone's favorite part."

"But you had some ordered?"

"Oh, yes. They never showed up. The caterer disavows all knowledge of what the pastry chef was up to. He washes his hands of it entirely."

"I see." Her brain was still shrieking, "No!"

"Have you tried the Swedish bakery?"

"They're closed. In fact, everyone is closed. You're our only hope."

Jill blinked. "So you called everyone else first?"

"Well…"

"Never mind." She made a face, but the lady couldn't see it. She took a deep breath. "Madeline, I'm afraid we just can't…"

Suddenly she was aware that Connor had grabbed her upper arm and was shaking her gently.

"Say 'yes,'" he hissed at her intensely.

"What?" she mouthed back, covering the receiver with her hand. "Why?"

"Say 'yes.' Never ever say 'no.'"

He meant it. She groaned.

"You're trying to build up a reputation," he whispered close to her ear. "You need to be the go-to person, the one they can always depend on. If you want to build your business up, you have to go the extra mile."

He was right. She knew he was right. But she was so tired. She really didn't want to do this.

"Say 'yes,'" he insisted.

She was too limp to fight it. Uncovering the mouthpiece, she sighed and handed the phone to him. "You do it," she said.

She turned around and looked at the mess they would have to wade through to get this done. Everything in her rebelled.

"You realize how many they need, don't you?" she asked when Connor hung up.

"Yes. We can do it."

"Can we? What makes you think you can say that?"

"I've seen you work. And I'm here to help you."

She winced. "How long do we have?"

"One hour."

Her mouth dropped open but no sound came out.

"Okay," Connor said quickly, hoping to forestall any forecasts of doom. "Think fast. What do you make that cooks in less than an hour?"

She shrugged. She felt like a wrung-out rag. "Cookies."

"Then we make cookies."

She frowned. "But that's not special."

"It is the way we make them." He looked at her expectantly. "What'll we do?"

She looked at him and she had to smile, shaking her head. She knew he was as beat as she was, but the call for desserts seemed to have given him new life. "You're the one who made the promises. You tell me."

"Come on. What's your signature cookie?"

She closed her eyes. "I'm too tired to think."

"Me, too," he agreed stoutly. "So we'll go on instinct instead of brainpower."

She began to laugh. This was all so ridiculous.

They'd just produced more baked product than she'd ever done before in one day, and now they were going to do more? Impossible.

"Cookies?" he coaxed.

"I guess."

They made cookies. Pecan lace cookies with a touch of cardamom, pressed together like sandwiches with mocha butter cream filling between them. Chocolate ganache on the base. A touch of white butter cream around the edges, like a lacy frill.

Connor used the mixer while Jill prepped the pans and got the chocolate ready to melt. Just as the first pan went into the oven, they heard the sound of giggling from the next room.

Jill looked at Connor. "Oh, no."

He nodded. "They climbed out again. We should have known they would." He looked at her. There was no time to spare and she was the chef. "I'll take care of them," he told her. "You just keep baking."

It took a couple of minutes to catch the boys and carry them back up, and all the while, he was racking his brain to think of some way to keep them in their beds. There was only one idea that just might work, but he knew instinctively that Jill wasn't going to like it. They didn't have much choice. He was going to have to do it and deal with the consequences later.

CHAPTER SEVEN

BY THE TIME Connor got back to the kitchen, Jill had at least sixty cookies cooling and was beginning assembly of the desserts.

"I don't hear the boys," she said. "What did you do?"

"Don't worry. I took care of it."

She stopped and looked at him through narrowed eyes. "You didn't tie them up or anything like that, did you?"

"No, nothing like that. I'd show you, but right now, we've got to hurry with this stuff."

She gave him a penetrating glance, but she was in the middle of the drizzle across the top of each confection and her attention got diverted.

"What do you think?" she asked him.

Connor looked the sample over with a critical eye.

"I don't know. It still needs something. Something to make it look special."

They both stared for a long sixty seconds.

"I know," he said. "We've got plenty of buttercream left. Get your decorating thingamajig."

"Why?"

"I've seen the flowers you can make with butter cream frosting. You're going to make one hundred and two rose buds."

"Oh." She looked at the clock. "Do you really think we can get them out in time?"

"I know we can." He grinned at her, then swooped in and kissed her hard on her pretty mouth. "We can do anything. We already have."

He took her breath away, but she stayed calm. At least outwardly. She stared at him for a few seconds, still feeling that kiss. Why was he doing things guaranteed to send her into a tailspin if she didn't hold herself together?

But she went back to work and she kept control and the job got finished. And at the end, they stared at each other.

"We did it."

"We did, didn't we?"

"But the delivery…"

"Quick. We're five minutes late."

He piled the desserts in boxes and headed for the door. Just before he disappeared, he called back, "Better check on the twins."

She was already on her way. There wasn't a sound as she climbed the stairs. When she opened the door, nothing moved. But somehow everything looked a little wrong. In the dark, she couldn't quite figure out what it was and she hated to turn on the light, but she had to. And what she saw left her speechless.

"What?"

One crib stood empty. The other had been turned

upside down. The mattress was on the ground, but the rest of the crib was above it like a cage. And on the mattress, her two little boys were sound asleep.

Her first impulse was to wake them up and rescue them, but then she realized they were probably better off where they were. After all, how was she going to get them to stay in their cribs without the bars?

She went back down, not sure what to do. She started cleaning up the kitchen, but then she heard Connor driving up and she went to meet him at the door.

He came in smiling. "They loved it," he announced. "People were asking for our card and I was handing them out like crazy."

She put her head to the side and raised her eyebrows as she listened to him. *"Our" card?* When had that happened? But she could deal with that later. Right now she had something else on her mind.

"Now do you want to explain what happened to the crib?"

"Oh." His face changed and suddenly he looked like a boy with a frog in his pocket. "Sure. I, uh, I had to turn it upside down."

"So I see."

He gave her a guilty smile. "Are they okay?"

She nodded. "Sound asleep."

"Good." He looked relieved. "That was the goal."

"But Connor…"

"They wouldn't stay in the cribs," he told her earnestly. "They kept climbing out. And that was just so dangerous. This was the only thing I could think of on the fly. And luckily, they loved it when I put them into their own special cage. I told them to be monkeys and they played happily until they went to sleep. Didn't they?"

"I guess so, but…"

"If I hadn't done it, they would still be climbing out and running for the hills. And we wouldn't have finished in time."

"Okay." She held up a hand and her gaze was steely. "Enough. I understand your logic. What I don't understand is how you could do such a crazy thing without consulting me first."

That stopped him in his tracks. He watched her and realized she was right. He thought he was doing what was best for her, but without her consent, it was really just what was best for him. He had no right to decide for her. They were her kids.

He'd goofed again and it pained him. Why was he always putting his foot in it where she was concerned? He had to apologize. He swallowed hard. That wasn't an easy thing to do. Taking a deep breath, he forced himself to do what had to be done.

"Jill, you're absolutely right," he said sincerely. "And I'm really sorry. I was wrong to take your agreement for granted. I won't do that again."

Now she had a lump in her throat. Few had ever said that sort of thing to her before, especially not a man. Could she even imagine Brad saying such a thing? Hardly. She felt a small sense of triumph in her chest. She'd asked for an apology and she got one. Wow.

"I guess the first order of business is to figure out

how to make a crib they can't climb out of," she noted, looking at him expectantly.

He feigned astonishment. "Who? Me? You want me to build a crib they can't climb out of?"

"Either that, or come up with a plan," she said, teasing him flirtatiously. "Aren't you here to help?"

His grin was endearingly crooked and he pulled her to him, looking down like a man who was about to kiss a very hot woman. She looked up at him, breath quickening, and she realized she really wanted that kiss. But a look of regret and warning flashed in his eyes. He quickly released her and turned away.

"You ready for that glass of wine now?" he asked, walking toward the wet bar at the end of the room.

She took a deep breath and closed her eyes before she answered. "Sure," she said. "Why not?"

He poured out two crystal glasses of pinot noir and they sat in the living room on a small couch. There was a gentle rain falling and they could see it through the huge glass windows that covered one side of the room.

"What a day," he said, gazing at her as he leaned back in his corner of the couch. The dim light left the wine in their glasses looking like liquid rubies. "It feels like it must have lasted at least a day and a half."

"Or maybe three and a half," she agreed. "And a few shocks to the system." She sighed. "But you came through like a trooper. I couldn't have done it without you."

"I'm glad I was here to help."

She met his gaze and then looked away too quickly. She felt her cheeks reddening and groaned inside. There was nothing to be embarrassed about. Why had she avoided his eyes like that? She coughed to cover up her feelings.

"So tell me the story of this cooking talent you seem to have discovered in the mysterious East," she said quickly.

He grinned. "So you can see the evidence of my expertise in my work even here," he said grandly.

The corners of her mouth quirked. "No, but you told me you were good, so I believe it."

"Ah." He nodded. "Well, it's all the fault of a young chef named Sharon Wong. We dated each other for most of the last year in Singapore. She taught me everything I know." He made a comical face. "Of course, that was only a small fraction of what *she* knows, but it was a start."

A woman was behind it all. She should have known. But it gave her a jolt. Connor had never seemed to have a special woman in his life. Lots of women, but no one special. Had that changed?

"A chef. Great. I'm partial to chefs. What kind of cuisine?"

"She specializes in Mandarin Chinese but she mostly taught me French basics. She claims every chef needs French cooking as a standard, a baseline to launch from. Sort of like learning Calculus for science classes."

She nodded. "That's why it's so important for Trini to go to the school she just left to attend. She'll get a great grounding in the basics."

He watched her for a moment, then asked, "Why didn't you ever go there?"

She shrugged and stretched back against the pillows, beginning to feel her body relax at last. "I took classes locally, but nothing on that level." Her smile was wistful. "Funny. I applied a few years ago. I got accepted on my first try. A scholarship and everything. But I didn't get to go."

"Why not?"

She gave him a bemused smile. "I married Brad instead."

"Wow, that was a bad decision." He looked pained at the thought. "You gave up going to the school of your dreams to marry Brad?"

"Yes." She threw him a reproving look. He was getting a little adamant about her life choices. "And I do regret it. So that's why I won't let her give it up for anything. She's got to go. She'll learn so much."

He was quiet and she wondered what he was thinking about. Something in the look on his face told her it still bothered him to think of her giving up her dream that way and she wasn't sure why he cared.

Everybody had to make choices. Everybody had to give something up now and then. It was part of life.

"I was just thinking about that time we went to San Francisco," she said a few minutes later. "Remember?"

He looked up and his smile completely changed his face. "Sure I remember. You had set up a weekend to celebrate Brad's birthday with a surprise trip to San Francisco and then you ended up taking me instead."

She nodded, still captivated by that smile.

"It was senior year, wasn't it?" he went on. "You got

a hotel just off Union Square and tickets to the ballet—
or so you said."

She nodded again. "That was my big mistake. Once
I told Brad that, he suddenly had somewhere else he
had to be that weekend."

She could hardly believe it. What a fool she'd been
in those days. "I was so mad, I told him I was going to
take you instead. And he said, sure, go ahead."

Connor smiled, recalling that sunny day. He thought
he'd died and gone to heaven. He was walking on air
when she asked him to go with her.

A whole weekend with Jill and no Brad. He hadn't
even cared if it was the ballet. But the beauty of it was,
she was just setting up a surprise, because the tickets
that she had were for the Giants in Candlestick Park.
The ballet thing was just a ruse to tease Brad and the
baseball game was supposed to be his big surprise. Instead it was Connor's.

She gazed at him speculatively. "Sometimes when I
look back I wonder why I didn't notice."

His heart gave a lurch. What was she reading into
his responses? "Notice what?"

She shrugged. "How little Brad actually cared for
me."

Oh, that. It had always been obvious to most of those
around her. Brad wanted her when he wanted her, but
he didn't confine his activities too close to home. Still,
looking at her now, he couldn't stand the haunted expression in her eyes. The last thing in the world she
should do was beat herself up over the past.

"He cared plenty," he said gruffly. "He wanted you for himself right from the first. Don't you remember?"

She shook her head and gave him a sad smile. "I think you know what I mean. Anyway, we had a great time in San Francisco, didn't we?"

"Yes, we did." He let his head fall back as he thought of it. That trip had planted dreams in his head. You could say he might have been better off without them, but he didn't think so. His feelings for Jill were a part of that time, even if she never knew it.

"Remember that night? We talked until almost dawn, and then we slept until noon."

"Yeah." They had two rooms, but he never went to his own. There were two beds in hers, one for each of them, and he just stayed with her. He never touched her, but he sure wanted to.

And best of all, it was on that night that he knew he was ready to try to have a real relationship. He'd spent the first few years in college wary of making any sort of commitment to any girl. His background had argued strenuously against it.

But Jill was different. He made up his mind that night that he was going to tell her how he felt about her once they got back to the university. And he was resolved— he was going to take her away from Brad. Somehow, someway, he would do it. He spent hours going over what he wanted to say, how he wanted to make her understand his feelings.

And then they got back to school, and there was Brad on crutches. He'd gone waterskiing and broken his leg. Suddenly he needed Jill. Connor felt himself fading into the background, like some sort of invisible man, and wondering why his timing was always so bad.

It was shortly afterward that he signed up to go to Europe for a semester. When he got back, he learned that Jill and Brad had broken up just after he left. From what he could see, Brad was busy dating every pretty girl on campus while Jill was busy trying to pretend she didn't care.

He took her to his favorite little Italian restaurant and they ate pasta and talked for hours. He ended up with his arm around her while she cried on his shoulder about how awful Brad was being to her. He restrained himself. He was going to do it right. He was going to take it one step at a time.

But once again, the timing wasn't in his favor. By the next afternoon, Brad was back in her life and all was forgiven.

That was when he'd hardened his heart. It had happened to him one too many times. He wasn't going to let it happen again—ever. Even today he was wary. What seemed like the opportunity to strike so often ended up as the chance to fall on his face instead. It wasn't worth it.

"I think of that trip to San Francisco as an island of happiness in an ocean of stress," she said softly. She looked at him with gentle speculation and a touch of pure affection. "Everything is always so easy with you. And it was always so hard with Brad."

Really? Really?

He stared at her, wondering how she could say such a thing. If that was so, why had she married the hard guy? He was tempted to come right out and ask her that question. That just might clarify a lot of things between them. But before he could think of a way to put it, she spoke again.

"So, was it serious?" she asked him.

He was startled. "Was what serious?"

"You and Sharon Wong?"

"Oh." He laughed, then considered for a moment. "Who knows? It might get to be. If I go back to Singapore."

She turned away. Why did she have such a sick feeling in the pit of her stomach? Was she jealous? Ridiculous. He deserved to fall in love. He deserved some happiness. Hadn't she just been counseling him to find someone to marry? And now she was going to go all green-eyed over a woman he obviously had some affection for? What a fool she was acting.

Connor was probably the best man she knew. He'd always been there for her—except when he took off for places like Singapore. Still, he'd always been a playboy in so many ways. She couldn't imagine him in love.

"I never knew any of your girlfriends in college," she noted. "Why was that? You never showed up with a girl on your arm. I knew they existed, because I heard about them. How come you never brought them around?"

He gazed at her and didn't know what to say. He'd dated plenty of girls in college. But why would he take any of them to meet the one girl he cared about above all others? They would have seen through his casual act in no time.

Funny that she never did.

He stared at her for a long, pulsing moment. "You could have had me anytime you wanted me," he said in a low, rough voice.

There. He'd said it. Finally a little hunk of truth thrown out into this sea of making everyone feel good about themselves. What was she going to do about it?

"Connor!"

She didn't seem to want to take it as truth. More like teasing. Did she really think he was making a joke?

"Be serious," she said, waving that away. "You know that's not true. You didn't want anyone to be your steady girl. You wanted fun and excitement and games and flirting. You didn't want a real relationship. You admitted it at the time." She made a face at him. "You have to realize that back then, what you wanted didn't seem to have anything to do with what I wanted."

He shook his head sadly. "I don't know how you could have read me so wrong."

"I didn't." She made a face at him. "You just don't remember things the way they really were. I was looking for the tie that binds, just like a lot of women at that age. It's a natural instinct. Nesting. I felt a deep need for a strong male, someone to build the foundation of a family with."

He almost rolled his eyes at her. Was she really so self-delusional? "So you chose a guy who didn't want kids."

Her shoulders sagged. He got her on that one. What had she been thinking? He was right. She'd known from the first that he didn't want children. Somehow she had buried that fact under everything, pretending to herself that it didn't matter. Maybe she wouldn't want children, either. Or, more likely, he would change his mind. After all, once it was a clear possibility, surely he would think twice and begin to waver. After all, he loved her. Didn't he?

"I didn't say I chose wisely." She hated to face it, but he had hit the nail on the head. Her mistakes had been easy to avoid, if she'd only been paying more attention. Sighing, she rose. "I want to check on the kids. And I think I'll change out of this uniform. Will you still be up or should I not come back and let you get some sleep?"

He looked at her and realized he wanted her back above all else. He wanted her in his bed, in his arms, in his life. But for now he would have to do with the minimum.

"Sure, come on back," he said, holding up his wine-glass. "I've still got a long way to go."

She was glad he'd said that. As she stopped in to look at her sleeping children, she sighed. The upturned crib was not a long-term solution. Something would have to give. She only hoped it wasn't her peace of mind.

She stopped by the guest room where she slept and changed into something more comfortable, then hurried back down, wondering if he would be asleep before she got back. But he was still staring at the light through his wine and he smiled to welcome her as she entered the room.

She flopped down on the little couch, sitting much closer this time. She was drawn to his warmth, drawn to his masculinity. Might as well face it. She loved look-ing at him, loved the thought of touching him. Would he kiss her good-night? That would be worth a little loss of sleep.

"Connor, how come I don't really know anything about your childhood? How come you never talk about it?"

He took a long sip of wine and looked at her through narrowed eyes. Then he put on his Sam Spade tough-guy voice. "It's not a pretty story, sweetheart. Full of ugliness and despair. You don't want to worry your pretty little head over it."

"Be serious for a moment," she asked. "Really. I want to know you better."

"Why? What more can there be? We've known each other for more than ten years and suddenly you don't know me?"

"Exactly. You've used our friendship as cover all this time. And now I want to know the truth. What were your parents really like? Not the cartoon version you dredge up for jokes. The real people."

He appeared uncomfortable for a moment, then thought for a second or two, and began.

"Let's just put it this way. As they say in the head-shrinking crowd, I've had lifelong relationship com-mitment problems, which can probably be traced back to my childhood environment."

"And that means?"

He stared at her. Did she really want him to go there? Okay.

"I learned early and firsthand just what kind of power women have," he said softly. "I watched my mother purposefully drive my father crazy. Payback, I think, for never making as much money as she felt she needed."

"Ouch." She frowned.

"Yes." He glanced at his ruby-red wine and thought back. "My father was a sweet guy in many ways. He tried hard to please her. But he just didn't have what it took to bring in a high salary, and she rubbed his nose in it every day."

"Oh, Connor," she said softly.

"I watched him go through all sorts of contortions to find some little way to bring a smile to her face, but that was virtually impossible. She nitpicked everything. Nothing was ever good enough for her." He threw her a lopsided grin. "Especially me."

"So she nitpicked you, too?"

"Oh, yeah. I think finding something to make me stammer out 'gee, I'm sorry, Mom,' was what made her day for her." He looked at her. "So I avoided going home. I hung around school in the afternoon, joined every sports team, every debating society, every club that would give me a place to hang out." His gaze darkened. "Meanwhile my father drank himself to death."

"Oh, Connor. I'm so sorry."

He nodded. "It was a waste, really. He was a smart guy. He should have had a better life."

"Yes."

He gazed at her levelly, wondering if he really wanted to get into the next level of this discussion. Did he want to cut a vein and just let it bleed all over the night? Not really. But he might as well explain a little more about why he'd been the way he was when they were younger.

"You know, for years I really was leery of having a relationship with a woman that lasted more than twenty minutes. It just didn't seem worth the risk from what I'd seen."

She wrinkled her nose at him, as if she thought he was being silly. Still, he plowed on.

"But I have a new perspective on it now. I spent the last eighteen months or so in Singapore working with a great guy name George who is married to a wonderful woman named Peggy. I lived in their house and saw their entire interaction, and it helped me understand that decent, loving relationships are possible. I had to look harder at myself and wonder if I had what it takes to have that. I mean, it may be possible, but is it possible for me?"

Jill stared at him. She'd had no idea he had such deep misgivings about lifetime relationships. It made her want to reach out to him, to hold his hand and reassure him. There were plenty of women in the world who didn't treat men the way his mother had. Didn't he know that?

"And what did you decide?" she asked tentatively.

He flashed her a quick grin. "The verdict isn't in yet."

She started to argue about that, but she stopped herself. How could she wrestle him out of opinions that had developed from real life experiences? She didn't have as many bad ones as he did. Maybe it got harder as they piled up.

"Where's your mother now?" she asked.

He shrugged. "I'm not sure. I think she moved to Florida to live with her sister, but we don't keep in touch."

She thought that was a mistake, but she held her tongue. Maybe later she would try to talk to him about how much could be lost when you lost your parents. Instead of going into it directly, she decided to tell him about her background.

"Here's what happened to me," she said. "And Sara. When my mother was alive, we were a happy family. At least, that's the way I remember it. But my father's second marriage was a horror show right from the beginning. That's why Sara and I never warmed to our stepmother, Lorraine." She shook her head.

"She was such a terrible choice for him. And it probably didn't help the marriage that we couldn't like her. He was a good guy, gentle, warm. And she was a shrew."

"Wow," he said, somewhat taken aback. He wasn't used to such strong disapproval from Jill. "That's a pretty negative judgment on the woman."

She shrugged. "Of course, I saw the whole thing through the perspective of a child who had lost her mother and found her father bringing home a new, updated version that didn't please her at all. We were very resentful and probably didn't give her much of a chance, especially after she had a baby. Little Kelly was cute, but it didn't make up for Lorraine. And she didn't like us any better than we liked her and she made it pretty obvious."

"Little Kelly is the one who died last week in a car crash?"

She nodded. "The one I wish we'd been kinder to." She shrugged, but her eyes were sad and haunted. "Too late now." She looked at him again. "And that's what I want you to think about. Don't wait until it's too late to contact your mother again."

He gave her a quizzical look. "Okay. Point taken."

She nodded, then yawned. He smiled.

"You look like a sleepy princess."

She'd traded in her uniform for a short fuzzy robe over the long lacy white nightgown and she looked adorable to him.

"What?" she said, laughing.

"In that gown thing. Even with the little robe over it. You look like you should be in a castle."

She was blushing. Connor had a way of letting her know how pretty he thought she was and she was so hungry for that, it almost brought tears to her eyes.

She smiled back. "I guess we'd better go to bed."

"You're right. We need sleep. I'm only glad we survived the day."

He rose and turned to pull her up beside him and he didn't let go of her hands once they were standing face-to-face, looking at each other.

"I'm glad you came back," she told him, her breath catching in her throat as her pulse began to race. Was he going to kiss her? Or was she going to have to do it herself?

"Me, too." His eyes went so dark, they could have been black instead of blue. He leaned closer, pulling her body up hard against his. "Jill…" he began, and at the same moment, the cell phone in his pocket began to vibrate.

She felt it right away. Sharply drawing in her breath, she stepped back and looked at him. He pulled the phone out, looking for a place to set it down. She reached out and took it from him. Flipping it up, she glanced at the screen and handed it back to him.

"Message for you," she said, and her voice showed no emotion. "How interesting. It's Brad." Her face didn't reveal a thing, but her eyes were strangely hooded as she turned away and started for the stairs. "Good night," she said over her shoulder.

He cringed, though he wouldn't show it. He stuck the phone back in his pocket and didn't answer it. He hadn't been answering Brad's calls all day. Why should he start now?

But he wished she hadn't seen that.

CHAPTER EIGHT

SLEEPING ON THE couch was getting old fast. Connor stretched and hit the armrest before he had his legs out straight.

"Ouch," he muttered grumpily, wondering why he was awake so early when he was still so tired. Then he noticed the problem. The twins were running around the furniture and yelling at the top of their lungs. He groaned. He really preferred a normal alarm clock.

He opened his eyes just enough to see them. They were pretty cute. But loud. He was going to have to give up any chance for more sleep. He stretched again.

"Great game, kids," he told them groggily, swinging his legs over the side of the couch and sitting up with a yawn.

The boys stopped and stared at him. He stared back. Tanner pretended to bark like a puppy. Timmy made a sound like a growling monster. He shook his head. They wanted him to respond. He could tell. And he couldn't resist.

Just like the day before, he burst up off the couch,

waving the covers to make himself look huge, and gave them a monster growl they wouldn't soon forget.

They screamed with scared happiness and charged out of the room, pushing and shoving to both fit through the door at once.

Jill came in and glared at him. "They won't be able to eat their breakfast if you rile them up too much," she warned.

He waved his sheet-covered arms at her and growled. She shook her head and rolled her eyes.

"How come you're not scared?" he complained.

"Because you look so ridiculous," she told him. She laughed softly, letting her gaze slide over his beautiful body. What on earth did he do in Singapore that kept him so fit? His muscles were hard and rounded and tan and a lot of that was on display. His chest was all male and his pajama bottoms hung low on his hips. He took her breath away.

"But you do look cute as a scary monster," she allowed, trying to avoid an overdose of his sexiness by looking away. "We might be able to use your skills at Halloween."

"Hey, no fair," he said as he looked her over sleepily. "You already changed out of your princess dress."

"I'm going incognito for the day," she told him. "They don't let princesses bake Bundt cakes."

"They should."

"I know." She smiled at him then asked with false cheerfulness, "What did Brad want last night?"

He shrugged. "I didn't answer it."

She stared at him for a moment, then looked away.

"I just checked my email. There are already two more orders from people who had cake last night. That makes four who want their cakes today, and two more for the weekend."

"I said you had star power. Didn't I?"

She reached out to take the sheet from him and he leaned forward and dropped a quick kiss on her mouth before she could draw back. She looked up into his eyes and the room began to swim around her.

"They should let princesses do whatever they want," he said softly, and then he reached out and pulled her closer and she slipped her arms around his neck and his mouth found hers.

Finally!

She'd been waiting for this kiss forever—or anyway, it seemed that way. She melted in his arms, taking in his taste and letting her body feel every hard part of him it could manage. His rounded muscles turned her on and his warm, musky smell sent her senses reeling.

And then the doorbell rang.

She collapsed against him, laughing and shaking her head. "Why does fate hate me?" she protested.

He held her close and buried his face in her hair, then let her go.

A timer went off.

"Oh, no, I've got to check that," she said.

"I'll go to the door," he offered.

"Really?" She looked at him skeptically, wondering who was going to get a stunning view of that magnificent chest and hoping it wasn't the church people. Then she rushed on into the kitchen to check her cake.

It definitely needed to come out. She set it on the cooling rack and looked around at the mess that still existed from yesterday. She usually made it a practice never to go to bed with a dirty pan left in the sink, but she'd broken that rule last night. Now she had a couple of counters full of pans that needed washing. She was working on that when Connor came into the kitchen.

"Who's at the door?" she asked distractedly.

Connor made a face. "The Health Department Inspector."

She turned to stare at him. "What? He just came last week."

He shrugged. "I guess he's back."

And so he was, coming into the kitchen and looking around with massive disapproval all over his face. Tall and thin, he wore glasses and had a large, fluffy mustache, along with a pinched look, that made him look like a bureaucratic force to be reckoned with.

Connor made a face at her and left to put on some clothes. The inspector sniffed at him as he left, then looked back at the kitchen.

"What the hell is going on here?" he demanded, looking at the pot and pan strewn counters.

Jill had a smart-alecky answer right on the tip of her tongue, but she held it back. This was the health inspector. He could ruin her if he wanted to. Shut her down. She had to be nice to him, much as it stuck in her craw.

"Look, this is such a bad time for you to show up. Unannounced, I might add. Aren't you supposed to make appointments?"

He glared at her. "Aren't you supposed to be ready at all times for inspection?"

She gave him a fake smile. "Sorry about the mess. I'm in the middle of cleaning it up. We had a huge, huge day yesterday. Things will be back in order in no time."

"That would be wise," he said. "I wouldn't want to have to write you up for kitchen contamination."

She gaped at him in outrage. "There's clutter, there's mess, but there's no contamination. Please!"

He shrugged, then turned as Connor reappeared, dressed in the same shirt and slacks he'd been wearing for three days now.

"What are you doing here?" he asked.

"Moral support," Connor responded simply. "I'm just a friend. I'm helping."

His eyes narrowed. "Helping how?"

Connor shrugged, instinctively knowing this might be a time to be careful and wary. "Odd jobs. Deliveries."

"Ah." He appeared skeptical. "Let's hope you aren't doing any of the baking. Because if you are, you're going to need to be screened for medical conditions. You'll need a blood test. And more. We don't want you touching the food if you're not healthy. Your papers must be in order."

Connor frowned at the man. "What papers?"

"The ones you need to qualify to do any cooking whatsoever."

Connor sighed and looked away. "Ah, those papers."

"Yes. Records of shots and tests, etc. Medical problems in the last ten years. You understand."

Connor made a face, but he said as pleasantly as possible, "Of course."

The man glared at him. "So? Where are your papers?"

"Really?" Connor said, beginning to get belligerent. "Hey, Mr. Health Inspector, let's see *your* papers."

The man produced a badge and a license and Connor stared at them, realizing he had no idea if they were authentic or not. But he was beginning to have his doubts about this guy.

Jill winced. Connor looked about ready to do something that would jeopardize her business and she had to stop him. Standing behind the inspector, she shook her head and put her finger to her lips, then jerked her thumb toward the other room. Connor hesitated, then followed her out into the hallway, leaving the inspector to poke around at will.

"Connor, don't antagonize him, for heaven's sake," she whispered. "He'll probably write me up for some little thing and then he'll have to come back to check if I've fixed it. But at least he'll go. So leave him alone."

Connor was frowning. "How often does this guy show up here?" he asked her.

"Too much if you ask me. I almost feel like it's harassment at this point. And the funny thing is, every time he comes, something seems to go wrong. I don't know if it's just that I get nervous and then I don't keep focused on what I'm doing or what."

Connor's gaze narrowed. "What sort of things go wrong?"

"Oh...one time the oven wouldn't work anymore and

I had to get a repairman out. Another time somehow the refrigerator got unplugged and it was hours before we knew it. A lot of supplies spoiled and I had to throw them out."

"No kidding." He frowned. "Is he the same official who comes every time?"

"No. But he does come the most. And he says the goofiest things. In fact, I called the health department to complain about him a few weeks ago. They claimed they hadn't sent anyone."

Connor's face was hard as stone. "That doesn't seem right."

"I know. But what can I do? I don't dare confront him. What if he pulls my license?"

Connor shook his head. "Jill, I don't buy it for a minute."

She stared at him. "What do you mean?"

"I think he's a phony. He's got to go."

"What?" She grabbed at his arm to stop him, but he pulled away and marched back into the kitchen, catching the stranger with a tiny camera in his hand.

"Get the hell out of here," he told the inspector in a low, furious voice.

"Connor!" Jill cried, coming in behind him. "You can't talk that way to the inspector!"

But the man seemed to take Connor quite seriously. He raised his hands as though to show he didn't mean any harm and said, "Okay, okay. Take it easy. I'm going."

And he turned around and left as quickly as he could.

Jill stared after him, then looked at Connor. "What the heck?" she cried.

He turned and gave her a look. "Jill, that man's not a real health inspector. Can't you see that?"

"No." She blinked in bewilderment. "What is he then?"

"A private investigator pretending to be a health inspector."

"But why would…?" Her face cleared. "Brad!"

Connor nodded. "That's my guess."

She sank into a chair. "Oh, my gosh. I can't believe that. Brad sent him to spy on me."

"And to sabotage your business, I would guess."

She closed her eyes and took a deep breath. "Why didn't I think of that? I knew there was something fishy about the way he kept showing up." She looked up at Connor. "I should have known."

But Connor was still thinking things over. "Okay, I'm ready to believe that was Brad at work. So the question is, what else has he been meddling in?"

She thought for a moment, then put a hand over her mouth. "Oh, my gosh." She grabbed his hand and held it tightly. "Connor, I don't know this for sure, but I was told that Brad tried to get them to disallow my license. Right at the beginning."

He lowered himself into the chair beside her, still holding her hand. "Why would he do that?"

"Well, he never wanted me to keep this house. He thought I ought to move to the mainland and get an apartment, put the kids in day care and get a regular job. He sort of acted like he thought I was trying to extort money from him by doing anything else."

His face was cold as granite. "Tell me more."

"It took a while to get started. At first, I didn't have any of the right equipment. I used every penny I got from Brad to help pay for the commercial oven, but I still needed to buy a three-unit sink and the special refrigeration I needed. When he found out what I was doing, he was furious."

"And stopped giving you money," he guessed.

She nodded. "Pretty much. Which only made it more important that I find a way to grow my business." She laced her fingers with his.

"You know, you hit a place where you can either move forward, or settle for something less, and get stuck in that great big nowhere land." She sighed. "In order to get to where I might make some actual profit, I had to take the chance. I needed funding. So…"

She met his gaze and looked guilty. "So, yes, I took out a loan so that I could finish buying the supplies I needed."

"What did you use to get a loan? The house?"

She nodded. "That's why it's so scary that this house is still underwater and they won't give me a mortgage modification."

"You've tried?"

"Countless times."

"You're in a tight spot."

She nodded. "I'm standing at the edge of the cliff, you mean. And the ground is starting to crumble under my feet."

His free hand took her chin and lifted her face toward his, then he leaned in and kissed her softly. "I'll catch you," he said, his voice husky. "I'm here, Jill. I won't let you hit the rocks."

She smiled, loving his generous spirit, but not really believing his words. How could he stop the chain of events that seemed to be overwhelming her? It wasn't likely. They'd had a good day yesterday and he'd made that possible. But goodwill—and cake sales—could only go so far. Every step forward seemed to bring on two steps back. She was beginning to lose hope.

He hesitated, then shook his head and drew back from her. "Okay, here's what I don't understand. This just really gets to me. Why do you let Brad still be such a huge part of your life?"

"I…I don't."

"Yes, you do. You're divorced. He's not even giving you the money you should be getting for the kids. He doesn't want anything to do with the children." He frowned, searching her eyes. "Why let him affect you in any way? Why maintain any ties at all?"

She blinked. It was hard to put this in words. How to explain how alone she felt in the world? In some ways, Brad was still her only lifeline. It was too scary to cut that off.

"The only real, legal ties we still have is the business," she said instead of trying to explain her emotional connection to her past. "I still own fifteen percent of it."

He nodded. He knew that. "Do you have a voting position on the board?"

She shrugged. "I'm not really sure if I do or not. I

think I'm supposed to but I've never tried to use it. I suppose I should ask a lawyer."

"At the very least."

"The only reason I keep it, to tell you the truth, is that emotionally, I just can't give up on it yet. It's still a part of my life, a part of my past, all those years we spent building it into the enterprise it is today."

He nodded. Did that answer the question? Her ties to Brad were still too strong. But were they that way from fear…or love? Hard to pull those two apart for analysis. And the answer to that meant everything.

Connor was so angry inside, both at Brad and at himself, he couldn't stay near her for now. Instead he went out and walked down to the ferry and then around the quaint little village and back again. He finally had something he wanted to say to Brad, but when he tried calling him, he found his old pal had turned the tables, and now he wasn't taking calls from Connor.

Voice mail was his only recourse. He waited for the beep.

"Hey, Brad. I just wanted to let you know that I know the health inspector is a phony. He's someone who works for you. If he comes here again, I'll have him arrested for impersonating a government employee.

"About those shares. If you really want them so badly, why don't you come and ask her for them like a man? Why don't you face her? And why don't you offer her something real? You never know what might happen.

"In the meantime, other than that, leave Jill alone. Go live your own life and forget about hers."

He clicked off and tried to tame the rage that roiled in him. Jill didn't deserve any of this. He only hoped she would let him stay here to help her get out from under all this. He knew she couldn't get Brad out of her system, but there wasn't much he could do about that. He didn't care about his own emotional involvement anymore. So, he was probably going to get his heart broken. So what? His love for Jill was too strong to try to deny any longer. And all he wanted was what was good for her. He had to stay.

When he walked into the house, he heard Jill singing in the kitchen. He had to stop for a moment and listen, marveling at her. What was she, some kind of angel? Whatever—she was everything he knew he wanted. And would probably never have.

"Hey," he told her as he came up behind her, putting his arms around her. She leaned back into him and smiled. "I'm getting pretty funky in these clothes," he said. "I think I'll run into town and get some fresh things from the hotel room. Can I bring anything back for you?"

She turned in his embrace and kissed him. "Just bring yourself back. That's all I need," she said.

He kissed her again and the kiss deepened. The way he felt about her grew every time he touched her. Right now, it seemed like fireworks going off in his chest. This was the way he wished it could always be.

Jill stood at the sliding glass door looking out at the grassy hill that was her backyard. Connor was outside playing with the twins, chasing them up and down the hill, laughing, picking up one and then the other to whirl about and land gently again. Her heart was full of bittersweet joy. Tears trembled in her eyes.

If only Brad could be this way. If he really met the boys, if he tried to get to know them, wouldn't he realize how wonderful they were? Wouldn't he have to love them? Wouldn't that make everything better?

As she watched, Connor fell, iron-cross style, into a huge bed of leaves, and the boys raced each other to jump on top of him. She could hear the laughter from where she was behind glass and it answered her own questions.

No. Brad would never love the boys, because he didn't want to. He wouldn't let himself. It was time she faced facts.

She heard the front door open and she turned that way.

"Jill!"

"In here, Sara." She frowned. Her sister's voice sounded high and strained. What had happened now?

Sara appeared, looking a little wild. "Did you get the letter?"

"What letter?"

"From Social Services." She waved an official-looking envelope. "Did you get one, too?"

"I don't know. Connor brought in the mail. I think he left it on the entryway table. Let me get it."

She stepped into the foyer and found the envelope Sara was talking about. Connor and the boys were coming back into the family room as she returned to it. The boys were jumping around him like puppies.

"I promised them ice cream," he said after nodding at Sara. "I'm hoping you actually have some."

"Don't worry." Jill put the envelope down and went into the kitchen. They all followed her and she pulled two Popsicles out of the freezer for them. "They'll accept this as a substitute," she said. "Now go on out and play in the sunroom. I don't care if you drip all over that floor."

They did as they were told, dancing happily on their toes. Connor laughed as he watched them go, then looked at Jill. They shared a secret smile.

Sara groaned. "Come on. Open the mail. You won't believe this."

"What does it say?"

"You need to read it for yourself. Go ahead. Read it. I'll wait."

Connor looked at Sara and said, "Hey, you look really upset."

Her eyes flashed his way. "Did Jill tell you about our stepsister? She died in a car accident last week."

"Yes, she did tell me. I'm sorry."

Sara nodded, then looked at Jill, waiting.

Moments later, Jill handed the letter to Connor and he noticed right away that her fingers were trembling. She turned and looked at her sister, wide-eyed. "I don't believe it."

Sara nodded, looking flushed. "Told you."

Connor glanced at the letter. It seemed to be about someone named Kelly Darling. Then he connected the name. It was the stepsister who had died the week before. Kelly Darling. It seemed that Kelly had a baby. A

three-month-old baby. Jill and Sara were her only living relatives that could be found. Would either of them
care to claim the child?

"A baby," he said. "And you didn't know?"

"No." Jill shook her head. "I guess she wasn't married. We hadn't heard from her for so long."

Sara nodded mournfully. "And now, a baby."

Jill felt tears threatening again. "Poor little thing."

Sara flashed her a look. "Kelly's baby." She shook
her head. "I don't think we've seen Kelly more than
three times in the last fifteen years."

"And that's our fault," Jill said mournfully. "We
should have made more of an effort."

Sara shrugged. "Why? She never liked us. The last
time I saw her, she was furious with me."

Jill looked surprised. "What happened?"

"She wanted to borrow five thousand dollars to help
pay for a certification class she wanted to take."

"Some kind of computer class?"

"No. It was to qualify as a professional dog trainer.
When I pointed out that I didn't see how she was going
to be able to pay me back on the salaries beginning dog
trainers make, she told me I was ruining her life and
she never wanted to see me again."

Jill sighed. "Well, she was an awfully cute little
baby."

Sara looked at Jill and bit her lip. "I'm sure they'll
find some relative we don't even know about to take
the child."

Jill frowned. "Maybe. But…"

"Jill!" Sara cried. "Don't you dare! There is no way you can take on another baby."

Jill looked pained. "What about you?" she asked.

"Me?" Sara's face registered shock. It was obvious that option hadn't even entered her mind. "Me?" She shook her head strenuously. "I don't do babies. I can barely manage to watch your little angels for more than an hour without going mad."

"Sara, she's our flesh and blood. She's our responsibility."

"How do you figure that? I don't see it. She was Kelly's responsibility, and now they'll find someone to adopt her. Tons of people want babies that age."

Jill was shaking her head. "I don't know...."

Sara groaned and looked tortured. Stepping closer, she took her sister's hands in her own. "Jill, I haven't come right out and told you this. I've tried to hint it, just to prepare you, but... I'm going to be moving down to Los Angeles. And my job is going to include almost constant travel, especially to New York. There's no room for a baby in that scenario." She had tears sliding down her cheeks. "And that also means I won't be here to help you. You can't even begin to think of taking this baby."

Jill looked at her and didn't say a thing.

Connor watched her. She was going to take the baby. He could tell. He tried to understand the dynamics here. This was another blow to Jill, another obstacle in her struggle to survive. And yet, that wasn't the way she was taking it. She didn't look at it as the end of her hopes and dreams, a financial and emotional disaster.

She was seeing it as another burdensome responsibility, but one that she would accept. He'd known her for years but he'd never realized how deep her strength went. Where had that come from? Where had she found the capacity to take on everyone else's problems? Was being the oldest sister the key? Or was it just the way her soul was put together?

"They'll find a good home for the baby somewhere, I'm sure," Sara was insisting. "Don't they have agencies to do things like that?"

Jill frowned. That just wasn't right and she knew it. "Sara…"

Sara closed her eyes and turned away.

"I've got to go. I'm expecting half a dozen calls and I've got to prepare myself." She looked back and hesitated, then said with fierce intensity, "Jill, you can't be considering taking that baby. I won't let you."

Jill winced. She knew what was going to happen. It was inevitable. She couldn't expect Sara to understand. Babies…life…family—that was what she'd been put on earth to deal with. So Brad hadn't worked out. Too bad. So her cake business was trembling on the brink and might just crumble. Okay. But turn down taking care of a baby? Her father's grandchild? Her own niece? No. Impossible. If Sara couldn't face it, that baby had only one chance.

She followed Sara to the door and touched her arm before she could escape. "Sara, I'm going to call them. I want that baby here with us."

A look of abject terror flared in her sister's eyes. Slowly, she shook her head, her lower lip trembling.

"You're crazy," she whispered. "Jill, I beg you. Don't do it." And then she turned on her heel and hurried to her car.

Jill came back into the house and went straight to Connor as though drawn by a magnet.

"Are you sure?" he asked her.

"About the baby?" She smiled. "Yes. There is no way I could let Kelly's baby go to strangers. I'm going to get in touch with these people right away. The sooner we get her here the better."

"Jill, your heart is definitely in the right place. But can you do it? You're already overextended. You're on the ragged edge with these two little boys. Can you take on another child like this?"

"I have no choice. I couldn't live with myself if I didn't do it."

His heart was overflowing with love for her, and he knew what she was doing courted disaster. His brain told him Sara was right, but his heart—it was all for Jill. "Come here. I have to hold you. You are so special…"

"Oh, Connor." She started to cry and he held her while she sobbed in his embrace. "It's scary, but it's wonderful, too. It's the right thing to do."

"I just hope it won't be too much for you," he said, kissing her tears away.

She kissed him back. "Sometimes I feel like I'm at my breaking point, but something always comes through to save the day. And right now, it's your arms around me. Connor, I'm so glad you're here."

And she started to sob again. He held her close, enjoying the feel of her and the sweet, fruity scent from her hair. He loved her and he would be there for her as long as she let him stay. But deep inside, he knew a time would come when she would want him to leave. He was prepared for that. He only hoped it didn't come for a long, long time.

CHAPTER NINE

AN HOUR LATER, Jill invited Connor to help her take the boys to the park to play on the swings and in the sandbox. They took little shovels and pails and made the trek on foot, through the residential streets and over the low-lying berm that marked the edge of the park area. The boys ran ahead, then came back for protection when dogs barked or a car came on the end of the street. Then they reached the park and the twins were in heaven.

When they tired of the swings, they got to work with the shovels, tossing sand and shrieking with happiness. After making a vain attempt to keep order, Jill and Connor sat back and let them play the way that seemed to come naturally to them. There weren't many other children around, so they gave them their freedom.

"I heard from Trini this morning," she told him. "I got an email. She's behind in a few classes, but she thinks she can catch up. She's thrilled to be there." She smiled happily. "She's going to keep me apprised with daily bulletins. That'll be great. It's just like vicariously going myself."

"I wish you could go yourself. We ought to be able to figure out a way…."

"We"? She looked at him sideways. But that seemed like a silly thing to have an argument about, so she moved on.

"So tell me more about what you were doing in Singapore all this time," she said, looking at the way his unruly hair flew around his head, much the way hers did, though his was dark as coal and hers was bright as sunshine. "You told me about the nice couple you lived with and worked for, and you told me about the chef you fell in love with—"

"Whoa! Hold on. I never told you that."

"Really?" Her eyes twinkled with mischief. "Gee, I don't know where I picked that up. I must have misheard it."

He knocked against her with his shoulder. "Come on, Jill. You know you're the only woman I've ever loved."

"Wow." She pressed closer to him. "It would be nice to think that was true."

He turned his head and said, close to her ear, "Count on it."

There was something in the way he said it that made her look up into his eyes. They were just kidding each other, weren't they?

"So tell me," she said after they sat down at the edge of the play area. She was sifting sand through her fingers. "Are you really going back or not?"

"That depends."

"On what?"

On whether I can make you fall in love with me. On

whether you can wipe Brad out of your calculations for your future. On whether you can believe in me.

But he sighed and actually said, "The company got bought out by a huge corporation. George made a fine haul on it. And under our contract, he gave me a nice chunk of change, too. So if I went back, it would be to link up with old George again and work on the next big idea."

She smiled with happy memories. "Just like the three of us did when we started MayDay."

"Exactly."

"Only Brad hasn't been bought out by anyone."

"No. Not yet."

She frowned, thinking that over. "And what are you going to do with your profits?"

He shrugged. "I don't know. Right now I'm pretty much looking around for a company to invest in. Some nice, clean little start-up. Preferably in the food business."

She looked at him suspiciously. "Are you teasing me?"

"Teasing you?" He looked shocked at the concept. "Why would I tease you?"

"Because you love to knock me off balance," she said with mock outrage. "You always have."

He leaned back against the rock behind him and laughed at her. She began to poke him in the ribs.

"You love it. Admit it. You love to have a good giggle over my naïveté. Fess up!"

He laughed harder and she began to tickle him. He grabbed her and pulled her down beside him and kissed her nose, making her laugh, too. And then he kissed her for real and she kissed him back and the warmth spread quickly between them.

"You're like a drug," he whispered, dropping kisses on her face. "I don't dare take too much of you."

"Good thing, too," she whispered back. "Because I only have that little tiny bit to give."

"Liar," he teased, kissing her mouth again.

She sighed, holding back the sizzle that threatened to spill out and make this inappropriately exciting. That would have to wait. But she had no doubt they would be able to explore it a bit more later.

"Hey," she said, pulling back up. "We're supposed to be watching the boys."

Luckily the two toddlers were still enchanted with the pails and shovels. Connor and Jill sat up and shook off the sand and grinned at each other.

"Okay," she said. "Now tell me what you're really going to do with the money."

"Just what I said. I've got my eye on a nice little Bundt cake bakery."

She didn't laugh this time. "No, Connor. I will not take charity from you."

He'd known she would react that way but it didn't hurt to start setting the background and give her a chance to think about it. "I'm talking about investing. I wouldn't put my money anywhere that I didn't expect to make a profit on it."

She was shaking her head adamantly. "I don't have shares to sell. That just won't work and you know it."

No, he didn't know it, but he had known she would be

a hard sell on the idea. Hopefully he would have more time to see what he could develop to do for her. "Jill…"

"Connor, I'm still bound to Brad by his company. I refuse to play that game again."

Ouch. That could make all the difference. He nodded slowly, frowning. "Jill, when you say you're still bound to Brad, what do you mean?" He looked her full in the face, searching her eyes for hints of the truth. "Do you still want him back?"

She thought for a moment, then looked at him, clear-eyed. "Connor, for a long time, I wanted Brad back. But not for me. I wanted him back for his children. What will it be like for them to go through life wondering why their father didn't want them? It breaks my heart." Her voice caught and she paused. "For so long, I was so sure, once he saw them, once he held them in his arms…"

He couldn't stand to see her still hoping. He wanted to smash something. Carefully he tried to tell her.

"He's just not made that way, Jill. Brad doesn't want to love a child. He doesn't want to complicate his life like that. He doesn't even want a wife at this point. He thinks he needs to keep the way clear so that he can think big thoughts and make cool-headed decisions. Human relationships only mess things up as far as he's concerned." He shrugged, grimacing. "I don't know why we didn't see that more clearly from the beginning."

"Maybe we did and we just didn't want to believe it."

She closed her eyes. She still had her dreams. She sometimes thought that maybe, if he saw her again, if they did come face-to-face, he would see what he'd once loved in her and realize what he'd lost—and want it back.

No. It wasn't going to happen. She'd given up on that fantasy a long time ago. So why did she still cling to the shards of that relationship?

"When did you start to figure out the truth about Brad?" Connor asked her softly.

Her smile was mirthless. "When I realized he was cheating on me."

He drew his breath in sharply. "You knew?"

She looked at him. "Connor, I'm not stupid. Gullible, maybe. Too weak to stand up for myself when I should, sometimes. But not dumb."

They were silent for a long moment, then Connor asked, "What do you think Brad will say about you taking on another baby?"

She laughed. "Luckily it doesn't matter what he says. Does it?"

The boys were tussling. One was hitting the other with a plastic pail and both were starting to cry. The inevitable end to a lovely time being had by all. Jill and Connor rose from their sitting place and started across the sand to mediate the battle, but on the way, they held hands.

Jill baked two more cakes once they got home and Connor put the boys down for their naps. They both fell asleep as soon as their heads hit their mattresses. He watched them for a while, amazed at how much he cared for them already. Then he went down to help Jill with the bakery business.

"So what's next?" he asked, sitting at the kitchen table and eating a nice large slice of Strawberry Treat. "What's the plan?"

She glanced back at him as she mixed up a fresh glaze. "Stay out of the way of the inspectors. Obey all regulations scrupulously. Grow my business. Hire some employees and get my own shop." She threw him a smile. "In other words, succeed."

He took another bite and nearly swooned with the deliciousness of it all. "You're the best Bundt cake baker on the island. Probably the best in all of Seattle. But all of Seattle isn't going to come here for their cakes. Your customers are basically the people on this island. Are there enough of them to let you be successful?"

She came to the table and dropped down into a seat across from him. "This is exactly my nightmare question. How can I get a large customer base?"

"And what's your answer?"

She shook her head. "I haven't really dealt with it because I'm scared of what it will take."

"And what is that?"

She frowned. "I have to branch out. I know it. I have to develop a full-blown bakery out of this. I have to make cookies and pies and éclairs and bear-claws and dinner rolls. I have to learn to do everything. It's my only hope."

"And your competition?"

She nodded. "There are two bakeries here, both run by older bakers who are about at the end of their bakery careers, I would think. So there should be room for me." She made a face. "If I can come up to the challenge."

He was impressed that she'd thought this out so fully. It gave him the reassurance that she really meant to make a go of it. Because she was going to have to work very hard to last.

"You've really developed a good business brain, haven't you?"

"I developed it right next to you. Remember when we used to brainstorm together during the early days at MayDay?"

"I do." He smiled at her. "But how are you going to do all this without someone here to help you? I can't even understand how you've done this much so far."

"It isn't easy."

He thought about that for a moment, then turned back and said, "You're going to have to have some help. Face it."

She nodded. "I know. I'm thinking of giving Mrs. Mulberry another chance."

"Great. I think she deserves it."

"She means well and she wants to do it. So there you go."

He nodded. "If you're with her most of the time, you can train her. And she'll begin to understand what the twins need. I'm sure it will go well."

She grinned at him. "I never realized what an optimist you are. Just a regular what-me-worry-kid."

"Sure. I learned long ago that being happy is better than being angry all the time."

He watched her work, nursing a cup of coffee and enjoying the smells of a working bakery. It all seemed too quiet and idyllic. Until you remembered that Brad was probably on his way. Most likely he would drive up from Portland. And then he would come here. Connor wanted to be here when he arrived. There was no way he was going to let Jill face him alone.

Jill was chatting about something or other. He wasn't paying much attention. He was too busy enjoying her, smiling at the flour on her face, watching the way her body moved, the way her breasts were swelling just inside the opening of her shirt, those long, silky legs. She'd always been his main crush, but now she was becoming something more. He wanted her and his body was letting him know the need was getting stronger.

From the beginning, it had seemed she was strangely dominated, almost mesmerized, by Brad. She'd been Brad's and he'd been crazy jealous, but he'd never thought he would have a chance with her. Now, he did. It all depended on how strong that bond between them still was.

He had his own bond with her—didn't he? Even if she didn't feel it, he did. She walked out toward where he was sitting at the table, talking about something he wasn't really listening to and stopping near him. Reaching out, he caught her wrist and tugged her closer. She looked down at him, saw the darkness in his eyes, and her own eyes widened, and then her mouth softened and she sank down beside him.

She hadn't hesitated. She'd come to him as soon as she saw he wanted her to. That filled him with a bright new sense of wonder. He wanted to hold her forever, make a declaration, make love to her and make her his own.

He wrapped her in his arms and she sighed as he

began to drop small, impatient kisses along the line of her neck. She turned, giving him more access to her body in a way he hadn't expected.

His heart was pounding now, filling him with a sort of excitement he hadn't felt for a long, long time. She was warm and soft and rounded in the best places for it. He kissed just under her ear and suddenly she was turning in his arms, moaning, searching for his mouth with hers, and then that was all there was.

The kiss. It took his breath away at the same time it put his brain into orbit. He couldn't think. He could only feel. And taste. And ache for her.

Jill felt his release, his acceptance of the desire swelling between them, and she was tempted to give way to it as well. She knew this had to stop but for the moment, she couldn't find the strength to make it happen. She hungered for his heat, longed for his touch, moved beneath his hands as though she couldn't get enough of him.

There was no way to stop this feeling. Was it love? Was it loneliness that needed healing? Or was it a basic womanly demand that smoldered deep inside all the time, hidden by the events of the day, and only revealed when the right man touched her?

That was it. She'd known passion before, but this was different. She not only wanted his body, but she also needed his heart and soul, and for once, she thought she just might have a chance to get that.

She was drowning in his kiss. His mouth tasted better than anything she'd ever known. She writhed with it, moaned and made tiny cries as though she could capture the heat and keep it forever in her body. And then reality began to swim back into focus and she tried to pull away.

It wasn't easy. His kisses were so delicious and his hands felt so good. But it had to be done. There were cakes in the oven. There were children waking up from their naps.

Reality. Darn it all.

"Jill," he murmured, his face buried in her curly hair, "we're going to have to find a way to do something about this."

"Are we?" But she smiled. Her body was still resonating with the trembling need for him, and she totally agreed. Somehow, they had to do something about it—soon.

The shadows were longer. Afternoon was flowing into evening. The boys were stirring and Connor went up to supervise their waking. He got them changed and brought them down to play in the playroom, listening as they called back and forth with what seemed like their own special language.

The doorbell rang and he stiffened. He didn't think Brad could have gotten here this fast unless he flew. But it was a possibility.

He went out into the entryway. It wasn't Brad. Jill was talking to the mailman and signing for a certified letter. She closed the door and ripped the letter open.

"What in the world is this going to be?" she muttered, her mind on her cakes. Then she looked at the letter. Frowning, she looked at it again.

"What does this mean?" she asked Connor.

He glanced over her shoulder and frowned. "It looks like the bank is calling your loan."

She gasped. "Are they allowed to do that?"

"Let me see the letter." He read it over more carefully. "Okay, it says here that their investigation has revealed that you have insufficient security and they don't trust your collateral." He looked at her. "You used this house, didn't you?"

She nodded, her eyes wide with alarm.

He went back to the letter. "They also claim that, if you study your contract, you will find it has a 'Due for Any Reason Clause' which allows them to call the loan without having to justify it." He stared at her in distaste. "Just because they want to." His face darkened as he thought that through. "Or because someone bribes them to do it," he suggested.

She stared at him and then she whispered, "Brad?"

He shrugged. "You probably won't ever be able to prove it."

She took the letter and read it again. That was what it said. Her loan was being called. There was no doubt in her mind that Brad had something to do with this.

She was shaking. Everything she tried to do seemed to fail. She wasn't getting anywhere. It was so hard—it was like running in quicksand. In her worst nightmares, she'd never thought of this. How could he do this to her?

"He won't ever cut me free, will he?" She raised her tragic gaze to Connor's blue one. "He doesn't want me, but he still wants to manipulate me. He still wants to control my life." Her voice got higher. "Am I doomed to be tied to this man forever? That's like being married without any of the perks. I just have to obey, forget the love and all that other stuff."

Connor took her shoulders and held her firmly.

"Jill, calm down. I know it's frustrating, but maybe if you find out exactly what he thinks he wants."

"Like what? For me to get rid of the boys?" She knew she looked wild. And why not? She felt wild. "You actually think I would consider something like that?"

"No, of course not." He hesitated. "But I don't think that's what he's after right now."

"Really? And why do you know so much about what he's after? Did he tell you?" Her face changed as she realized what she'd said. "That's it, isn't it?" She stared at him. "You know what he wants. You just haven't told me yet."

He had a bad feeling about where this train of thought was leading. He took a deep breath. "Jill…"

She backed away from him. "Okay, Connor," she said coldly, her face furious. "Are you finally ready to tell me what Brad wants from me? What he sent you to tell me?"

He tried to touch her but she pulled away.

"Tell me," she demanded.

He shook his head, knowing she was in no mood to hear this and think logically. But he didn't have any choice. He had to tell her. He should have done it sooner. But still he hesitated, not sure how to approach it.

"Brad asked me to talk to you," he admitted. "But I never told him I would. And once I saw you again, I knew I would never do his dirty work for him. If he wanted to ask you something he had to come and do it himself."

"I see," she said cynically. At this point, she was ready to believe the worst of anyone and everyone. "So you decided for some reason, I wasn't ready. I wasn't softened up enough. You decided to go slow. You needed to sweeten me up, flatter me a little, get me ready for the slaughter."

"Jill..." He shook his head, appalled that she would think that.

She drew in a trembling breath. "I can't believe you would gang up on me with Brad this way."

That was like a knife through his heart. "I'm not."

She wasn't listening. "So how about it, Connor? Am I ready now? Are you going to stop lying and tell me the truth?"

He shook his head. He might as well get this over with. "Okay, Jill. What Brad wants is those company shares he gave you when you divorced. He thinks he needs them back."

She looked surprised. "Why?"

He shrugged. "I think he's having a fight with some of the other shareholders. He wants to stop a power play by some who are getting together to outvote him on some company policies."

She pressed her lips together and thought about that for a moment. Then she glared at him again.

"Is that all? Really? Then why didn't you tell me the truth from the beginning?"

He turned away, grimacing. Then he turned back. "I asked you before, Jill, and I'm going to ask you again.

You've hinted now and then that you would take Brad back if you could. Do you still feel that way?"

She thought for a moment, pacing from him to the glass door and back again. "What I really want is to have my life back. Do you understand that? I chose Brad to be at my side forever and I gave birth to two angels, two gifts for him." She stared at him with haunted eyes. "So why did he reject them? Why did he reject me and the life we'd both created together? I want that life."

He winced. That wasn't really what he'd wanted to hear.

"I want things to be like they used to be. I want my life back."

"So you still want Brad back."

She didn't answer that.

Who was he to tell her it couldn't happen? Stranger things had.

"Nothing has changed?" he asked her, incredulous.

She shook her head. "Of course. Everything has changed." Anger flashed through her eyes like flames from a fire. "And now you've proven you stand with Brad."

He grimaced. He couldn't let her think he wasn't behind her one hundred percent. "Jill, listen to me. Seeing you again, I realized how much I care for you. How much I missed you and all you've always meant to me. I want you for myself. I don't want Brad to have anything to do with...with our relationship."

She stared at him as though she hadn't heard a word he'd said. "But you've kept in constant contact with him, haven't you? Isn't he always calling on your phone?"

"Yes, but…"

"Connor, you lied to me!"

"No, I didn't. That's ridiculous."

"Yes, you did. You led me to believe Brad didn't really want anything. And now I come to find out, he wanted it all."

Tears filled her eyes and she turned away, walking back into the kitchen. That was her default position. The kitchen was the center of her world. She went to the counter and turned to face him, hugging her arms in around herself.

"Jill," he said as he caught up with her. "I know this looks bad to you, but I didn't lie. When you asked, I just didn't answer."

"That's the same as a lie." She shook her head. "I can't trust you."

"Okay, Jill. I understand that you're really angry, and I'm sorry. But…"

She narrowed her eyes and hardened her heart. "I think it's time for you to leave, Connor. Way past time."

He shook his head. Pain filled him, pain and regret. "Don't do this, Jill. Wait until you've calmed down. Think it over. I…I don't want to leave you here on your own."

"You have to. I can't trust you. I want you to go."

His eyes were tortured but she didn't relent. She had to have some time and space to think, to go over all that had happened in the last few days and decide if she could ever, ever talk to him again.

He winced. "You know that at some time soon, Brad will be coming, don't you?"

She blinked at him. "Why?"

"Because he wants those shares. He's not going to rest until he gets them. If he has to come here to do that, he will."

She was seething. "If you knew that, why didn't you tell me before? Why didn't you warn me?"

He had no answer for that.

"Go," she said. "You've helped me with some things, but you've undermined me at the same time. I need you to go."

He started to say something, but she pointed toward the door. Shaking his head, he turned away. Then he looked back and said over his shoulder, "Call me if you need me," and he left.

She watched him walk away until tears flooded her eyes and she couldn't see anything anymore.

"Connor, Connor, how could you betray me like this?" she murmured.

The one person she thought she had in her corner, that she could count on when things got rough, the only one that she could really trust in this world besides Sara had turned out to be lying to her. And now it turned out all she had left was Sara.

She sank to the floor of the kitchen and hung her head and cried.

Connor was headed back to the mainland, but before he went, he had one last thing he had to do. He knew Sara lived only about a mile away, but her bungalow was right on the beach. Turning down the narrow road, he found her house easily. He'd been there before.

Walking up to the front door, he saw Sara in the side yard, trimming roses. He approached carefully but she still jumped when she saw him.

"Hey, Sara," he said. "We need to talk."

She backed away looking wary. "Connor, I don't want to talk to you. I already know how I feel about everything and I don't need you messing with my mind."

"Sara, come on. You know we both love Jill. Right?"

Sara made a face, but she nodded reluctantly.

"And you know that she's not going to let that baby go anywhere else, don't you? Not if she can help it."

Sara looked away.

"If you won't take her, your sister will. There's just no two ways about it."

Sara turned and looked at him pleadingly. "Can't you talk her out of it?"

"You know the answer to that. Nobody can talk her out of it." He looked down and kicked the dirt. "And we both know that taking on another baby is going to be hard. She doesn't need to have something that hard. She's already got far too much on her plate, far too much that she has to handle alone." He looked up at her. "So there's only one thing left to do. And you know what it is."

She shook her head with a jerky motion. Her face was a study in tragedy. "No," she said. "I can't."

He was quiet for a minute and she snipped off a few more dead blossoms. He listened to the water lapping against the shore not too far from where they stood. Seagulls called and a flock of low-flying pelicans swooped by.

Her hair was still slicked back into a bun at the back of her head. She'd changed into slacks and a fuzzy pullover, but she managed to look like a fully functioning professional anyway. There was something about her that spoke of competence and dignity. But when he looked at her face, all he saw was fear and sadness.

Finally he spoke to her quietly.

"Sara, come sit down with me."

She edged closer, but she still acted as though she was afraid he might have something catching.

"Come on." He sat down on a wicker chair and nodded toward the little wicker couch. She walked over slowly and sat down, but she wouldn't look at him.

"Thanks, Sara. I want to tell you about someone I got to know well in Singapore. Her name is Sharon Wong. She's a very fine chef. A few years ago, her neighbor died, leaving behind a three-year-old girl. Sharon had gotten to know them both during the neighbor's illness. She took her broths and things and watched the child for her at times.

"When the woman died, Social Services came to take away the child, and Sharon realized what a nightmare that baby faced. Who knew who would end up caring for her? Maybe someone good. Maybe not. Maybe she would be in an institution for the rest of her childhood. She watched how the Social Services people treated that little girl and she made up her mind that she couldn't let this happen.

"So she stepped in and took the baby herself. When I met her, the girl was six years old, bright as a penny and sweet as candy. A delight. And Sharon told me that this little girl had enriched her life like nothing she'd ever dreamed might happen to her."

"And then she told me about a saying she'd heard lately. No one on their deathbed ever says they should have spent more time at the office. When you get down to what really counts, it's family."

Sara turned tragic eyes his way. "But I don't really have that kind of family," she said softly.

"Not now. But that doesn't mean you won't."

She stared at him, shaking her head. "Connor, if I had a choice right now between having a terrific career, or meeting a terrific guy, I'd take the career. I've had enough disappointment with terrific guys."

He shrugged as he rose to leave. "Guys are one thing. Babies are another." Reaching over, he kissed her cheek. She didn't turn away. She caught his hand and held it for a moment, looking deep into his eyes.

"See you later, Sara. Do the right thing, okay?"

And he walked away.

Jill was wandering through her house like a ghost. It was after dark and she hadn't put on any of the down-stairs lights yet. The boys were in bed and sound asleep. She was alone.

Her mind was a jumble of thoughts, none of them very coherent. She was so angry with Connor, and at the same time, she was so hurt that he would still be on Brad's side after all he'd seen her go through. Why had he come all the way back just to prove to her that she really wanted him—only to say, "Sorry, I'm with

Brad. He's such an old friend." That thought made her furious all over again.

She heard the front door opening and she stopped in her tracks, heart beating wildly. Who was this going to be?

"Anybody home?"

She let her held breath out in a whoosh. It was Sara.

Seconds later, Sara came into the family room where Jill was standing.

"What's going on? How come no lights?"

She wasn't going to tell her it was to hide her swollen eyes and tear-stained face. She would see that for herself soon enough.

Sara went ahead and turned on the overhead without asking permission. It must have seemed a natural thing to do.

"Hey, Jill. I've got to talk to you." Compared to the last time Jill had seen her, she seemed to be brimming with energy.

Slowly Jill shook her head, staying to the shadows as much as she could. "Sara, sweetie, not now."

She thought Sara would notice from her voice that this was not a good time, but no. Sara charged ahead as though she hadn't said a thing.

"Wait. I'm sure you're busy, but this will just take a minute and it may help take a load off your mind."

Jill threw up her hands in surrender. "Anything that will do that," she muttered and tried to smile. "What is it?"

Sara came and stood before her, looking as earnest as Jill had ever seen her look.

"I've thought about this long and hard. I've looked at all the angles. And I've decided. I want to take Kelly's baby."

That was a jolt from the blue. "What are you saying? You can't possibly do that and take the job in L.A. Can you?"

"No." She shook her head. "I'm turning the job down."

"What? Oh, Sara, no!"

"Yes. A job is just a job. A baby is a human being. And this human being is even a part of our family, whether we like it or not." She smiled. "And I've decided to like it."

It was true that she looked much better, much healthier, than she had earlier that day when she had been so frightened of the entire concept. That was good. If it was really going to last.

She took her sister's hands in hers. "But, Sara, why?"

"It's a funny thing. I wanted a traditional life so badly. I planned my wedding from the time I was five years old. You know that. But every romance I tried to have ended badly. I just couldn't seem to find a man who fit me. I finally got hurt one too many times and I gave up all that. It's just too painful. No more romance. No more man who was wrong for me."

Jill nodded. She'd been there and watched it all. "I know all this. But what does it have to do with taking the baby?"

"I decided maybe I was going at it from the wrong side. Maybe if I find a baby who fits me, I'll have my family without having to find a man first."

Oh, no. Sara had lost her mind.

"Sara, babies don't provide miracles. Please don't go into this thinking it's going to be a piece of cake. Don't depend on a baby to make you happy, to solve all your problems."

She waved that away. "Oh, please, Jill. Give me some credit. I know that. I've been with you enough with the twins to know that raising a child is no picnic."

"You got that right."

"But anyway, you're the one who always picks up the slack for everyone else. You do your big sister routine and go all noble on me, and I let you, because then I get out of doing things I don't want to do."

"Oh, Sara, please. We're not kids anymore."

"No, but we're still sisters." She gave Jill a hug. "So I decided. It's time I took my turn. I want Kelly's baby."

Jill took a deep breath and realized, suddenly what a weight she'd been carrying. "Oh, Sara, I hope you know what you're doing."

"I do."

She hugged her again and held her close, then leaned back and looked at her. "What changed your mind? What made you see it that way?"

"Connor."

"Connor?" She was thunderstruck.

She heaved a heavy sigh. "Yes, it was Connor. He gave me a good talking-to and then told me about a friend of his. Some woman in Singapore…"

"Sharon Wong?"

"That's the one. Do you know her?"

"No."

"Well, he sat me down and made me take a more realistic look at life."

"He did?" Jill felt dizzy.

"Yeah. Where is he?"

"He's a…"

"You know, that is one great guy. You'd better not let him slip away. He's a treasure." She looked around the room and toward the back porch. "So where is he, anyway?"

"I, uh, he left."

Her head swung around. "Left? Where did he go? What happened?"

"I told him to leave."

"Oh, Jill… You didn't!"

"I did. I told him to go. I was so angry."

"Why?"

She took a deep breath and tried to remember it all, including the incredible pain she'd felt. Quickly she explained to Sara about the loan being called, and how Connor thought Brad was behind it. Then she went on to fill in her problems with Connor.

"He didn't tell me the truth about what Brad wanted and when I found out that he wanted me to sell him the shares I swore I would never give up, I just…I felt like he was manipulating me. Like I couldn't trust him. Like he was on Brad's side again. Why didn't he prepare me to know what Brad was up to?"

"You think he's on Brad's side?"

Jill nodded.

Sara stared at her. "What are you, nuts? You do realize he's crazy in love with you, don't you?"

She shook her head. "Sara, I don't think—"

"You can see it in the way he looks at you."

She hesitated. "Do you really think so?"

"Come on, he's always had a crush on you. And now I think it's developed into full-blown mad love. He's insanely in love with you."

Jill was feeling dizzy again. "We've always been friends."

"No. It's more than that." Sara threw up her hands. "He wants you, babe. Don't let that one get away."

"I just got so frustrated. And…and so jealous."

"Jealous?"

She nodded. "I mean—is he my friend or Brad's? It makes a difference."

Sara nodded wisely. "I told him that the first day he was here. I told him if he was going to be your friend, he had to get rid of Brad. And you know what? He was ready to do it."

Jill wasn't so sure. Sara could go off like a runaway train at times. But she listened to her sister and they talked about how she was going to manage to take care of a baby, and after she left, she went back over what she'd said about Connor and she felt more confused than ever.

There was no doubt about it, she wanted Connor back. For the past couple of days, he'd been her shelter against the storm. Why on earth was she making him go?

But maybe it was for the best. After all, she didn't want him to be here if he was Brad's friend more than he was hers. What was the truth? She was overwhelmed by the emotions churning inside her.

But she knew one thing: it was time to face facts. She loved Connor. She'd probably loved him for years and hadn't been able to admit it to herself. But she could remember countless times that she'd been frustrated with Brad and wished he could be more like Connor. She'd known forever that Connor fit her better than Brad did. They looked at life through much the same lens. They liked the same things, laughed at the same jokes. Brad always seemed restless and disapproving. Why had she put up with it for so long?

And Connor was so darn sexy. She'd always felt a certain buzz around him. Brad was more demanding, more dominant. Connor was more easygoing. More her type. What a fool she'd been all these years.

She loved Connor. Wow.

Except for one little tiny problem. No matter what Sara said, she was pretty sure he didn't love her. He liked her fine, he always had. But he liked a lot of girls. And when push came to shove, he was better friends with Brad than he was with her. And that hurt.

In fact, it cut deep. Brad had been so awful to her. It had taken time, but she'd finally come to a place where she could look into the past and face the truth. She'd been blinded by a lot of things when she'd thought she loved Brad. A lot of those things were not too flattering to her. She'd been a fool. Now she could look Brad squarely in the eye and say, "Brad, you're a real jerk." At least, she thought she could.

She had to get that out of her system because, like it

or not, Brad was her boys' father. There was no hiding from that. Even Brad couldn't pretend it didn't matter. They would always be tied to him in ways he couldn't control.

So Connor had tried to help her in his way, and now she'd kicked him out. Maybe that wasn't the wisest thing to do, but she couldn't pretend with Connor. She was in love with him. What if he knew that? What if he saw it in her face, in her reactions? Would he use it against her? She didn't know, because she really couldn't trust him.

Why hadn't he told her the truth right from the beginning so that she could get prepared for any sort of attack from Brad? Now she was going to have to deal with Brad on her own.

That was going to be hard to do. Brad had a domineering way about him and she'd been trained over the years to yield to him. It almost came naturally to her. She was going to have to fight against that impulse. She couldn't let him walk all over her. And once he realized she wasn't going to obey him, what next? He would find some way to make her pay. Brad was capable of doing almost anything.

Life was becoming impossible. What was she going to do? She was probably going to lose her house and lose her business. She couldn't meet the loan call. She was going to go under like a small boat in heavy swells.

The only way out she could see was to sell her shares to Brad. She didn't want to do it. She especially hated to do anything that might make him happy. But she wasn't going to have any choice. Her options had just become even more limited.

Well, she might end up that way, but she intended to put up a fight as long as she could. She would see how well she could stand up to Brad when she really tried. Live and learn.

In the meantime, all she could do was sit here and wait for Brad to show up.

CHAPTER TEN

CONNOR CHECKED BACK into his hotel. As he started for the elevators, he heard "Mambo!" coming from the dining room dance floor and he couldn't resist looking in to see if Karl was back. Sure enough, and dancing with a bewildered looking redhead. Connor ducked back out quickly. He didn't want to scare Karl off.

He ordered something from room service and watched the news and then he turned off the TV and went out and walked the Seattle streets for a couple of hours. This was a city he knew well. He'd grown up not far away in a small town, and then gone to the University. The years after college had been spent right here. It was home in a sense. He could live here. He didn't need anything else.

Except Jill. He needed Jill more than he needed air to breathe.

His cell received a text and he flipped it out to see who it was. Brad had finally answered him.

"You're right," he said. "I need to come and get what I need myself. I'll be there in the morning."

So Brad was coming to work his magic on Jill. What

did he think—that he could walk in and hypnotize her into doing things his way? Or was he ready to give her what she'd always wanted—marriage and a promise to try to be a father to his kids?

That night he couldn't sleep. He spent the time staring at the ceiling and going over what had happened over the last few days. He knew he was following a familiar pattern. He'd begun to let his feelings for Jill come out and actually show themselves, but once Jill backed away, so did he. He'd walked off and left the field to Brad so many times, it seemed the natural thing to do.

But it wasn't. It was time he made up his mind, declared himself, and claimed Jill for himself. This was probably his last chance to do it. What the hell was he waiting for?

Damn it, she needed him. He was the only one who loved her the way she needed to be loved. He was the only one ready to protect her and make her happy, the only one who was ready to help her raise her kids. The only other person he needed to convince was Jill herself. And that was the only part he was still a little shaky on.

He was a realist and he knew there was a chance that Brad would offer to take Jill back, and he knew there was a chance she would take him up on it. She yearned to have the boys' father back fulfilling his role, giving them what they needed. Whether she yearned for the man himself in the same way, he wasn't sure. But he wasn't going to let things take their natural course and see what happened. No. Not this time. He was going to fight for the woman he loved.

He ate an early breakfast in the coffee shop and then he headed for the ferry landing. He got out of the car during the crossing and looked up at the house Jill and Brad had bought together when their marriage was young and the company was all they cared about. How quickly things could change.

He was pretty sure Brad would show up sometime today. And how Jill reacted to that would tell the tale. He meant to play a part, regardless. And if he had to tell a few home truths to his old friend, he was ready to do it. He drew in a lungful of sea air and began to prepare for what he was going to do.

Jill had the children up and dressed and ready to go first thing in the morning. She'd hardly slept at all but she had done a lot of thinking. She was definitely staring at a fork in her life's road. Would she bow to Brad, or would she fight for Connor? Could she find a way to make Connor want her more than he wanted to be friends with Brad? If she couldn't do that, it was all over. But if she didn't even try, how would she ever know?

She planned to leave the twins with Sara and then she was heading to the mainland. She was going to go and find Connor and tell him she loved him. Her blood pounded in her ears. She was so scared. But she had to take the chance. Like Sara said, she couldn't let him slip away.

She'd let the boys out to play in the backyard while she got things ready and she was just about to get them and put them into the car when she heard the front door close. She stopped, listening.

"Sara?" she called at last. "Is that you?"

There was no answer. She swallowed hard, glancing toward the side door and thinking of making a run for it, one child under each arm. But before she could try that out, Brad appeared in the doorway to the kitchen.

"No," he said, watching her coolly. "It's me."

It was still early and once Connor got across the channel, he decided to take a run around the island before he went up to the house. The trip was as pretty as it had ever been, with trees and a lush growth of flowers that was almost tropical in its glory. What a wonderful place to choose to raise a family.

As he came back around, he stopped at a light and looked down at the ferry landing. The next one had arrived, and the first car coming off was a silver Porsche. He knew right away that had to be Brad.

Staying where he was, he watched as the car climbed the hill and turned into Jill's driveway, then parked in front of the entryway. Brad got out and headed for the front door, and Connor gritted his teeth and counted to ten. He had to force back the rage that threatened to overwhelm him. If he came face-to-face with Brad right now, he would surely end up bloodying the man's nose. He had to give it a minute.

Once he was calmer, he turned his car up toward the house, parking on the street. He got out just as he saw Brad disappearing inside.

Striding quickly up the hill, he went around back,

quietly opening the door to the screened-in porch, which opened onto the kitchen. Ten to one she would be there. He stopped and listened.

Jill was shaking. She only hoped Brad couldn't tell. How many times had she imagined this scene? Here he was, in the flesh.

This was the first time he'd been back to their house since the divorce. The first time she'd seen him in over a year. She shoved her unruly hair back behind her ears and tried to smile.

"It's good to see you, Brad," she said breathlessly.

His eyes had been cold as steel when he'd first come in, but as she watched, they began to warm. "Jill," he said, and held out his hands to her.

She hesitated for a few seconds, but she took them. They were warm. He was so cool and confident. And here she was, rattled and skittish as a baby bird.

"I've missed you," he said.

She blinked at him. Why did his lies always sound so sincere?

"Where's Connor?" he asked.

"Oh, he...he left. Last night."

"Ah," he said, and she could tell he thought Connor had left because he was coming. "Probably a good thing," he said almost to himself. "Did he ever give you my message?" he asked.

She took a deep breath. "Why don't you just tell me what that message is?"

"I don't want to rush things. How about a cup of coffee while we talk over old times?"

He was so cool, so ready to treat her like dirt and pretend she deserved it. She dug deep inside. She couldn't let him maneuver her. This was her home and he was the invader.

"I...I don't have any coffee ready," she told him. "Why don't you just get on with it? I'd like to know where we stand."

He didn't like that. She could see the annoyance flash in his eyes. "Okay," he said shortly. "Here's the deal. I need those shares, Jill. You have fifteen percent of my company. I'm going to have to ask for them back."

"Really? And what if I want to keep them?"

He looked as though he could hardly believe she was being so obstinate. "No, don't you understand? I need them. I'm fighting off a mini rebellion and I need them to regain the advantage." He frowned. He could see she wasn't bending for him the way he thought she should. "Listen, I'll make it worth your while. I'm prepared to pay you quite handsomely for them."

He named a figure that didn't sound all that handsome to her. If he could pay that for shares, why couldn't he pay child support? But she knew the answer to that. Because he didn't want to.

"I'm being attacked by some of the other shareholders who are conspiring against me. I need those shares to defend myself. And of course, if you ever hope to get any more money out of me, you'd better help."

She found herself staring at him. The fear had melted away. He was just a big jerk. There was no reason to let him intimidate her.

"Brad, I'm not interested in selling. I feel that those

shares are a legacy of sorts for the boys. I want them to be there for them when they grow up, both as an investment and for traditional reasons."

His jaw tightened. "All right, I'll double the offer."

She shook her head. "But that's not the point. I want the boys to have something from their father. I'm just sorry you don't feel the same way."

"Are you crazy? What do those brats have to do with my company?"

She glared at him. Didn't he have any human feelings at all? "We built that company together, you, me and Connor. It was a work of joy and friendship between us all at the time."

"That's a crock. I had the idea, I worked out the plans, I did the development. You two were filler. The company is mine. You had very little to do with it." He grunted. "And those kids didn't have anything to do with it."

Her fingers were trembling but she was holding firm. "Whether or not you want to acknowledge them, those kids are yours. They have your DNA. They wouldn't exist without you. Though you may never be a real father to them, this will give them something to know about you, to feel they've been given a gift from you."

"That's ridiculous. It's sentimental garbage." He shook his head as though he just couldn't understand her attitude. "Jill, what's happened to you? You were once my biggest supporter. You would have done anything to help me. And now…"

For just a moment she remembered him as he used to be, so young and handsome, with the moonlight in his

eyes and a kiss on his mind. She thought of how it was
when they were first married and he had let her know
how much he wanted her, every minute of the day. She'd
thought it would always be like that. She'd been wrong.

But thinking about what used to be had the effect of
cooling her anger. They did have a past. She couldn't
ignore that. She took a deep breath and made her voice
softer, kinder, more understanding.

"Brad, I did support you for so many years. But what
you've done has undermined that. Lately you have done
nothing but stand in my way. And you expect me to
bend over backward for you?"

He controlled his own anger and tried to smile. "You
know what, you're right. And that wasn't really fair of
me." He tried to look sincere. "But everything I do is
for the good of the company. You know that."

She shrugged. That wasn't good enough to justify
what he'd done.

He stared at her for a long moment, then nodded and
adjusted his stance. He was good at sizing up the other
side and finding a way to adapt to new facts.

"Okay, Jill. I understand. You need something more."
He nodded, thinking for a moment. "Here's the deal. I
want full ownership of the company. I need it. I'm willing to take you back to get it."

She almost fell over at his words. "You'll take me
back?"

"Yes, I will."

Unbelievable. "And the boys?"

He turned and looked at the twins playing on the hill
behind the house. "Is that them?"

She nodded.

"Sure, why not?" He turned back, his eyes hard and cold as steel. "Have we got a deal?"

She stared at him. What could she say? Did she have a right to hand away her children's connection with their father? But what was that connection worth? Why hadn't she ever seen the depths of his vile selfishness before? His soul was corrupt.

"Brad, you've really surprised me with this. I never thought you would make such an offer."

"So what do you say?"

"She says 'no.'" Suddenly Connor was in the room with them.

"Hello, Brad," he said, his tone hard and icy. "She says 'no deal.' Sorry."

She looked from Brad to Connor and back again, confused. Where had he come from? She wasn't sure, but suddenly he was there and suddenly Brad didn't look so smooth and sure of himself.

"Connor," Brad said, looking annoyed. "I thought you were gone."

"I was. But I'm back."

Brad looked unsure. "This is just a matter between me and Jill."

"No, it's not. I'm afraid there's been a change." Connor stood balanced, his stance wide, like a fighter. In every way, he was exuding a toughness she didn't think she'd ever seen in him before. "I'm involved now."

Brad looked bewildered. "What the hell are you talking about?"

"You're not married to Jill anymore. In fact, since

you won't acknowledge your own children, and from
what I understand, you hardly ever give them any
money, the only real substantial tie they have with you
is those shares."

He turned and looked at Jill. "Here's my advice.
Give him the shares. Let him buy them from you. Once
they're gone, and you and I are married, he won't have
any reason left to contact you in any way or have any
part in your life. You'll be free of him." He reached out
and touched her shoulder. "But of course, it's up to you.
What do you say?"

Jill stared at Connor. She heard his words but she
was having some trouble understanding them. Did he
mean…? Wait, what did he say about marrying her?
A bubble began to rise in her chest—a bubble of happiness. She wanted to dance and laugh and sing, all at
once.

"Connor?" she said, smiling at him in wonder. "Are
you feeling okay?"

He gave her a half smile back. "I'm feeling fine.
How about you?"

"I think I'm going to faint." She reached out and he
caught hold, steadying her against him. She put an arm
around his waist and pulled even closer, looking up at
him with laughter bubbling out all over.

He gazed down at her and grinned. He had a good
feeling about how this was turning out. There was only
one last test. Was she ready to cut all ties to Brad?
"What do you think about selling back the shares?"
he asked her.

She nodded happily. Suddenly she knew that she just

didn't care about the shares. All her excuses had been hogwash meant to give her an excuse to not do what Brad wanted. But she didn't care about that anymore. She didn't have to care about Brad. She was going to care about her family, and he wasn't in it. He'd given up that chance long ago.

"I think you're right," she said. "I liked that second offer."

Brad looked uncertain.

Connor shrugged at him. "There you go. Hand over the money, Brad. Let's see the glint of your gold."

"Hey, she just said…"

"I don't care what you heard. She'll take the second offer. Or would you rather have her contact the people in the company who are fighting you and see how much they'll offer?"

Brad frowned at him, shooting daggers of hate, but he pulled out his checkbook. He wrote out a check and handed it to Jill. She looked at it, held it up to the light, then nodded and put it down, leaving the room to get her documentation. In a moment she was back.

"Here are the shares," she said. "There you go. It's all you now, Brad. You don't need me for anything anymore. Right?"

Brad didn't say a word.

"Let's make a pact," Jill said. "Let's not see each other ever again. Okay?"

He seemed completely bewildered. "Jill. Don't you remember what we once had together?"

She snorted. "Don't you remember what you did to me eighteen months ago?"

One last disgruntled look and Brad headed for the door. Connor pulled Jill into his arms and smiled down at her.

"I hope you don't feel like I coerced you into that."

"Not at all. I think it was the perfect solution. If he'd come and asked me in a humble, friendly way, I would have handed them back to him at any time. It was just when he acted like such a jerk, I couldn't stand the thought of giving in to him."

"At least you made him pay for them."

She shook her head and laughed. "It is so worth it to get him out of my life."

He searched her dark eyes. "You're sure there's nothing left? You don't love him?"

"How can you even ask that?" She touched his face with her fingertips. "I love you," she said, her voice breaking on the word. "It's taken a while to get that through my skull, but it's true."

He shook his head, laughing softly. "That's quite a relief. I wasn't sure."

She smiled and snuggled into his arms. "I'm not even going to ask if you still consider Brad your best friend. Actions speak louder than words. You showed me."

"You're my best friend," he told her lovingly.

She pursed her lips, looking up at him with her brows drawn together. "And the new baby?" she asked, just testing reality. "Are you really willing to take that one on with me?"

"Of course. It's going to be crazy around here with all these kids, but I think I can handle it." He went to the sliding glass door and called the boys and they came running.

"Well," Jill said, "the truth is, Kelly's baby is going to be living with Sara."

He turned and looked at her. "Ah. She came around, did she?"

"Thanks to you."

He shook his head. "She was going to get there eventually. It just took some time for the shock to wear off."

Jill looked at him with stars in her eyes. He was so good and so ready to be a part of this family and commit to them all, even to her sister. And the new baby. She hardly knew how to contain her happiness.

The twins roared in and headed for the sunroom and she went back into Connor's arms. This was where she really belonged. This is where she was going to stay. Forever was a long, long time, but she was ready to promise it.

"I love you," she whispered to him.

"I've always loved you," he told her, his gaze dark with adoration and longing. "So I win."

"Oh, no, my handsome husband-to-be. If anyone is a winner here, it's me." And she kissed him hard, just to make sure he knew it.

* * * * *

DADDY'S DOUBLE DUTY

STELLA BAGWELL

To my late father,
Louis Copeland Cook,
who always said don't do anything
unless you intend to do it right.
I hope he thinks I have.

Chapter One

His secretary was crying!

Conall Donovan stared at the woman behind the cherrywood desk. Vanessa Valdez had been in his employ for more than two months and during that time she'd been nothing but cool and professional. He could hardly imagine what had brought about these waterworks. In the past hour, he hadn't even yelled once! And even if he had, it wouldn't have been directed at her. She was the epitome of a perfect, professional secretary.

Cautiously, he approached the desk. "Vanessa? Is something wrong?"

With one slender hand dabbing a tissue to her cheek, the petite brunette glanced at him. At thirty-five, she looked more like twenty-five, Conall thought. And though he wouldn't describe her as gorgeous, she was an attractive woman with honey-brown hair brushing the tops of her shoulders and curling in pretty wisps around her head. Usually, her large brown eyes were soft and luminous but presently her eyes were full of tears.

"I'm sorry," she said in a strained voice. "It's... I... Something has happened."

"Your father? Has he taken ill?" he demanded.

Vanessa paused and he could see her throat working as she tried to swallow. The sight of her discomposure struck him unexpectedly hard. In spite of her being an old family acquaintance, they hardly shared a close bond. For the most part, the woman kept to herself. The only reason he knew she'd lost her mother two years ago, and that her aging father now resided in a nursing home, was because he happened to attend the same small church where her parents had been regular members. Still, these past months, Vanessa had become a quiet and dependable fixture in his life and he'd come to respect her dedication to this job and the subtle finesse she used with clients in order to make his life easier.

"No," she answered. "It's not my father."

When she failed to elaborate, Conall fought back an impatient sigh. He hardly had time to play mind reader.

"Do you need to take the rest of the afternoon off?" he asked bluntly. There was still a hell of a lot of work that he needed finished by the end of the day, but if necessary he'd somehow manage without her. Even if it meant calling on his mother, Fiona, to fill in for the remainder of the afternoon.

Shaking her head, his secretary sniffed and tried to straighten her shoulders. Even so, Conall could see tears sparkling upon her smooth cheeks and he was shocked at the sudden urge he felt to round the desk and wipe them away.

Hell, Conall, you've never been good at consoling women. Just ask your ex-wife. Besides, women and tears don't affect your iron heart. Not anymore.

While he shoved that unbidden thought away, she finally answered in a ragged voice, "I—I'll be all right, Conall. Just give me a few moments to…get over the shock."

Shock? As usual, the phone had been ringing all afternoon. The Diamond D Ranch was a huge conglomerate, with business connections all over the world. With it being the middle of summer, they were in the busy height of Thoroughbred racing season. His office was only one of several set in a modern brick building situated north of the ranch yard and west of the main ranch house. His younger brother Liam, the ranch's horse trainer, also had his own office along with a secretary, and then there was the general accounting for the ranch, which took up several rooms. As for Conall's job, he rarely saw a quiet moment during working hours and the overflow of correspondence kept his secretary extremely busy. Especially now that he'd also assumed the job of keeping the Golden Spur Mine operations running smoothly.

"Look, Vanessa, I realize I'm asking you to handle an undue amount of work for one human being. But it won't always be like this. I have plans to hire an assistant for you, just as soon as I have a chance to go over a few résumés."

Her brown eyes widened even more. "Oh, no, Conall, it's not the work!" She gestured toward the piles of correspondence lying about on her desk. "I can easily handle this. I just received a call from Las Vegas," she attempted to explain. "It was…horrible news. A dear friend has passed away. And I…well, I just can't believe she's gone. She was—"

Suddenly sobs overtook the remainder of her words and Conall could no longer stop himself from skirting the desk and taking a steadying hold on her trembling shoulders.

"I'm very sorry, Vanessa."

Averting her face from him, she whispered, "I'm okay. Really, I am."

Whether she was trying to reassure him or herself, or the both of them, Conall didn't know. In any case, she was clearly an emotional wreck and he had to do something to help her, even if it was wrong.

"No, you're hardly okay," he said gruffly. "You're shaking. Let me help you over to the couch."

With firm hands, he drew her up from the rolling desk chair and with an arm at her waist, guided her to a long leather couch positioned along the far wall.

"Just sit and try to relax," he ordered as he eased her small frame down. "I'll be back in a minute."

Once she was safely settled, Conall hurriedly crossed the room and stepped into his private office, where he kept an assortment of drinks to offer visiting business-men. After pouring a mug half-full of coffee, he splashed in a hefty amount of brandy and carried it out to her.

"Here," he told her. "Drink this. All of it."

With trembling hands wrapped around the heavy cup, she tilted the contents to her lips. After a few careful sips that made her gasp and cough, she lowered it and cast him an accusing glance.

"That has alcohol in it!"

"Not nearly enough," he said dryly.

"It's more than enough for me." Straightening her

shoulders, she offered the cup back to him. "Thank you. I can talk now."

Relieved to see a faint bit of color returning to her face, Conall took the cup and after placing it on the floor, he eased down beside her. "All right," he said gently. "Tell me what happened to your friend."

Closing her eyes, she pressed slender fingers against her forehead. Conall couldn't help but notice the long sweep of her lashes as they settled against her damp cheeks. Her complexion reminded him of a pink pearl bathed in golden sunlight and not for the first time he thought how her skin was the most fetching thing about her. Smooth and kissable.

Now why the hell was he thinking that sort of thing, especially at a time like this? Kissing a woman's soft skin was all in his past. And that was where it was going to stay.

With her eyes still closed, she began to speak. "I became friends with Hope Benson not long after I arrived in Las Vegas. We both worked as cocktail waitresses in the Lucky Treasure casino."

Conall was stunned. He'd not known that Vanessa had ever worked as a cocktail waitress. Not that it mattered. Everyone had to start somewhere. And she'd obviously climbed the ladder. A few months ago, when she'd left Nevada, she'd been a private secretary to a casino executive.

"I didn't realize you ever worked as a waitress," he mused, speaking his thoughts out loud.

The guttural sound in her throat was self-deprecating. "What did you expect, Conall? I left Hondo Valley with nothing. It took lots of long, hard hours to put myself through college."

Of course he'd known that Vanessa was from a poor

family. She was the same age as his sister Maura, and
the two women had been good friends ever since el-
ementary school. During those years, Vanessa had often
visited the ranch. Being two years older, Conall hadn't
paid much attention to her. With the house full of six
Donovan kids, there were always plenty of friends hanging around and Vanessa had simply been one more. The
main thing he recalled about her was that she'd been
very quiet, almost to the point of being a wallflower.

After Conall had gone away to college, he'd heard in
passing that Vanessa had moved to Nevada. That had
been fifteen years ago and since then he'd not heard
anything else about his sister's old friend. In fact, she'd
completely slipped his mind until two months ago, when
she'd called him about the secretarial job.

She'd moved back to Hondo Valley to stay, she'd told
him, and she was looking for a job. He was secretly
ashamed to admit that he'd not expected Vanessa to
be qualified. As a teenager, she'd seemed like the shy,
homemaker sort, who'd want to devote her life to raising a house full of kids and keeping a husband happy.
He couldn't imagine her as a career woman. But out of
courtesy to his sister, he'd invited her to come out to
the ranch for an interview. When she'd walked into his
office, Conall had been stunned to see a very professional young woman presenting him with an equally
impressive résumé. He'd hired her on the spot and since
that time had not once regretted his decision.

The soft sigh escaping her lips caught his attention
and he watched her eyes open, then level on his face. For
the moment her tears had disappeared, but in their place
he saw something that amounted to panic. A strange
emotion to be experiencing over a friend's demise, he
couldn't help thinking.

"Sorry," she said. "I didn't mean to sound defensive. God knows how He's blessed me. And now...I just don't know what to think, Conall. You see, Hope was pregnant. Something happened after she went into labor—I'm not exactly sure what. The lawyer didn't go into details. Except that she had to have an emergency C-section. Shortly afterward, she died from some sort of complications. I assume it had something to do with her heart condition—a genetic childhood thing. But she always appeared healthy and I thought the doctors were keeping everything under control. In fact, each time I'd talked with her, she'd assured me that she and the babies were doing fine."

Conall's attention latched on to one word. "Babies? Are you talking plural?"

Vanessa nodded. "Twins. A boy and a girl. They were born three days ago and Hope's lawyer has just now had a chance to go over the legalities of her will and wishes."

"And what does this have to do with you?" Conall asked.

Across the room the telephone on Vanessa's desk began to ring. She started to rise to answer it, but Conall caught her shoulder with a firm hand. "Forget the phone," he ordered. "Whoever it is will call back or leave a message. I want to hear the rest of this."

Groaning, Vanessa dropped her head and shook it back and forth as though she was in a dream. "It's unbelievable, Conall! Hope wanted me to have custody of her babies. I—I'm to be their mother."

"Mother?" The word burst from Conall's mouth before he could stop it. "Are you...serious?"

Her head shot up and for a brief moment she scowled

at him. "Very serious. Why? Do you think I'm incapable of being a mother?"

A grimace tightened his lips. Leave it to a woman to misread his words, he thought. "I don't doubt your abilities, Vanessa. I'm sure you have...great motherly instincts. I was questioning the validity of your friend's wishes. Isn't the father around?"

Her shoulders slumped as she thrust a shaky hand through her hair. "The father was only in Hope's life for a brief period before they went their separate ways. When she learned that she was pregnant, she contacted him with the news, but he wanted nothing to do with her or the babies. Seems as though he was already paying a hefty amount of child support to his ex-wife and he wasn't keen on adding more to his responsibilities. By then Hope had already come to the conclusion that he wasn't the sort of man she'd ever want back in her life. And she certainly didn't want him to have any claims to the babies. When she confronted him with legal documents, he was only too glad to sign away his parental rights."

"What a bastard," Conall muttered.

Vanessa sighed. "I knew she was making a mistake when she first got involved with the creep. But she really fell hard for him. Poor thing, she believed he loved her and she desperately wanted a big family. You see, she was adopted and didn't have many relatives."

"What about her parents?"

"If you mean her real parents, she never looked for them. She considered the Bensons to be her true parents. But when Hope was still very young, they were killed in the Loma Prieta earthquake in California," she said ruefully. "Luckily, Hope escaped being physically injured, but I don't think she ever got over the emotional loss of her parents."

"Damn. Sounds like your friend didn't have an easy life."

"No. Life is never easy for some," she sadly agreed. "Hope was forty-two. She figured this would be her last and only chance to have children. That's why she risked carrying the babies. Even though doctors had warned her about being pregnant with her type of heart condition, she wanted them desperately."

"Had you discussed any of this with your friend?" Conall asked. "I mean, about you becoming their mother if something happened to her?"

Vanessa nodded glumly. "At the very beginning of her pregnancy Hope asked me to be their godmother. I agreed. How could I not? The two of us had been good friends for a long time. We...went through some tough times together. And I wanted to reassure her that no matter what, I'd see that the babies would be well cared for. But I also kept telling her that she was going to be okay—that everything with her and the babies would be fine. I wanted her to concentrate on the future she was going to have with her children." Tears once again filled her eyes. "Oh, Conall, I didn't think... I refused to believe that Hope might die."

Conall hated himself for not knowing the right words to ease the grief that was clearly ripping her apart. But he'd learned with Nancy that he wasn't good at dealing with women's problems.

"None of us ever wants to consider losing someone we're close to, Vanessa. But we can't go around thinking the worst. Where would that get us?"

Where indeed, Vanessa wondered dazedly. Swallowing at the painful lump in her throat, she rose to her feet and wandered aimlessly across the room.

For years now, she'd desperately wanted children. But as she'd struggled to obtain a degree in business management, she'd set aside having a family. Then when she'd finally achieved that goal, she'd slowly begun to work her way off the casino floor and into the business offices. First as a simple file clerk, then on to secretarial assistant, then a jump to office manager, and finally a great leap to personal secretary to the CEO of Lucky Treasures. During that climb, she'd met her now ex-husband, and she'd believed her dreams of having a family of her own were finally going to become a reality. But Jeff had turned out to be nothing but a hanger-on, a man only too happy to let his wife support him while he went his free and fancy way.

Vanessa supposed it was a good thing that children had never come from their short marriage. But since the divorce, she'd grieved long and hard for what hadn't been and prayed that someday her fate would change. Still, she'd never expected to become a mother in this shocking fashion and the news was almost too much for her to absorb.

"I suppose you're right, Conall. We can't dwell on what might go wrong. But I—" She stopped in front of the huge picture window that framed a view of the mountain ridge that ran along the north edge of the massive horse ranch. "Right now I'm...stunned. In the next few days, the lawyer expects me to be in Vegas to pick up the babies! There's so much I'm going to have to do! I live in my parents' house. Do you remember it?"

Vaguely, Conall thought. It had been a long time since he'd driven through that mountainous area northeast of the Diamond D, but he did recall the tiny stucco home where the Valdez family had resided for so many years. The place had always needed work. And to give him credit, Mr. Valdez had done the best he could on a carpenter's salary. But his four sons had been the worthless sort, never lifting a hand to help their parents or themselves. As far as Conall knew, Vanessa's brothers were all gone from the area now and all he could think was good riddance. She didn't need any of them trying to mooch her hard-earned money.

"Yes, I remember," Conall told her. "Are you living there by yourself? I mean, do you have enough extra room to accommodate the babies?"

"It's just me living there," she replied, "so there's enough room. But the place isn't equipped to handle two infants! You see, I came back to Hondo Valley, so that I'd be around to see after my father's needs. I know he has great medical care in the nursing home, but he needs my emotional support—especially now that Mama is gone. And since I'm divorced now I never dreamed about raising a family there! Dear heaven, there are so many things I'll have to change—buy—to make a nursery for the babies!"

She jerked with surprise when she felt his hands fold over the back of her shoulders. She'd not heard him walk up behind her, but even if she'd been warned of his approach, his touch would have been just as jolting to her senses. Conall Donovan was like no man she'd ever known. For a time, when she'd been a sophomore in high school and he a senior, she'd had an enormous crush on him. He'd been one of those rare guys who'd possessed brains and brawn. He'd also been a perfect gentleman, who'd been nothing but nice and polite to his sister's poor friend. Now after all these years, he was her employer, and she'd done her best to forget about the crush. Until a few minutes ago, when he'd touched her for the very first time.

"Tell me, Vanessa, do you want these babies in your life?"

The question caused her to whirl around to face him and just as quickly she wished she'd kept her back to him. The man's presence was always overwhelming, but up close like this, it was downright rattling her already ragged senses.

Nearly black hair lay in undisciplined waves about his head, while one errant hank teased a cool gray eye that peered at her beneath a heavy black brow. His features were large, rough and edged with a haggardness that could only come from working long, hard hours without enough rest. His clothes, which ranged from faded jeans to designer suits, always fit his tall, well-honed body as though they'd been tailored for him. And probably had been, she thought wryly. He was certainly rich enough to afford such an extravagance.

As far as Vanessa was concerned, she always thought of Conall Donovan as dark, dangerous and delicious. And something totally beyond her reach. And standing only inches away from him like this only reinforced those descriptions of the man.

Nervously licking her lips, she attempted to answer his question. "Of course I want the babies! There's nothing I want more." She didn't tell him that during her short marriage she'd wanted children, but her husband had insisted he loved her too much to want to share her with a child. Now Vanessa very nearly gagged when she thought of how phony those words had been. Jeff hadn't loved her. He'd only loved himself. But Conall didn't want to hear about the personal mistakes she'd made. Besides, they were far too humiliating to share with a man like him.

"I've always wanted children. And I want Hope's twins to be loved. I'm positive that I can give them that love and raise them as if I gave birth to them myself. But I'm not sure how I can handle all the changes I need to make right now. I have very little time and—"

"Whoa! Slow down, Vanessa. Let's take one thing at a time," he said. "What do you need to do first?"

Behind her, the phone began to ring again, but the subtle change in his expression was telling her to, once again, forget the telephone.

Turning her palms upward, she tried to breathe normally and assure herself that this man's sexual aura wasn't going to suffocate her. "I suppose the first thing is to go to Vegas and collect the babies. They've already been released from the hospital and placed in temporary care at a Catholic orphanage."

With a dour frown, he turned away from her and began to pace back and forth in front of her desk. Momentarily relieved by the space between them, Vanessa drew in a much-needed breath.

"I'm sure they're being well cared for," he said suddenly. "But I'm certain you'll feel better once we fetch the children back here as soon as possible."

We? Where had that come from? This was her problem. Not his. But that wasn't entirely true, she reminded herself. Conall was depending on her to keep his office running smoothly. Bringing two infants all the way from Vegas and getting them settled was going to chop into her work time. Naturally, this whole thing was going to affect him, too, she thought sickly. And what was that going to do to her job? A job that she'd quickly come to love, and now, more than ever, desperately needed.

"I'm sorry, Conall. I suppose I'll have to ask for time off while I make arrangements to fly out and collect the twins. If you feel you need to let me go permanently," she added ruefully, "then I'll understand."

Stopping in his tracks, he scowled at her. "Let you go? What the hell, Vanessa? Do you think Donovans fire our employees whenever they need help?"

Seeing she'd offended him, she drew in a deep breath and blew it out. "I didn't mean it like that. You obviously have tons of work to deal with. You can't do it alone and you put your trust in me to be here every day. I can't expect you to suffer just because I have a problem."

He waved a dismissive hand through the air. "This isn't like you're asking for time off to go on a shopping binge or some other frivolous excursion," he barked, then resumed pacing. "I'll deal with the problems here in the office. Mother will step in your place for the time being. As for me, I suppose I could ask Dad to deal with my most pressing obligations. He doesn't know anything about the mining business. But he can always call me with questions," he went on, more to himself than to her. "I'll discuss this with my parents tonight. In the meantime, you get on the phone and buy plane tickets for tomorrow. You can be ready by then, can't you?"

Vanessa was accustomed to his rapid-fire orders. Some days he rattled them off as though she were a tape recorder. But this afternoon, she'd been knocked off-kilter and the sudden personal attention Conall was giving her wasn't helping her brain snap into action. She stared at him with confusion.

"Tickets? Pardon me, Conall, but I only need one round-trip ticket."

Walking back to her, he held up two fingers. "You need to purchase two tickets. I'm going with you."

She gasped and he smiled.

"What's wrong?" he asked. "Afraid you'll fall asleep on the plane and I'll see you with your mouth open?"

Was he saying something about her mouth? she wondered fuzzily. And had something gone wrong with the room's thermostat? Sweat was popping out on her forehead and upper lip. Her legs felt oddly weak and there was a loud rushing noise in her ears.

"Conall— I—"

The remainder of her words were never uttered as she slumped forward and straight into his arms.

Chapter Two

"Poor little thing. The shock must have gotten to her."

From somewhere above her, Vanessa could hear Fiona Donovan's concerned voice, but try as she might, she couldn't open her eyes or form one word.

"Her pulse is getting stronger. She's coming around."

This statement came from Bridget Donovan, the doctor of the family. Vanessa could feel the pressure of the young woman's fingers wrapped around her wrist.

"Well, if the truth be known, Conall probably forced her to work through lunch," Fiona continued in an accusing tone. "She probably hasn't had a bite to eat all day."

"Mom, I don't force Vanessa to do anything," Conall said brusquely. "She probably stopped long enough to eat a sandwich or some of that gooey stuff from a carton that she seems to favor."

"You don't know whether she ate or not?" Fiona shot back at her son.

"Hell, no! I've been in my office since before daylight and didn't come out until a few minutes ago when I found her crying. I don't know about her lunch! But you can see she's not starving. She has plenty of meat on her bones."

His last remark was enough to spike Vanessa's blood pressure and with a weak groan, she slowly opened her eyes to see she was lying on the couch in her office. Bridget was kneeling over her, while Conall and his mother stood just behind the young doctor.

"Hello, pretty lady," Bridget said with a bright smile. "Glad to see you're back with the living."

Vanessa's fuzzy eyesight darted over the redheaded doctor and then slowly progressed up to Conall's dour face. Next to him, Fiona was smiling with happy relief.

"What...happened?" Vanessa asked weakly. "I was talking to Conall and the next thing I knew there was a strange rushing noise in my ears."

"You fainted," Bridget explained. "Thankfully Conall caught you before you hit your head on the desk or the floor. When he called over to the house for help, I happened to be home on a break from the clinic. How are you feeling now?"

"Weak and groggy," Vanessa admitted. "But better."

"Good. Your color is returning," she said. "Conall tells me you received a bit of a shock about your friend."

"Yes. I was feeling a bit shaky, but I never dreamed I'd do anything like...faint! This is so embarrassing." She glanced back at Conall to see his expression was still grim and she figured he had to be terribly annoyed for all this interference in his work schedule. Over the past couple of months, she'd learned his work was his life and he didn't appreciate anything or anyone intervening. "I'm sorry, Conall. I've disrupted the whole office and your family."

"Nonsense!" Fiona blurted out before her son had a chance to utter a word. "You had every right to have a little fainting spell. Most women have nine months to prepare to be a mother. From what Conall tells us, you didn't have nine minutes."

"I'm just glad I happened to be home," Bridget quickly added. "Conall feared you were having a heart attack." She clamped a strong hand on Vanessa's shoulder. "Sit up for me and let's see how you do now."

With the young woman's help, Vanessa rose to a sitting position. "I'm fine. Really," she told the doctor. "I feel much stronger now and my head isn't whirling."

"Well, from what I can see, you had a simple, garden-variety faint. It happens to the best of us sometimes," Bridget assured her. "But if you have any more trouble— weakness, dizziness or anything like that—please get to your doctor for a checkup. Okay?"

"Yes. I promise. Thank you, Bridget."

"No problem," she said, then with a broad smile, she rose to a standing position and pointed a direct look at her brother. "I've got to get back to the clinic, so I'm leaving the patient in your hands, Conall. You might go lightly on her the remainder of the day."

"Vanna is going to get the rest of the afternoon off," Fiona spoke up, using the shortened name that Maura had given Vanessa many years ago when the two had been teenagers. "In fact, Conall is going to drive her home."

Vanessa opened her mouth to argue, but quickly decided not to make the effort. Fiona could be just as formidable as her son and with Bridget agreeing that Vanessa could clearly use some rest, she had no choice but to go along with the family's wishes.

Once Bridget had departed the small office, Conall said to Vanessa, "I'll get your things and we'll be on our way."

While Conall collected her sweater and handbag from a tiny closet located in the short hallway separating her office from his, Fiona was already taking a seat at Vanessa's desk.

"While you two are gone," she said to Conall, "I'll take care of the plane tickets and see to organizing anything else you might need for the trip to Vegas. If there are still empty seats, do you want the first flight out?"

"That would be great, Mom. See what you can do."

With her things thrown over his arm, he walked over to the couch and slipped a hand beneath Vanessa's elbow.

"Think you can stand okay now?" he asked gently.

Since she'd gone to work for this tall, dark powerhouse of a man, he'd been polite enough to her, but mostly he was all business. It felt more than strange to have him addressing her about personal things and even more unsettling to have him touching her.

"Yes," she assured him, then feeling her cheeks warm with an embarrassed flush, added, "I don't think you need worry about having to catch me again."

Not bothering to make a reply, he began to guide her toward the door. Across the room, Fiona flung a parting question at her son.

"Conall, the hotel rooms. How many nights do you need reserved? Or do you have any idea about that?"

"No idea," he said. "Better leave that open."

"Right," she replied, then tossed a reassuring smile at Vanessa. "Don't worry, Vanna. Everything is going to be just fine. Why, in no time you'll have those little babies of yours home and in your arms."

Vanessa thanked the woman for her kind thoughts and then Conall ushered her out to a shiny black pickup truck with the Diamond D brand emblazoned on the doors.

After he'd helped her into the cab and they were barreling past a fenced paddock filled with a row of busy mechanical horse walkers, he said, "You gave me a fright back there when you fainted. Are you sure you're okay?"

He was staring straight ahead and Vanessa could read little from his granite-etched profile. For the most part, she'd always thought of him as an unfeeling man, but maybe that was because he didn't allow his feelings to show on his face. He was certainly going out of his way to help her. Which created an even bigger question in her mind. Why? Even if she was his one and only secretary, her personal problems were none of his responsibility.

"I'm okay, Conall. Really. I just feel...silly for causing you and your family so much trouble." Her gaze turned toward the passenger window as they curved away from the Donovan ranch house. The structure's stalwart appearance hadn't changed since she'd left the Hondo Valley more than fifteen years ago. And she liked to think the big Irish family that lived inside hadn't changed, either—that if she stepped inside, she'd still feel like Cinderella visiting the castle.

"Forget it," he practically snapped.

She looked at him. "But you—"

He interrupted before she could say more. "Let it rest, Vanessa."

Sighing, she smoothed the hem of her skirt over her knees and stared ahead. One minute everything had been going along fine. As fine as it could be for a divorced woman with her family split in all directions and an aging father too debilitated from a stroke to leave the nursing home. Yet those problems seemed small in comparison to what she was facing now.

Still, Vanessa realized she couldn't give in to the overwhelming shock. She had to straighten her shoulders and take up the reins of her life again. But taking them out of Conall's hands was not going to be an easy task. He was a man who was all about using his power to bend operations to his liking. And she was all about independence. She didn't want to be beholden to anyone and that included her boss. Yet this was one time that agreeing to a little help might be the sensible thing for her to do. Especially for the babies' sake.

"You don't like accepting help from anyone, do you?" he asked as he steered the truck off Diamond D ranch land and onto the main highway.

The man must be a mind reader, she thought. "I like taking care of myself," she answered truthfully, then realizing how ungrateful that probably sounded to him, she glanced over and added, "But this is one time I can't take care of things entirely on my own. And I am grateful to you, Conall. Please know that."

He didn't say anything for a while and she was wondering if she'd offended him, when he said, "You can tell me if I'm getting too personal, Vanessa, but what about your brothers? If I remember right, you had four of them. Are any of them close enough to help you with the babies?"

Vanessa choked back a mocking laugh. Her brothers couldn't care for themselves, much less two needy babies. "My brothers all moved far away from here. They conveniently forgot their parents and only sister. And that's fine with me, 'cause I wouldn't ask them for the time of day," she said flatly.

"That's too bad."

She heaved out a heavy breath. "It's probably for the best, Conall. None of them have ever made much effort to become responsible men. The only one who comes close to it is Michael—the one your age. And he's hardly in the running for sainthood," she added.

He didn't make any sort of reply to that and Vanessa figured he was thinking badly of her. The Donovan family had always been a strong unit. They lived together, worked and played together, and stuck close even when life's problems crashed in unexpectedly. He probably couldn't understand why she and her brothers lacked the love and devotion it took to keep the Valdez family bonded. But then, she'd never understood it herself.

"Sorry," she said quietly. "I didn't mean to sound so…judgmental. But believe me when I say there are no relatives around to help. Not with the babies, my father, the home place, anything."

In other words, she had her hands full, Conall thought grimly. As he'd suspected, the Valdez brothers had left Lincoln County. He'd not seen any of them in years and even when they had still been around, Conall hadn't associated with any of them. He'd never been into strutting around in black leather and begging for scrapes with the law. Some time back, he'd heard the eldest son had served time for distributing drugs over in El Paso, but as far as he knew, no gossip had ever surfaced about the remaining three.

Conall cast a brief glance at her. What had her life been like these past years she'd been away from the valley? She'd certainly climbed the workforce ladder. But in spite of her having more financial security, she was more or less alone in life. Like him.

Which only proved that riches didn't always come in the form of money, he thought.

Ten minutes later, on a five-acre tract of land near the tiny settlement of Tinnie, Conall pulled the truck to a stop in front of a rickety picket fence. Beyond the whitewashed barrier was a small stucco house of faded turquoise. One mesquite tree shaded the front entrance, while a short rock walkway crossed a bare dirt yard. A brown-and-white nanny goat stood on the porch as she reared on her hind legs and nipped at a hanging pot of red geraniums.

Even though he'd not been by the homestead recently, the Valdez home looked pretty much as it always had. Seeing the family's modest existence normally wouldn't have affected Conall one way or the other. Rich and poor was a fact of life. Not just in the New Mexico mountains, but everywhere. Yet now that he was beginning to know Vanessa, he was struck by the stark simplicity of the place. She'd left a very high-paying job to return to this, he thought incredibly. All because her father had needed her. How many women would do such a thing?

As she collected her handbag and jacket, Conall walked around to the passenger door to help her to the ground.

"I'll walk with you to the door," he told her. "Just in case your knees get spongy."

With his hand at her back, they walked through a sagging gate and down the rough walkway. To the east, far beyond the house, clouds had gathered over the Capitan

Mountains, blotting out the sun and hinting at an on-coming rainstorm.

When they reached the porch, the goat ignored them as they stepped up to the door. "Would you like to come in?" she asked.

He smiled. "Some other time," he assured her. "If we're going to leave in the morning, I have a hundred things to tend to before we go. Richardson is coming about the pool at three. I need to be there to see what sort of ideas he has. And to get his estimates for the cost."

The idea of discussing plans to enlarge the swimming pool for Diamond D racehorses, while Vanessa was worrying how she was going to house two needy infants, made him feel rather small and out of touch. But it was hardly his fault that their worlds were so different.

"Sure," she said, then suddenly looked up at him. Her features were taut with stress. "Could you let me know about our flight time? Since my vehicle is still at the ranch, I suppose I'll need someone to pick me up and take me to the airport."

Placing his forefinger beneath her chin, he passed the pad of his thumb slowly along her jaw line. "Relax," he said softly. "I'll take care of everything, Vanessa. Just pack your bags and let me do the rest."

She nodded and then her gaze skittered shyly away from his and on to the closed door behind her shoulder. Conall told himself it was time to drop his hand and back away. But something about the tender line of her cheek, the warm scent emanating from her hair, made him bend his head and press a kiss to her temple.

For one moment her small hand fluttered to a stop against the middle of his chest, and then just as quickly she was pushing herself away and hurrying into the house.

Conall stared after her for long moments before he finally moved off the porch and walked back to his truck.

Later that evening, as Vanessa attempted to pack what things she needed for the trip to Vegas, the phone rang.

Praying it wasn't another call from Hope's lawyer, she picked up the phone located on the nightstand by her bed and was surprised to hear Maura's voice on the other end of the line.

Even though the two women had been longtime friends, Maura had a husband and two young children to care for, along with her part-time job at Bridget's medical clinic in Ruidoso. She was too busy to make a habit of calling.

Without preamble, Conall's sister exclaimed, "Bridget just told me about your friend—and the babies! Dear God, I can't imagine what you must be feeling right now!"

Swiping a weary hand through her hair, Vanessa said, "I feel like every ounce of energy has been drained from my body, Maura."

"Bridget told me about you fainting. Thank God Conall was there with you. How are you feeling now?"

"Physically, better. I'm packing for the trip right now. But my mind is racing around in all directions. How can a person feel grief and happy excitement at the same time? I feel like I'm being pulled in all directions." She eased down on the edge of the bed. "But mostly, Maura, I'm scared."

"Scared? You?" Maura scoffed. "You're one of the

strongest and bravest women I've ever known. What do you have to be scared about, anyway?"

Brave? Strong? Maybe at one time, years ago when she'd first headed out to Las Vegas on her own, she'd been brave and determined to make a better life for herself. But her mistakes with Jeff had wiped away much of her confidence.

"Two little infants, that's what! You've got to remember I've never had a baby. I don't know the first thing about taking care of one."

Maura's soft laugh was meant to reassure her friend. "Trust me, dear friend, giving birth doesn't give you an inside corner on taking care of babies. It's a learn-as-you-go thing. Believe me, you'll be fine. And isn't it wonderful, Vanna? You with children! You've wanted some of your own for so long now."

As tears stung, Vanessa squeezed her eyes shut. "That's true. But I didn't want them this way—with my friend dying. She was...well, I've talked about her to you before. She was such a generous person and so fun and full of life. She was planning to...come back here for a visit later this summer to show me the babies and see where I grew up. Now—" her throat tightened to an aching knot, forcing her to pause "—I'll be bringing the babies back without her."

Vanessa could hear Maura sniffing back a tear of her own. "Yes, it's so tragic, Vanna. I would have loved to meet her. But it wasn't meant to be and you can't dwell on her death now. You have to concentrate on the babies and remember how much your friend wanted them to be loved and cared for."

"You're right, Maura," Vanessa said as she tried to gather her ragged emotions. "I have to move forward now."

Maura cleared her throat. "Well, Bridget says that our brother is traveling with you to Vegas. Frankly, I'm shocked about this, Vanna. The rare times he leaves the ranch are only for business reasons."

Surely Maura could see that Conall considered Vanessa a business reason and nothing more. "I tried to tell him it wasn't necessary."

"Oh. I thought you might have asked him to go."

Vanessa drew in a sharp breath. "Are you serious? I would never ask Conall to do anything personal for me! He just made all these decisions on his own. And I have no idea why."

"Hmm. Well, his last secretary was a real bitch," Maura said bluntly. "And everyone in the family has heard him singing praises about your work. I'm sure he wants to keep you happy."

Vanessa released a short, dry laugh. "I've been told that good secretaries are hard to find." But earlier this afternoon, when he placed that brief kiss on the top of her head, she'd definitely not felt like his employee, she thought. She'd felt like a woman with something worthwhile to offer a man.

Dear God, the shock of losing Hope and becoming a mother all at once had numbed her brain. Conall Donovan would never look at her as anything more than his employee. Socially, he was several tiers above her. And even though he wasn't a snob, he was still a Donovan.

"Doesn't matter why he's going," Maura said. "I'm just glad he is. You need someone to support you at a time like this. And Conall has a strong arm to lean on."

Vanessa had no intentions of leaning on Conall. Certainly not in a physical way. But she kept those thoughts to herself. "Yes. Your brother is a rock."

"I wouldn't exactly call him that. Yes, he can be hard. But there's a soft side to him. You just have to know where to look for it," Maura explained. "There was a time—" She broke off, then after a long pause, added in a rueful voice, "Let's just say Conall wasn't always the man he is now."

Shying far away from that loaded comment, Vanessa said, "Well, I'm hoping we can wrap up everything in Vegas quickly."

"And I'd better let you go so that you can finish your packing," Maura replied. "Is there anything I can help you with while you're gone? Check on your father? Your house?"

"It's kind of you to offer, but I'll keep in touch with the nursing home. And I think the house will be okay for a couple of days. But just in case, you know where I leave an extra key so that you can get inside."

"Yes, I remember. In the little crack behind the window shutter."

"Right," Vanessa replied. "But I doubt we'll be gone for that long. Besides, the best thing you can do for me is share your experienced mothering skills. I'm definitely going to need advice."

Maura laughed. "Just wait, Vanna. You're going to see that a woman can never learn all there is to know about mothering. You just have to go by instinct and you happen to have a good one."

"I can only hope you're right," Vanessa murmured.

The next afternoon, after the short flight to Las Vegas, Conall dealt with their luggage, then picked up their rental car and headed to their hotel. Thankfully Fiona hadn't booked them into one of the resort monstrosities that lined the busy strip, but a nice peaceful villa on the desert outskirts of the city.

After checking in and sending their bags to adjoining rooms, they drove straight to the lawyer's office to deal with the legalities of claiming the twins and arranging to store Hope's ashes.

By the time they finally arrived at the orphanage, an old, ivy-covered Spanish-style building located on the outskirts of town, Vanessa's exhaustion must have been clearly showing. As they followed a silent Sister down a wide, empty corridor, Conall brought a steadying hand beneath her elbow.

"I'm thinking we should have waited until tomorrow to see the babies," he said in a low voice. "I'm not sure you're up to this."

Vanessa straightened her shoulders as best she could. For the life of her, she wasn't about to let this granite piece of man think she was made of anything less than grit and determination.

"I'll be fine. And seeing the babies is the best part of this trip," she assured him.

Conall studied her pale face and wondered what his secretary could possibly be thinking. Even for the strongest of women, she was receiving a heavy load to carry. Especially without a man to help her.

He didn't know anything about Vanessa's marriage or divorce. In fact, he'd only known she was divorced because she'd stated it on her résumé. Of course he could have questioned Maura about her friend and most likely his sister would have given him an honest account of what had occurred. But Conall had never been one to pry into another person's private life, unless he believed there was a good reason to. He liked his privacy and tried his best to respect everyone else's. And even if she was his employee, he didn't consider Vanessa an exception to that rule. Except there were times, he had to admit to himself, that he was curious about her.

He gave her a wry smile. "To be honest, I'm looking forward to seeing them, too."

At the end of the corridor, the kindly nun ushered them into a sunny nursery filled with rows of cradles and cribs, all of them occupied with babies ranging from infancy to twelve months old. Three more nuns were moving quietly around the room, tending to the needy children, some of whom were crying boisterously.

"The twins are over here in the corner," the Sister said, motioning for the two of them to follow.

When she finally stopped near a pair of wooden cradles made of dark wood, she gestured toward the sleeping babies. Since the newborns were yet to be named, the two were differentiated with blue and pink blankets, while paper tags were attached to the end of each cradle, one reading Boy Valdez and the other Girl Valdez.

"Here they are," she announced. "Take as much time with them as you'd like. And if you need anything, please let me know. I'll be just down the hall in Mother Superior's office."

Conall and Vanessa both thanked the woman as she left and then they turned their entire attention to the sleeping twins.

Both babies had red-gold hair with the boy's being a slightly darker shade than his sister's. To Conall, they appeared extremely tiny, even though the Sister had told them earlier that each baby weighed over five pounds, a fair amount for newborn twins.

"Oh. Oh, my. How…incredible," Vanessa whispered in awe as she stared down at the babies. "How perfectly beautiful!"

She bent over the cradles for a closer look and Conall watched as she touched a finger to the top of each velvety head. And then suddenly without warning, she covered her face with one hand and he could see her shoulders began to shake with silent sobs.

Quickly, he moved forward and wrapped an arm around her waist. "Vanessa." He said her name softly, just to remind her that she wasn't alone.

She glanced up at him, her brown eyes full of tears. "I'm sorry, Conall. I thought I could do this without breaking down. But...I—" Her gaze swung back to the babies. "I can't believe that I've been blessed with two beautiful babies. And yet I look at them and...can't help thinking of Hope."

His hand slipped to her slender shoulder and squeezed. "Your friend had the perfect name. Through you, she's given her children hope for the future. Remember that and smile."

She let out a ragged sigh. "You're right, Conall. I have to put my tears for Hope behind me and smile for the babies." Glancing up at him, she gave him a wobbly smile. "I've chosen names for them. Rose Marie and Richard Madison. What do you think?"

"Very nice. I'll call them Rose and Rick, if that's all right with you."

Her smile grew stronger. "That's my plan, too. Shall we pick them up?"

He stared at her, amazed that she wanted to include him. "We? You go ahead. I'm just an onlooker."

She looked a bit disappointed and Conall realized he felt a tad deflated himself. But whether that was because he actually wanted to hold the babies and was stupidly pretending indifference or because he was disheartening her at this special time, he didn't know.

Frowning, she asked, "You don't like babies or something?"

"Of course I do. I have baby nieces and nephews. But I didn't hold them when they were this small. Come to think of it...none of them were ever this small." He gestured toward the twins. "I might do it all wrong."

"I might do it all wrong, too," she suggested. "So we might as well try together."

Realizing it would look strange if he kept protesting, he said, "All right. I'll watch you first."

She bent over Rose's cradle and after carefully placing a hand beneath the baby's head, lifted her out of the bed and into her arms. After a moment, Conall moved up to the other cradle and, in the same cautious manner, reached for the boy.

Once he had the child safely positioned in the crook of his arm, he adjusted the thin blue blanket beneath little Rick's chin so that he could get a better look at his face. It was perfectly formed with a little pug nose and bow-shaped lips. Faint golden brows framed a set of blue eyes that were now wide open and appeared to be searching to see who or what was holding him.

Vulnerable. Needy. Precious. As he held the child, memories carried him back to when he and Nancy had first married. In the beginning, he'd had so many dreams and plans. All of them surrounding a house full of children to carry on the Donovan name and inherit the hard-earned rewards of the Diamond D. But those dreams had slowly and surely come crashing down.

Now as Conall experienced the special warmth and scent of the baby boy lying so helplessly in the crook of his arm, Conall wasn't sure that Vanessa yet realized what a treasure she'd been handed. But he did. Oh, how he did.

"Conall?"

Reining in his thoughts, he pulled his gaze away from the baby to find her staring at him with a faintly puzzled look on her face. Had she been reading his mind? Conall wondered. Surely not. Down through the years he'd perfected the art of shuttering his emotions. Baby Rick wasn't strong enough to make him change the longtime habit.

"Am I doing something wrong?" he asked.

For the first time Conall could remember, his secretary actually smiled at him with those big brown eyes of hers.

"No. You look like you were tailor-made for the job of Daddy."

Her observation struck him hard, but he did his best to keep the pain hidden, as though there was no wide, empty hole inside him.

"Not hardly," he said gruffly. "I'm not...daddy material."

One delicate brow arched skeptically upward. "Oh? You don't ever plan to have children of your own?"

For some reason her question made him pull the baby boy even closer to his chest. "That's one thing I'm absolutely certain I'll never have."

Clearly taken aback by his response, her gaze slipped away from his and dropped to the baby in her arms. "Well, everyone has their own ideas about having children," she said a bit stiffly. "I just happen to think you're making a sad mistake."

A sad mistake. Oh, yes, it was a sad mistake that she was misjudging him, Conall thought. And sad, too, that he couldn't find the courage to tell this woman that at one time he'd planned to have at least a half-dozen children.

But if he let her in on that dream, then he'd have to explain why he'd been forced to set it aside. And why he planned to live the rest of his life a lone bachelor.

Hardening himself to that certain reality had changed him, he knew. Even his family often considered him unapproachable. But none of them actually understood the loss he felt to see his siblings having children of their own, while knowing he would always be cheated out of one of life's most blessed gifts.

"You have a right to your opinion, Vanessa. Just like I have a right to live my life the way I see fit."

She cast him a pained look, then turned her back to him and walked a few steps away as though she'd just seen him for the first time and didn't like what she was seeing.

Well, that was okay, Conall thought. What his secretary thought about him didn't matter. It wasn't as if they were romantically linked, or even close friends.

He looked down at the baby in his arms and felt something raw and sweet swell in his chest. Vanessa would no doubt provide the twins with love. But they needed a father. And at some point in the future she would probably provide them with one. Then her family circle would be complete and that was only right.

Yet strangely, the idea left Conall with a regretful ache.

Chapter Three

Later that evening, long after their visit to the orphanage had ended, Vanessa sat in a quiet courtyard behind their villa-style hotel, and tried to relax from the hectic pace of the day. Along with the busy schedule of flying, meeting with lawyers and visiting the babies, her cell phone had rung continually all afternoon. Most of the calls were from people here in Vegas who'd been mutual friends of her and Hope and were just now hearing about the tragedy. Vanessa appreciated their concern and interest, but she was exhausted from explaining about the twins and sharing her grief over Hope's death.

Finally, in desperation, she'd left the phone in her room and walked outside to enjoy the cooling desert air. Now as she sat on an iron bench beneath a huge Joshua tree and watched darkness fall on the distant mountains, she wished she could turn off thoughts of Conall as easily as she'd turned off the phone.

The man was an enigma. After weeks of working with him, she still didn't understand what made Conall tick or what drove him to work long, trying hours for the ranch. Clearly he was ambitious. Every morning he arrived at the office at least two hours ahead of her, which meant he went to work before daylight. And when she left in the evenings, even after working overtime herself, he remained at his desk making calls or meeting with horse-racing connections. Running the Diamond D was clearly more than a job to him. It was the entire sum of his life. Did he invest so much of himself because the ranch was family owned and operated?

She could only guess at the answer to that question. But there was no doubt that Conall was a man of striking looks with plenty of money to match. The ranch could easily afford to hire an assistant in order to free Conall from his grueling schedule. With part of his workload eased, he'd be able to travel the world and indulge in all sorts of lavish recreations, with a trail of willing women trotting behind him. Yet none of those things appeared to interest him in the least. She seriously doubted he would accept the help of an assistant, even if the person volunteered to work for free. He was a man who wanted things done his way and refused to trust just anyone to carry out his orders.

Vanessa often wondered if he was still bitter over his divorce, or perhaps he was still in love with his ex-wife and wanted her back. Maura had never mentioned the cause of her brother's divorce and Vanessa wasn't about to question her childhood friend about him. The hopes and dreams and feelings going on inside Conall weren't her business. Or so she kept telling herself. But ever since she'd looked up in the orphanage and seen him standing there with her baby son in his arms, she'd been consumed with unexpected emotions and questions.

The fact that he didn't want or expect to ever have children had shaken her deeply. Of all the men she'd met through the years, Conall had always seemed like a man who would love and welcome children into his life. True, he had a dark and dangerous appearance but it belied the responsible man beneath. He wasn't a roamer or playboy with a wild lifestyle. Why would he not want children? Because there was no room in his heart for them? No. Vanessa couldn't believe he was that cold or stingy with himself. Not after seeing the way he interacted with the twins.

"Vanessa?"

The unexpected sound of Conall's voice had her glancing over her shoulder to see him walking a narrow brick pathway toward her. Figuring something had to be wrong for him to come all the way out here to find her, she rose from the bench and met him on the footpath.

"I'm sorry," she quickly apologized. "I left my phone in the room. Has the lawyer or orphanage been trying to reach me?"

Impatience creased his forehead. "You need to quit all this worrying, Vanessa. No one has tried to reach you through me. The lawyer seemed very competent. I'm sure he'll have the last of the papers for us to sign before we catch our flight out tomorrow afternoon. And from what Mother Superior told us, the babies are perfectly healthy and able to travel."

Shaking her head, Vanessa forced the tenseness in her shoulders to relax. "I am a bit on edge," she admitted. "My phone has been ringing all evening and—"

Before she could finish, the cell in his shirt pocket went off and after a quick glance at the caller ID he said,

"Sorry, Vanessa, I've been having the same problem. This won't take but a minute or two."

With a quick nod, she turned her back and took a few steps away to where water trickled over a three-tiered fountain and into a small pool. As she watched colorful koi swim in and out of water plants, she heard him say, "No. That won't do....I understand you mean well. But nothing used....Everything new....Yes, classic....No. Something like cherry and antique....Got it?...Yeah. And anything else you can think of that will be needed." There was a long pause as he listened to the caller and then he replied. "Yeah. Thanks, sis....Good night."

His sister? That could be Maura, Dallas or Bridget, she thought. Apparently they were planning something together and the notion sent a sad pang through Vanessa. She'd never had a sister to conspire with and share experiences, only older brothers who'd mostly caused great agony for her parents. Now with Esther, her mother, gone and her father, Alonzo, still having trouble communicating with his halting speech, she couldn't look for family support. Unlike Conall, who'd always been surrounded by loving siblings, parents and grandmother.

"Well, now that I have that out of the way," Conall announced behind her, "I came out here to see if you'd like to go to dinner somewhere? We've not eaten in hours."

Vanessa glanced down at herself. She was still wearing the simple pink sheathe she'd started out with this morning, minus the matching bolero sweater, but it was wrinkled and even without the aid of a mirror she knew her hair was blown to a tumbled mess. "I really don't feel like dressing up for dinner, Conall. You go on without me."

He chuckled and the sound took her by surprise. He

was a man who rarely laughed and when he did it was usually about something that she didn't find amusing. Now as she looked at him, she was jarred by his jovial attitude.

"Have you taken a look at me?" he asked. "I'm wearing jeans."

Dragging her gaze away from the charming grin on his lips, she slowly inspected the blue denim encasing his muscled thighs and the pair of brown alligator boots he wore. He was one of those few men who looked comfortable dressed up or down, which meant he would probably look even better without any clothes at all.

Dear, God, what was she doing? Now wasn't the time for those sorts of indecent thoughts, she scolded herself. As far as Conall went, there would never be a time for them. And she had more important issues to focus on. Like two little tots with golden-red hair and blue eyes.

"I am hungry," she admitted. For food. Not for a man like him, she mentally added.

"Great. There's a little restaurant right across the street that looks good."

"Just give me a moment to fetch my purse and sweater from the room," she told him.

A few minutes later, they were seated at a small table in a family-type restaurant that featured Italian dishes. Vanessa ordered ravioli while Conall chose steak and pasta. As they waited for their salads and drinks to be served, Conall glanced around the long room decorated with early dated photos of Las Vegas and simple, home-style tables covered in brightly striped cloths.

Seated directly across from him, Vanessa asked, "Is this place not to your liking? We can always find another restaurant."

Surprised by her suggestion, he turned his gaze on her. "I'm perfectly satisfied. Why do you ask?"

One of her slender shoulders lifted and fell in a negligible way. "I don't know. The way you were looking around and frowning."

"I frown all the time." A wry smile touched one corner of his mouth. "At least, that's what my mother tells me."

"Mothers don't like to see their children frown," she reasoned. "Mine never did. She always told me to smile and count my blessings."

As Conall's gaze dwelled on his secretary's face, he was surprised at how easy and pleasurable it was to look at her and be in her company. He'd not expected to enjoy any part of this trip. He'd only done it because she was a woman alone and in need, and she was a dedicated employee. But he was quickly discovering that Vanessa was more than an efficient secretary, she was a lovely woman and, like it or not, desire was beginning to stir in him for the first time in a long, long time.

"You must miss your mother terribly," he said. "I was surprised when I heard about her passing. The last time I'd seen her in church she seemed very spry."

Her gaze suddenly dropped to the tabletop, but Conall didn't miss the sadness on her face. The image bothered him almost as much as her tears had yesterday. And for some reason he felt guilty for not attending Mrs. Valdez's funeral services. Even though he'd not known the woman personally, he should have made the effort for Vanessa's sake. But at that time, she'd not been working as his secretary; she'd merely been a past acquaintance, who'd left the valley years ago.

"Yes. Mama appeared to be a picture of health. That made her sudden heart attack even harder to take," she said quietly, then lifted her gaze back to him. "Her death was one of the main reasons I left Las Vegas and returned to Tinnie. I missed the end of my mother's life. I want to be around for my father as much as I can before…he leaves me."

Other than the twins, she certainly didn't have much in the way of family. The idea troubled Conall, although he wasn't sure why. Plenty of people he knew had lost their parents or were lacking family of any kind and they didn't necessarily garner his sympathy. At least, not the deep sort of regret he felt for Vanessa.

"You gave up a very good job to return to your family home and your father," he commented. "I have to admire you for that, Vanessa."

Her eyes were full of doubt as they connected with his.

"I'm not sure that I made the most sensible decision, Conall. I did have a good job and a little house in a nice part of town. Materially speaking, I had much more here in Vegas than I ever had in the valley. But…" Pausing, she let out a long sigh. "Money isn't a cure-all."

No one knew that any better than Conall. Money couldn't change the fact that a childhood fever had killed his chances to ever father a child of his own. Nor had money been able to fix his shattered marriage. In fact, being rich had only compounded the problems he'd endured with Nancy. But since his divorce he'd tried his best to bury those painful personal details. They certainly weren't matters he wanted to discuss with a woman, and that included Vanessa.

"You're not worried about the twins' financial future, are you?" he asked. "Hope's life insurance appears to have left them set up nicely for college."

"I'm not worried about the financial part of this," she

replied. "My parents raised six children. Surely I can manage two."

"But you're not married," he pointed out.

From the stiff line of her shoulders to the purse of her lips, everything about her looked offended by his comment.

"You think having a man around would be a help?"

The bitterness in her short laugh was something he'd never heard from her before. The idea that this gentle woman might hold any sort of hard streak inside her took him by surprise. "I'm a man," he answered. "I like to think we're a helpful gender."

Frowning, her gaze left his to travel to an insignificant spot across the room. "Look, Conall, I've already had one husband I had to support, I don't want another. I can do just fine without that added burden."

So she'd ended up marrying a man just like her parasitic brothers. No wonder there was bitterness on her tongue. But how and why had she made such a mistake in judgment? He would have thought she'd seen enough freeloading men to spot one at first glance.

Yeah. Just like you'd been able to spot Nancy's twisted character. You didn't use good judgment with her, either. You allowed love to lead you around. And around. Until you were walking down a path of destruction.

Clearing his throat, he tried to ignore the mocking voice going off inside him. "I wasn't trying to suggest—"

Shaking her head, she interrupted, "Forget it, please. I...didn't mean to sound so catty. It's just that after Jeff... Well, I resent the idea of being told I need a man."

Like he resented his family telling him he needed another woman in his life, Conall thought. Hell, getting hooked up with another woman like Nancy would finish him. And finding a nice, family-oriented woman that he could love wasn't as simple as it sounded. Oh, he'd tried. Once the initial blow of his divorce was over, he'd returned to the dating scene and attempted to put his heart into starting his life over with another woman. But as soon as he made it clear that he couldn't father children, all his dates had backed away from him. Sure, for the most part they'd all been kind and empathetic to his problem, but in the end none of them had wanted to start out their lives with a man that couldn't give them a family of their own. After a while, Conall had grown so weary of being rejected over and over that he'd finally given up on finding love, marriage and anything in between. And for the past few years he'd pretty much convinced himself that he was better off being alone and focusing all his attention to his job.

Vanessa's cynical remark was still dangling in the air between them when the waitress arrived with their drinks and salads. After the young woman served them and went on her way, he could feel Vanessa's gaze on him and he paused from the task of stirring sugar into his tea to glance at her. Clearly, from the expression on her face, she wanted to speak her mind about something.

"What?" he prompted.

She hesitated before giving her head a slight shake. The gentle waves of hair lying on her shoulders shook with the movement as did the blue teardrops dangling from her earlobes. Suddenly Conall was wondering how it would feel to thrust his fingers into her silky hair, to nibble on the perfect little shell of her ear.

"I don't know how to say this, Conall, without making you angry."

Trying to concentrate on her words instead of the erotic images in his mind, he asked, "What makes you think I'll be angry? I've not gotten angry with you yet, have I?"

He would admit that he often got frustrated with business dealings and the roadblocks he encountered while dealing with the multitudes of details that went into managing a ranch the size of the Diamond D. But he'd never gotten upset with Vanessa. She'd always given more than a hundred percent to her job and he appreciated her effort.

She reached for the pepper shaker and shook it vigorously over her salad. "Because you're going to think I'm ungrateful. And I'm not. I'm actually very indebted to you for making this trip with me and…everything else you've taken care of. But I —"

A faint smile curled up one corner of his mouth.

"You don't want me telling you how to take care of the twins or what you might need in your personal life. Is that it?"

She studied him for a long moment and then laughed softly under her breath. Conall likened the sound to sweet music.

"That's about it," she answered.

Amused by her streak of independence, he finished stirring his tea. "In other words, while we're on this trip I need to forget that I'm your boss and you're my secretary."

The tip of her tongue came out to moisten her lips and Conall found himself gazing at the damp sheen it left behind. What would she taste like? he wondered. Honey? Wine? Or simply all woman? He certainly didn't need to know. But he sure as hell wouldn't mind making the effort to find out.

She said, "Uh, well, I suppose that's a way of putting it."

The smile on his face deepened and he realized with a start that he was flirting. Something he'd not done in years or, for that matter, even wanted to do.

"Good," he said.

One of her winged brows shot upward. "Good? I thought you were a man who always wanted to be the boss."

Chuckling softly, he reached across the table and enfolded her small hand with his. "Not tonight. I'd rather just be a man having dinner with a beautiful woman. What do you think about that?"

She grimaced, but he could see a faint swathe of pink rushing over her cheeks and her breasts rising and falling with each quick intake of breath. The notion that he was affecting her, even in this small way, was like a heady drink of wine to him, and in the far back of his mind, he wondered what was coming over him. Clearly he wasn't himself. He'd not been himself since yesterday when he'd walked through the office and found Vanessa with tears on her cheeks.

"I think there's something about this town that makes people forget who and what they are. But I never thought you'd be the type to fall prey to its lure," she said dryly. "The next thing I know you'll be saying we should take a stroll down the strip and take in the lights."

"Hmm. That's a great idea. We'll go as soon as we finish eating."

Less than an hour later, after the two of them found a parking space and made their way to the busy sidewalks lining the city's most famous boulevard, Vanessa was still wishing she'd kept her mouth shut. Spending time with Conall away from the office was something she'd often dreamed about, but she was smart enough to realize it was risky business.

In spite of what he'd said back at the restaurant, he was her boss and she depended on him for her livelihood. Allowing herself to think of him as anything more than the man who signed her paychecks would be like inviting trouble right through the front door. Yet here she was walking close to his side and enjoying every second of it.

"Is this the first time you've ever visited Las Vegas?" Vanessa asked as they slowly made their way southward along the busy sidewalk running adjacent to the congested street.

"No. Believe it or not, I was here once with my parents. We'd gone out to Santa Anita to watch one of our horses run in a graded stakes race. On the way back Mom wanted to stop off and play the slots. So Dad and I endured while she had fun."

The night had cooled to a balmy temperature and as the light wind caressed her face, Vanessa realized this was the first time she'd relaxed since she'd gotten the call from Hope's lawyer.

"You don't like to gamble?" she asked.

"Not that much."

She smiled with amused disbelief. "How can you say that, Conall? You're in the racehorse business. That's a big, big gamble."

He chuckled. "That's true. But in my business I pretty much know what I'm investing in. At least I can see my venture and put my hands on it." He gestured to one of the massive casinos to their right. "In there you're placing your money on pure chance."

"Like the stock market," she joked.

"Exactly," he said with another short laugh, then added, "I didn't realize you could be a funny girl."

"I have my moments."

She was thinking what a nice deep laugh he had and how much she enjoyed hearing it when his arm suddenly slid around the back of her waist and drew her even closer to his side. The sudden contact nearly took her breath, yet she did her best to hide the havoc he was causing inside her. After all, she wasn't that same teenager who'd had such a crush on him so many years ago. She'd grown up, dated, married and divorced. Men weren't a big deal to her anymore. Or so she'd believed. Until tonight. When Conall had suddenly started to treat her like a woman instead of a secretary.

"Even though it's not my cup of tea, I have to admit there's something magical about this town. Do you miss all this?" he asked, as he gestured toward the elaborately designed buildings, the endless lights and the bumper-to-bumper traffic on the strip.

"No. I never was into the bright lights and glamour of this place. I only saw it as a town of opportunities. And I took them. Before I ever left the valley, I decided if I had to work my way through college waitressing, I might as well do it where I could make the most money."

"I certainly don't blame you for that."

No. He wouldn't, Vanessa thought. He was the sort of person who never looked down on anyone because they had less than him. And he admired any person who worked hard for a living.

Conall gestured to an area several feet away where a low curved wall contained a shallow pool with spraying spouts of water. "Let's take a rest over there by the pool," he suggested.

"Sounds good to me," she agreed.

Beneath a huge palm tree they took seats on the wide concrete wall. As the two of them made themselves comfortable, he dropped his arm from her waist and Vanessa was trying to decide if she was relieved or disappointed at the loss of contact, when he reached for her hand and folded it casually within his.

Staring out at the street of heavy traffic and gawking pedestrians, Conall grunted with dismay. "After working in this town, the Diamond D must seem mundane."

"The Diamond D is a busy place, too," she disagreed. "Only in a different way."

The idea that his thigh was pressed slightly against hers and that the heat from his hand was radiating all the way up to her shoulder was making every nerve inside Vanessa tighten to the screaming point. Why was he getting this close to her? She'd worked for the man for more than two months and he'd never touched her in any form or fashion until yesterday when she'd fainted straight into his arms. Now he was behaving as though he had every right to put his arm around her or hold her hand.

If she had any sense at all, she'd put a stop to it, Vanessa argued with herself. She'd tell him to keep his hands to himself and remember that she was his secretary and nothing more. But she'd already made the foolish mistake of telling him to forget about being her boss while they were here in Vegas. And she'd be lying to herself, and to him, if she tried to say she wasn't enjoying the feel of his warm fingers wrapped so snugly around hers.

Clearing her throat, she said, "I have to confess that when I first returned to Lincoln County, I did so with intentions of getting a job at the Billy the Kid Casino. I have a friend there who works in the business office and he would have given me a glowing reference. But I'd already worked in that industry for so long that I thought a complete change might be good for me. And then I read about your job opening and I..." She paused long enough to give him a wry smile. "I almost didn't call you."

One of his black brows lifted slightly and as her gaze wandered over his cool gray eyes and dark profile, she felt her heart thud into a rhythm that actually scared her. The man wasn't supposed to be making her feel light-headed. He wasn't supposed to be making her forget they were hundreds of miles away from the office or reminding her they were in a town that urged people to be a little reckless.

"Why?" he asked. "You didn't think you'd like working for me?"

"That wasn't the reason. I didn't want you giving me the job just because I was Maura's old friend. But I should have known you were the type of man who'd never put sentimentality over business. You'd never be that easy with...anyone."

Suddenly his expression turned solemn and Vanessa felt her heart kick to an even faster rate.

"If it makes you feel any better, Vanessa, I can assure you that you got the job on your own merit. Not through a friendship with my sister."

She nervously licked her lips and wondered why she couldn't tear her eyes away from his rugged face. All around her there were fabulous sights that should be monopolizing her attention. But none of them, she realized, could compete with Conall.

"I'm glad you told me," she said, her voice dropping to a husky note.

"And are you glad you took the job?"

How could she answer that without incriminating herself? This man had no idea that he was the thing that fueled her, pushed her out of bed in the morning and made her want to hope and dream again, even after she'd thought her future had died.

"So far," she said lowly. "What about you? Do you wish you'd offered it to someone else?"

A sexy grin suddenly exposed his white teeth and Vanessa was mesmerized by the sight. She'd never seen this side of him before and the notion that he was showing it to her was almost more than she could take in.

"Giving you the job was one of the smartest decisions I've ever made." Leaning closer, he gently pushed his fingers into her windblown hair and smoothed it away from her cheek. "And coming on this trip with you was even smarter."

By now her breathing was coming in shallow sips and she had to swallow before she could finally form one word. "Why?"

His head drew so close to hers that she could see little more than his mouth and nose.

"Because it's opened my eyes. And I'm beginning to see all the things I've been missing."

"Conall." His name passed her lips as she hesitantly pressed a hand against his chest. "This...you... I don't understand."

"That makes two of us."

"But we—"

"Don't talk," he whispered. "Talking won't change the fact that I want to kiss you."

Even if she could have said another word, she doubted it would have stopped what he was about to do. What *she* was about to do.

His thumb and forefinger closed around her chin and

then his lips settled over hers. Vanessa closed her eyes and for the first time in a long time, she stopped thinking and simply let herself feel.

Chapter Four

The desert wind teased her hair and brushed her skin, but it did little to ease the heat building inside Vanessa. Conall's mouth was like a flame licking, consuming, turning her whole body to liquid fire.

Beyond them she could hear the movement of the crawling traffic and among the nearby pedestrians, the occasional burst of conversation punctuated with laughter. Above their heads, the fans of the palm trees whipped noisily in the wind. Yet none of these distractions were enough to jerk Vanessa back to sanity.

Instead, she simply wanted to sit there forever, tasting his mouth, feeling his hands move against her skin. This wasn't the same as the fantasies she'd had of Conall while they'd been teenagers. This was very, very real and so was the effect it was having on her body.

She was melting into him, her senses totally absorbed with his kiss when somewhere behind them voices called out loudly. The interruption broke the connection of their lips and Conall finally lifted his head to gaze down at her.

What could she possibly say to him now? she wondered. Or should she even try?

He cleared his throat and she suddenly realized his hand was cupped against the side of her face. The skin of his palm was rough and raspy, yet his touch was as gentle as a dove's. She wanted to rub her cheek against the masculine texture, experience the erotic friction.

"I guess we'd better be moving along," he said huskily. "Or I...might start forgetting we're in a public place."

Start forgetting? Vanessa had forgotten their whereabouts a long time ago. Like the first moment his lips had touched hers! The idea that she'd become so lost and reckless in his arms was downright terrifying. She couldn't afford to get entangled in an affair with this man. He had the power to hurt her emotionally, not to mention the right to terminate her job whenever the whim hit him.

Trying to put her focus on her new babies, rather than the growing need in her hungry body, she turned and scooted several generous inches away from him.

"I think you're right." Her voice was raw and awkward, but that was better than appearing totally speechless, she thought with a bit of desperation. "And it's getting late. I think we should head back to the hotel."

Apparently he agreed, because he took her by the arm and helped her up from the low concrete wall. Without exchanging any more words, he guided her back onto the busy sidewalk and in the general direction of their rental car.

Close to ten minutes passed before he finally spoke

and by then Vanessa had decided he was going to totally ignore what had happened. No doubt he was regretting giving in to the impulse of kissing his secretary. Especially kissing her as though he was enjoying every moment their lips had been locked together.

Oh, God, what had she done? What was he thinking now? That she was easy and gullible and helpless? That she was so stupid she'd allowed his kiss to go to her head and her heart?

"I hope you're not angry with me, Vanessa."

Stunned by this statement, she glanced his way. "I'm not angry. Why should I be?"

He stared up ahead of them and she could see they had reached the parking area where they'd left the car.

He answered, "Because I wasn't behaving like myself back there. Because I shouldn't have taken advantage of the moment like that. You've been through a lot these past couple of days."

So it hadn't really been him kissing her back there, she thought dismally, just a part of him that had succumbed to impulse. Well, that shouldn't surprise her. Conall was normally a calculated man and under normal circumstances he would never plan to make a pass at her. The notion bothered her far more than it should have.

"I'm a big girl. I could have pushed you away."

"Yeah, but—"

She groaned. "Let's forget the kiss, Conall."

"I don't want to forget it. I want to repeat it."

That was enough to stop her in her tracks and she looked at him with faint amazement.

She mumbled, "That's not going to happen."

He moved closer and when his hand came to rest on her shoulder, she felt herself melting all over again.

"Why?" he asked. "Because you liked it?"

Deciding now was the perfect time to be totally honest, she answered, "Yes. And to let anything start brewing between us now would be a big mistake."

A deep furrow appeared between his black brows. "Maybe you're right," he murmured, then before she could make any sort of reply, he placed a hand at her back and ushered her on toward the car. "But I'm not totally convinced that you are. Yet."

A shiver of uncertain anticipation rolled down Vanessa's spine. From now on she was going to have to stay on guard whenever she was with this man. Otherwise, she might wake up and find herself in his bed.

The next morning as Vanessa stepped out of the shower and slipped into a satin robe, a knock sounded on the door. Knowing it was far too early for housekeeping, she glanced through the peephole to see Conall standing on the opposite side of the door.

The sight of him surprised her. It wasn't quite seven yet. Last night when they'd returned to the hotel and parted ways, he'd not mentioned anything about meeting this early.

"It's me, Vanessa."

Drawing in a bracing breath, she opened the door and stared at him. He was already dressed in a pair of dark, Western-cut slacks and a crisp white shirt. His deep brown hair was combed back from his face and there was a faint smile on his lips, a soft sort of expression that she'd never seen on him before.

Her heart beating fast and hard, she blurted, "I'm not dressed yet."

His gray gaze slowly left her face to slide all the way to her bare toes. Vanessa had never felt so exposed in her life.

"I wasn't planning on us going out just yet," he explained. "I wanted to talk with you. Before we left the hotel."

Knowing she would look childish and prudish to send him away, she pulled the door wider and gestured for him to enter her room.

As he stepped past her, she clutched the front of her robe to her breasts and hoped he didn't notice the naked shape of them beneath the clinging fabric.

"Is something wrong?" she asked as she shut the door after him.

"No. And why do you always suspect something is wrong whenever I show up? You act like I'm some sort of bearer of bad news."

Her cheeks warmed with color as she joined him in the middle of the room. "I just…wasn't expecting you to be out so early. That's all. And all this legal stuff with the babies is not like anything I've dealt with before. I'll be glad when I sign the final documents this morning, before anything can go wrong."

"Nothing is going to go wrong," he said gently, "and the babies are what I'm here to talk to you about."

She stared at him, her brows lifted in question. "What else is there to talk about?"

Vanessa saw his eyes slide to the king-sized bed. The covers were rumpled and she'd left a set of black lacy lingerie lying atop the white sheet. She wondered what he was thinking. Was he remembering the kiss they'd shared last night or the intimate times he'd shared with his ex-wife?

"A few things," he said pensively, then focused his gaze back on her face. "I'll call room service for breakfast and we can eat out on the patio while we talk."

It was a statement, not a question, and for a moment

she bristled at his authoritative attitude. She wanted to remind him that they were in a hotel room—her room to be exact—and he was supposed to be behaving as a supportive friend, not a boss. But she kept the thoughts to herself. Asking him to forget he was her boss while they were here in Vegas had already caused problems. Now wasn't the time or place to take that risk again.

"All right," she told him. "While you call I'll get dressed."

Crossing to the bed, she snatched up her lingerie, then walked to the closet to take down her dress. Behind her, she heard him picking up the phone.

"What would you like?" he called to her. "Fresh fruit and yogurt?"

Frowning, she turned to look at him. "You mean I get to order for myself?"

A sheepish smile settled over his face and that was all it took to turn her insides to mushy oatmeal.

"Sorry, Vanessa. I don't mean to be bossy but it—"

"Just comes natural to you," she finished with an understanding smile. "I'll bet you always tried to tell your younger siblings what to do and how to do it."

He laughed. "Somebody had to."

This was not the Conall she'd been working for the past two months, Vanessa thought. This man was far more approachable and endearing. He was also far more dangerous.

"Well, I do like fresh fruit and yogurt, but I need something more substantial this morning. Make it bacon and eggs and wheat toast."

"A woman who likes to eat in the morning. I like that," he said.

She was afraid to ask what he meant by that remark, so she simply excused herself and hurried to the bathroom to dress.

By the time she'd finished pulling on her clothes, swiping on a bit of makeup and combing her hair into casual waves around her face, she heard room service arriving.

She stepped from the bathroom just as Conall was handing the server a hefty tip. As the young man headed out the door, he turned to Vanessa.

"Everything is waiting out on the patio," he announced.

"Great. I'm starving."

Outside the morning was perfect with a blue, blue sky and a warm, gentle breeze. The table holding their breakfast was situated on a red brick patio edged by a row of palm trees. Thick blooming shrubs and tall agave plants acted as a privacy fence between the rooms. As Conall helped her into one of the rattan chairs, Vanessa couldn't help thinking the villa would be a perfect place for a honeymoon.

A honeymoon, she thought wryly. That kiss Conall had given her last night had messed up her thinking and had her dreaming about things she had no business dreaming about. She'd had her chance at love and marriage. It hadn't worked. And now she seriously doubted she'd ever find a man who would truly love her. A man she could trust with all her heart.

"I'm sure you've been wondering what I wanted to speak with you about," he said as the two of them began to eat.

Vanessa fortified herself with a long sip of strong coffee as she watched him slather a piece of toast with apricot jam.

"I am curious," she admitted.

"I've been thinking about your housing situation," he said before he bit into the toast.

"What is there to think about? I have my parents' home."

"Yes. But there's a house on the ranch that was vacated only a few days ago. It was just remodeled only last year with new flooring and up-to-date appliances. You'd have plenty of room for yourself and a nursery. And you'd be on the ranch—close by—in case you needed help."

Stunned and just a little vexed, Vanessa looked at him. "You know what my salary is, Conall. I couldn't afford to lease the house."

"Why not? It wouldn't cost you a penny."

All she could do was stare at him. "It's obvious you don't know me, Conall. Otherwise, you'd know that I don't go around looking for, or expecting, handouts."

He leveled a frustrated frown at her. "If you think I'm making you a *special* offer because you're my secretary, then you're in for a surprise. Not all of our employees are housed on the ranch and that's fine, too. But the housing we do supply for our ranch hands and house staff is considered a part of their salary, one of the benefits for working for the Diamond D. As I see it, you are an employee and the house is there—empty for now—but I can assure you, not for long."

Vanessa felt more than a little embarrassed. She'd quickly jumped to the conclusion that he was offering her an exclusive deal. All because he'd made this trip with her and given her that one long, mind-shattering kiss. How foolish could she be? He was a man who liked to help people whenever the opportunity arose. And he'd apparently enjoyed that kiss he'd given her. He'd said he wanted to repeat it. But in spite of that pleasant physical exchange, Conall Donovan didn't view her as anything special. She was simply his secretary.

"I'm sorry, Conall. Since the general-managing office handles that sort of thing I wasn't aware that the Diamond D offered housing to its employees free of charge."

A faint smile touched his lips as his gaze slid curiously over her face and Vanessa wondered how a pair of gray eyes could look so warm or how their gaze could feel even hotter to her skin.

"I see. So does that change your mind about moving to the ranch? I'd certainly feel a lot better about you and babies knowing you had close neighbors."

Up to a point, she could understand his thinking. Her parents' home was fairly isolated, with the nearest neighbor being a good five miles away. And even though the Valdezes' had raised five children in the tiny stucco structure, the rooms were small and limited to what she could do with them.

Still, the home was hers now and she was proud of it. She didn't need the best of things to be happy and that's the way she wanted her twins to be raised—without the need for material trappings. He ought to understand that. He ought to know that for him to merely imply she needed to find some place "better" was offensive and hurtful to her. Besides, after dealing with Jeff, she wanted her independence. Needed it, in fact. But she didn't want to go into that now with Conall.

Reaching for the insulated coffeepot, she added a splash of the hot liquid to her cooling cup. "I thank you for the offer. But, no. It doesn't change my mind. Until I get the hang of it, taking care of two newborns is going to be...well, challenging. I need to be in a place where

I feel comfortable and at home. And that's at my own place." Her gaze met his. "I hope you understand."

Conall dropped his attention to his plate as he shoveled up a forkful of egg and wondered why he felt so disappointed. It wasn't as if he was a green teenager and she'd turned him down for a date. Last night, after he'd left her at the door of her room, the idea of offering her housing had entered his mind and once he'd gone to bed, he'd lain awake for some time imagining how it would be to have her and her new little family close by. He'd liked the idea so much that he'd rushed over here early to tell her about it. Now, seeing how she didn't want his help, he felt deflated and foolish.

"I understand that you women have your own ideas about things," he said. "I can accept that."

Even though her sigh was barely discernible, he heard it. The sound put a faint frown between his brows as he wondered why anything she was thinking and feeling about him should matter. Hell, she was just his secretary. Just because she'd become the sudden mother of twin infants didn't make her any different than the woman who'd worked in his office for the past two months, he reasoned with himself.

Yet this whole thing with the babies had forced Conall to see Vanessa in a more personal way. And last night, when he'd succumbed to his urges and kissed her, something had clicked inside him. Suddenly he'd been feeling, wanting, needing. All at once he'd felt the dead parts of him waking and bursting to life again.

Conall realized it was stupid of him to hang so much importance on one kiss. But he couldn't put it or her out of his mind.

"I'm glad," she said, "because I don't want to appear ungrateful."

He smiled at her. "Good. Because I have another offer for you. Especially since you turned the last one down," he added.

Her brows lifted with faint curiosity and Conall couldn't help but notice how the early morning sun was kissing her pearly skin and bathing it with a golden sheen. Last night, when he'd touched her face and laid his cheek against hers, he'd been overwhelmed at the softness and even now a part of him longed to reach across the table and trail his fingers across her skin, her lips.

"Don't you think you've already offered me enough?" she asked dryly.

Reaching for his coffee, he tried to sound like he was discussing business with a client. "Not yet. This is something essential to you and to me. I don't want to lose you as a secretary, so while you're at work you're going to need child care services. I insist that the ranch provide you with a nanny. Two, if need be."

She fell back against her chair and Conall could see he'd shocked her. Clearly, she'd not been expecting him to offer her any sort of amenities simply because she was a Diamond D employee. In fact, she acted as though it would be wrong for her to accept anything from him. Which was quite a contrast to his ex-wife, who'd grabbed and snatched anything and everything she could, then expected more.

"Don't you think you're going a little overboard?" she asked after a long moment.

"Not really. When I think back through some of the secretaries I've endured in the past, hiring a nanny to keep a good one like you is nothing more than smart business sense."

Actually, there was nothing businesslike going

through Conall's mind at the moment, yet he was playing it that way. Otherwise, he knew Vanessa would balk like a stubborn mule at his suggestion.

"Things have happened so quickly I've not yet had time to think of day care for the babies. There might be someone in Hondo to care for the twins while I'm at work," she said a bit tentatively. "Or Lincoln."

He smiled to himself. "Vanessa, we both know you'd be lucky to find a babysitter in either community. And making such a long drive every morning and evening with the babies wouldn't be practical."

She absently pushed at the egg on her plate. "Sometimes a person has to do things that are...well, not the most convenient."

"Why would you need to do that when I can hire someone to watch the babies right in your home? You wouldn't have to disturb them or drag them in and out in the weather. As far as I can see, it's the perfect solution."

She nodded briefly and he could see a range of emotions sweeping across her face. She clearly wanted to resist his help and Conall couldn't understand why. If he'd ever been harsh or cold with the woman, he didn't recall it. And though they'd never visited about things out of the office, he'd never treated her with indifference. He could understand, up to a point, her wanting to be independent. But now wasn't the time for her to worry about showing off her self-reliance. She had more than her own welfare to consider now. Maybe the only way she could think of him was as her boss, instead of a friend offering help. The idea bothered him greatly, although he couldn't figure why it should. He'd stopped caring what women thought of him a long time ago.

She let out a deep breath, then lifted her coffee cup

from its saucer. "I'll be honest, Conall. I've been trying to budget in my head and the cost of child care is going to take a big hunk out of my salary. I'd be crazy to turn down your offer of a nanny. At least until the babies get older and I can get my feet planted more firmly."

Relief put a smile on his face. "Now you're making sense. I'll start making calls as soon as we finish breakfast."

"There is one condition, though, Conall."

He paused in the act of reaching for a second piece of toast. "Yes?"

Her brown eyes met his and for a split second his breath hung in his throat. He was slipping, damn it. None of this should feel so important to him. Yes, the babies were adorable and yes, Vanessa's kiss had been like sipping from a honeycomb. But Vanessa and the children weren't supposed to be his business or responsibility.

Her answer broke into his uneasy thoughts. "I also want to have a say in who you hire for the job."

In spite of his internal scolding, Conall began to breathe again. "I wouldn't have it any other way," he assured her.

By the time they finished the last bit of business at the lawyer's office, picked up the babies and boarded a plane back to Ruidoso, Vanessa felt as though she'd gone around the world and back again. The excitement of becoming an instant mother had finally caught up to her, along with the fact that she had no idea of how to deal with this new and different Conall.

The cool, aloof boss that she'd worked with for the past two months appeared to be completely gone. On the flight home, he'd been attentive, reassuring and helpful. When Rick had stirred and began to cry, he'd insisted on cradling the tiny boy in his arms and feeding him one of the bottles the nuns had prepared for their flight.

Seeing the big rancher handle the baby with such gentleness had overwhelmed her somewhat. He was such a man's man and she'd never seen him display much affection toward anyone or anything, except his grandmother Kate and the baby colts and fillies that were born every spring on the Diamond D.

She'd often wondered if his hard demeanor was the thing that had sent his ex-wife, Nancy, running to other pastures. But seeing him interact with her new son had given Vanessa a glimpse of a Conall that she'd never seen or knew existed. There was a soft side to him. So there must have been another, more complicated reason for his divorce.

For weeks now, Vanessa had told herself she didn't want to know what had happened to end her boss's marriage. After all, it wasn't her business and she'd had her own heartbreaking divorce to deal with. But now that Conall had kissed her, now that she'd seen for herself that he could be a hot-blooded man with all sorts of feelings, she'd grown even more curious about his marriage and divorce.

Trying to shove aside the personal thoughts about Conall, Vanessa glanced over her shoulder to see the twins sleeping soundly in the two car seats they'd purchased back in Las Vegas for the trip.

"I doubt the twins will feel any jet lag," Conall commented as he skillfully steered the truck over the mountainous highway toward Tinnie. "They've slept for nearly the entire trip."

She straightened in her seat and as she gazed out the window, she realized she was nearly home. So much had happened since they'd left for Vegas that she felt as though she'd been gone for weeks instead of two days. "That's what newborns mostly do, sleep. Unless they have colic and I'm praying that doesn't happen."

He glanced her way. "You know about babies and colic? I thought you were the youngest of the family."

"I am. But my mother used to reminisce to me about her babies. She said two of my brothers cried with the colic until they were six months old and she hardly got any sleep during that time."

"I don't suppose she had anyone to help, either. I mean, your dad worked hard and probably needed his rest at night. And she didn't have any older daughters to help out with a crying infant."

"No. My mother didn't have much help with anything. But she was a happy woman." Wistful now, she glanced at him. "I wish Mama could've seen the twins. She would have been so thrilled for me and so proud to have been their grandmother."

To her surprise he reached over and touched her hand with his. "I figure somewhere she does see, Vanessa."

Many of her friends and acquaintances had expressed their sorrow to Vanessa when her mother had died unexpectedly and she'd appreciated all of them. Yet, these simple words from Conall were the most comforting anyone had given her and she was so touched that she was unable to form a reply. The best she could do was cast him a grateful little smile.

He smiled back and she suddenly realized he didn't need or expect her to say anything. He understood how she felt. The notion not only surprised her, but it also stunned her with uneasy fear. She couldn't allow her feelings for this man to tumble out of control. She had to keep her head intact and her heart safely tucked away in the shadows.

Minutes later Conall parked the truck near the short board fence that cordoned off the small yard from the graveled driveway. After he cut the motor, he said, "Give me the keys and I'll open up before we carry the babies in."

Vanessa dug the house key from her purse and handed it to him. "I'll be unstrapping the twins," she told him.

When he returned, he gathered up Rose from her car seat while Vanessa cradled Rick in the crook of her arm.

Nudging the truck door shut with his broad shoulder, he said, "I'll come back for your luggage and diaper bag later. Right now let's get the babies inside and settled."

Vanessa started to the house with Conall following her onto the tiny porch and past the open door leading into a small living room.

Pausing in the middle of the floor, she glanced around with faint confusion. "Someone has been inside and left the air conditioner on," she said. "I told Maura where the key was but when I last talked to her she didn't mention driving over here."

A sheepish expression stole over his lean face. "I confess. I sent Maura over here to…take care of a few things. I guess she had the forethought to turn on the air conditioner so it would be comfortable when you arrived." He inclined his head toward an arched doorway. "Are the bedrooms through there?"

Vanessa wanted to ask him what sort of things Maura would be doing here. She'd already arranged for a young neighbor boy to feed the goats and the chickens. But seeing he was already changing the subject, she let it pass. She'd be talking to Maura soon enough anyway, she thought.

Nodding in response to his question, she walked past him and he followed her through the doorway and into a tiny hall. As she made a left-hand turn that would lead them to the bedrooms, she said, "My bed is queen-sized so I guess for now, until I get a crib, I'll have to put the twins with me and surround them with pillows."

"Vanessa, why don't you put them in the spare bedroom?"

"Because there's only a narrow twin bed in there. And everything in there needs to be dusted badly."

"It couldn't be that dusty. And a small bed might work better. Let's look at it."

Vexed that he wanted to argue the matter, she paused to frown at him. "Conall, I told you—"

"Just humor me, Vanessa," he interrupted. "Let me see the room. That's all I'm asking."

How could she deny him such a simple request when he'd just interrupted the past two days of his life to help her? Not to mention absorbing the expense of the trip.

With an indulgent shake of her head, she muttered, "Oh, all right. But I'm beginning to think you'd have been better suited to raise mules than Thoroughbreds, Conall."

He chuckled. "I have a lot of Grandmother Kate in me."

The door to the spare bedroom was slightly ajar and she reached inside to flip on the light before pushing the door wide.

Glancing around at him, she pointed out, "Your grandmother Kate is wonderful. Not stubborn."

"That's what I mean."

The grin on his face made her heart flutter foolishly and she quickly turned her attention away from him to push the bedroom door wide.

"Oh!" The one word was quietly gasped as she stared in complete shock. The dusty drab room that she'd been planning to refurnish one day had been transformed into a fairy-tale nursery. Twisting her head around, she said with stunned accusation, "You knew about this!"

He motioned for her to step inside the room. "Perhaps you should take a look before you decide to chop off my head."

Dazed, she moved slowly into the room while her gaze tried to encompass everything at once. The walls had been painted a soft yellow and bordered with wall-paper of brightly colored stick horses. A classic crib made of dark cherrywood with carved spokes stood in one corner while on the opposite wall a matching chest and dresser framed a window draped with Priscilla curtains printed with the same theme as the wallpaper. Behind them, in another available corner, a full-sized rocking horse made of carved wood, complete with a saddle and a black rag-mop mane and tail waited for lit-tle hands and feet to climb on and put him in motion.

"This is...unbelievable," she said in a hushed voice. "It's lovely, Conall. Truly lovely."

"The crib is especially made to connect another one to it later on," he said. "Maura tells me most parents let their twins sleep together until they get a little older. So we thought the one would do for now."

Vanessa stepped over to the bed to see it was made up with smooth, expensive sheets and a yellow-and-white comforter. At the footboard, a mobile with birds and bees dangled temptingly out of reach.

"I think—" She paused as a lump of emotional tears clogged her throat and forced her to swallow. "It's all perfect, Conall."

She pulled back the comforter and placed Rick

gently on the mattress. Conall bent forward and laid Rose next to him. Her throat thick, Vanessa watched as he smoothed a finger over the baby girl's red-gold hair, then repeated the same caress on the boy.

Once he straightened away from the babies, he rested his hand against her back and murmured, "I'm glad you think it's perfect, Vanessa. I wanted this little homecoming to be that way for you."

She looked up at him as all sorts of thoughts and questions swirled in her head. "I don't know what to think...or say. The cost, all the work—"

"Don't fret about any of that, Vanessa," he said quickly, cutting her off. "The cost wasn't as much as you think. And the two stable hands that Maura borrowed from the ranch to help her were only too glad to get out of mucking stalls for a couple of days."

Even though Maura and others had worked to prepare the nursery, no one had to tell her that Conall had been the orchestrator of the whole thing and the fact left her totally bewildered. For a man who said he would never have children, Conall was behaving almost like a new father.

What did it mean? Was he doing all this for her? Or the babies? None of it made sense.

Yes, innately he was a good, decent man, she reasoned. And he could afford to be generous. Being his secretary, she personally dealt with the charities he supported, and the people he helped, some of whom he didn't even know. She could almost understand him paying for the trip, the nursery, the nanny. Almost. But the kiss, the touches, the smiles and easy words, those hadn't been acts of charity. Or had they?

"Vanessa? There's a tiny little frown on your forehead. Is something wrong?"

Hoping that was all he could read on her face, she said, "I'm just wondering."

"About what?"

She couldn't answer that, Vanessa decided. If he knew her thoughts had been dwelling on his kiss he'd most likely be amused. And she couldn't stand that. Not from him.

"Nothing. Just forget it," she said dismissively.

He studied her face for a quiet moment, then bent his head and placed a soft kiss on her forehead. "I'm going to go get the rest of your things from the truck," he said gently.

As Vanessa watched him leave the nursery, she realized the twins had done more than made her an instant mother. For now, they'd turned her boss into a different man, one that was very dangerous to her vulnerable heart.

Chapter Five

A week and a half later, Conall stood inside the only
barn on the Diamond D that was still the original structure their grandfather, Arthur Donovan, had erected back
in the 1960s when the ranch was first established.

The walls of the structure consisted of rough, lapped
boards while the wide span of roof was corrugated iron.
Down through the years loving attention had allowed
the old building to survive the elements and to this day
the building was, in his opinion, the prettiest on the
ranch.

Conall would be the first person to admit he'd always
been attached to the old barn. It held some of his earli-
est and fondest childhood memories, many of which
included his stern grandfather warning him not to climb
to the top of the rafter-high hay bales.

"This old building is a tinderbox just waiting for
a match or cigarette to come along and ignite it," his

brother Liam commented as the two men stood in the middle of the cavernous barn.

For the past few years Liam had been the sole horse trainer for the Diamond D and for the most part Conall allowed him to dictate how the working area of the ranch was laid out and what equipment was needed to keep the horses healthy, happy and in top-notch running and breeding condition. But the old barn was a different matter. It was full of history. It was a point of tradition and Conall was just stubborn enough and old-fashioned enough to insist it remain the same.

"Liam, I've heard this from you a hundred times. You ought to know by now that I have no intention of changing my mind on the subject."

Rolling his eyes with impatience, Liam answered, "Fine. If you don't want to tear the firetrap down, then at least you can renovate and replace the lumber with cinder block."

Conall groaned. "Sorry. I'm not doing that, either. I don't want our ranch to look like the grounds of a penitentiary."

Slapping a pair of leather work gloves against the palm of his hand, Liam muttered, "I don't have to tell you what a fire would do to this place."

The sun had disappeared behind the mountains at least forty-five minutes ago and for the first time in months Conall had left his office earlier than usual with plans to drive to Vanessa's. He didn't want to waste his time going over this worn-out argument with Liam.

"Liam, I might not have my hands on the horses every day like you do, but I do understand their needs and how to care for them. You damn well know that I'm aware of the devastation a fire causes to a horse barn or stables. But—" he used his arm to gesture to the interior of the building "—we're not housing horses in here now. Besides that, we have the most modern and up-to-date fire alarm system installed in every structure on the ranch. Not to mention the fact that we have security guards and stable grooms with the horses around the clock. The horses are safer than our own grandmother is when she's sitting in a rocker on the back porch. So don't give me the fire argument."

Liam let out a disgruntled grunt. "You've got to be the biggest old fogey I know, Conall. What about the argument of updating the barn to make it more usable and efficient? Right now all we have in here are hay and tractor tires!"

"This barn worked for Grandfather and it's still working for us. And right now, it's getting late. Let's get to the house," Conall told him.

With both men agreeing to let the matter drop for now, they stepped out into the rapidly fading light. As they walked to the main house, Liam kept his steps abreast of Conall's.

"I'm going over to the Bar M after dinner," he announced abruptly. "Want to come along?"

Mildly surprised, Conall glanced at him. "The Bar M? The Sanderses giving a party or something?" he asked, then shook his head. "That was a stupid question of me, wasn't it? You don't do parties."

Beneath his cowboy hat, Liam's lips pressed together in a grim line. "Why do you have to be a bastard at times, Conall?"

Conall bit back a sigh. It was true he'd purposely asked the question to dig at his younger brother. But he'd not done it out of meanness as Liam seemed to think. He'd done it out of care and concern. But trying to explain that to his younger brother would be as easy as making it rain on a cloudless day, he thought dismally.

"I don't know—just goes with my job, I suppose," he quipped.

Liam grunted. "Compared to my job, yours is like a day off. You should be smiling and kicking your heels."

Even though Conall put in long, stressful hours, his job couldn't begin to be compared to Liam's. His younger brother was up at three in the morning in order to be at the stables at four and most nights he didn't fall into bed until long after the rest of the household was sound asleep. When Ruidoso's racing meet wasn't going on, he was shipping horses to tracks in the mid-south and on to the west coast. And their health and racing condition was only a part of his responsibility. He had to make sure each one was strategically entered in a race that would enhance his or her chances of winning.

"I know it," Conall admitted. "That's why you're going to have to give in and replace Clete. Or you're going to end up in the hospital with a heart attack."

Three years ago, Liam's longtime assistant, Cletis Robinson, had died after a lengthy illness. The death of the seventy-five-year-old man had shaken the whole ranch and especially the Donovan family, who'd valued Clete's friendship for more than thirty years. Liam grunted again. "According to Bridget I don't have a heart."

"She doesn't believe I have one, either," Conall half joked. "I guess our little sister thinks we should be like those namby-pamby guys she went to med school with."

"Bridget is too soft for her own good," Liam muttered.

"So why are you going over to the Bar M this evening?" Conall asked as they approached a side entrance to the main ranch house.

"Chloe has a two-year-old gelding she's thinking about selling. I think he might be good enough to earn some money."

Pausing with surprise, Conall looked at him. "There has to be a catch. Chloe would never sell a good runner."

"Normally, no. But she was forced to geld this one. And Chloe doesn't like to invest time or money into a horse that can't reproduce."

Conall tried not to wince as he reached to open the door. "Yeah," he said, unable to keep the sarcasm from his voice. "Throwing offspring is the most important thing."

Close on his heels, Liam cursed. "Hell, Conall—"

"Forget I said that," Conall quickly interrupted. "You do what you think about the gelding. I have plans to see the twins tonight."

The two men entered the house and started down a long hallway that would take them to the central part of the house.

"The twins," Liam repeated blankly. "You mean Vanessa's new twins?"

"What other twins do we know?" Conall countered.

Liam stepped up so that the two of them were walking abreast of each other. "Well, there's the Gibson twins. You know, the ones we dated in high school."

Conall chuckled. "So you haven't forgotten them, either?"

Liam grunted with faint humor. "Forget two blonde tornadoes? They might have been short on intelligence but they were long on entertainment," he said, then glanced at Conall. "So what's the deal with Vanessa's twins? I thought after that trip to Las Vegas you had everything taken care of?"

Vanessa and the twins were settled now and from what she'd told him over the phone, everything was going fine. So why was he giving in to the urge to tear over to her house, Conall asked himself? Because ever since that evening they'd returned from Vegas he'd been dying to see the babies again. And more than that, he missed Vanessa, missed seeing her at her desk and talking with her, however briefly, throughout the busy day.

"They're fine. I have a gift for the babies that I want to deliver."

Liam studied him faint dismay. "Making a trip out to Vegas and bringing them home wasn't enough of a gift?"

Apparently Liam didn't know about the new nursery he'd funded for the twins or the fact that he was in the process of hunting for a full-time nanny. And Conall wasn't about to tell him. What went on between him and Vanessa was none of Liam's or anyone else's business, he decided.

"No. I wanted to give them something personal. After all, Vanessa is my secretary. And it's not like she had a baby shower." Seeing they'd reached the staircase that led up to the floor where his bedroom and several others were located, he broke away from his brother's side. As he started the climb, he threw a parting comment over his shoulder. "Good luck with Chloe. You're going to need it if you try to deal with her. She's tough."

"She might be tough, big brother, but she's not dangerous."

Conall glanced behind him to see Liam was still standing at the bottom of the stairs staring thoughtfully up at him.

"What does that mean?" Conall asked.

With a dismissive wave, Liam began to move on down the hallway. "You figure it out," he called back to Conall.

From the Diamond D to Vanessa's place, the highway meandered through pine-covered mountains then opened up to bald hills spotted with scrub pinion, twisted juniper and random tufts of grass, and this evening he took in the landscape with renewed appreciation. It wasn't often that Conall left the ranch for any reason. Unless there was an important conference or horse-racing event for him to attend, there wasn't a need for him to leave the isolated sanctuary of his home. Clients came to him, not the other way around.

Going to Vegas with Vanessa had definitely been out-of-character for him. And this trip tonight was even more so, he admitted to himself. Especially since he'd sworn off women and dating.

So what was happening to him? he wondered as he rounded a bend and the turnoff to Vanessa's house came into view. Had two little babies reminded him that his life wasn't over? Or was he simply waking up after a long dormant spell? Either way, it felt good to be getting out, good to think of seeing the babies, and even better to envision kissing Vanessa again.

Vanessa was at the back part of the house in a small alcove used for a laundry room when she heard a faint knock at the front door. Surprised by the unexpected sound, she used her hip to shove the dryer door closed and hurried through the house. In the past few days she'd had a few old friends and acquaintances stop by to see the babies, but it was getting far too late in the evening for such a neighborly visit.

Before opening the door, she peeked through the lacy curtain covering a window that overlooked the front porch. The moment she spotted Conall standing on the tiny piece of concrete, her heart momentarily stopped. He'd not been here since the evening they'd returned from Las Vegas and a few days had passed since she'd talked to him on the phone. It wasn't like her rigidly scheduled boss to show up unannounced on her doorstep. But then it wasn't like Conall to leave the Diamond D, much less leave it to come here.

Momentarily pressing a hand to her chest, she drew in a bracing breath, then pulled the door wide to greet him. This evening he was dressed in old jeans and a predominately white plaid shirt with pearl snaps. A black Stetson was pulled low over his forehead and she was struck by how much younger and relaxed he looked. This was Conall the horseman—not the businessman— and rough sexuality surrounded him like an invisible cloud.

She released the breath she'd been holding. "Hello, Conall."

A sheepish smile crossed his lean features. "Sorry I didn't call first, Vanessa, but I didn't want you thinking you needed to rush around and tidy things before I got here. Am I interrupting?"

Her insides were suddenly shaking, making her feel worse than foolish. For weeks she'd worked with this man every day. It wasn't like he was a stranger. But actually he was a stranger, she thought. This man on her porch wasn't the same as the tough-as-nails boss who ran a multimillion-dollar horse ranch; he was a man she was just beginning to know and like. Far too much.

"Not at all. Won't you come in?" she asked.

"Thanks," he murmured as he stepped through the door.

As he walked to the middle of the small living room, his male scent trailed after him and as her eyes traveled over his broad shoulders and long muscular legs, Vanessa felt her own knees grow ridiculously weak.

"Please have a seat," she offered, "or would you rather take a look at the babies first? They're in the kitchen. Asleep in their bassinet."

Two days after they'd returned from Las Vegas, a delivery truck had arrived at the door with a double bassinet fashioned just for twins. The card accompanying it had simply read, *I thought you might need this, too.*

She'd immediately called Conall and thanked him for the gift, but now that he was here in the flesh, now that his gaze was on her face, she felt extremely exposed and confused. Why was he really here? For her or the babies?

With a guilty little grin, he pulled off the black Stetson and placed it on a low coffee table in front of the couch. "If you don't mind I'd love to see the babies."

"Sure. I was just about to eat. Have you had dinner?" she asked as she motioned for him to follow her out of the room.

"I didn't take time to eat," he admitted. "Liam had me cornered and then it was too late to join the family at the dining table."

"I'm sure Kate wasn't too pleased about that."

He chuckled. "You've heard about Grandmother's strict rules of being on time for dinner?"

Vanessa smiled fondly. "Years ago, when I visited

Maura at the ranch, Kate's rules were the first things I learned about the Donovan household. I remember being very scared to enter the dining room."

"Why? Grandmother always loves having young people around."

Shrugging, she entered the open doorway to the kitchen while Conall followed closely behind her. "I always thought I looked too raggedy to sit at her dining table or that I'd say something stupid or wrong."

He shook his head. "Grandmother has never been a snob. Strict, yes, but not a snob. And she made sure the rest of us weren't, either."

"I know. But I always felt a little out of place in your home, Conall." She laughed softly and gestured to the small room they were standing in. It was neat and clean, but the wooden cabinets were more than fifty years old and the porcelain sink chipped and stained. The ceiling was so low that Conall had to duck in order to keep from hitting his head on the light fixture and though the appliances were still chugging along, they'd seen better days. "This isn't quite the same as the kitchen in the Diamond D."

"No," he admitted. "But it's very homey and inviting. And it's yours. That should make you proud."

His comments made her feel warm and good. "It does," she agreed, then motioned to the bassinet sitting near a double window. "I know the babies can't see yet, but I put them by the window just in case they can pick up the movement of lights and shadows. But I think they notice music more than anything. Whenever I sing to them they usually fall right to sleep. To end the torture, I guess."

Chuckling, Conall crossed the small room and bent over the sleeping babies. "They've grown," he said just above a whisper. "And their skin doesn't look as ruddy."

"They're losing that just-born look," she told him.

He said, "Before you know it they'll be rolling, then crawling and walking. It seems incredible that they start out so tiny and grow into big people like us."

He gazed at them for several long moments before he finally straightened to his full height. When he turned away from the bassinet Vanessa caught sight of his profile and was immediately struck by the wistful expression on his face.

Were the twins softening him? she wondered. Perhaps changing his stance about not having children? She wanted to think so, although she didn't know why the issue was important to her. Whether Conall ever raised a family or not would depend on the next woman he married. Not her and the twins.

He walked over to where she stood by the cabinet counter. "I don't mean this in a bad way, Vanessa, but you look exhausted. I assume the babies are keeping you up at night?"

Unwittingly, she touched a hand to her bare cheek. Without makeup and her hair pulled into a messy knot at the back of her head, she no doubt looked terrible. She hated having him see her like this, but it was too late to worry about her appearance now.

"Some nights are more broken than others," she admitted. "If the babies would both wake at the same time it would be a big help. But Rick always wakes far before his sister and then about the time I get him fed and asleep and I'm about to crawl back into bed, she starts fussing." She smiled at him. "But I'm not complaining. Having the babies...well, it's like a dream come true."

He reached out and rubbed a hand up and down her

arm in what was meant to be a comforting gesture. But for Vanessa, it was like flint striking stone. The friction was igniting a trail of tiny flames along her skin, making it difficult for her to breathe.

"You need help, Vanessa. You can't continue to handle two infants alone. I'm sorry it's taken so long for me to find a nanny, but things have been hectic in the office since you've been away."

She sighed. "I'm sorry I've gotten everything out of whack. I did call Fiona and thank her for filling in for me at the office. I hope the job isn't wearing her out."

Conall chuckled. "Wearing Mom out? Not hardly. She thinks she's still in her twenties instead of entering her sixties."

"She had six children and I'm letting two wear me down," Vanessa said with a grimace. "That makes me feel like a wimp."

"She didn't have two at once. That would wear anyone out. But today I think I might have found a nanny and if things go as planned she'll be over tomorrow or the next day for your approval."

Her interest sparked, Vanessa asked, "Do I know this woman?"

"I doubt it. Her name is Hannah Manning and she's a retired nurse that Maura used to work with at Sierra General."

"Oh. Well, if she's a nurse, she ought to be qualified for the job. I'll look forward to meeting her."

His hand was still on her arm, sending sizzling little signals to her brain, and she could only hope he couldn't guess how much she wanted to touch him, kiss him again. In spite of her days and nights being consumed with caring for the twins, she'd not been able to quit thinking about the man.

"I've stewed a pot of *carne guisada* for dinner," she said, her gaze awkwardly avoiding his. "Would you like to join me?"

"I'd love to," he murmured, "but I'd like to do something else first."

She was wondering what *something else* could possibly be when his forefinger slid beneath her chin and lifted her face up to his. Their gazes clashed and Vanessa's heart began to thud so hard she could scarcely breathe.

"Conall, this…is…not good," she finally managed to whisper.

His mouth twisted to a sexy slant. "How do you know that? We haven't done it yet."

She groaned with misgivings but the sound didn't deter him. Instead, both his hands came up to frame the sides of her face. The tender intimacy shot her resistance to tiny pieces and as his head lowered toward hers, she closed her eyes and leaned into him.

This time the meeting of their mouths was not the fragile exploration they'd exchanged in Las Vegas. No, this time it was all-out hunger, and what little breath Vanessa had beforehand was instantly swept away by the crush of his hard lips.

Instinctively her hands grabbed for support and landed smack in the middle of his chest. She gripped folds of his cotton shirt as the heat of his body infused hers with heady warmth and his hands began a lazy expedition against her shoulders.

Certain she was going to dissolve in a helpless puddle if the kiss went any further, Vanessa frantically tore herself away and turned her back to him.

She was fiercely trying to fill her lungs with oxygen, when his lips pressed against her ear and she closed her eyes as he began to whisper, "I'm not going to apologize for that, Vanessa. It felt too right."

She couldn't argue that point. Until now, until Conall's lips had touched hers, no man's kiss had ever spun her away to such a fairy-tale world. And that was the problem, she thought desperately. Conall was a prince and he wasn't looking to make her his princess.

She swallowed hard. "I don't expect you to apologize," she said in a faint voice. "I'm just—" Stiffening her resolve, she turned back to him. "I don't know what's going through your mind, Conall. But I think you should understand that I'm not a woman who plays around."

For a fraction of a second, he looked astounded and then a grimace tightened his features. "Do you think I'm a man who plays around?"

Her eyes searched his. "I've never thought so. But you're starting to make me wonder."

He let out a mocking snort. "I haven't touched another woman in a long, long time. Does that sound like a man that's on the prowl?"

It sounded like a man who was still in love with his ex-wife, or one that had been wounded so badly he'd turned away from love altogether. Either way, Vanessa thought, the notion was a bleak one.

Sighing heavily, she stepped around him and crossed over to a small gas range. Giving one of the knobs a savage twist, she ignited a flame beneath a blue granite pot.

After a moment, she answered his question. "No. It sounds to me like a man that's confused."

"Confused, hell," he muttered.

She glanced over her shoulder to see him striding toward her and before she could stop it, desire washed through her like a hot wave, knocking down her defenses before she could even get them erected.

"Well, if you're not mixed up, I am," she admitted.

He stopped within a few inches of her and though he didn't touch her, Vanessa could almost feel his hands, his gaze, roaming her face, her body.

"Explain that, would you?"

A war exploded inside her and she was trying to decide if she wanted to throw herself in his arms or scurry out of the room, when he shifted closer.

She tried to swallow but her throat was so dry she nearly choked in the process. Finally, she managed to say, "I don't understand any of this, Conall."

He was looking at her with that same stony expression she'd seen on him in the office when things weren't going his way.

"It would help if I knew what *this* was," he stated.

The fact that he was deliberately being ignorant made her clench her jaw tight and suddenly all the doubts and emotions that had been swirling around in her for the past two weeks boiled to the surface. "You know what I'm talking about, Conall!" she burst out. "I've worked for you every day for more than two months and you hardly took a moment to look at me, much less touch me. Now all of a sudden you behave as though I'm irresistible. It's—it's ridiculous! That's what it is."

Behind her the stewed beef began to boil rapidly and the sound matched the blood pounding in her ears. Twisting around to the stove, she automatically lowered the flame as she sucked in a deep breath and tried to calm herself. But the effort failed completely as soon as his hands settled upon her shoulders.

"Vanessa, I don't understand why you're so worked

up over a kiss," he murmured. "I'm not asking you to jump into bed with me."

The mere idea of making intimate love to this man was enough to make her face flame and her body burn. And she suddenly felt terribly, terribly embarrassed. Maybe she was acting foolish and naive. Maybe she was making a mountain out of a molehill.

Forcing herself to turn and face him, she said, "I'm sorry, Conall, but this change in our relationship has caught me off guard. I wasn't expecting any of this and—"

"Do you think I was? Hell, Vanessa, like I said before I've not even looked in a woman's direction in years. And even after you came to work for me I wasn't thinking of you in this way, but..."

She waited for him to finish, but he appeared to be lost for words.

"But what, Conall? I receive word about the babies and suddenly you're looking at me as though you've never seen me before."

"That's true," he admitted.

Incredulous, Vanessa stared at him. "It is?"

Clearly frustrated, he swiped a hand through his dark brown hair. "I can't give you a solid reason for my behavior, Vanessa, except that the day you fainted in the office I began to see you as a woman."

Grimacing, she peered around him to the opposite side of the room. Thankfully, the twins were still sleeping soundly in their bassinet.

"And what was I before?" she asked dryly, "A robot that answered the phone and dealt with your correspondence?"

He groaned. "I'm trying to explain."

"You're not doing a very good job of it," she pointed out.

His hands slipped from her shoulders and slid down her arms until they reached her hands. Then, like a pair of flesh-and-bone handcuffs, his fingers clamped around her wrists.

"You're not making the task any easier, either," he countered.

Nervously moistening her lips, she focused her gaze to the middle button on his shirt. "I suppose I'm not," she admitted. "But try to see things from my angle, Conall. Suddenly you're making the twins a nursery, buying them gifts and—and handling me as though... you want to! What am I suppose to think? Are you playing up to me just so you can be around the twins?"

"That's damned stupid!"

Surprised by sharpness in his voice, her gaze flew up to his face.

"I care about the twins," he went on. "But I'm pretty sure you'd let me visit them whether I kissed you or not."

Desperate for answers, she spluttered at him, "So why are you kissing me? Because your libido has woken up and I'm handy?"

His nostrils flared as his fingers tightened on her wrists. "Vanessa, none of this is hard to understand. I'm simply being a man. A man that has found himself attracted to a woman. A kiss is...well, I'm trying to tell you that I think we should get to know each other better. On a more personal level."

She groaned with disbelief. "That wasn't a get-to-know-you kiss, Conall. That was more like an I-missed-you-like-hell kiss."

To her amazement, a tempting little grin spread

across his lips. "Finally, you're getting something right," he murmured, his eyes settling softly on her face. "I have missed you like hell."

His admission sent a foolish thrill rushing through her, spinning her heartbeat to a rapid thud.

"That's very hard to believe," she said, in a breathless whisper.

"Then maybe I'd better give you another demonstration. Just to prove my point."

Making his intentions clear, his head bent toward hers and though Vanessa told herself she'd be smart to make a quick escape, she couldn't make a move. Instead, she stood transfixed and waited for his lips to capture hers.

Chapter Six

Just a few more moments, Vanessa promised herself, and then she'd gather the strength to step away from the heated search of Conall's lips. She'd get her breath back, along with her senses, and then she'd remind herself why being in his arms was as dangerous as sidling up to a sizzling stick of dynamite.

But so far the minutes continued to tick away and she'd not taken that first move to end their kiss. Instead, she couldn't stop her lips from parting beneath his, her arms from sliding around his waist.

She was leaning into him, her whole body buzzing with the anticipation of getting even closer to his hard body, when she caught the sound of Rick's faint whimpers.

The pressure of Conall's lips eased just a fraction, telling her that he must have picked up on the baby's subtle call. Even so, he didn't bother to end the kiss until the tiny boy let loose with an all-out cry.

Lifting his head, he drew in a ragged breath and glanced over his shoulder toward the bassinet. "That child needs to learn better timing," he said with humor, then glancing back to Vanessa, he added, "Sounds like duty calls."

Struggling to regain her composure, she said in a husky voice, "It's Rick. I can tell by his cry. He's probably thinking it's time for his supper, too."

After switching off the fire beneath the *carne guisada*, she walked over to the bassinet. Conall followed close on her heels.

"Can I help?" he asked.

She lifted the fussing Rick from the bed. "It would be a big help if you could hold him while I heat a bottle."

Conall eagerly held out his arms. "I'd be glad to hold him, just don't expect me to make him stop crying," he warned. "I wouldn't know how."

She carefully placed the baby in the crook of Conall's strong arm. "Just rock him a little," she suggested. "And don't worry if he keeps on crying. He's not hurting, just exercising his opinion."

Chuckling, he looked down at the fussy baby. "Oh, well, we men have to do that from time to time."

Pausing for just a moment, Vanessa couldn't help but take in the sight of Conall with tiny Rick cradled against his broad chest. The man looked like a born father, she thought, certainly not a guy that had sworn off having children.

Shaking away that disturbing notion, Vanessa hurried to the refrigerator to fetch the bottle. She was about to place it in the microwave, when Rose decided to let loose with a wail.

"I think you'd better make it two bottles," Conall said, raising his voice above the crying.

"So I hear."

Vanessa collected another bottle from the refrigerator and quickly heated them to a wrist-warm temperature. By the time she handed Conall one of the bottles and went to gather Rose from the bassinet, the girl was howling at the top of her lungs.

"I think you'll find it easier to feed him if you're sitting down," Vanessa told Conall, then she picked up Rose and crooned soothingly to the baby while carrying her over to the dining table.

After taking a seat, Vanessa propped the baby in the crook of her arm and offered her the bottle. Rose latched on to the nipple and began to nurse hungrily.

On the opposite side of the table Conall was trying to emulate Vanessa's movements. "I've never fed a baby before," he admitted. "I'm not sure I'm doing any of this right."

From what Vanessa could see the Donovan family had been having babies left and right with Maura's two boys and Brady's little girl. She found it difficult to believe that Conall hadn't given at least one of them a bottle. Especially Brady's daughter, since the two brothers lived together in the main ranch house. Sure, he was a busy man, she reasoned, but not that busy. Perhaps the babies had all been breast-fed. That might account for his lack of experience, she thought.

"There's nothing to it," she assured him. "Just keep his head supported and the bottle tilted upward so he won't suck air. He'll do the rest."

He shifted Rick to a comfortable position and offered him the bottle. Once the baby was nursing quietly,

Conall looked over at Vanessa and smiled. "Hey, that's quite a silencer. Does a bottle always do the trick?"

Vanessa chuckled. "Unfortunately, no. Sometimes they cry when they aren't hungry and I have to try to figure out what's wrong and what they're trying to tell me."

He nodded. "Like a horse. They can't talk with words, but they have other ways of communicating."

It wasn't a surprise to Vanessa to hear Conall use equine terminology. Even though he didn't spend his days down at the barns as Liam did, he was equally as knowledgeable about the animals. In fact, the first time she'd seen Conall up close was when she'd visited the Diamond D and she and Maura had walked down to the training area where Conall had been breezing a huge black Thoroughbred around an oval dirt track. At the time he'd been a lean teenager, not the muscular man he was now. Yet she'd remembered being impressed by his strength and the easy way he'd handled the spirited stallion.

Needless to say, from that moment on he'd been her dark, secret prince and she'd dreamed of how incredible it would be to be the object of his affection. But then he'd graduated from high school and left for college. Vanessa had put away her crush for the rich Donovan boy and focused on the reality of her future, one that included leaving Lincoln County, New Mexico, and her adolescent dreams behind.

"Vanessa, you've gone far way. What are you thinking?"

Unaware that she'd gotten so lost in her thoughts, her face warmed with a blush as she glanced over at him. "Actually, I was thinking back to the first time I saw you," she admitted.

The lift of his dark brows said she'd surprised him. "Really? You remember that?"

Clearly his memory bank didn't include the first time he'd seen her, but then she hardly expected him to recall such a thing. He'd been older and had moved in much higher social circles than she. He'd always been associated with the brightest and prettiest girls on the high school campus. He would have never bothered to give someone like her a second glance.

"I do. You were on the track, exercising one of your father's horses."

He chuckled with fond remembrance. "Hmm. That must have been when I was thirty pounds lighter."

"You were about seventeen."

With a shake of his head, he murmured, "So long ago."

"I had a huge crush on you."

The moment the words passed her lips, Vanessa expected amusement to appear on his face, or even a laugh to rumble out of him. Instead, he studied her thoughtfully for a long, long spell and Vanessa got the impression he was thinking back to those carefree days before either of them had met their respective spouses.

"I didn't know," he said finally.

She felt the blush on her face sting her cheeks even hotter. To escape his searching gaze, she bent her head over Rose's sweet little face.

"No," she murmured, as she absently adjusted the receiving blanket around the baby's shoulders. "I would have died with embarrassment if you'd found out. In fact, I never told anyone about my feelings for you. Not even my mother."

"And why was that?" he quietly asked.

That pulled her attention back to him and she smiled

wanly. "Mama was a realist. She would have given me a long lecture about crying for the moon."

His brows formed a line of disapproval. "You make it sound like I was some sort of unattainable prize, Vanessa."

"To me you were."

His head swung back and forth. "I was just a young man, like millions of others in the world."

Not to her. Not then. Not now, Vanessa thought. With a shake of her head, she gave him a patient smile. "Con-all, look around. You didn't pick your girlfriends from this sort of background. Nor would you now."

Rolling his eyes toward the ceiling, he mouthed a curse under his breath. "I don't have girlfriends now. I've already told you that." He lowered his gaze back to her face. "Unless I count you as one."

Her heart gave a jerk. "Is that what I am to you?"

A slow grin tilted the corners of his lips. "I think that's a subject we need to discuss, don't you?"

Was he serious? No. He couldn't be. But, oh, his kiss had felt very, very serious. And that scared her. She wasn't emotionally capable of dealing with a man like him. "No. That's out of the question."

"Why?"

She couldn't stop the tiny groan from sounding in her throat. "I could give you a whole list of reasons. The main one being we have to work with each other."

"So? I can't see that posing a problem. Neither of us are married or committed to someone else."

"It would make things awkward," she said flatly. "Impossible, in fact."

Seeing that Rose had quit nursing and fallen asleep, Vanessa placed the near empty bottle on the table. Rising to her feet, she carefully positioned the baby against her shoulder and gently patted her back. As soon as she heard a loud burp, she carried the sleeping girl back to the bassinet.

"I think he's finished eating, too," Conall told her. "But he's not asleep. His eyes are wide open."

"He probably won't cry now if you put him back by his sister," she suggested as she crossed the room to pull dishes from the cabinet. "But you need to burp him first."

"I might need a little help with that."

Leaving the task of the dishes behind, she walked back over to where he sat holding the baby. "Place him against your shoulder or across your lap," she instructed.

Slowly, he adjusted the boy so that he was reclined against his shoulder.

"Now what?"

"Pat him gently on the back."

He frowned at her. "I don't know what you consider gentle."

She rolled her eyes. "Well, I don't mean pat him like you would a horse's neck!" Deciding it would be easier to show him, she picked up Conall's hand and placed a few measured pats against Rick's back.

"Okay, I get—"

Before he could complete the rest of his sentence, Rick made a belching noise, which was immediately followed by Conall's yelp.

Vanessa didn't have to ask what had happened. She could see a thick stream of milk oozing from Rick's mouth and rolling down Conall's back.

"Uggh! Is that what I think it is?" he asked, twisting his head around in order to get a glimpse of his soggy shoulder.

"Sorry," she said, and before she could stop herself she began to laugh.

He flashed a droll look at her. "I didn't know being vomited on was so funny."

"It isn't. But—" She was laughing so hard she couldn't finish, but instead of him getting angry, he began to grin.

He said, "I didn't know you could laugh like that."

She calmed herself enough to say, "I didn't know you could look so...dumbfounded, either."

He thrust the baby at her. "Here, you'd better take the little volcano before he erupts again."

Still chuckling, Vanessa lifted Rick from his arms. While she cleaned the baby's face, Conall snatched up several paper towels and attempted to wipe the burp from the back of his shirt.

"I'll help you do that," Vanessa told him. "Just let me get Rick settled back in the bassinet."

Once she had both babies nestled together in their bed, she walked over to where Conall stood at the kitchen sink.

"You smell like formula," she said.

"No kidding."

She motioned for him to turn his back to her. When he did, she groaned with dismay.

"Oh, Conall, this is beyond wiping. You're going to have to take off your shirt and let me wash it for you."

"That's too much trouble. Surely the mess will dry."

"Eventually," she agreed. "But I don't think either of us will enjoy eating our supper with that smell at the dining table." She motioned with her hand for the shirt. "Give it to me. I have other things to wash anyway. And

if you're worried about sitting around half-naked, I'll
find you one of Dad's old shirts."

"All right, all right," he mumbled, then quickly began
to strip out of the garment.

Vanessa tried not to stare as the fabric parted from his
chest and slipped off his shoulders. Still, it was impossible to keep her gaze totally averted from his muscled
chest, the dark patch of hair between his nipples and the
hard abs disappearing into the waistband of his jeans.

"I'll put it right in the machine," she said in a rush,
then hurried out of the room before she made a complete
idiot out of herself.

A man's anatomy was nothing new to her, she reminded herself as she tossed Conall's shirt into the
washing machine and followed it with a few more gar-
ments. She'd been married for five years and Jeff had
been a physically attractive man. Yet looking at him
without his shirt hadn't left her breathless or tongue-tied,
the way looking at Conall had a moment ago.

Trying not to reason that one out, Vanessa went to a
closet where she'd stored some of her father's clothing in
hopes that one day he'd get well enough to come home
and wear them again. Now she pulled out a dark blue
plaid shirt and hurried back to the kitchen.

When she stepped through the doorway, she spotted Conall sitting at the table and she swallowed hard
as she walked over and handed him the shirt. "Here's
something to wear while you're waiting. It might be a
little big," she warned. "Dad was pretty fleshy before
he had the stroke."

"Thanks, I'm sure it'll be fine."

Rising to his feet, he plunged his arms into the sleeves
of the cotton shirt. To her surprise the shirt wasn't all
that big, proof that her eyes hadn't deceived her when

they had taken in the sight of his broad shoulders and thick chest.

"So now that the babies are settled and you don't smell like a half-soured milk factory, are you ready to eat?" she asked.

"Sure. Can I help with anything?" he asked as he followed her over to the cabinets.

"Have you honestly ever done anything in the kitchen? Besides eat?"

"Well, I—" He thought for a moment, then gave her a sly grin. "I put the teakettle on to boil whenever I need steam to reshape my hat."

She let out a good-natured groan. "Oh. So you know how to boil water. That's something."

He chuckled. "Maybe you could teach me a few things. Just in case the Diamond D kitchen staff ever go on strike."

His comment reminded Vanessa of the privileged life he led, the fortune he'd been born into.

"I wouldn't worry about it," she replied. "You can always hire someone else to do the job for you."

As she began to pull down plates again, he came to stand close behind her.

"Do you resent that fact, Vanessa? That I…and my family have money? I never thought so. But—" One hand came to rest against the back of her shoulder. "We've never talked about personal things before."

She gripped the edges of the plates as unbidden desire rushed through her.

"We were always too busy to make personal chit-chat." She glanced over her shoulder. "But as far as you being wealthy, I don't resent that. You work harder than anybody I know."

"Not Liam," he corrected.

With the plates pressed against her chest, she turned to face him. "No. Maybe not Liam," she agreed. "But you're just as dedicated."

He gently brushed the back of his knuckles against her cheek and Vanessa wanted to slip into his arms.

"I'm glad you think I earn what I have. And I'll tell you something else, Vanessa, I like spending it on you—and the babies. I like making things better for you. It makes all the work I do mean more to me."

Every cell inside her began to tremble. "That's not the way it should be, Conall. We're—the babies and I... well, you should be doing all of that for a family of your own. Not us."

Slowly, he eased the plates from her tight grip. "Yeah," he said, his quiet voice full of cynicism. "That might be good advice, Vanessa. But I don't happen to have a family of my own."

He carried the plates over to the table and all of a sudden she was struck by the fact that in spite of Conall's wealth, in spite of his long list of valuable assets, he didn't have what she had. He didn't have two tiny babies who needed and cried for his touch or quieted at the soothing sound of his voice. He didn't have anyone to call him Daddy. And from what he'd told Vanessa, he never would.

Hot moisture stung the back of her eyes and as she turned to fish silverware from a small drawer, she wondered whether the unexpected tears were for Conall or herself.

Chapte Seven

Nearly two weeks later, Conall was sitting at his desk, watching dusk settle across the ranch yard when Fiona stepped into the room and announced she was quitting for the day.

"Your father and grandmother will be ready to eat in thirty minutes. Will you be there?" his mother asked.

"Uh…no." Struggling to focus his thoughts back to the moment, he glanced over to Fiona. The woman had been working nonstop all day at Vanessa's desk, yet she looked nearly as fresh as she had when she'd started at eight this morning. Her graceful femininity was a guise, he couldn't help thinking. She was actually a lioness, always fierce and never tiring. "I'm afraid not. I still have a few calls to make before I leave the office."

She grimaced. "Have you talked to Liam?"

"No. Why?"

"He wanted to speak with you about Blue Heaven—

the two-year-old. Something about paying her futurity fees."

Leaning back in his chair, he looked at her with puzzlement. "Why would Liam want to talk to me about the filly? Liam is the trainer, he enters any horse he wants into whatever race he wants. He certainly doesn't ask my opinion on the matter."

Frowning with impatience, she stepped farther into the office until she was standing at the end of his desk. Conall felt as if time had traveled back to when he was ten years old and he'd slipped off to the horse barn instead of doing his homework.

"Does it ever cross your mind that your brother needs your support? That he might want your advice on these matters?"

His gaze dropping away from his mother, he picked up a pen and began to tap it absently against the ink blotter. He wasn't in the mood for one of Fiona's family lectures. He was missing Vanessa like hell and though a nanny for the twins had been hired more than a week ago, she'd not yet returned to work. And damn it, he wasn't going to push her, even though he wanted to. "Not really."

To his surprise Fiona muttered a curse under her breath. It was rare that he ever heard his mother utter a foul word and he couldn't imagine this trivial matter pulling one from her mouth.

"Not really," she mimicked with sarcasm. "I should have known that would be your answer. I doubt you actually think about your brother for more than five minutes out of the day!"

Startled by her unexpected outburst, he jerked his head up to stare at her. "What in the world are you talking about, Mom? Is this 'feel sorry for Liam' day or something?"

"Don't get smart with me, Conall. This is as much about you as it is about Liam working himself to death."

Conall tossed down the pen. "Maybe you haven't noticed, but I'm not exactly taking a vacation here," he muttered, then immediately shook his head. "Sorry, Mom. I...shouldn't have said that."

"No. You shouldn't have."

Sighing with exasperation, he swiveled his chair so that he was facing her head-on. "Liam is working too hard. But what can I do about it? I've been after him to hire an assistant. But he doesn't think anyone could measure up to Clete. Until he decides that he's not going to find another Clete and hires someone to help him, there's not much I can do."

Fiona sighed. "That's true. But I wish...well, that you would take time for him and he would take time for you. You're both so damned obsessed with work that—" Pausing, she shook her head with regret. "Forget it, Conall. I can't change either of you and it's wrong of me to try. I just want you to be happy. But Liam goes around pretending everything is just dandy when it's anything but. And you—sometimes I think you've simply given up. A son of mine," she added with disgust, "I never thought I'd see it."

It wasn't like Fiona to be so critical. Even when she was angry with her children, she managed to display it in a loving way. But something seemed to have stirred her up. As for him giving up, it was no secret that his parents wanted him to get back into the dating scene and find himself a wife. To the Donovans, a person had nothing unless they had a family. And they both had the Pollyanna idea that if he found the right woman, she would understand and accept his sterile condition. Maybe there were a few out there, he thought dully. But would one of them be a woman he could love?

Hell. What kind of question is that, Conall? You don't believe in love anymore. Not after Nancy. Why can't you settle for someone to simply cozy up to and grow old with? Your heart doesn't have to be involved.

His jaw tight, he said firmly, "I'm sorry you've had to work so hard these last few weeks, Mom. I thought Vanessa would have been back by now. But—"

She looked at him sharply. "I can manage this office with one hand tied behind my back. That's not—" She waved a dismissive hand at him and started out the door. "I've got to get back to the house for dinner. And you won't be seeing me at Vanessa's desk in the morning. She called a few minutes ago to say she'd be returning tomorrow."

His boots hit the floor with a thump. "Vanessa called? Why didn't she speak to me?"

"You were on the phone with the fencing company. She didn't want to disturb you."

Or maybe she'd simply wanted to avoid talking to him, Conall thought as his mother slipped out the door. But that was a stupid notion. She was coming back to work tomorrow. She'd be spending her days with him. But it wasn't exactly the days that Conall had been thinking about before his mother had walked in and abruptly interrupted his musings.

With a heavy sigh, he rose from the deep leather chair and walked over to a large framed window overlooking part of the stables. Resting his shoulder against the window seal, he gazed out at the lengthening shadows. Ranch hands were busy with the evening chores and no doubt Liam was in one of the barns, making sure his latest runners were pampered and happy.

Liam goes around pretending everything is just dandy when it's anything but. And you—sometimes I think you've simply given up.

Fiona's words were still rattling around in his head and though Conall tried to tell himself they were simply a mother expressing dissatisfaction with her sons, he had to admit she was, at least, partially right. He couldn't speak for Liam, but as for himself, he supposed he had given up on some aspects of his life.

Didn't his mother realize it was easier for him to focus on his work instead of the mess he'd made of his personal life? The mess he would make if he tried to marry again?

You should be doing all of that for a family of your own. Not us.

Close on the heels of his mother's words, Vanessa traipsed through his mind, reminding him just how much she and the twins had changed his life, had re-opened the old dreams and wishes that he'd started out with as a young man.

Although he'd talked with Vanessa on the phone about hiring the nanny, he'd not seen her since the night Rick had burped all over him. Every night since then, he'd wanted to go back to her house. He'd wanted to sit across from her at the little table, eat warm tortillas, talk about mundane things and simply watch her beautiful face. Over and over he'd thought about the way she'd felt in his arms when he'd kissed her and the way she'd looked afterward. For the first time in a long time he'd wanted to make love to a woman. And though he'd told himself he'd been too busy to make the trip over to Tinnie to see her, a part of him knew he'd been hiding these past few days, afraid to admit to himself or to her that she and the babies were the family he'd wanted for so long.

Three days later, Vanessa was relieved that Friday had finally arrived. If she didn't get out of the office and away from Conall soon, she was either going to break into pieces or throw herself into his arms and beg the man to make love to her. Neither option was suitable for a secretary who'd always considered herself a professional. And she was beginning to wonder if the job she'd once loved was now going to have to come to an end.

Drawing in a bracing breath, she rapped her knuckles on the door separating their offices. The moment she heard him calling for her to enter, she stepped into his domain and shut the door behind her.

"I have the contract for the trucking company ready for you to sign," she said as she approached his desk. "I've also alerted Red Bluff that a new trucking company will be in place at the mine by the middle of next month."

"Good. I'm glad to get that settled." He glanced up as she leaned forward to place the papers in front of him. "Did Red Bluff seem to have any problem with the idea of new haulers?"

It was after five in the evening and though he'd started out the day in a crisply starched shirt and matching tie, the tie was now loosened and the top two buttons of his shirt were undone while the sleeves were rolled back on his forearms. His nearly black hair was rumpled and she knew if she were to rub her cheek against his, she'd feel the faint rasp of his beard.

"Not at all," she said as she straightened to her full

height and tried to bring her thoughts to the business at hand.

"Good. I only wish raising racehorses was as easy as digging gold from a mountainside." He picked up a pen and scratched his name on the appropriate lines. Once he was finished, he handed the document back to her and smiled. "But my grandfather used to say that nothing was worthwhile, unless it was earned. Gold mines eventually peter out. Horses will always be."

"Yes, well, I'll get this in the outgoing mail before I leave this evening," she told him, then quickly turned to start out of the room.

She'd taken two steps when his hand closed around her upper arm and with a mental groan, she turned to face him.

"Was there something else?" she asked.

Grimacing at her businesslike tone, he muttered, "Hell, yes, there's plenty more! I want to know why you've been acting as though I have a contagious disease. Ever since you've started back to work, you've been tiptoeing around me like I'm some sort of hulking monster."

Shaking her head, she looked away from him and swallowed hard. "I'm sorry if it appears that way, Conall. But I'm just trying to keep things in order."

"What does that mean?"

"It means—" Her gaze slipped to her arm, where his fingers were pressed like dark brown bands around her flesh. "I'm trying to keep our relationship professional here in the office."

He stepped closer and her heart began to knock against her ribs. "What if I don't want it to be professional?" he asked softly.

She cleared her throat, but it didn't clear away the

huskiness in her voice when she spoke. "Like I told you before, Conall, we can't—"

Before she could get the rest of her words out, he jerked her forward and into his arms. The instant his lips covered hers, Vanessa understood why she'd been fighting so hard to keep this very thing from happening.

Tasting his kiss again, having his arms holding her close against his hard body, felt incredibly delicious and impossible to resist. She couldn't hide or ignore the desire rushing through her, urging her to open her mouth to his and slip her arms up and around his neck.

All at once the kiss heated, deepened and surrounded her senses in a hot fog. The room receded to a dim whirl around her head. She heard his groan and then his hands were sliding down her back, splaying against her buttocks and dragging her hips toward his.

Crushed in the intimate embrace, Vanessa forgot they were in his office and that anyone could walk in on them. She forgot, that is, until the phone in her office began to ring and stop, then ring again.

Summoning on all the strength she could find, she jerked her mouth from his. "Conall—the phone, I—"

"Forget the phone," he ordered huskily as his mouth descended toward hers for a second time. "The caller can leave a message."

Panicked by just how much she wanted to do his bidding, she burst out, "No!"

Twisting away from his embrace she started to hurry out of the room, but halfway to the door, she realized at some point during their kiss she'd dropped the contract.

Turning back, she groaned when she spotted it lying to one side of his boots. As she walked toward him to retrieve it, he said softly, "That was a quick change of mind."

"I haven't changed my mind." She bent down to retrieve the typed pages that were held together with a heavy paper clip. "I'm retrieving the contract. That's all."

Gripping the document with both hands, she straightened back to her full height and before she could step away his hand came out to catch her by one elbow.

"All right, Vanessa, you can pretend you're indifferent, but I won't believe it," he murmured.

She swallowed as her heartbeat reacted to his nearness. "Conall, I'm not going to deny that I like kissing you. But—"

"Good," he interrupted before she could go on. "Because I plan on us doing a lot more of it."

"No," she repeated. "It won't take us anywhere. Except to bed!"

A corner of his mouth curled upward. "For once we agree on something."

She stared at him as her mind spun with questions and images that left her face burning with red heat. "Well, you might as well go over to your desk and write this down on your calendar, Conall—it ain't gonna happen!"

He laughed in a totally confident way, but instead of the sound irking her, it sent a scare all the way down to her feet. To make love to Conall would be the end of her. He'd have her eating out of his hand, waiting and begging for any crumbs of affection he might throw her way.

"You look very pretty when you use bad grammar. Did you know that?"

She muttered a helpless curse and then the phone

began to ring again. "The one thing I do know is that I have to get back to work and—"

"No. You don't. It's quitting time," he said, his voice quickly slipping back to boss mode. "And right now I want to speak with you about tomorrow night."

She arched her brows at him. "Tomorrow night? Are you having a special meeting or something and I need to attend to take notes?"

He shook his head. "Not even close. Sunday is Grandmother Kate's birthday and the family is throwing her a party. Not anything as huge as we did for her eightieth. But since this is her eighty-fifth we thought she deserved more than just a cake and a few gifts from her family."

"What does this have to do with me? You'd like for me to pick up a gift or flowers for you to give to her?"

He frowned. "Not hardly. I know how to buy gifts for women. Even one as hard to please as Kate." His hand departed her elbow and began a hot glide up her bare arm and onto her shoulder. "I'd like for you to attend the party with me. Will Hannah be available to watch after the twins?"

He was inviting her to his family home? As his companion? She couldn't believe it. Sure, as a young teenager she'd been inside the small mansion many times. But that had been totally different. She'd been there as Maura's friend, not as a so-called date for the eldest Donovan son.

"So far I can't get Hannah to take any time off, so she will be available. But I'm not keen on the idea of being away from the babies for that long. I know that probably sounds silly to you, but just being apart from them while I'm here at the office has been hard for me to deal with these past three days."

He smiled with understanding. "It's not silly. You're a new mother. But it's not a problem, either. You can bring the twins to the party with you."

Her jaw dropped. "To the party? Conall, they're only a few weeks old."

"I'm well aware of how old they are. Everyone will love seeing them. In fact, the whole family has been asking about them."

How could she turn down the invitation now, she wondered, without appearing to be indifferent to his family? She couldn't. "If you think no one will mind," she said hesitantly.

"Grandmother will love seeing the babies. Bring Hannah, the nanny, too," he added. "That way you won't be babysitting the whole time. And Hannah is acquainted with Maura and Bridget, so I'm sure she'll enjoy the outing, too."

Another reason why she couldn't refuse, Vanessa thought wryly. Hannah, the nanny that Conall had hired for the twins, was a lovely widow and worked tirelessly to keep the babies healthy and happy. So far she'd not taken a night off for any reason and Vanessa knew the woman needed a break of some sort.

"All right. We'll be there. But I don't understand any of this, Conall. Why invite me? Now? Since I've come to work for you, your family has held several parties for one reason or another. You didn't ask me to attend any of those," she couldn't help pointing out.

"Look, Vanessa, whatever you might think or want, the two of us aren't going back to the impersonal relationship we had before the twins arrived. Things have changed with you and with me. Surely I don't have to spell that out to you."

Things have changed. That was certainly an understatement, she thought. If she wasn't with the man, she was thinking about him. And when she was with him all she could think about was being in his arms. She was in a predicament that was very unhealthy to her state of mind and try as she might, she couldn't seem to do a thing about it.

"I think—" She broke off abruptly as the phone began to ring again.

"You think what?" he prompted.

She shook her head. Now wasn't the time or place to say the things she needed to say to him. Tomorrow night would be soon enough to let him know he was sniffing around the wrong tree. "Nothing. I'll be at the party, Conall. With Rose and Rick. Right now I'm going to get this contract in the mail, then go home."

He looked like he wanted to say more, or maybe it was more kissing he had on his mind. Whatever it was she read on his face, she didn't hang around to let him put his wants into action. She hurried out of the room and purposely shut the door between them.

Apparently Mother Nature didn't want to disappoint the Donovans. With Kate's party being held in the backyard beneath the pines and the cottonwood trees, the early August weather couldn't have been more perfect. Even the mosquitoes seemed to forget to come out after night had fallen and the colorful party lanterns were glowing festively over the tables of food that had been served more than an hour ago.

Conall had told her the party was going to be small, but to Vanessa it was anything but. People, most of whom she didn't know, filled the yard and the back porch where Kate was presently ensconced in a rattan chair surrounded by family and friends. Music was playing and down by the pool the more active guests were laughing and splashing and swimming in the crystal blue water.

Tilting the long-stemmed glass to her lips, Vanessa drained the last of her punch while wondering how soon she could leave without appearing unsociable. She'd already spoken to Kate and expressed her well wishes. She'd chatted at length with Maura and exchanged a few words with the rest of the Donovans. Except for Conall. So far she'd seen him for all of two minutes and that had been when his grandmother had blown out the candles on her cake. After that, he'd disappeared into the house and left her wondering for the umpteenth time why he'd invited her in the first place.

Moving from her spot beneath a giant pine, she started walking toward the far end of the porch where the twins were sleeping in their double stroller. A few steps away, Hannah and Bridget were engaged in a lively conversation, but both women looked around as she approached.

"Vanessa, come have a seat with us," Bridget insisted. "Hannah was just telling me what it's like at the twins' bath time."

Vanessa laughed. "I can tell you in one word. Chaos. And in a few weeks I'm sure it's going to get a lot wilder and a whole lot wetter."

She started toward an empty chair to the left of the two women, but before she reached the seat, a hand came down on the back of her shoulder. At the same time Bridget said, "Conall, it's about time you showed your face around here. Where have you been anyway?"

"Business, as usual," he answered. "A phone call I couldn't ignore. But that's finished and now I'm more than ready for a piece of cake. What about you, Vanessa?"

Turning toward him, she tried not to notice how sexy he looked in close-fitting jeans and a black T-shirt that clung to his hard torso and exposed his muscled arms. "I've already had more than my share," she told him.

"Then you can come watch me have my share," he said with a grin for her, "but first I want a look at Rose and Rick. Are they enjoying the party?"

"At least they're not howling," Hannah answered with a laugh.

He moved over to the stroller and squatted on his heels in front of the twins. Rick was asleep, his head tilted toward his sister's. But Rose was awake, her blue eyes wide, her arms pumping through the air as though she could hear the music.

"Hey, little doll, your brother is missing the party. But you'd like to dance, wouldn't you," he said in a soft voice to the baby girl. Not bothering to ask permission, he eased Rose from her side of the stroller and cradled her in the crook of his arm. Then after letting her tiny fingers curl around his forefinger, he began to slowly two-step around the porch.

"Aww, look," Bridget gushed, her gaze resting fondly on her brother and the baby in his arms. "She loves that, Conall."

"So do I," he replied with a broad grin. "I've never had a better dance partner. She's not even complaining about me stepping on her toes."

"We need him around when Rose is crying at two o'clock in the morning," Hannah joked to Vanessa.

Her eyes taking in the precious sight of Conall dancing with her daughter, Vanessa felt her throat thicken with unexpected emotions. Years ago, she'd often dreamt of Conall waltzing her around a ballroom floor. Back then she could have never imagined him holding her baby, dancing her around as though she was a special princess.

"He wouldn't be any use to you then," Bridget observed. "My brother sleeps like a rock."

Dismissing his sister's remark with a chuckle, Conall carried Rose back to the stroller. After he'd placed her back beside his brother, he pressed a kiss on her chubby cheek. "Thank you for the dance, little Rose."

To Vanessa it seemed as though he remained bent over the babies for an exceptionally long time before he finally straightened and walked back over to her. After placing his hand around Vanessa's arm, he nodded to the other two women. "Excuse us, ladies."

He guided Vanessa off the porch and across the yard to where a table held a massive three-tiered cake and an assortment of beverages.

"Sorry I had to leave the party," he said as he gathered a plate and fork. "Have you been bored?"

"No. But I should be leaving soon. By the time Hannah and I get home with the babies, it will be getting late."

"You can't leave yet."

She watched him ladle a huge hunk of cake onto the plate. "Why? Is your family waiting to give your grandmother a surprise gift?"

"No. Kate doesn't want gifts. Says she has everything she wants. Personally, I think she needs a man in her life, but then she'd be hell to put up with, if you know what I mean."

Vanessa folded her arms against her breasts as he began to wolf down the cake. "No. I don't know what you mean. Kate might be strict and opinionated, but she wouldn't marry a man unless she loved him."

His brows lifted faintly as he looked at her. "You're probably right. She was crazy about Granddad, which always amazed me because he was a mean old cuss most of the time."

"I doubt he was mean to her. Kate is too strong of a woman to put up with that."

"Yes, but—"

"But what?"

His expression was nothing but cynical as he glanced at her. "Love makes people put up with behavior they wouldn't ordinarily tolerate."

Was he speaking from experience? Vanessa wasn't about to ask. Even though things had changed between them these past few weeks, he wasn't the type of man who poured out his personal life to anyone, including her.

Raking a hand through her hair, she looked away from him and over toward the twins. In spite of the night being pleasantly cool, she felt uncomfortably hot. "You haven't explained why I need to stay at the party a little longer," she reminded him.

He placed the now empty plate on the table and reached for her arm. "I'll explain as we walk. Let's go to Kate's rose garden. It'll be quieter there."

As the two of them disappeared into the shadows, Vanessa wondered if anyone had noticed their leaving. But why that should even matter, she didn't know. She was a grown woman and what went on between her and the manager of the Diamond D Ranch was no one's business but theirs. Yet at the same time, she had to concede that other people's opinion of her did matter. Maybe because as a poor girl growing up she'd heard the nasty whispers at school, she'd heard the gossip that Vanessa Valdez would turn out no better than her worthless brothers. And down through the years she'd worked hard to prove those people wrong, to make herself respectable and successful.

"If you needed to say something to me, you could have said it back there at the party," Vanessa told him as they trod along a graveled path that was lined with dim footlights and wound through head-high rose bushes.

"Not what I want to say."

The softness to his voice caught her attention and she paused to swing her gaze up to his shadowed face. Her heart jerked. He looked so serious, yet so sexy that her breath flew away and refused to come back.

"Conall—"

"Not here," he said. "Let's go sit in the gazebo."

Maura had told her that the gazebo had been built the same time as the huge ranch house. Now, after more than forty years, the board seats were worn smooth, along with the planked floor. A pair of aspen trees sheltered one side of the structure and as they sat down together on one of the secluded benches, the leaves rattled gently from the evening breeze.

Vanessa welcomed the cool air against her hot skin, yet it did little to chill her racing thoughts. Was he about to suggest that the two of them become lovers? That she become his mistress? She didn't know what to expect. Only one thing was clear to her—sitting in the dark with the heavenly scent of roses wrapping around them was going to be a heck of a test on her resistance.

"When my sisters were teenagers I used to tease them about sitting out here dreaming about marrying a prince or a frog. Whichever they could catch first," he said with amusement. "But after we all got older, I realized the place had a nice, calming effect. Now I think I visit the place more than they do."

"Is that why you brought me out here?" Vanessa asked wryly. "To calm me down?"

He chuckled as he reached for her hand. "That's one thing I like about you, Vanessa, you make me laugh. Something I'd almost forgotten how to do."

As his warm fingers tightened around hers, Vanessa wasn't about to let herself think she had that much of an effect on the man. To do so would simply be dreaming. And during her doomed marriage she'd learned that a person had to be responsible for their own happiness, instead of relying on someone else to provide it for them.

She sighed. "Sometimes that's easy for a person to do—forget how to laugh." She glanced over at him, but the shadows were too deep to pick up the expression on his face. "So why are we here instead of mingling with the party guests?"

"I wanted to talk to you about…several things."

The humor was gone from his voice now and her heartbeat slowed to a heavy dread of drumbeats. "Is this about my job?" she asked.

"Actually, it is."

He'd never been evasive or short on explanations before and she wondered yet again what had brought about this change in him. Before the twins he'd been cool, work-driven and predictable. Now she couldn't begin to anticipate what he might say or do next. It was more than unnerving.

Finally, he said, "I think I need to find a different secretary."

She sucked in a sharp breath and bit down on the urge to scream at him. "You invited me to a party to fire me? Why?" she demanded. "Because I refused to make love to you?"

His lazy chuckle infuriated her.

"No. Because I've come to realize that you were right. It's too damn hard to get any work done in the office when all I want to do is lock the door and make love to you all day."

Feeling the desperate need to escape, she tried to pull her hand from his, but he held her tight, making it clear that he had plenty more to say and expected her to hang around and listen.

"Conall—"

"Wait, Vanessa, before you get all huffy, this isn't... well, it's not just about the two of us making love. It's more than that."

Confused now, she squared her knees around so that she was facing him head-on. "What *is* this about?"

He looked away from her and if Vanessa hadn't known better she would have thought he was nervous. But that couldn't be so. Conall Donovan didn't allow anything to rattle him.

Eventually he began to speak and his husky voice slid over her skin like warm, summer rain and filled her with the urge to shiver, to lean in to him and invite his kiss. She clamped her hands together and tried to concentrate on his words.

"I've been thinking about us, Vanessa. A lot. And the more I think about it the more I realize there's a perfect solution to our problem."

She swallowed as all sorts of questions raced through her head. "Problem? You mean now that you want to fire me and get another secretary?"

He grimaced. "I don't want to fire you. I mean, I

do, but only because I have something different in mind—for you...for us."

Bending her head, she sucked in several deep breaths and prayed the nausea in her stomach would disappear. "Look, Conall, I like my job. I like being here on the ranch and you Donovans are excellent people to work for. But I don't appreciate the fact that you're trying to... extort sex from me! I'm not that needy. Like I told you, I can easily get a job at the casino at Ruidoso Downs and—"

"Extort sex from you! What are you talking about?"

His interruption whipped her head up. "Why, yes, isn't that what this is all about? You want me to quit my job and be your mistress?"

With a groan of disbelief, he clasped his hands over both her shoulders. "Oh, Vanessa, I'm sorry. I must be doing this all wrong. I don't want you to be my mistress. I want you to be my wife."

Chapter Eight

If he'd not been holding on to her, Vanessa was sure she would have fallen straight backward and onto the floor of the gazebo.

"Your wife!" she said in a shocked whisper. "Are you…out of your mind?"

There was no smile on his face, no glimmer that he was anywhere near teasing.

"Not in the least. The twins need a father. And you and I…well, we obviously get on together. I think it's the perfect solution for all of us."

Stunned, she rose to her feet and walked to the other side of the gazebo. In her wildest imaginings, she'd not expected this from Conall. Twenty years ago, when she'd viewed him as a knight on horseback, she'd fantasized how it would be to receive a kiss from him, or even go on a date with him, but even her fantasies had known when and where to stop. Men like Conall didn't marry women like her.

She heard his footsteps approaching her from behind and then his hands came to rest upon her shoulders. As their warmth seeped into her skin, she closed her eyes and wondered why she suddenly wanted to weep.

"Vanessa, what are you thinking?"

Her throat was aching, making her voice low and strained. "I'm...very flattered, Conall. But marriage needs to be more than a solution."

His sigh rustled the top of her hair. "I'm trying to be practical, Vanessa. Marriage—making a family together—would be good for all four of us."

Maybe it would, she thought sadly, but what about love? He'd not mentioned the word, but then he hardly needed to explain his feelings. She already understood that he didn't love her.

Turning, she demanded, "How would it be good for you, Conall?"

His arms slipped around her waist and drew the front of her body up against his. "Just having you next to me would be good," he murmured.

She groaned as a war of wanting him and needing his love erupted inside of her. "I'm sorry, Conall, but it hasn't been that long since I got out of a horrible marriage. I don't want to jump into something that...well, I'm just not sure about."

He frowned. "Do you think I'm taking this whole thing lightly? That I proposed to you on impulse? Hell, Vanessa, my marriage turned out to be a nightmare. For a while after the divorce I tried to date again, to find a woman I could build a relationship with. But the past refused to let that happen so I finally gave up trying.

So if you think you're the only one who has a corner on being hurt by a spouse, then think again."

"That's exactly why this is all so crazy!" she exclaimed. "Why would you want to marry a divorced woman with two newborns when..."

"Finish what you were going to say, Vanessa. When...?"

Pressing her lips together, she looked away from him. Through the lattice covering the side of the gazebo, she could see the lights of the party twinkling through the pine boughs. Shrieks of laughter were coming from the pool and closer to the house she could hear several voices singing "Happy Birthday" to Kate. The fact that Conall had chosen this night to propose to her while his family was celebrating seemed surreal.

Biting back an impatient curse, she turned away from him. "Don't play dumb with me, Conall. It doesn't suit you at all. You know what I was about to say. You're a Donovan. You don't have to go around looking for a woman to marry. All you have to do is get the word out and they'll come running to you. You certainly don't have to settle for your secretary."

His face stony, he caught her by the shoulder and spun her back around. "Why are you doing your best to insult me and yourself? Me being a Donovan has nothing to do with us marrying!"

Amazed, her head swung back and forth. "Conall, that's a fact that can't be buried or swept under the rug!"

His nostrils flared. "Why do you think so little of yourself?"

Tears were suddenly burning her eyes. "Because... oh, you can't understand anything, can you? I've already had one husband who didn't love me! Do you honestly think I want another?"

Before he could answer, she twisted away from him and dashed out of the gazebo. As she hurried along the lighted footpaths, she did her best to stem the hot moisture threatening to spill onto her cheeks.

She'd made a fool of herself, she thought bitterly. Of course, Conall couldn't understand her reaction to his proposal. He couldn't know that she loved him and, perhaps, had always loved him. She was just now beginning to realize that herself.

At one time in his life, long before he'd learned of his sterility, Conall had been comfortable with women. As very young men, Liam had struggled to converse with the opposite sex, while Conall had instinctively known exactly what to say or do to make a woman adore him. Long before he'd met Nancy, he'd dated a lengthy list of beauties and he could safely say that each of the relationships had eventually ended on his terms, not his partner's. Whether his success with women had been partly due to his being a Donovan was a question he'd not considered that much. Until last night when Vanessa had flung the fact in his face.

Obviously he'd lost his touch. Or maybe the long marriage battle he'd endured with Nancy had taken away his innate ability to deal with a woman. Whatever the reason, he'd clearly done everything wrong when he'd proposed to Vanessa last night.

Glancing at his watch, he noted it was a quarter to eight. Normally Vanessa had arrived by now. Especially on a Monday. But he'd not heard any stirrings in the outer office and he was beginning to wonder if she'd decided to skip work altogether today. Or maybe she was going to quit and was planning to call and let the gavel drop on him.

Thrusting fingers through his dark hair, he pressed fingertips against his scalp. Tiny men were pounding sledgehammers just beneath his skull, a result of drinking too many beers last night after Vanessa had taken the babies and gone home, he thought grimly. He'd never been one to indulge in alcohol, but after the fiasco in the gazebo, he needed some sort of relief. Now he was paying for it with a doozy of a headache.

A hard knock on the doorjamb had him wincing and he glanced around to see Liam striding into his office.

"What's with all the roses in Vanessa's office? Did someone break into a florist shop this morning or something?" he asked.

With an awkward shrug, Conall admitted, "I broke into Grandma's rose garden. I knew it would be useless to drive to town and try to bribe a shop owner to open up and deliver this morning."

His brows arched with curiosity, Liam glanced over his shoulder toward the outer office. "I didn't realize your secretary was that important to you. What is today, secretary's day or something? If it is, Gloria is out of luck."

Conall grunted. "The only thing Gloria ever expects from you is win photos to put on the wall behind her desk."

"That's all?" he countered with sarcasm. "It would be a hell of a lot easier to raid Grandma's flower garden and blame it on the gardener."

Conall walked over to the coffeepot and refilled his mug. "Coffee?" he asked his brother.

"No. I'm in a hurry. I'm missed you at breakfast, so

I wanted to let you know I was shipping Red Garland to Del Mar today, along with a few others."

He looked around at Liam. "To Del Mar? Now?"

Liam rolled his eyes with impatience. "Have you forgotten she's entered in the Debutante? That's only a month away and I want her to get accustomed to the Pacific climate and the Polytrack before race time."

Actually it had slipped Conall's mind that the filly would be traveling to the west coast to run in the prestigious race at one of the most famous tracks in California. "Sorry, brother, I guess the time has slipped up on me."

"Geez, Conall. What's going on with you? From the moment she was born Red Garland has always been your darling. And you've forgotten about her first stakes debut?"

Conall had been in the foaling barn, watching when Red Garland entered the world. Only hours later, the baby girl had left her mother's side to investigate Conall's outstretched hand and something about her trust had touched him, had gotten to him in a way no human ever had. Since then, she'd grown up to be an outstanding runner that had quickly stunned race fans with her ability to outdistance herself from the rest of the pack. Conall was extremely proud of her. He was also very attached to the filly. Something he normally didn't allow himself to be with the horses they raised and raced.

Conall glanced at his brother's incredulous expression. "Maybe you haven't noticed but I've had a lot going on here lately," he said, then shoved out a heavy breath. "Anyway, I'm glad you came by to say you were leaving. I…well, I'll be honest, I hate for her to be shipped all the way to California."

Liam frowned. "Why? We ship horses out there all the time."

Conall felt like a soppy idiot. "I know. It's just that…anything might happen. That Polytrack surface is unpredictable."

"So is the dirt."

"She might hurt herself. With an injury that could end her career or even kill her," Conall pointed out, even though both men were already well aware of that fact. "But you're the trainer. You know what she can handle best."

Liam shook his head. "Hell, Conall. You're my brother. I don't want to do anything against your wishes."

With a self-effacing grunt, Conall placed his coffee mug on the edge of the desk. "What's the matter with me, Liam? I've never gotten this soppy over any of our horses before. I've never let myself. Because…well, we both know anything can happen to lose them."

"Sometimes something or someone comes along to remind us we're not machines," Liam said thoughtfully, then added, "I'll scratch Red Garland from the Debutante and leave her here. We'll lose the entry fee, but what the hell. She's already won that much a thousand times over."

"No, she's going," Conall said with sudden firmness. "She deserves her chance to be great."

A wry smile touched Liam's lips. "Well, she stands a good chance to win a pile of money."

"Yeah. But money isn't everything," Conall replied.

Liam grunted in agreement. "Sometimes it doesn't mean anything at all."

Satisfied that things were settled with the situation,

Liam turned to leave the room, but before he disappeared out the door, Conall called to him, "Thanks, again, Liam. For coming by and reminding me about Red Garland's race. Will you be following the horses out today or tomorrow?"

"Today and I'm taking three grooms with me."

Conall lifted his hand in farewell. "Travel safely and I'll see you when you get back."

"You want to drive to the airport and see Red Garland off this afternoon?" Liam asked in afterthought.

"No. I'd rather meet her there when she gets back."

With a nod of understanding, Liam left the office and Conall forced himself to sit down at his desk.

Five minutes later, he heard the outer door to the office open and close and then Vanessa's light footsteps cross the tile. Normally, she went straight to the closet they shared to store away her purse and whatever sort of wrap she was wearing but so far the closet hadn't opened.

He forced himself to wait another minute before he walked through the open door and into her section of the office. He found her standing in front of the desk, staring at the massive vase of pink roses he'd left for her.

Upon hearing his approach, she whirled around to face him. "What are these?"

Conall walked toward her. "Roses. To say I'm sorry if I hurt you last night. I didn't mean to. I didn't have any idea a marriage proposal would be so harrowing to you."

Bending her head, she closely examined the petals on the tea roses. "I'll be honest, Conall, I considered not coming to work this morning. But I didn't want Fiona to have to fill in for me. So I made myself drive over here." Turning slightly, she leveled her brown eyes on him. "I'm sorry, too, Conall. I overreacted about you— about everything. I was expecting too much from you. I realize that now."

Relieved that she no longer appeared angry, he walked over to her. "I'm glad you're here," he confessed. "And if you don't want to talk about things right now, we won't."

Her glaze flickered away from his face and back to the roses and Conall was struck by how very beautiful she looked this morning. Her hair was swept up and off her neck, while a heavy fringe fell in a smooth curtain over one eyebrow. Her dress was white, the neckline fashioned in a deep V. Faint freckles dotted her chest and lower down a hint of cleavage teased his senses. The pale pink color on her lips reminded him of a seashell and he realized he'd like nothing better than to kiss the shimmery color away, kiss her until her lips were ruby-red and swollen.

"There's nothing to talk about," she said wearily. "I can't marry you."

Desperate to touch her, he planted his hands on either side of her waist. "Listen, Vanessa, I have no idea what happened in your marriage or what kind of man your husband was, but please don't compare me to him."

To his surprise she laughed with disbelief. "Oh, Conall, you can't imagine how...well, how opposite you are from Jeff. He didn't have an ounce of ambition. He was perfectly content to let me support him."

Trying to understand, he shook his head. "I'm guessing you didn't know this about him before you married?"

Grimacing, she stepped away from him. "Of course I didn't! When I first met him he was doing contract electrical work for the casino where I was employed. At that time he owned a small building company and he and his men had more jobs than they could handle. He made very good money, plus he was from a nice respectable family that had resided in Bullhead City for many years. There was nothing about Jeff that warned he would turn out to be a deadhead."

She started into his office and Conall followed her to the coffee machine. As she poured herself a mug and stirred in a measure of half-and-half, he couldn't stop himself from asking, "When did you learn he was less than ambitious."

Cradling the mug with both hands, she turned to face him. "About six months after we were married. He began to find all sorts of reasons not to take jobs. Mainly he would use the excuse that he wanted to spend more time with me—because I was so irresistible he didn't want to leave me for a minute of the day," she added with sarcasm. "Dear God, was I ever stupid to believe his lines. But he...well, he had a charming, lovable way about him that was hard to resist and I—" Pausing, she shook her head with self-reproach. "I guess he'd come along in my life at a time when I was feeling very alone. My brothers were long gone and I was watching my parents grow old. I wanted a family of my own and Jeff kept promising we'd have one. I hung on hoping and praying he'd change. But in the end, I think all he ever wanted was to have fun and a woman to take care of him while he was having it. I should have seen that from the very beginning, but I didn't. And it's taken me a long time to convince myself that I'm not a fool. That I'm worthy of better than...him."

The faint quiver Conall heard in her voice touched a spot in him that he'd long thought dead and he was amazed at how much he wanted to take her into his arms, to whisper how beautiful and precious she was to him. Did that mean he loved her? No. It couldn't mean that. He'd forgotten how to love. But he'd not forgotten how to want and he wanted Vanessa in his life. He wanted to be a father to Rick and Rose.

I wanted a family of my own.

Her words had pierced him right in the heart and twisted home the reality of his condition, his failed marriage and the total emptiness he'd carried inside him for all these years. Maybe he should confess to her right now that he couldn't father a child. But she was already reluctant to trust him, to believe they could have a good marriage together. He didn't want to wham her with that kind of revelation. She would automatically think he was only interested in the twins. Later, he told himself. Later, after he'd convinced her to marry him, he would explain it all. He would make her understand just how perfect the four of them were for each other.

"Oh, Vanessa," he said lowly, "you are worthy of better. And I like to think I can give you better."

Her gaze dropped awkwardly to the brown liquid in her cup. "Yes, you could give me better in so many ways," she conceded. "Except you can't give me what I need the most."

She sounded so defeated, so sure, and that worried Conall more than any words she could have said to him.

"What is that?" he asked.

She looked up him and he spotted a mixture of defiance and resignation swimming in the depths of her brown eyes.

"Love."

The one word caused Conall to rear back and unwit-

tingly drop his hands from her waist. "Love," he repeated, rolling the word around on his tongue as if he'd
never spoken it before. "You mentioned that word last
night, but you didn't give me a chance to have my say
on the matter."

"All right," she said in a faintly challenging tone.
"I'm giving you the chance right now."

Finding it difficult to face her head-on, Conall moved
away from her and over to the huge plate glass window
overlooking the stables. "And I'm telling you right now
that love is a fairy-tale state of mind. That's all. It's just
a euphoric condition that doesn't last. In fact, it only
makes living with a person worse."

Her light footsteps sounded behind him and he turned
to see she'd joined him at the window, but she wasn't
looking out at the busy shed row, she was looking at
him with so much disappointment that she might as
well have struck him physically.

"No wonder your marriage crumbled."

Now, a voice inside his head shouted, *now is the
time to explain everything, to defend yourself and your
actions.* But he couldn't push the words off his tongue.
She was already looking at him with disenchantment;
he didn't want to add even more to it.

The tiny hammers pounding at his skull grew harder
and he wiped a hand over his face in hopes of easing
the pain. "I loved Nancy when we married," he said
with gruff insistence. "And I loved her for a long time
afterward. But love can't hold up to life's interventions.
At least, it didn't for me."

She didn't reply and he used her silence as an opportunity to plead his case. Latching a hand over her
shoulder, he pressed his fingers into her warm flesh.
"Think about it, Vanessa. Love didn't give your marriage

a happily-ever-after ending. Nor did it mine. But you and I have the chance to build a marriage on a solid foundation. Not something that crumbles at the slightest hint of trouble."

Her nostrils flared with disdain as she drew in a deep breath and let it out. "I've never heard of anything so… unfeeling," she muttered.

Before she could guess his intentions, he took the mug from her hands and placed it on the wide window ledge.

"There is nothing unfeeling about this, Vanessa. Maybe I ought to show you."

Pulling her into his arms, he fastened his lips roughly over hers. A moan sounded in her throat at the same time her mouth opened like flower petals seeking the hot sun. His tongue thrust past her teeth and began to explore the sweet, moist contours.

With his hands at her back, he pulled her closer, until her small breasts were flattened against his chest, until he felt the mound of her womanhood pressing into his thigh. Heat was rushing through him, gorging his loins with the unbearable need to get inside her. His sex was rock-hard and pushing against the fly of his jeans.

He couldn't remember the last time, if ever, he'd wanted a woman like this, and when her arms slid around his waist and her soft body arched into his, it was all he could do to hang on to his self-control, to lift his head and speak.

"Let me go lock the door," he said hoarsely.

His words must have hit her like a cold wall of water. Jerking away from him, she stumbled backward and pressed a hand against her throat. "No! You've made your point, Conall. You want me physically. And I admit

I want you. But that's not enough. I'm not going to let it be enough. Not now. Not again."

She started toward the door and though Conall wanted to go after, he realized it wasn't the time or the place to press her. But, oh, God, he desperately wanted to.

"I'm going to work," she said over her shoulder. "If that isn't enough for you, then hire yourself another secretary!"

He stood where he was until the door between their offices shut firmly behind her. Once it was obvious she wasn't going to reappear or change her mind, Conall stalked over to his desk and sank into the lush leather chair.

Damn, damn, damn. What would it take to make her cozy up to the idea of marrying him? Or would she ever come around to his way of thinking? She wanted love, but how could he give her the one thing he didn't have?

With a frustrated oath, he picked up the phone and punched in Liam's cell number. His brother answered after the third ring.

"Yeah. What's up?

"I...just wanted to see what time the plane with the horses would be departing the airport."

"Probably around eleven this morning. Why?"

Pinching the bridge of his nose, Conall closed his eyes. "I've changed my mind. I've decided I want to see Red Garland off."

Liam grunted. "What's brought this on?" he asked bluntly.

Conall grimaced. "Do I have to explain myself?" he countered gruffly. "Maybe I want to see her one last time. In case...she doesn't come home."

The line went silent for long moments, then Liam gently cursed, "Hell, Conall. I promise I'll bring the filly back."

"You can't make promises like that." He swallowed hard and glanced at the closed door between him and Vanessa. "Don't let the plane leave until I get there."

The next two days Vanessa was bombarded with an extra flurry of work while Conall was continually tied up with issues both in and out of the office. She'd done her best to deal with tractor dealers, feed suppliers and tack salesmen even as she plowed through mounds of paperwork.

Being busier than usual was a good thing, she supposed. That gave her less time to dwell on Conall. Since that fiery kiss they'd exchanged, they'd been polite and civil to each other, but the words and the touches they'd exchanged had hung in the air between them like a heavy humidity, leaving Vanessa uncomfortable and emotionally drained.

At the end of the second day, Vanessa was sitting at her desk, finishing a phone call and wrapping up her work for the evening, when Conall strolled through the door and eased a hip onto the edge of her desk. After two days of tiptoeing around each other, his casual nearness jolted her.

Looking up at him, she asked briskly, "Is there something you need?"

"I need a lot of things, but I won't have you make a list now." He gestured toward her work. "Are you nearly finished?"

"Yes. As soon as I make a few notes in my message book. Why?"

The faint grin on his face was the warmest thing she'd

seen since the morning he'd wanted to lock the two of them in his office and his gray eyes had been hot with lust. She had to wonder about the abrupt change.

Folding his arms against his chest, his expression turned sheepish. "I wanted to see if you've forgiven me enough to have dinner with me this evening?"

Forgiven him? She'd not been expecting anything like this. Maybe a request for her to work later than usual, but not anything sociable, like having dinner together.

"You've been all business the past couple of days," she bluntly pointed out.

"So have you."

Her gaze dropped from his face to the vase of roses he'd given her a few days ago. She should have thrown them out or at least taken them home and given them to Hannah. But they were still as pretty as the morning she'd found them on her desk and she couldn't bring herself to get rid of them.

When she didn't reply, he said, "I thought we both needed some time to cool off."

That was an understatement, Vanessa thought wryly. Her gaze flickered back up to his face. "And you think we've *cooled off* enough to have dinner together? Alone?"

"We've eaten together alone before," he reminded, as if her memory needed refreshing. "At your house. And in Vegas."

She sighed. He'd been so sweet, so helpful during that trip to Las Vegas and for as long as she lived, she would never forget the look on his face when he'd held the twins for the first time. He'd looked at them with affection and tenderness and for those few moments she'd seen the part of him that she admired, wanted, loved.

"I remember," she told him.

"I'd like to do it again. Would you?"

She'd be lying if she told him no. These past couple of days as she'd kept her distance, she'd constantly argued with herself that it was better that way. The only thing she could ever expect to get from the man was sex. Yet even knowing that hadn't been enough to stop the hunger inside of her, the need to be near him in all the ways a woman could be near a man.

"Yes," she answered. "But—"

"What? Afraid you might find out that you like me after all?"

In spite of her torn emotions, she chuckled. "Oh, Conall, you know that I like you. Very much. That's the whole problem." She closed the small book where she scribbled down daily notes and stuffed it away in the top drawer of the desk. "We... Well, I'm not going to go into any of that tonight. Going out with you is out of the question. I've already promised my father I'd visit him after I got off work. And I'm not going to disappoint him for any reason."

"I wouldn't want you to disappoint him. We'll go by and visit him together," he said.

While she looked at him her thoughts swirled. "He's in the nursing home."

"I'm well aware of that, Vanessa."

Jeff would have never stepped foot in a nursing home, she thought. Not for anyone. In that way he'd been a thoughtless man. Unfortunately, she'd learned about Jeff's unpleasant traits after they'd been married, a fault she could only place squarely on herself. She'd been so eager to be loved, so anxious to be a wife and mother, that she'd been blinded by Jeff's charms and his quick press for them to marry.

With a mental sigh, she did her best to shove away the dark memories before she glanced down at the simple wrap dress she was wearing. The pale green geometric print still looked fresh enough, but it wasn't exactly what she would have picked to wear for a date with Conall. A date? If that's what this was supposed to be then he was going backward, she thought. Dates were supposed to come before marriage proposals, not after. But then she could hardly forget that Conall's proposal had not been the conventional sort, where a man promised his love for a lifetime.

"We can't go anywhere fancy," she finally said. "I'm not dressed for it."

He reached over and plucked one of the dark pink roses from the bouquet he'd given her. "You are now," he murmured as he tucked the flower behind her left ear. "A rose in your hair to match the roses on your cheeks."

Clearing her tight throat, she said, "I didn't know you could flirt."

He grinned. "I'll be happy to show you what else I can do."

Forbidden images raced through her mind. "I'll go get my handbag so we can be going."

Rising from the chair, she purposefully moved away from him and the desk before she lost all sense and reached for him, before she could tell him that the only place she wanted to go was straight into his arms.

Chapter Nine

A few minutes later they were traveling toward Ruidoso in Conall's plush black truck. Only moments ago they'd watched the sun slip behind the mountains, and now in the western sky rich magenta threads laced together a cloak of purple clouds.

Being cooped up in the cozy cab with Conall was a temptation in itself and so far she'd been doing her best to concentrate on the scenery instead of his long, lean presence. But since they'd departed the ranch, he'd been in a surprisingly talkative mood and she'd found her gaze lingering on him far more than it should have.

"How long has Alonzo been in the nursing home?" he asked as he capably maneuvered the truck over the steeply winding highway.

Back at the office, he'd tugged a black cowboy hat low on his forehead and now as Vanessa glanced at his profile, she could only think that this man was living his days out not really in the way he wanted, but as he thought he was expected to. As a teenager she'd spent enough time on the ranch to see that Conall had been an outdoorsman, a horseman. She sensed that deep down, he would much rather be working hands-on with the horses than dealing with business issues. But apparently he considered managing the ranch his family duty and from what she could tell about the man, Conall would never shun his family responsibilities. In that aspect, he would be an excellent husband and father. But did duty mean more than love? Not to her.

"About six months," she answered. "After his stroke he was in the hospital for nearly a month before he was well enough to go to the nursing home. He's doing much better now, but he still has a way to go. I've hired a speech therapist to work with him and that's made a great difference. He's actually beginning to talk again with words that are understandable."

He nodded. "Do you think he'll ever get to come home?"

"If he continues to improve, his doctor says it's highly possible. But he'll not be able to live alone." She sighed. "I'm hoping when, or maybe I should say if, that happens, the twins won't be so demanding of me."

Chuckling lowly, he shook his head. "I'm sorry, Vanessa, but I don't think it's going to work that way. I have a feeling that the older the twins get, the more they're going to demand of their mother. Especially since—"

He broke off as though he had second thoughts about his next words. Vanessa didn't press him. She simply waited.

"Well," he finally said, "no matter about the twins. I'm sure you'd love to have your father well again and back home. If it was my father, I certainly would."

She smiled wanly. "More than anything. He's all alone. And I have a feeling the twins would be good for him."

"The twins are very special," he said with undisguised warmth. "But you would be good for him, too. You have a way of making people around you feel better about themselves."

With a shake of her head, she said, "You don't have to overdo it, Conall."

He mouthed a curse under his breath. "I'm not overdoing anything, Vanessa. If you... Well, you've made me realize that divorcing Nancy didn't make me a criminal or a devil. Nor did it end my life."

Curiosity sparked in her and she couldn't stop herself from asking, "You were the one who wanted the divorce?"

He grimaced. "Yes," he answered bluntly.

"Why?"

Sighing, he said, "We had fundamental differences in what we thought was important to our lives and our marriage. But in the end she...betrayed me in a way that was unforgivable."

Had Nancy cheated on Conall with another man? She'd never met the woman who'd once been in the Donovan family, but she found it hard to imagine her committing adultery on a man that was breathtakingly sexy, unless the cheating had been more about her unhappiness. "You don't believe in forgiveness?" she asked.

A wry twist to his lips, he said, "I can forgive, Vanessa. But forgiving wouldn't have fixed the problem."

"Oh."

He looked at her. "Let's not waste this evening talking about such things. It's in the past and that's where it's going to stay. So tell me some of your favorite foods and we'll decide where to eat."

He obviously wanted to change the subject and Vanessa could understand why. She didn't particularly enjoy talking about Jeff and the mistakes she made with him. No doubt Conall felt the same.

"All right," she agreed, "I like anything I can eat with my hands. How about a hamburger?"

He flashed her a grin. "I knew we'd be perfect together. You just proved it."

Groaning inwardly, Vanessa could have told him there wasn't such a thing as being perfect together. Maybe for a few minutes at a time, but not for a lifetime. But she kept the cynical thought to herself. Now that she'd agreed to spend the evening with Conall, she didn't want to spoil their time together with more useless arguments.

Once they reached town, Vanessa started to give Conall directions to the nursing home, but he quickly interrupted.

"I know where it is, Vanessa. I've been there many times."

She looked at him with surprise. "I didn't realize any of your family had been incapacitated. From what Maura's told me, your grandfather's death was rather quick."

"I've not had a family member living in Gold Aspen Manor. But Liam's assistant stayed there until…his death."

By now they had reached the one-story, ranch-style building that sat in a carved out area of a wooded foothill. Slanted parking slots skirted a wide front lawn where sprinklers were going and a gardener was meticulously edging the sidewalk. It was a quiet and beautiful place, but Vanessa cringed each time she walked through the doors. She wanted her father to be whole and well again. She wanted him to be back on his little patch of land, scratching out a small garden and tending his goats.

"I didn't realize Liam ever had an assistant," she admitted. "I took it for granted that he'd always worked alone."

Conall cut the motor, but didn't make any hurried moves to depart the truck. "No. Before Liam was experienced enough to take on the task of being head trainer, Cletis—we called him Clete—was the man. He mentored Liam, then after handing the reins over to him, continued to work alongside my brother until about three years ago when his health began to fail. Liam's not been the same since the old man passed away."

"I can understand that. I've not been the same since my mother passed," Vanessa sadly admitted. "Everything that once was important to me now looks so different, almost trivial."

His expression suddenly sober, he let out a long breath. "Yeah. Well, Clete didn't have a family. He regarded Liam as a son. And Liam doesn't think anyone could ever fill Clete's boots. That's mainly why he continues to work himself to death instead of hiring a new assistant." With a wry expression, he reached over and touched her hand. "Come on, that's enough about that stuff. Let's go see your father."

To Vanessa's delight they found Alonzo outside, seated around a patio table with a group of men who were also patients at the Gold Aspen Manor. As soon as the older man spotted her approach, he rose from his chair and held out his arms to her.

Leaving Conall's side, she rushed to her father and

hugged him tight. After he'd kissed both her cheeks, he put her away from him with a strength that surprised her.

"Wow, you're awfully spry this evening," she said with a happy laugh. "What have they been feeding you around here, spinach?"

Alonzo's dark wrinkled face split into a grin for his daughter. "Can't stand that stuff. Meat. Fresh meat. That's what's done it."

Pressing her cheek against his, she hugged him once again, before gesturing toward Conall, who was standing a few steps behind her. "I brought someone with me tonight, Dad. You remember Conall?"

The old man's brown eyes flickered with surprise, quickly followed by pleasure. "Sure, sure. Donovan. That right?"

Smiling, Conall stepped forward and reached to shake her father's hand. "That's exactly right, Mr. Valdez. It's good to see you again."

The other man nodded with approval. "Good to see you. Yes."

Looping her arm through his, Vanessa asked, "Do you think you can make it over to that empty table where we can sit down and talk?"

To her surprise, he pushed away her helping hand. "Show you. Watch," he said proudly.

Moving aside, she stood next to Conall and watched as Alonzo walked slowly but surely the twenty-foot distance to the empty table.

"Your father looks like he's doing great to me," Conall said under his breath.

She glanced up at him with pleased wonder. "I've never seen his back so straight and he's actually lifting his feet and putting them down instead of shuffling. He's improved so much from just a week ago."

Giving the side of her waist an encouraging squeeze, he inclined his head toward Alonzo. "Let's join him."

For the next forty minutes the three of them talked about the twins, then on to several local happenings, until finally the two men began to reminisce about the time Alonzo restored one of the Diamond D horse barns. Vanessa hadn't been aware that her father had ever contracted work for the Donovans or that he'd known the family so personally. But that didn't begin to describe the shock she felt when Conall suddenly scooted his chair close to Vanessa's and curled his arm around her shoulders in a completely possessive way.

"Alonzo, has your daughter told you that I've asked her to marry me?"

The old man appeared stunned and then he turned accusing eyes upon his daughter. "She did not tell me."

Conall shot her a devilish smile. "Why haven't you told your father about us?"

It was all Vanessa could do to stop herself from kicking his shins beneath the table. "Because it—" Jerking her eyes off Conall's expectant face, she looked over to her father. "Because I told him no!"

Alonzo studied her closely. "Why?"

"Yeah, why?" Conall echoed the older man's question.

She wanted to kill the man for putting her on the spot like this in front of her father. And yet, a part of her felt ridiculously warm and wanted and a bit like a princess to have Conall Donovan declaring to her father that he wanted to marry her.

"Because I—" She turned a challenging look on Conall. "I want a husband who will love me."

Alonzo's sharp gaze leveled on Conall and then after a moment he chuckled. The sound didn't just stun Vanessa, it also angered her.

"That'll come," Alonzo said with beaming confidence. "Later."

Jumping to her feet, she tugged on Conall's arm. "We've got to be going. Now!"

Conall didn't argue and after she gave her father a quick goodbye, the two of them hurried around to a side exit of the building and on to the parked truck.

As he helped her climb into the cab, she hissed under her breath, "What the hell were you doing back there?"

"Telling Alonzo my intentions toward his daughter," he answered easily. "As far as I'm concerned, that's the respectable thing for a man to do."

"But you did it on purpose!"

"Of course I did it on purpose." As she settled herself in the seat, he shut the door and rounded the truck. Once he was under the wheel and starting the engine, he said, "I don't say things just to be saying them, Vanessa."

Groaning helplessly, she swiped a hand across her forehead. "Now Dad is going to be wondering about us and expecting—"

"What?"

"Me to marry you. That's what. He likes and respects you and he's been telling me that I need a husband. It's all simple logic to him."

Conall smiled. "He did appear pleased about the whole thing. But I always did think your father was a wise man."

Latching on to his last words, she jerked her head around to stare at him in wonder. "You never cease to surprise me, Conall."

"Why?" he asked with a puzzled frown. "What have I done now?"

Suddenly her heart was melting like candy clutched in a warm palm. Maybe he didn't love her outright, but he was good in so many other ways that she was beginning to wonder if she was crazy for refusing to marry him. "Nothing. You complimented my father. Did you really mean that when you called him wise?"

He backed the truck onto the street and directed it down the steep street. "Like I said, I don't say things just to be saying them. Your dad has weathered plenty of storms and he's done it without bending or begging. He's worked hard all his life and managed to hold his land and his home together. That takes wisdom." He glanced at her. "Plus he knew how to keep your mother happy. I could see that each time I saw them together in church. They looked at each other the same way my parents look at each other."

She swallowed hard as emotions thickened her throat. "You mean...with love?"

His features tightened ever so slightly. "I'd rather call it respect."

Vanessa couldn't argue that respect was a key ingredient in a marriage. But it wasn't enough to keep her heart warm and full. It didn't thrill her or fill her with hunger or need or joy.

"By all means call it that if it makes you feel safer," Vanessa told him as she unconsciously reached up and touched the rose he'd placed above her ear. "I prefer to call it what it is."

They ate at a tiny café on the northwest side of town called the Sugar Shack, in tribute to the decadent home-made desserts that were served there. Over the casual dinner, all mention of love and marriage, or anything close to it, was avoided by both of them and eventually Vanessa was able to relax and enjoy the good food.

Once the meal was over and they exited the building, she pressed a hand to her stomach and groaned. "I've not eaten that much in ages. I'll probably have nightmares tonight after stuffing myself."

"I have a perfect place for you to walk some of that meal off," he suggested slyly.

Spend more time with this man? Alone? The sane, sensible and smart thing for her to do would be go straight home. He made her crazy and on edge, yet at the same time he made her undeniably happy. She was at a loss as to how to deal with the contradictory feelings, especially when a part of her was screaming to simply give up and give in to her desires.

"I really should get back home and give Hannah some relief."

He moved his arm around the back of her waist and guided her toward the truck. "I promise you, Hannah and the twins can make it without you for a little while longer. And if you don't feel like doing any walking, we can always do a little stargazing."

Her mouth opened to utter another protest, but that was as far as her resistance would take her. "All right," she conceded. "It would be nice to stay out a little longer."

"That's exactly what I was thinking."

Once they were back in the truck, he drove northwest until most of the town was behind them. After turning onto a narrow dirt road, they wound upward through a tall stand of pines and spruce trees until they were near the crest of the mountain. Just when she'd decided he was probably taking her to a state campground, the road ended and the forest opened up. Beyond the beam of headlights she could see some sort of house constructed of cedar wood and native rock.

"Is this your place?" she asked as he parked the truck near a big blue spruce.

"It belongs to the Diamond D," he answered. "We have guests, horse buyers, or out-of-town friends fly in to attend the races and this place is a lot closer to the track than the ranch. Our city friends especially enjoy the privacy." He reached to release his seat belt. "Let's get out and I'll show you around."

Once he helped Vanessa down from the truck, he took a firm hold on her hand. "Be careful and watch your step," he warned as they started toward the house. "Dad doesn't want to install a yard light up here. Says it would ruin the effect. So at night it's dark as hell."

"The moon is rising," she remarked as she cast an observing glance at the eastern sky. "That gives us walking light."

The back part of the structure sat on the edge of the mountainside, while the front was supported with huge wooden pillars. She figured the Donovans considered this a mere mountain cabin, but to regular folks like her it was more like an opulent getaway.

The two of them climbed long steps up to a wide planked deck that also served as a porch. Conall led her over to the far end and they leaned against a waist-high wooden railing to gaze beyond the surrounding forest to a majestic view of the valley below.

"It's beautiful up here!" she said with quiet wonder.

He said, "Well, you can't exactly get the full effect of the view in the moonlight, but we'll come back again when the sun is out and the weather is nice. You'll really appreciate it then."

His suggestion implied that he planned to spend more personal time with her. The idea thrilled her, yet troubled her. No doubt the more time she spent with him, the more she would fall in love with him. And where would that eventually leave her? Loving a man who was unable to love her in return?

No. She didn't want to think about that right now. Since her divorce more than a year ago, she'd kept a high fence around herself. Before she'd taken even the tiniest of steps, she'd stopped and looked in all four directions to make sure she wasn't about to be waylaid by something or someone. Careful, cautious and controlled, that was how she'd lived her life since her marriage had ended. Now she was struck with the reckless urge to break free of those cold boundaries, to let herself live and feel again. No matter the painful consequences.

Sighing, she turned toward him. "I'm glad you asked me out tonight," she admitted.

His smile was full of doubt. "That's hard to believe. I haven't exactly been one of your favorite people since... well, since that morning at the office when I wanted to make love to you."

The memory of that incident still had the power to heat her cheeks and she was grateful the darkness masked the telltale color on her cheeks. "Make love to me? Don't you mean you wanted to have sex with me?"

In the silver moonlight she could see a grimace cross his face. "I was trying to be tactful. Making love sounds better."

"I'd prefer honesty over sounding nice." She directed her gaze away from his face to a dark corner of the deck.

"Actually, I should tell you that I was angrier at myself that day than I was with you."

His hand released hers only to wrap around her upper arm. Since her dress was sleeveless, the feel of his fingers against her bare skin was like throwing drops of water into a hot skillet. The sizzle vibrated all the way down to her toes.

He said, "I don't understand."

She dared to look up at his shadowed face. "You should understand, Conall. It's not smart of me to want you. But I do," she added in a whisper.

Suddenly the hand that had been burning a ring around her arm slid upward until his long fingers were curved against her throat. No doubt he could feel the hammering of her pulse and knew exactly what his touch was doing to her. But then, he'd probably always known how weak and utterly helpless he made her.

"You shouldn't have been angry with either one of us," he murmured. "And if it's honesty you want, I can truthfully say I want you, Vanessa. More than I've ever wanted any woman."

From any other man, a trite line like that would have garnered a groan of disgust from Vanessa, but coming from Conall she wanted to believe it was uttered with sincerity. Oh, yes, to think he desired her over any other woman was more than a heady thought. But thinking, wondering, deciding what was right or wrong was quickly taking a backseat. Instead of her brain, her heart had taken control and it was urging her body to press against his, begging her arms to wrap around his waist.

"Don't say any more, Conall. Just show me."

She heard him suck in a sharp breath and then his lips were suddenly hovering over hers.

"Vanna. Vanna."

The repeated whisper of her nickname was like a warm, sweet caress and she sighed ever so slightly before his lips latched on to hers, his hands slid to the small of her back and pressed her body into his.

She'd expected his kiss to be a lazy, searching seduction, but it was anything but. His lips were rampaging over hers, taking her breath and searing her senses with the depth of his desire. She tried to match his movements, tried to give back to him, but he'd taken total control and all she could do was surrender to the ravaging passion.

By the time he lifted his head, her legs were trembling and she was clutching the front of his shirt just to keep herself upright.

He whispered, "I think we should go inside, don't you?"

Her lips felt swollen, prompting her to run the tip of her tongue over them at the same time she sucked in deep, ragged breaths. And though she should have taken the time to regain her senses and consider his loaded question, she didn't wait. She was tired of waiting.

"Yes," she murmured. "We should."

She followed him over to the door, which he quickly unlocked with a spare key hidden beneath a pot of cacti. Once they were inside, he switched on the nearest table lamp and beneath the dim glow Vanessa caught a brief glance of expensive, rustic-style furniture, a polished pine floor scattered with braided rugs and a wall of glass overlooking the deck. Beyond that, she saw nothing but Conall's dark face as he pulled her into his arms and began to kiss her all over again.

For long, long moments, they stood just inside the door, their bodies locked together, their lips clinging, tasting and searching for a closeness they couldn't quite attain. Unlike his ravaging kiss on the deck, this time his lips were slow and hot, luring her to a place where there was nothing but mindless pleasure.

The concept of time faded, along with their surroundings. When he finally ended the embrace and took her by the hand to lead her out of the room, she followed blindly and willingly down a narrow hallway with doors leading off both sides.

At the far end, they entered a bedroom with a wall of glass similar to the one they'd just left. Beyond it, the moon was a bright orb in the sky and its silver light illuminated the layout of the room, the king-sized bed and matching cedar armoire, a pair of stuffed armchairs by the window and a nightstand that could also be used as a desk.

Leading her toward the bed, Conall said, "This is the room I stay in whenever I'm up here. But that's not often."

"Why is that?" she asked huskily.

Their legs bumped into the side of the mattress and he quickly spun her into his arms. "Because you're not here," he said with a hungry growl.

She groaned with disbelief. "Oh, Conall."

He pulled her down onto the mattress and with the two of them lying face-to-face, he cupped a hand against her cheek. "It's true, Vanessa. Until you came to work for me, I think I'd forgotten about living. And I'd sure as hell forgotten about this."

With his arm around her waist, he urged her forward until the front of her body was pressed tightly to his. Vanessa's heart was pounding like a drumbeat deep in a hot jungle as his lips settled against her cheek, then slid open and wet to the side of her neck.

Desire bubbled within her before spreading like fingers of hot lava to every part of her body. Certain she was paralyzed by the incredible heat, she moaned and waited for a sense of normalcy to return to her limbs. It didn't. And in the back of her mind, she suddenly realized that everything about this and about Conall was different and new.

"I think…I might have forgotten, too," she whispered as his lips continued their heated foray against her throat. "Or maybe I never knew that it could feel like this."

Lifting his head, he gazed wondrously at her. "Vanna. Oh, baby."

It was all he said before his lips moved over hers and then his kiss was telling her how much he needed and wanted her. And for the moment that was enough for Vanessa. Words could come later.

Like a man wandering through a parched desert, Conall craved to drink from her lips, to bury himself in the moist folds of her body and restore the dry emptiness inside him. And though he was trying his best to control himself, to give her time to get used to being in his arms and to accept the idea of making love to him, the weeks, days, hours of wanting her had left him simmering far too long.

Before he could stop himself, he was tugging at her clothes, tossing them every which way until his hands and mouth had nothing but smooth skin beneath them. She felt like the petal of a flower and tasted even sweeter. Without even knowing it, a groan rumbled deep in his throat as he explored her tight nipples, then on to the hollow of her belly, the bank of her hipbone and the tender slope of her inner thigh.

Above his head, he could hear her soft whimpers of

need and the sound fueled him, thrilled him, empowered him in a way he'd never felt before. And when her fingers delved into his hair, her hips arched toward his searching mouth, he realized that without even trying she was giving him everything his body, his soul, had been craving for so long.

Desperate to have her, yet please her, he slipped his hand between her thighs, then his fingers into the very warm center of her. Her reaction was to suck in a harsh breath and then she released a guttural groan as his slow, tempting strokes caused her to writhe and beg for relief.

"Conall...please...I can't...wait!"

Her choked plea prompted him to pull his fingers away and quickly replace them with his tongue. As he lathed the moist folds, she began to pulsate and he supped at her pleasure, inhaled the unique scent of her until the ache in his loins threatened to overtake him.

While her body was still riding on a crested wave, he moved up and over her, then sealing his lips over hers, he thrust deep inside her.

The intimate connection was so overwhelming it took his breath, and not until her legs wrapped around his waist and her hips arched toward him did he realize his body had gone stock-still. He used the moment to lift his head and gaze down at her face and for one split second he wished he'd looked elsewhere, anywhere but at the tenderness, the raw emotion radiating from her eyes. What he saw in the deep brown depths looked so much like love that he wanted to embrace it and run from it all at the same time.

Cupping a hand against her cheek, he tried to speak, to tell her with words exactly how much this moment meant to him. But nothing would form on his tongue except her name and it came out on a hoarse whisper.

"Vanna. My beautiful sweetheart."

Reaching up, she curled a hand around the back of his neck and pulled his face down to hers. "Make love to me, Conall."

Love. She wasn't labeling it as sex anymore. She was calling it love. And Conall couldn't argue the point. In spite of his effort to put a brake on his free-falling emotions, everything inside his heart was shouting that he loved this woman. And he could no more put a halt to his feelings than he could stop his body from moving against hers, from seeking the pleasure that only she could give him.

Chapter Ten

With her cheek resting against his damp chest, the sound of his rapid heartbeat merged with the blood rushing through her ears. Her hair was a damp tangle around her face while the rest of her body was covered with a fine sheen of sweat. Beyond Conall's shoulder she could see the glass wall, which was partially covered with dark drapes.

Sometime after they'd entered the bedroom, clouds had covered the moon and now bolts of lightning were streaking across the peaks of the distant mountains. The ominous threat of rain matched the turmoil going on inside of her and though she tried to push the dark feelings away, tried to focus on the sheer wonder of being in Conall's arms, she couldn't prevent a wall of tears from stinging her eyes and thickening her throat.

When his hand rested on her head and his fingers began to push through her hair, she did her best to speak.

Talking would break the spell, she told herself. Talking would make her realize that what just happened between them was normal and nothing out of the ordinary. The earth hadn't shattered nor had her heart. It was still beating in her chest and the world was still turning on its axis. So why did she feel as though everything had suddenly changed?

"It's going to rain," she said.

He murmured, "Not in here. We're dry and cozy."

His hand left her hair to settle on her shoulder and Vanessa's eyelids drifted closed as his fingers made lazy circles across her skin. She wanted to stay in his arms forever. She wanted to pretend that he loved her, that each time he'd touched her, his heart had been guiding him. But that would be fooling herself. And she wasn't going to be a fool a second time around. No matter how good he made her feel.

"It's getting late," she reminded him. "I have to be going home soon."

His sigh ruffled the top of her hair. "It's already late. Being a little later isn't going to make much difference."

Tilting her head back, she looked at him. "Explaining this to Hannah is not going to be easy."

One side of his lips twisted upward. "Hannah isn't your mother. And why don't you simply tell her the truth? That you were out with me?"

She bit down on her bottom lip. "I don't know."

"Why? Are you ashamed of being here with me?"

"Not exactly."

His jaw thrust forward. "What is that supposed to mean?"

She swallowed as the raw thickness returned to her

throat. "I guess what I'm trying to say is…that I'm feeling more sad than anything."

A puzzled frown puckered his forehead and then his expression quickly turned to one of concern. "Sad? Why, did I hurt you? Did I do something wrong and you're too embarrassed to tell me about it?"

A rush of pure love for him overcame her and she scooted her body upward until she could press her lips against his cheek. "Oh, Conall, you did everything right. Perfect. I could make love to you over and over if…well, I suppose I'm just feeling sad because I know this is the end."

Next to hers, she could feel his body tense.

"End?" he asked inanely. "I thought it was just the beginning."

Easing out of his arms, she sat up on the side of the bed. Except for the intermittent flashes of lightning, the interior of the bedroom was completely black. She was glad the darkness was there to hide her tears.

"I can't keep being your secretary now, Conall. Not after this. It would never work."

The sheets rustled as he shifted toward her and then his hand was pushing the hair away from the back of her neck. As he pressed a kiss against her nape, he murmured, "I'm glad you said that, Vanessa. Like I said before, I don't want you to be my secretary. I want you to be my wife."

Groaning, she bent her head and squeezed her eyes against the burning tears. "Oh, Conall, please don't do this to me," she pleaded in a whisper. "Not tonight."

With his hands on her bare shoulders, he twisted her upper body toward him. "What am I doing to you that's so wrong, Vanna? I'm asking you to be my wife, to be at my side for the rest of our lives. A few minutes ago you said you could make love to me over and over. Did you mean that?"

"Yes. But marrying you—I can't. I can't live in a loveless marriage." She gestured toward the center of the bed. "Yes, the sex between us would be good—for a while. But after the initial luster wore off everything would feel empty...be empty. I want more than that."

His hand smoothed the hair back from her forehead and as her gaze flickered over his shadowed features, she suddenly felt as though she was looking at a different man. The soft and gentle expression in his eyes was something she'd never seen before and she didn't know what to think or expect.

"I want more than that, too, Vanna."

Wide-eyed, with her lips parted, she stared at him. "What are you saying?"

One corner of his mouth lifted. "You don't want to make any of this easy for me, do you?"

"Easy? Nothing about this is easy for me," she said flatly. "I've made too many mistakes, Conall. I don't want to keep making more."

A heavy breath slipped past his lips. "Neither do I," he admitted. "That's why...you have to know...that I love you."

Stunned, she shifted her body so that she was facing him directly. "Love? Who are you trying to kid? Me or yourself?" Angry and confused, she slipped off the bed and reached for her dress. "Either way, Conall, I'm not sure I can forgive you for this!"

Leaping off the bed, he snatched the dress from her hands before she could step into the garment. "What the hell are you talking about?" he demanded. "I'm trying to tell you how I feel about you—about us!"

"Sure. Sure you are." Since he'd confiscated her

dress, she glanced around for something to cover her nakedness. Luckily his shirt was at her feet and she quickly jammed her arms into the sleeves and buttoned the front between her breasts. "What do you think I am? An idiot? A fool?"

Tossing her dress aside, he reached for her and though she wanted to resist, she couldn't. As soon as his hands wrapped around her shoulders, as soon as the front of his hard, warm body was pressed against hers, she was lost to him.

"Vanna," he began gently, "maybe I did pick the wrong time to confess my feelings. Maybe it does look all contrived to you. But I can't help that. I'm a rancher not some sort of Romeo or playboy that knows exactly what to say or how to say it."

She wanted to believe him. Every beat of her heart was longing for his words to be true. But the scarred, wary side of her held back, refused to believe that this man could have changed. Especially for her.

"Maybe you're forgetting, Conall. You told me that you didn't believe in love. That it was a fairy-tale existence. Not a firm foundation for a marriage."

A mixture of regret and frustration twisted his features. "That was the bitterness in me doing the talking, Vanna. For a long time now I'd quit looking for a woman to love. I'd decided it wasn't worth the pain. But then you walked into my life and...oh, Vanna, believe me, I've tried not to love you. I've tried telling myself that you're just another woman, you're nothing special and I could do without you. But none of that has worked. I want you by my side. I need you in my bed, my life, in every way a man can need a woman. I love you. Pure and simple."

Even though she felt the safety barriers inside her begin to crumble, she tried her best to withstand his gentle persuasion. "And us just having sex had nothing to do with this sudden realization of yours," she said with skepticism.

His hands left her shoulders and began to roam against her back and farther down to the curve of her bottom. The familiar touch of his hands, even through the fabric of his shirt, was heating her flesh, reminding her body of the delicious pleasures he could give her.

"Would you call what just happened between us sex?" he countered. "You don't believe that. And neither do I. And as for realizing that I loved you—" dipping his head, he nuzzled his cheek against hers "—I think that happened a long time ago, Vanna. Even before that day you fainted in my arms. That's why I did my best to keep everything between us business. I didn't want to give myself the chance to let my feelings for you grow."

In spite of all the misgivings traipsing through her thoughts, Vanessa's heart began to beat with hope. Tilting her head back she gazed at him through shimmery eyes. "I didn't want to love you, either," she whispered, "but I do."

With a groan of relief, he captured her lips with his and with their mouths still locked, he lowered them both back onto the bed.

As he shoved his shirt off her shoulders and began to nibble eagerly at one breast, she groaned in defeat. "Conall, the babies—"

"Are going to have me for a daddy," he murmured, his words muffled by her heated skin.

"But tonight—"

"You'll be getting home late. Very late."

* * *

More than a week later, Conall was standing beneath the shady overhang of a long shed row talking with Walt. In his early seventies with a face as wrinkled as a raisin, he was rawhide-tough and as dependable as the rise and fall of the sun. For longer than Conall had been alive, he'd been the man who made sure the barns, the stalls, the gallopers, the hot walkers, the grooms and everyone in between had what they needed to make their jobs easier and keep the horses in top-notch condition.

A stickler for making lists, Walt's hand-scribbled notes normally went to Liam's office first and then on to Conall's. But with Liam still out in California at the Del Mar track, he was making sure Conall was personally handed the written requests.

"Not asking for much this time, Mr. Conall," he said as Conall scanned the short piece of paper. "Mainly shavings and clippers. Had two pair of them burn up this week. They just ain't made to last like they used to be."

Even though it had been more than forty years since Walt had migrated over to New Mexico from South Texas, he still insisted on the mannerly form of putting the *Mr.* in front of Conall's name.

"Shavings, huh?" Conall mused out loud. "I just had a thousand yards of those delivered to the ranch last week. We already need more?"

"Yes, sir. That brother of yours has stalled nearly every two-year-old on this place and I think half of 'em needs to be turned to pasture. Save plenty of shavings like that. But you know Mr. Liam, he thinks they're all runners."

Conall grunted with amusement. "He's supposed to

think like that, Walt. Otherwise, he might accidently turn a champion out to pasture."

The older man's grin was sly. "Well, we couldn't have that, could we?"

Giving Walt a companionable swat on the shoulder, Conall said, "It's time I got back to the office. Why don't you take the rest of the day off, Walt," he suggested. "You work too hard."

A scowl wrinkled Walt's features even more. "Look who's talkin'. Besides, I gotta help Travis repair the water trough in the yearling pen. Anything mechanical boggles that boy's mind. This younger generation is helpless. Slap-dab helpless."

Still muttering about Travis's incompetence, Walt turned and walked away. Conall headed in the opposite direction and was nearly at the end of the shed row when he spotted Brady, his younger brother, striding toward him.

Being a deputy for the Lincoln County sheriff's department kept Brady working random shifts, which didn't give Conall much opportunity to spend time with him. This evening Brady was still dressed in his uniform and Conall didn't have to ask if his day had been long. The man put in an extraordinary amount of hours on the job, yet even now there was a grin on his face, albeit a weary one.

If Conall was being totally honest with himself, he'd often been envious of his youngest brother. Brady had grown up to be the strong-minded, independent one of the Donovan boys. He'd chosen to go outside the family tradition of horse racing and take on a job that he quite obviously loved. Moreover, Brady had never experienced a moment's guilt over the decision. Whereas Conall had often felt bound, even restricted, by the duty of being the eldest son; the one that was meant to hold the Diamond D together for future generations.

"Hey, Conall," he greeted. "Are you heading toward the house or the office?"

As Brady took off the felt hat he was wearing and slapped it against his thigh to remove the dust, Conall gestured toward the part of the ranch yard where the office buildings were located.

"The office. And I'm glad you interrupted. I get damned tired of being cooped up."

Brady chuckled slyly. "With Vanessa? That's hard to believe."

Conall frowned. "Vanessa took the day off to go shopping with Maura. Mom's been sitting in for her, but she's already left me, too. One of these days I've got to take the time to hire an assistant to take over whenever Vanessa or Mom can't be around."

Clearly amused, Brady walked over to the nearest stall where a chestnut horse was poking his nose eagerly over the wooden gate that had him safely fastened inside the small square space. As he stroked Hot Charlie's nose, he said, "Mom probably hightailed it to the house 'cause you were too cranky to put up with."

Smiling, Conall walked over to join his brother. "What are you talking about? I'm always Mr. Nice Guy."

"Well, maybe now that Vanessa has tamed you," he conceded. "You two set a wedding date yet?"

"Not yet. But we will soon."

"That's good." Brady glanced at him. "I haven't had a chance to tell you how glad I am that you're getting married again. I've been hoping for a long time that you'd find somebody special—like I found Lass."

Conall smiled ruefully. When Brady had first fallen

in love with Lass, Conall had been worried sick about his younger brother and the whole situation he'd gotten himself into. At the time, Lass had been suffering from amnesia and hadn't known who she was or even if she had a home somewhere. Conall had been certain she was going to take Brady for a disastrous ride. He and Brady had even had cross words over the woman. But Conall would be the first to admit he'd been dead wrong about Lass. She'd made Brady a loving and devoted wife.

"Well, I didn't find her on the side of the road like you found Lass," Conall joked, "but she's definitely the right one for me."

Turning away from the horse, Brady gave him a weary smile. "That's all that matters. When's Liam coming home?"

"I don't know. Probably not until Del Mar closes on Labor Day. So let's hope he's taking a liking to all that sun and surf."

Brady laughed out loud. "Liam in the surf? That'd be the day. He's spending every waking moment on the backside of the track. That's what he's doing." He slapped a hand over Conall's shoulder. "I've got to get going. Dallas is staying at Angel Wings an hour later tonight to accommodate a little girl who's just gotten over a long illness, so Lass is expecting me to drive over and fetch her before dinnertime. And since my wife and I haven't had dinner together in the past two weeks, she'll kill me if I'm late."

"I doubt it. Other than Vanna, I don't know of any woman who's more understanding than Lass."

Brady started to stride away, then at the last minute turned back toward Conall. "Oh. By the way, I came down here to tell you that we found out who crashed their vehicle through the fence—a teenage boy from over around Alto. The father found the damage to the truck and pressed his son for answers. The man is offering to pay for the fence repairs. I told him I'd discuss it with you and let him know."

Conall shook his head. "Money isn't the issue. I'd rather the boy do the labor to repair the fence. Teach him a hell of a lot better lesson than his dad bailing him out with money."

"That's exactly what I was thinking. I'll have a talk with the father and see what we can work out," Brady said, then grinned. "By the way, I hope Vanessa knows what a hell of a daddy those twins are getting."

Brady lifted his hand in farewell, then turned to hurry on to his waiting truck. Conall remained beside Hot Charlie's stall as all sorts of emotions swirled inside of him.

These past few days, he'd been torn between complete euphoria and stark terror. When Vanessa had made love to him and agreed to marry him, the joy he'd felt had put him on a cloud. She was everything he'd ever wanted in a woman and wife. Being with her, loving her, made his life complete. Yet in his quieter moments, nagging fear tried to intrude on his happiness.

There was going to be trouble—big trouble—if he didn't take Vanessa aside and talk to her about his condition. But since their night at the mountain cabin, when she'd agreed to marry him, things had quickly begun to barrel out of control. Not that he could use a hectic routine as an excuse. If he'd been any sort of man at all, he would have told her that night. But at the time, he'd not had the courage or the confidence to risk smashing the progress he'd made with her. He'd felt...no, he'd *known* that Vanessa needed more convincing of his love and he needed more time to do that convincing.

But that had been more than a week ago and now his mother and grandmother were already planning an engagement party for the two of them. In a matter of days, the ranch house would be full of friends, family and acquaintances. Everyone would be expecting them to announce their wedding date. But would there even be a wedding, he wondered, once Vanessa discovered he was sterile?

Once he returned to the office there was a stack of business calls he still needed to make. But business would have to wait, he decided, as he reached for the cell phone in his shirt pocket. Talking to Vanessa couldn't. If she was the wonderful, understanding woman that he believed her to be, then she would accept and empathize with the circumstance that had never been his fault.

Buoyed by the thought, Conall punched in Vanessa's cell number. After the fourth ring he was expecting her voice mail to end the call when she suddenly answered.

"Hello, Conall," she said. "This is a surprise. I expected you to still be working."

"I am. Sort of. I've been down at the shed rows talking with Walt. But I'm on my way back to the office to make a few calls before I quit for the evening."

"Oh, do you need information? Maura and I are at the Blue Mesa having coffee. I can probably talk you through it."

He smiled to himself. No matter what the situation, Vanessa was always the consummate secretary. "Everything is okay here. I'm calling to see about us getting together tonight. I thought I'd drive over to your place. That way I could see the twins. And we could…talk."

Her low chuckle was sexy enough to curl his toes. "Talk? You really think that would happen?"

He closed his eyes as the images of her naked and writhing beneath him rolled into his mind. Talking to Vanessa tonight was going to be difficult. In more ways than one. "Well, we do have things to discuss. Important things. Like making a date for our wedding. And…other things," he added. He drew in a deep breath and blew it out. "Will you be in town for much longer?"

"Not much, I don't think. Let me check with Maura," she told him. She went off the line, but in the background he could hear the faint sounds of music and the casual chatter of voices, intermingled with street traffic. When she finally returned, she said, "We'll be leaving here soon, Conall. So I'll be home by the time you get there."

"Great. I'll see you then, darlin'."

Vanessa closed her cell phone and reached for her cooling coffee. Across the outdoor table, Maura smiled shrewdly.

"So what's my brother doing? Already giving you orders before you even get married?"

Chuckling, Vanessa said, "He's my boss. He's supposed to give me orders."

With a good-natured groan, Maura shook her head. "It's clear that he has you right where he wants you."

After a long sip of coffee, Vanessa looked over the rim of her cup at her longtime friend. "I can truthfully say I'm right where I want to be."

Smiling with approval, Conall's eldest sister sliced her fork into a piece of blueberry pie. "Hmm. Well, I can honestly say that Conall appears to be right where he wants to be, too." She chewed, swallowed, then released a sigh of contentment. "This is so nice, Vanessa, the two of us getting out like this together. Since you've returned to Lincoln County we've hardly had any time to spend together. I hope that changes and we can have more days like this. You've not even been out to see the Golden Spur yet."

"I will soon," Vanessa promised. "After we're married Conall wants to find someone to help me in the office. He thinks I need to be home with the twins for at least half of every workday and I agree with that. I want the twins to bond with me and know me as their mother, not just a woman they see in the mornings and at night. Still, I don't want to give up working completely. Does that sound selfish?"

"Not to me," Maura said between bites of the rich dessert. "After Riley was born I cut my weekly work hours down to half. And since Clancy arrived back in April I've cut them even more. But I've not quit nursing entirely. I believe some women need outside interest, too. Like me. Otherwise we'd become as dull as dishwater. And no man wants a dull wife."

Vanessa took a long sip of coffee before she replied, "Well, working a half day will be plenty for me until the twins get older."

Maura smiled suggestively. "And who knows, by then you and Conall might want more children."

Vanessa felt a blush creep across her cheeks. If she'd not had the forethought to stay on the oral birth control she'd used during her marriage, she would probably be pregnant with Conall's child at this moment. That night they'd first made love, she'd been so besotted and lost in the man she'd forgotten to mention she was protected and apparently he'd forgotten to ask. Later, when she tried to assure him that there was nothing to worry about, that she was on oral contraceptives, he'd quickly dismissed the whole thing. As though getting her pregnant would be a welcome idea with him.

She'd not yet talked with him about having any future children. But she had no doubts that he would want them. As crazy as he was about the twins, she couldn't imagine him wanting to stop with just the two.

"Maybe," Vanessa said, then before she could stop it, a happy laugh slipped past her lips. "Oh, Maura, it's still hard for me to take everything in. First the twins and now becoming Conall's wife. In my wildest imaginings I couldn't have pictured this happening to me. I look back now and wonder why I was fighting Conall so hard and refusing to accept his proposal."

Her pie gone, Maura pushed the plate aside and reached for her coffee. "I remember the feeling well. I fought Quint for a long time before I ever agreed to marry him. But a woman wants to know she's loved for herself, not because of a baby. And Gilbert had done such a job of deceiving me that I...was scared to trust any man. Thank God Quint was persistent."

"I'm very happy that Conall didn't give up on me, either."

Vanessa placed her empty cup back on its saucer and reached for her handbag. "If you're ready we should probably be going. I need to tidy up the house—and myself—before Conall gets there."

Reaching across the table, Maura placed her hand over Vanessa's. "Before we go, I just wanted to say how glad I am that you're going to be my sister-in-law. I couldn't have picked any better woman for my brother. He's been so...well, dark and lost after the mess he went through with Nancy. I was afraid he'd never let himself love again. But you've made him so happy and I know you always will. You'd never try to hurt or manipulate him like she did. And you'd certainly never stop loving him just because of his condition."

Vanessa suddenly froze. "Condition?" she repeated blankly.

Maura's auburn brows pulled together. "Why, yes. You know—*his condition.*"

Thrown for a loop, Vanessa's mind began to race down a tangle of dark roads. If there was something personal about Conall that she wasn't aware of, something he should have told her already, the last thing she wanted was for Maura to explain. That could only cause trouble between brother and sister. And whatever it was, she wanted to hear it directly from the man she planned to marry.

"Oh, yes," she said with feigned dawning. "That... None of that matters to me."

Maura's smile was full of approval and relief. "That's one of the reasons I've always loved you, Vanessa. You don't expect a person to be perfect."

Her mouth suddenly felt like she'd walked through Death Valley in mid-July. She reached for her water glass and after a long drink, tried to speak casually. "I'm hardly perfect myself, Maura. I can't expect others to be."

Just as Maura started to reply, her cell phone went off and the other woman quickly began to fish the device from her handbag. Vanessa was grateful for the diversion. She couldn't continue to fake this train of conversation.

"Excuse me, Vanessa, it's Quint. I'd better see what he needs."

While Maura exchanged a few short words with her husband, Vanessa's mind tumbled end over end. What could be wrong with Conall? A recurring health problem? That was hard to believe. During the time she'd worked for him, she'd never seen him sick or even close to it. He appeared as healthy as the horses he bred and raised.

The snapping sound of Maura's phone being shut jerked Vanessa out of her whirling thoughts and she looked across the table at her friend's apologetic face.

"I hate to end the day so abruptly, Vanna, but Quint's grandfather is feeling a bit puny and he wants me to drive out to Apache Wells and check on him before I go home. It's forty minutes from here, so I need to hit the road."

As she stood up, she tossed several bills onto the table. "That ought to take care of everything here."

Rising to her feet also, Vanessa quickly grabbed up the money and thrust it back at the other woman. "Here. I'll take care of things."

"No arguments. It's my treat today, sweetie." She pressed a quick kiss on Vanessa's cheek. "See you soon. And I promise you that Conall's eyes are going to pop out of his head when he sees you in the dress we found today."

Smiling as brightly as she could, Vanessa waved her friend off, then went to pay the check. A few minutes later, she was on the highway, driving home to Tinnie as fast as the speed limit would allow.

Conall had never been known for being a nervous person. In fact, his brothers had often accused him of having ice water in his veins and his mother had regularly referred to him as a piece of unmoving granite. But if they could see his insides now as he drove to Vanessa's place, they would all believe they were looking at some other man, not him. His stomach was clenched into a tight, burning knot and his heart was hammering at such a rate, the blood was pounding like a jackhammer against his temples.

He'd never agonized over discussing anything with anyone. Especially when he knew he'd be talking to a level-headed, sensible person. And Vanessa was definitely both of those things. Plus, she was understanding. So he had nothing to worry about, he told himself as he pulled his truck to a stop in front of the small Valdez house. Except his whole future.

Chapter Eleven

Vanessa answered the door after his first knock and before he stepped over the threshold, he pulled her into his arms and placed a long, reckless kiss on her lips.

"Mmm," she exclaimed with a little laugh. "Gauging by that greeting I'd say you've missed me a little today. Maybe it's a good thing I told Hannah she could have the evening off."

His arms tightened briefly around her waist and as the sweet scent of her rose to his nostrils, he desperately wished the only thing he needed to say to her were words of love and longing.

He peered over her shoulder. "She's not here?"

Vanessa stepped back and allowed him to enter the house. As she shut the door behind him, she said, "No. She left a half hour ago. I've been feeding the twins and now they're both down for the count."

"Oh. I was hoping they'd still be awake," he said as

they gravitated away from the door, to the middle of the small living room. "It seems like ages since I've had a chance to hold them."

"It seems like ages since you've held me," she replied.

With an eager groan he pulled her into his arms and kissed her again, but this time he sensed she wasn't fully focused on him and when he lifted his head, he could see there was a tiny frown creasing her smooth forehead.

"What's wrong?"

"Nothing. I hope." Turning away from him, she gestured toward the kitchen. "Would you like something to eat?"

"No. Maybe later."

She clasped her hands in front of her. "All right. You said you wanted to talk. Let's talk."

For some reason he couldn't figure, she was on edge, even a tad cool, and he realized her unusual mood was only going to make his task harder.

"I'm trying to decide if we should discuss anything right now." Rather than make his way toward the couch, he continued to search her face. The closer inspection revealed a paleness he'd not noticed when she'd first answered the door. "You're not yourself tonight."

Her shoulders suddenly sagged and she let out a long breath. "Okay, I confess. I'm not myself. I'm actually worried sick about you."

Conall frowned with amused confusion. "Me? I'm great. Everything about me is great. And it'll be even better after we set our wedding date."

With a look of enormous relief, she sagged limply toward him and rested her cheek against the middle of his chest. "Oh, thank God. I thought…well, I've been imagining all sorts of horrible things."

Totally confused, Conall wrapped his arms tightly around her. "Why would you be doing that, honey? Surely you can see that everything is fine with me."

"I know," she said with a tiny sniff. "But I was afraid that…well, after what Maura said, that you might have a recurring disease or something. Since she's a nurse and—"

For once Conall felt as though there was actually ice water in his veins and it was freezing him with dread. "What exactly did Maura say?" he asked stiffly.

Leaning back, she looked up at him. "Nothing particular. Just something offhand about your condition. I didn't press her to explain. Whatever it is, I wanted to hear it from you."

With a sinking feeling in the pit of his stomach, he took her by the arm and led her over to the couch. "I think we'd both better sit," he said.

By the time they were settled and facing each other on the cushions, her brown eyes were dark with concern. Conall reached for one of her hands and clasped it tightly between the two of his.

"What is it, Conall? The way you're looking at me—it frightens me."

"I'm sorry. I didn't mean to." He shook his head, then lifted his face toward the ceiling and closed his eyes. "I'm not doing this right. But then, I don't guess there is a right way," he murmured. "I should have told you about this days ago. Weeks ago, even. But I couldn't bring myself to."

"Why?"

Struggling to keep the bitterness from his voice, he

said, "Because the information has always produced a negative reaction. Especially with women."

Her brows arched with surprise. "Women? I don't understand. You're certainly not frigid or impotent."

If he hadn't felt so sick inside he could have laughed. "No. I'm glad you figured that out."

Her free hand moved over his and squeezed tightly. "I don't know what this is about. But there's nothing you could tell me that would make me stop loving you, Conall."

"I hope to God that's true, Vanessa. I hope a few days from now we'll remember this moment and smile."

Her lips gently curved at the corners. "Being with you anytime makes me smile," she said, then laughed softly. "I sound like a hopeless cornball, don't I?"

Leaning forward, he pressed a kiss against her forehead. "And I've never seen a more lovely cornball."

She sighed. "Oh, Conall, even if you are ill I can deal with it. We'll deal with it together."

Easing his hand from beneath hers, he touched the side of her face. "I'm not ill, Vanessa, I promise. But I was once. When I was a very young child just learning to walk I had a viral infection that caused me to have a very high fever. I ended up having convulsions and my parents feared for my life. But eventually my body fought off the infection and I got well without any lasting effects, it seemed."

Her head swung back and forth. "Why are you telling me this now, Conall? I don't understand."

His eyes caught hers as he forced the words off his tongue. "Because you need to know why—why I can't have children."

She stared and he could see from the confusion crossing her face that she was having difficulty absorbing what he'd just said.

"Do you mean...you—"

"I'm sterile, Vanessa. The fever affected my reproductive system. It doesn't occur often, but it does happen from time to time. And I didn't even know that anything was wrong until Nancy and I tried to get pregnant."

"Oh. Oh, Conall...this is—" Her whole body sagged as though the air had literally been knocked from her. "I wasn't expecting anything like this."

Slowly, she pulled her hand from his and rose to her feet. Conall stayed on the couch and watched as she began to absently move about the small room. Eventually she stopped at a small end table and picked up a framed photo of her parents. There was raw pain on her face as she studied the image and in that moment Conall hated himself. If he'd not fallen in love with her, if he'd not pushed her to marry him, she would have eventually found someone else, someone who could give her everything. Now, God only knew what all this was doing to her.

"I'm sorry, Vanessa," he said hoarsely.

She didn't respond and after a moment he rose to his feet and walked across the room. As he came to stand beside her, she placed the photograph back on the table, then turned to face him.

"I'm sorry, too, Conall, that such a terrible thing ever happened to you. But mostly I'm sorry that you felt you couldn't tell me—long before—before I fell in love with you!"

Tears began to stream down her face and he realized there was an ache in the middle of his chest that made it almost impossible to breathe. If he was having a heart attack he probably deserved it, he thought. But he wasn't ready to die. No, there was so much that he wanted for the two of them and the twins.

"You're right. I should have. But...you weren't exactly warming up to the idea of having any sort of relationship with me. If I'd suddenly blurted out the fact that I was sterile, you would have turned your back on me and not given us any chance for a future together."

Her mouth fell open. "How do you know that I would have reacted that way? You didn't try!"

He curled his hands over the top of her shoulders. "Would you have given us a chance, Vanessa? Answer me truthfully."

Her tear-filled eyes were full of agony as she searched his face. "I don't know. I've always wanted children. Jeff wouldn't give me any and—"

"You have two children now," he pointed out. "Two beautiful, wonderful children. I want to be a father. Just like you want to be a mother."

A perceptive light suddenly flickered in her eyes. "Ahh. I wasn't thinking. But I am now," she said stiffly. "You want to be a father and I have two babies." She rapped her fist against side of the head. "What a fool I've been! That's what this has been about all along. Everything you've done and said was all for the babies! I was just a...side dish for you!"

His face felt like a stiff clay mask as he spoke in a low, purposeful tone, "I thought...I hoped and prayed that you would be different from the others. That's one of the reasons why I fell in love with you. Because deep down I believed you would accept me for the man that I am instead of persecuting me for what I can't be. I can see now that I was wrong. Again," he added bitterly.

Her expression incredulous, she shook her head.

"Don't try to make me the culprit, Conall! You asked me to marry you because of the twins!"

In spite of the pain ripping through him, the corners of Conall's mouth tilted into a wan smile. "You finally got something right about this whole situation, Vanessa. The twins were the very reason I proposed to you. I like to think they need me just as much as I need them. But mainly I figured you having the twins would make my sterility easier for you to accept. You already had two children and I was hoping they and me would be enough for you. I can clearly see we're not."

Not bothering to wait for any sort of reply she might give him, he snatched up his hat, levered it onto his head and quietly let himself out of the house.

The next morning, after a night that had passed like a wide-awake nightmare for Vanessa, she dragged herself out of bed before daylight, and chugged down a cup of coffee before she finally found the courage to reach for the phone.

As she'd hoped, Conall wasn't yet in the office and she felt a measure of guilt when the voice mail answered. But she was in such a raw, emotional state she knew the mere sound of his voice would break her into sobs. Talking directly to him would only make matters worse.

Her throat aching, she swallowed and forced herself to speak. "This is Vanessa. I'm calling to let you know I won't be in to work today. If you…feel you need to replace me permanently I'll understand. Goodbye."

As soon as she snapped the phone shut she began to weep and when Hannah walked into the kitchen, tears were still seeping from Vanessa's eyes.

On the way to the coffeepot, the woman yawned and swiped a tangle of dark hair from her face. "My, you're up early," she exclaimed. "Do you have to go into work earlier than usual this morning?"

Vanessa hurriedly made an effort to wipe her eyes. "No, I'm not going in today. I—I'm not sure I'll be working for...the Diamond D anymore."

Pausing as she reached for a mug, Hannah glanced over her shoulder and suddenly noticed Vanessa's tearstained face. "What in the world is going on?"

Swallowing hard, Vanessa answered in a hoarse voice, "I don't know where to begin, Hannah. Everything is...over."

Forgetting the coffee, the woman hurried over to where Vanessa sat at the small dining table and curled an arm around her shoulders. "Are you ill? I'll get the babies ready and drive you in to town to see a doctor."

Since Hannah had become the twins' nanny, the two women had grown to be fast friends and Vanessa was beginning to think of her more as a sister than anything. At this very moment she felt like falling into Hannah's arms and sobbing her eyes out.

"No. I—I'm not ill." She looked away from the other woman and struggled to gather her composure. "Something happened last night—between me and Conall. I— We're not going to be getting married...like we'd planned."

Stepping back, Hannah looked at her. "Oh, no! I'm not going to believe this, honey. You two—why, you're perfect for each other."

Closing her eyes, Vanessa pressed fingertips against her burning eyelids. Last night when Conall had walked out the door, she'd felt her heart rip right down the middle and for a few moments, she'd almost run after him. She'd wanted him to understand just how wrong he was about her. It wasn't his sterility that was a problem with her. It was the fact that being a father to the twins appeared to be far more important to him than being a husband to her.

But she'd not run after him. Pride, confusion and anger had all stopped her. Now, as the morning sun was beginning to creep across the kitchen floor, she wondered if she'd saved herself from another loveless marriage, or ruined the best thing that could have ever happened to her.

Sighing, she said, "Nothing is perfect in this world, Hannah."

"It's clear you're not thinking straight this morning, Vanessa. And I'm not going to pry into what happened. I'm just going to tell you to give yourself time. Whatever happened between the two of you will work itself out. I just know it."

Vanessa wished she had the other woman's optimism, but at the moment all she could see was a long bleak road ahead of her. Even if she'd misjudged Conall's motives for marrying her, she'd hurt him deeply with all her accusations. She seriously doubted he would ever want anything else to do with her.

"I seriously doubt it, Hannah. And I...well, I hate to bring it up, but if Conall fires me then I won't be able to keep you on as the twins' nanny." The idea of losing both Conall and Hannah brought a fresh spurt of tears to her eyes. "I'm so sorry."

Squeezing Vanessa's shoulder, she said, "Look, honey, quit borrowing trouble. Conall is the one who hired me for this job and he's the one who signs my checks. Until he tells me otherwise, I'll be here. Now put your chin up and help me fix us a bit of breakfast before the twins start yelling for theirs."

* * *

Almost two weeks later, Vanessa was surprised by a call from Gold Aspen Manor. The doctor had pronounced Alonzo fit enough to leave the nursing home for a few hours and she'd wasted no time in fetching him away from the facility and bringing him to the only home he'd known for the past sixty years.

Playing with the twins had left a sparkle in his eyes and now that they'd fallen asleep, her father was exploring the backyard, the patch where he'd grown vegetables and the acre-sized pen that held his beloved goats. At the moment, one of the nannies had trotted up to him and Vanessa's eyes misted over as she watched him stroke the goat's head.

Having her father home again, even for a few short hours, was the only bright thing that had happened since her break with Conall.

Break. Was that the right word for it? she wondered bleakly. It felt more like a dead-end crash to her.

With a heavy sigh, she turned her gaze to the pot of white daisies sitting in the middle of the patio table. *He loves me. He loves me not.* Plucking the petals couldn't tell her, Vanessa thought sadly. And as for Conall, he'd not even bothered to try.

Since the morning she'd called and left a message, she'd only talked to him once and that was when he'd called her later that same day. He'd been cool and brusque as he'd informed her that he'd gotten her message and that she needn't worry about coming in to work today or any day—he could handle things without her. She'd tried to get in a reply, to explain that she needed time to think things through, but he'd not given her a chance to say anything. Instead, he'd quickly ended the call with a cool goodbye and she'd not seen or heard from him since.

Had she really expected to hear from him? she miserably asked herself. Perhaps. Deep down she'd hoped and prayed that she'd been wrong about him, about his motives, about all the harsh things she'd accused him of. But he'd not made any effort to prove her wrong. And she couldn't humble herself to ask him to.

I believed you would accept me for the man that I am instead of persecuting me for what I can't be.

For the past couple of weeks Conall's low voice had sounded over and over in her head. His words continued to haunt and confuse her. Was she blaming him, punishing him for simply being unable to have children? No. She wasn't that sort of woman. She was using common sense. She was simply refusing to jump into another loveless marriage.

The feel of her father's warm hand on her shoulder had her looking up and she did her best to smile at him. "The goats are happy to see you," she said.

"They're fat. You've been feeding them good." He eased onto the chair opposite his daughter while glancing over to a shaded part of the patio where the twins were sleeping in a portable playpen. "The babies are growing fast. They'll soon walk."

Vanessa's gaze followed her father's and as she watched the sleeping babies, her heart swelled with a mixture of emotions. Even if she'd given birth to the twins herself, she couldn't love them any more. They were her children to raise and nourish, to teach and guide, to love and cherish. No matter how a child came in to a person's life, it was a precious gift and she'd been given not one, but two gifts.

Now, each time she looked at Rose and Rick, she

thought of Conall. Unless he married a woman who already had children, or adopted some of his own, he would never know the joys of being a father. It wasn't right or fair and her heart ached for his loss. But the ache didn't stop there. Missing him, wanting and needing him, filled her with such pain she doubted she would ever recover.

Pulling her thoughts back to her father's remark, she said, "Yes, in a few months they'll be walking and I'll be chasing after them."

Even though Conall hadn't formally fired her, when he'd told her goodbye over the phone there'd been finality in his voice. He'd obviously decided she couldn't bring herself to work for him. And he clearly wasn't going to ask her to return to her job. As for Hannah, the woman had stuck to her guns. Unless Conall terminated her position, she insisted on staying with Vanessa and the babies. And so far, he'd not told Hannah that her job as the twins' nanny was finished.

Vanessa didn't know what to think about the situation. Did he love the twins that much?

"What are you going to do about a job?"

Caught off guard by Alonzo's remark, she looked across the table to see he was studying her closely. It was almost like her father had been reading her thoughts. But then, she'd never been able to keep anything from either of her parents. She was as transparent as a piece of cellophane tape, until it came to Conall. He'd been unable to see how much she loved him, how much she wanted his love in return.

"What do you mean?"

He grimaced. "I know about your job at the Diamond D, my daughter. And your fight with Conall."

Vanessa drew in a sharp breath. Since she'd picked up

her father earlier in the day, he'd not mentioned anything about Conall or even asked why she wasn't working today. Vanessa had been putting off telling her father that she'd quit her job and her relationship with Conall. She'd known it would upset him and she'd been trying to think of some way to approach the subject without making it sound like her life was in a mess.

But it was in a mess. And avoiding the issue wasn't going to make her or her father feel any better about it, she decided.

"Who told you?"

"Conall. He came last week to see me. And explain." Alonzo shook his grizzled head. "I'm not happy, Vanessa. You're wrong. Wrong."

Sighing heavily, Vanessa looked away from her father's penetrating gaze. "I'm sorry I've disappointed you, Dad. But things…just didn't work out for us. That's all. I'm moving on. He's moving on. I'll get another job soon. In fact, Eric has already offered me a job at the Billy the Kid and I'll probably take it. So everything will be okay."

"Will it?"

Her lips pressed together, she rose from the chair and walked over to the playpen. Rick was beginning to stir, so she reached down and picked up her son. The warm weight of the baby cradled against her breasts was momentarily reassuring.

"Why not?" Vanessa countered his question with one of her own. "I've been supporting myself for years now. Jeff rarely lifted a hand to help me make ends meet. I'm not worried."

Alonzo spit out several curse words, further proof that his speech and his health was rapidly returning.

"What is this? You talk about money? Money is nothing. Nothing."

With Rick snuggled in her arms, she walked back over to her father. "It's something when you don't have it." She cast him a censuring glance. "Isn't that why you wanted me to marry Conall? So that I'd be financially secure?"

More curse words slipped past his lips and Vanessa shook her head. "It's a good thing the twins aren't old enough to hear you, otherwise I'd have to cover their ears."

"Hearing me cuss—you think that's bad?" He snorted. "Not near as bad as you explaining to them why Conall won't be their daddy."

Vanessa sat back down and positioned her son against her shoulder. As she patted Rick's back, she asked, "Just why do you think I'm not...marrying Conall?"

"Because he can't give you any more babies. The twins aren't enough for you, I guess."

Vanessa had thought she couldn't hurt any more than she had these past two weeks, but she was wrong. Her father's impression of her had always been important to her. Ever since she was a tiny girl, she'd wanted him to admire her, be proud of her. When she disappointed him it cut something deep inside her.

Trying to swallow away the tears burning her throat, she said, "You have this all wrong, Dad. I'm not marrying Conall because he's sterile! Even if I didn't have the twins, that wouldn't matter to me. It's because he doesn't love me—he was using me to become a father. That's all!"

Alonzo sadly shook his head at her. "I hope to God your mama is not hearing you. Tears would be in her eyes."

"I guess as a daughter I've been a disappointment to you both," Vanessa said flatly. "But can't you see, Dad? I made a bad mistake with Jeff. I don't want to repeat it with Conall. I—" Her eyes pleaded with him to understand. "I just can't go through that sort of pain again."

"You think Conall only wanted the twins? I thought you were smarter than that, my daughter. Conall isn't ugly or stupid or poor. There're plenty of single women around that need a daddy for their children. You aren't the only one. Wonder why he isn't proposing marriage to them?"

"Probably because he hasn't gotten off the ranch to meet any of them yet," Vanessa retorted.

Alonzo snorted. "And what about all those orphanages with babies that need a home? If all he wanted was to be a daddy, he could do that without you. He asked you to marry him because he loves you. But you can't see that. All you can see is Jeff. You're still hung up on that sorry excuse for a man."

Outraged, Vanessa shot straight to her feet. "That is not true! I love Conall! You know that!"

Nodding, Alonzo said, "I know it. But does Conall? Maybe you should be telling him instead of me."

Vanessa sank weakly back into the chair. Her father was making sense, a lot more sense than she'd made this past couple of weeks. Which made her feel even more like a fool. But what could she do about it now? Conall appeared to have already washed his hands of her. "I'm not sure he'd want to hear it," she mumbled uncertainly.

For the first time since he'd sat down at the table, Alonzo smiled. "It'd be worth a try."

Easing Rick from her shoulder, she cradled the baby

against her breasts and as she gazed down at her son's tiny face, she knew she had to see Conall, she had to convince him that she loved him for the man he was and nothing else mattered.

Chapter Twelve

The next morning, shortly after daylight, Conall broke from the normal routine of reading his messages and walked the quarter-mile distance to the training track. Now, as he stood next to his father at the pipe railing, he tried to focus his attention on one of the ranch's most promising runners.

Like a gull skimming the ocean, the dark brown filly was moving smoothly over the track, floating as though she had wings on her hooves. Her neck was level and outstretched, her ears perked with reserve energy. On the last turn, she lay close to the rail and then sprinted down the homestretch.

"Look at that!" Doyle practically shouted. "Juan didn't even have to ask her to change leads!" His father punched the button on the stopwatch before turning to look at Conall. "Kate's Kitten is going to be a queen, boy! She's not only fast, she's smart. When was the last time we got a combination like that?"

"When Red Garland was born," Conall was quick to answer.

Doyle stared at him with surprise and then he chuckled. "You got me there. But Kate's Kitten is right behind her. We're going to have two queens on our hands."

A wan smile touched Conall's lips. Even though the sight of the galloping filly had been beautiful, he couldn't work up near the enthusiasm that his father was displaying. But then, there wasn't much of anything that could lift his spirits these days. Not since he'd walked out of Vanessa's house. He'd not looked back that day. But he'd not needed to look back to see that he'd left his heart in her hands.

Everything you've done and said was all for the babies! I was just a...side dish for you!

Even now, after nearly two weeks had passed, the accusation that Vanessa had flung at him still had the power to hurt. Unlike an aching tooth that could be pulled out and thrown away, the words continued to claw at him and he didn't know what to do to dull the pain, much less make it go away.

"Liam will be thrilled to hear you say that about Kate's Kitten," Conall remarked. "And Grandmother will be happy to hear that her namesake has yet to disappoint."

Doyle frowned at his eldest son. "Hell, Conall, *you're* supposed to be thrilled, too. Instead you look like you did when you were a kid and I just ordered you to your bedroom to study for exams."

Conall held back a weary groan. With Vanessa no longer sitting at her desk, nothing seemed the same, felt the same. He'd walked down here to the track this morning in hopes of giving his mind a short reprieve of her image, of the tortured thoughts he couldn't cast away. But so far he'd not felt one moment of relief.

"Sorry, Dad. I am excited about Kate's Kitten. It's just that…I've had a lot of things on my mind here lately."

Doyle stuffed the stopwatch in his shirt pocket as Conall absently watched the jockey jump to the ground and hand the filly's reins to the waiting hot walker.

"Guess it doesn't have anything to do with that little secretary of yours."

Conall grimaced. "She was more than my secretary, Dad. She was the woman I was planning to marry. Now she…well, she's not even my secretary anymore."

The tall dark-haired man's expression turned to one of concern as he eyed his son. "Hell, Conall, we all knew you were planning to marry Vanessa and we all know those plans went awry. But no one has mentioned anything to me about Vanessa quitting her job."

Conall's gaze dropped to the toes of his boots. "I haven't exactly told anyone that Vanessa has quit. Since Mom is filling in at the office, I just explained to her that Vanessa was taking some time off, that's all."

"Instead, Vanessa quit. Is that it? Because you two can't see eye-to-eye on your romance." Squinting at a far off group of horse barns, he said in a gentler voice, "Well, that's not surprising. When a woman gets angry she doesn't want a man getting too close. If he does get near, she'll raise her hackles and hiss. I can see where she wouldn't want to be cooped up in an office with you."

Conall wiped a hand over his face. He couldn't remember the last time he'd slept the night through and his lack of rest was only compounding the mental agony he was going through. "She accused me of wanting to marry her just for the twins."

Doyle sighed. "In case you didn't know, your sister Maura is heartsick. She thinks she's the cause of all of this."

Shaking his head, Conall turned his gaze back on the exercise track. At the moment a chestnut colt was being trotted around the mile oval, but Conall wasn't really seeing the beautiful Thoroughbred, he was seeing Vanessa's face, the way she'd looked when he'd told her that he couldn't have children. It was like he'd punched her in the stomach.

A grimace tightened his weary features. "Maura isn't to blame for anything. I wasn't planning to marry Vanessa without telling her about my condition. Maybe I should have done it sooner, but I kept thinking our relationship needed to be more solid before I sprung something like that on her. Apparently there wasn't anything solid about it," he added bitterly.

Stepping closer, Doyle rested a comforting hand on Conall's shoulder. "You think she turned her back on you because you can't give her children, don't you?"

Filled with agony, he looked at his father. "Oh, God, Dad, what hurts the most is that I really thought she was different. That she would accept me just the way I am. I don't want to believe that she's like Nancy or the others that backed away from me like I was a ruined man."

"Conall, just because I'm your father doesn't make me an expert on women. God knows I've only loved one all of my life and she's more than enough to keep me confused. But from the little time I've been around her, Vanessa seems like a very sensible woman."

Conall grunted. "What does that make me, an idiot?"

"Sort of."

"Thanks, Dad," Conall said with sarcasm. "That really makes me feel better."

"Hell, son, I'm not trying to make you feel better. I'm trying to help you fix things. Forget about Nancy and what came about with her. Forget about the other women that turned tail and ran. Nothing is going to be fixed with you and Vanessa until you first start accepting yourself. You need to realize that siring a child doesn't necessarily make a man a man or a father a father. You're much a man in my eyes, son. And I think you are in Vanessa's, too. Don't give up on her."

Doyle gave him one final pat on the back, then strode off in the direction of Kate's Kitten and the hot walker. Watching him go, Conall continued to lean against the white railing as his father's words reverberated in his head.

Had he been too hard on himself all these years? God knows, he'd tried hard to live up to the role of being the eldest Donovan son. He'd tried his best to always be the strong one, the one who rarely, if ever, failed, the one who would leave an admirable pattern for his younger brothers to follow.

When he'd learned of his inability to have children, he'd felt like a total failure, like he'd let his family down in the worst kind of way. But in the tradition of his role, he'd glued on his iron-man image and pretended to his family and acquaintances that he was tough enough to swallow anything life handed him.

Scrubbing his face with one hand, he turned away from the track and lifted his gaze toward the far mountain range where Vanessa's little house sat near a shrubby arroyo. It was no wonder, he thought, that Vanessa had struggled to believe that he truly loved her. For most of his adult life he'd been pretending, making an art out of hiding his feelings.

If he ever hoped to have another chance with her, he was going to have to go to her, open himself wide and hope that she could see what was truly inside of him.

His strides long and purposeful, he hurried back toward the office. If his mother had arrived to fill in at Vanessa's desk, he would send her home and reroute all his calls to the ranch's general office, he decided. If he hurried, he could drive over to Vanessa's house in twenty minutes.

His thoughts were so caught up in his plans that when he arrived back at the block of offices, he didn't notice the car parked next to his Ford truck at the side of the building. When he stepped inside, he glanced over, expecting to see his mother. Instead, Vanessa was sitting at the desk, sifting through a stack of correspondence as though she'd never been gone.

"Vanna!"

He didn't know whether he'd shouted her name or whispered it. All he knew was that she looked like a beautiful dream come true and his boots couldn't carry him across the room fast enough.

She looked up as he approached her desk and as their gazes met, her lips parted and he could see the movement of her throat as she swallowed.

"Hello, Conall."

"Where is Mom?"

She tried to smile and he was amazed to see that she was pale and nervous. Didn't she realize that she was holding all the cards, his very heart in her hands?

"When Fiona found me here, she went back home." She placed the papers she'd been holding back on the desktop and then with her eyes still on his face, folded her hands together in a tight steeple. "Since you never formally fired me I was hoping you needed your secretary back."

Amazed and shocked, he stared at her while his heart began to bump and thump with hope. "Did you honestly think I wouldn't want you here?"

Her head jerked back and forth. "I...didn't know. You walked out and—"

"That was a stupid stunt on my part."

Her eyes wide and hopeful, she rose to her feet. "You were hurt," she said in a raw whisper. "And I should have never said those awful things to you."

Fast as lightning, he streaked around the desk and tugged her into his arms. "Vanna! Oh, God, I'm so sorry. I've done everything wrong and—"

She placed a shushing finger against his lips. "So have I. Maybe we both have. But that doesn't matter now. Does it?"

For an answer, his lips swooped down on hers. The sweet, familiar taste of her kiss was a soothing balm to his battered heart and it was a long, long time before he ever lifted his head.

"My darling, I...when I stepped through the door a few moments ago I was about to tell Mom to forget about working today. I'd already planned to drive over to see you—to see if you'd be willing to listen to me."

"Listen? You don't need to explain anything, Conall. I—"

Before she could finish, he grabbed her by the hand and led her into his office. After shutting the door behind them, he urged her over to the couch. After they were sitting, their knees together, hands clasped tightly, he said, "I need to explain a lot of things, Vanessa. I need to say them as much as you need to hear them."

Nodding, she said, "All right. But first, I just want to say...I love you. That I never stopped loving you."

His heart was so full he thought it would burst; he lifted a hand and reverently touched her cheek. "Vanessa, I was wrong in not telling you about my condition long before anything started to develop between us. But I guess it was something—well, I was trying to convince myself that with you it wouldn't matter."

Through a mist of watery tears, she smiled at him. "It doesn't matter if we can't have more children the conventional way," she assured him. "I don't care about that. I didn't care the day you told me about it. I wanted to be the reason you wanted to marry me. Not the twins. That's all. And I was quick to jump to the wrong conclusion. Because I guess I never believed I was good enough to deserve your love. I never could totally believe that you wanted me, needed me in that way."

Amazed by her confession, he shook his head. "Oh, Vanna, that's awful. How could you think such a thing? You're the most precious woman I've ever known."

Bending her head, she murmured, "Jeff squashed my ego, Conall. He never saw me as a wife that he loved and cherished. He saw me as a workhorse, a provider for him. And I could only think that you saw me as a way to have children—not as a wife."

Sighing, he pushed his fingers gently into the rich brown hair at her temple. "And I thought you couldn't love me because I was sterile." His mouth twisting to a wry slant, he went on. "You see, when Nancy and I married, I had no idea that I was unable to father children. When we started trying to get pregnant and nothing happened, we both went through a battery of health tests. The minute the doctor gave us the news, something twisted inside of her, warped her into someone that I hardly recognized."

Lifting her head, Vanessa searched his face. "Didn't she stop to think that the two of you could adopt?"

Conall snorted. "She wouldn't even consider the option. She wanted a baby of her own and she was determined to get one no matter what she had to do."

Vanessa's brows peaked with questions. "So what options did that leave?"

Fixing his gaze to a spot on the floor, he said, "She wanted to go to a fertility clinic and get impregnated by a donor."

"Oh."

"Yeah. I understand that's a suitable solution for some childless couples. But at the time, the whole idea revolted me. I was young and full of masculine pride. I didn't want to see my wife pregnant with another man's child, much less have her giving birth to one. I tried to explain that it would leave me feeling as though I was on the outside of things. I argued that adoption would be a better option for the two of us. An adopted child wouldn't be more hers than mine—it would be ours."

"She couldn't understand your feelings? Or she didn't want to try?"

Dropping his hand from her hair, he released a long, heavy breath. "Nancy was a headstrong woman determined to have her way. She accused me of being selfish and robbing her of the right to be a mother. A 'real' mother in her terms."

Sickened by what she was hearing, Vanessa laid her hand on Conall's forearm. "So she didn't believe an adopted child would be a 'real' child," Vanessa mused out loud. "Well, I could tell her, or anyone, that the twins are just as much my children as if I'd given birth to them."

As he turned his gaze back on her, a wan smile tilted his lips. "Yes. But you're not Nancy. It took me a few horrendous days without you to figure that out." He turned his gaze to the picture window framing the wall in front of his desk and this time when he spoke his voice was reflective and full of doubts. "I suppose I was equally responsible for the breakdown of our marriage. Perhaps I was selfish for not letting her have her way. Anyway, I've stopped trying to figure it out. We wanted different things and nothing could change the way each of us felt."

Her fingers slid back and forth over the warm skin of his forearm as she searched for the right thing to say. "You both had different values and ideas about things. That never works—unless one of you sacrifices everything. And that wouldn't have made you happy, would it?"

"No." His expression pained, he said, "You know, I believed I'd married a woman that loved me, but after a while I realized I didn't really know her at all. And that made me the biggest fool who ever walked down the aisle."

A self-deprecating frown turned down the corners of Vanessa's lips. "Forget it, Conall, I hold that honor," she told him, then asked, "What finally happened? You two could never come to terms about having children, so you agreed to divorce?"

"I wish it had simply ended that way."

"What do you mean?"

"Like I mentioned before, something twisted in Nancy—I don't know what. I'm not even sure a psychiatrist could tell you. But she became an obsessed woman.

She wanted to become pregnant. Anyhow, anyway that she could. She kept hounding me about going to a clinic and selecting a donor. I kept refusing and she continued to hound."

"I'm surprised she didn't ask for a divorce," Vanessa mused. "But love binds and I'm sure she didn't want to lose you."

His grunt was a cynical sound. "Nancy probably did love me in the beginning. At least, I want to think so. But after she learned I was sterile, I think all that died. She hung around because she liked being in the Donovan family. She liked the luxuries and privileges, the social standing that went along with the name."

"I see," Vanessa murmured thoughtfully, "Was she originally from a poor family?"

Conall shook his head. "No. Her family wasn't rich by any means, but they were financially comfortable. Nancy was the youngest of three children and I think after the other two grew up and left the nest, her parents doted on her. I'm guessing she learned at an early age that she could bat her eyelashes and quiver her lips and get most anything she wanted. After a while I grew weary of her demands, but I didn't ask her for a divorce. I wanted our marriage to make it and I suggested that we needed counseling to help us work out our problems."

"So did she agree? Did you two go for counseling?"

Rising to his feet, he crossed the room and rested his shoulder against the window frame. As he stared out at the busy ranch yard, he spoke in a flat voice. "She laughed and said that all we needed was a baby to make us happy again. At that time I didn't know what was going on in that head of hers. And I would have never known if Liam hadn't come to me and told me."

Frowning, Vanessa asked, "Liam? What did he have to do with any of this?"

Turning his head, he looked straight at Vanessa. "Nancy went to him and begged him to get her pregnant. In her twisted mind, she was sure that I would accept the baby. After all, it would be a true Donovan, she reasoned."

Vanessa gasped. "That's—insane! And how did she plan to explain her pregnancy?"

His lips took on a wry slant. "Divine intervention. She believed she could convince me that the medical tests were wrong and by some miracle I had gotten her with child. And if she couldn't convince me, then she was gambling that I could never turn away from my own brother's baby."

"How terribly sad," Vanessa said pensively. After a moment, she went to him and rested her palms against his chest. "Oh, God, Conall, I didn't know that any of this had ever happened to you. Maura or anyone in your family never spoke to me about your marriage or why it ended. And I've not asked. You must have been so crushed when Liam revealed what Nancy had done. And I can't imagine what it must have done to him to have to tell you that your wife…well, that she was disturbed."

He cupped her face with his hands and she was relieved when the dullness in his eyes flickered to a bright and shining light of love.

"Actually, in some strange way the whole incident brought him and me closer. But that was the only good thing to come out of the mess. After the divorce, everything else about me was pretty much numb and I guess I stayed that way until I met you." He lowered his head until their foreheads met and his lips were hovering close to hers. "For years, I got damn good at hiding my feelings. I didn't want anyone guessing that I might be vulnerable or hurting. I didn't want anyone thinking I was anything less than a man. I guess I must have perfected my acting ability. Otherwise, you would have seen how much I love you."

"Oh, Conall, yesterday evening I got to bring Dad home for a visit and while he was there we had a long talk about you and me. He made me see how stubborn I was being and how much the twins and I were going to lose if I didn't get you back in our lives."

Smiling now, Conall rubbed his nose against hers. "Thank God for fathers. Not more than an hour ago, mine pretty much said the same thing to me."

Rising on her toes, she brought her lips up to his. "And thank God you're going to be the twins' daddy. And if they're not enough to turn your hair gray we can always adopt a whole house full of babies to go with them."

Wrapping his arms around the back of her waist, he clamped her tightly against him. "Hmm. You'd do that for me?"

"Only if you think you can handle the double duty."

He chuckled as he pressed his cheek against hers. "Double duty? I think you'd better explain, my darling."

She sighed as the warmth of his body and the goodness of his love filled her with pure, sweet contentment.

"That you'll always love me just as much as you love our children."

His lips moved to the side of her neck where he began to mark a trail of kisses. "You're going to quickly learn, my lovely, that I always honor my family duties."

* * *

A month later, early autumn had moved in to predict the winter to come. The night air was sharp and clear and sometime before dawn frost would lace the fading roses in Kate's garden. But inside the Donovan ranch house no one cared about the chilly weather. The lights were blazing, music filled the great room and there was no end to the dancing and plates of good food. Family and friends had gathered to celebrate the marriage of the eldest heir of a horse-racing empire and no expense had been spared for the party.

Two weeks ago, Conall and Vanessa had decided they couldn't wait for a big, traditional wedding to be planned. Instead they'd flown to Las Vegas and married in a little wedding chapel not far from the spot where they had first kissed. Afterward, Vanessa had insisted they spend their week's worth of honeymoon, not in Jamaica, where Conall had initially planned to take his new wife, but at Del Mar, where they'd played in the sand and surf and watched Red Garland race to victory in the Debutante.

The fact that Vanessa had remembered how Red Garland held a soft spot in Conall's heart, much less that she'd be willing to accommodate their honeymoon to catch the filly's race, had amazed him. And he knew those special days they'd spent loving each other on the California coast would be relived in his mind on each and every wedding anniversary.

Now, as Conall moved Vanessa around the dance floor to a romantic waltz, she gazed up at him, her face glowing. "When your mother said she was planning a little get-together for us, I was expecting a gathering of twenty to thirty people. This reception is incredible. I never expected to see so many people. So much food. So much…everything!"

Happy that she was so pleased, Conall squeezed her hand. There was never a time that Vanessa didn't look beautiful to him, even in the mornings when her face was puffy from sleep and her skin bare of makeup. But tonight, dressed in an ice-blue concoction that provocatively draped her curves, she looked especially lovely. And as they danced, he kept asking himself why he'd been so blessed, while at the same time thanking God that he had been.

"And I never expected to be enjoying it all so much," he confessed. "Normally when my parents throw parties, I'd always find an excuse to make a quick exit. But not tonight. We're going to dance until dawn."

The sparkling light in her brown eyes warmed him with loving promises. "Just dance?" she teased.

Grinning, he whirled her out of another couple's path. "Ask me that question later—when we're climbing the stairs to our bedroom."

Since their marriage, he and Vanessa and the babies had taken up residence in an upstairs suite of rooms that were connected to his original bedroom. As for the little Valdez house where Vanessa had been living, Alonzo had been able to move back home, thanks to live-in assistance that Conall was only too happy to provide. His father-in-law's health was continuing to steadily improve and tonight the older man was clearly enjoying being here at the party, chatting with friends and acquaintances and watching his daughter dance with her new husband.

As the music finally paused, she said, "I'm having a lovely time, Conall, but would you mind if we took a few minutes to slip upstairs and check on the twins? A couple of hours have passed since Hannah had them down to meet the guests."

"You've been reading my mind," he agreed. "Let's go give Hannah a little break, so that she can come and enjoy the festivities."

With his hand still wrapped around hers, he led her out of the crowded great room and down a long hallway until they reached a polished staircase. Side by side, they climbed the steps until they reached the second floor. At the end of the landing, Conall tapped lightly on a carved door. When they entered the room, Hannah was sitting at the end of a long couch. The dim glow of a table lamp illuminated the book in her hands.

She looked up in surprise. "Don't tell me the party is already over."

"It's just now getting fired up," he assured the devoted nanny. "We thought we'd better come see how you and twins have been getting along."

"In other words, you wanted to come up and play with your son and daughter," Hannah teased.

Vanessa laughed. "How did you ever guess?"

Laying her book aside, Hannah gestured toward a nearby door that led into a room that had been transformed into a beautiful nursery. "The last time I peeked in they were both asleep."

His hand still latched around his wife's, Conall began to urge her toward the nursery. "Get out of here, Hannah. Go on down and enjoy the party. We'll take care of things up here for a while."

The woman glanced down at her jeans and fitted sweater. "I'm not dressed for a party. But I will go down to the kitchen and test the food," she told him.

"Whenever you need for me to come back up just let me know."

As Hannah slipped out the door, they both thanked her before making their way into the quiet nursery.

Near the head of the crib, an angel-shaped nightlight illuminated the slumbering babies and Conall's throat tightened with emotions as he leaned over the rail and touched a finger to each sweet face.

"I never dreamed I would have one child," he said murmured. "Now I have two."

Vanessa's arm slipped around his back and as always, whenever she touched him, he felt strong and sure of himself. But most of all he felt loved. Utterly loved.

"Whenever we first went to the orphanage to see the babies, you told me then that you were certain you'd never have children. I thought it was because you didn't want any," she admitted. "And I couldn't fit that notion with the Conall I knew and loved."

Rick's tiny fist was lying outside the blanket. Conall picked it up between his thumb and forefinger while imagining how his son's hand would look in a few years after he'd grown to be a man. Other than being a husband to Vanessa, being a father was the richest gift he'd ever been given and he was cherishing every moment with his new family. "I'd already decided that I would never find a woman I could love again, much less one with children. I'm so happy you proved me wrong, my darling."

After placing a kiss on each baby's cheek, he pulled Vanessa over to a wide window that faced the southwest part of the ranch. Through the boughs of the pine trees, a ridge of mountains could be seen reaching up to the star filled sky.

Vanessa sighed with pleasure as he pulled her into his arms and kissed the crown of her head. "See that break in the mountain? Way over to the west?" he asked.

Vanessa's gaze followed his instructions. "Yes, I see it."

"I want to drive you over there tomorrow," he said, "I want you to take a look at the view and see if you like the spot enough to build our new home there."

Leaning her head back, she stared wondrously up at him. "New home? You don't like living with your family here in the big house?"

"I love living with my family. It's the only home I've ever known. But the Donovan family is changing and growing. Brady and Lass already have a daughter and I suspect they're already planning for another baby. And who knows, Liam might shock us all and marry again. Plus, there's Bridget and Dallas. This old house can't hold us all. Besides," he added, as his hands moved to the small of her back to gather her closer, "our children deserve a home of their own, one that they can pass on to their children."

"Mmm. Family tradition. I wouldn't expect anything else from you, my dear husband." She slipped her arms around his waist. "I only ask that our new home be simple and homey. And that you make a big fenced yard for our children to play in."

Smiling, he brought his lips down to hers. "You're such a demanding woman."

She kissed him softly, then easing slightly back, whispered, "How long do you think it will be before our guests realize we're missing?"

With a wicked chuckle, his arms tightened around her. "Long enough."

* * *

At the same time, down in the kitchen, Brady was doing his best to persuade Hannah to join the rest of the merrymakers while Bridget was at the far end of the cabinet, holding one hand over her ear while straining to hear the voice on the other end of the telephone.

With her hand over the receiver she scolded, "Brady! Shhh! I can't hear a thing." Turning her attention back to the caller, she finally managed to pick up the sound of a male voice and as she did her face grew pale, and her heart kicked to a rapid thump. "On the res, you said?... Oh....Yes....Yes, I remember....I'll be there as soon as I can make the drive."

When she hung up the telephone, she started toward a door that exited to the outside of the house. Thankfully, she'd left her coat and medical bag in her car and wouldn't have to waste time fetching it or dealing with prolonged goodbyes.

"Sis! Are you leaving?" Brady called after her.

Her hand on the doorknob, she paused to glance over her shoulder. "Yes. An emergency has come up."

Leaving Hannah, he trotted over to his sister. "Is it that important? This is your brother's wedding reception," he pointed out, as though she needed reminding.

Tossing him an impatient look, she said, "You know as well as I do that emergencies don't pick and choose their times to happen. Explain to the family why I had to go and give my love to Conall and Vanessa."

"Sure." He gave her quick kiss on the cheek. "Are you headed to the hospital?"

Shaking her head, she stepped through the door and out into the cold night. "No. But I might end up there," she called back to him.

Before he could ask more, Bridget hurried away from the house. She didn't want her brother to know that it had been his old friend Johnny Chino that she'd been speaking with on the phone. And she especially didn't want Brady to know that she was driving straight to the Mescalero Apache Reservation. He wouldn't understand why Johnny had summoned *her*. And frankly, Bridget didn't, either.

* * * * *